Pat

THE SPEAR

THE SPEAR

A Novel

by
Louis de Wohl

IGNATIUS PRESS   SAN FRANCISCO

Original edition published by
J. B. Lippincott, Philadelphia and New York

Cover design by Riz Boncan Marsella
Cover art by Christopher J. Pelicano

This edition published with permission of
Mrs. Ruth Magdalene de Wohl
Executrix of the Estate of Louis de Wohl
and with permission of Curtis Brown, Ltd.

Published in 1998 Ignatius Press, San Francisco
ISBN 0-89870-604-1
Library of Congress catalogue number 97-76863
Printed in the United States of America

TO MY WIFE

Ruth Magdalene

BOOK ONE

I

The Lady Claudia Procula was amused. Whirlwind courtships were not exactly new to her, but this young man seemed to wish to make up within a few weeks for all the time he had spent at some impossible outpost of the empire. Otherwise there was nothing extraordinary about him. He was fairly tall, with good bone structure, eyes the color of black cherries, and rather heavy, dark eyebrows that made him seem serious even when he was laughing. He came from a good family; the Longini had been soldiers for many generations, and his father was a retired general.

She had met Cassius Longinus first at a garden party in the house of Nerva Cocceius, and he would not leave her side even when a proconsul and two senators tried to get rid of him. A few days later she met him again in the house of Senator Pomponius and observed that he paid no attention at all to his host's dazzlingly beautiful daughter, although she flirted with him quite shamelessly.

And now he had turned up at Marcus Balbus' dinner party.

When the Lady Claudia found him sitting on a corner of her dining couch, she laughed. "You again! We seem to have a good many friends in common."

Cassius beamed at her. "I am doing my best to see to that, Domina. If it weren't for you, I wouldn't have come here."

"You would have been wrong there. Balbus' parties are famous."

He laughed. "They say he's almost as rich as he is fat. If that's true he must be horribly rich."

She raised her eyebrows. "Careful! He is not fond of such remarks, and he's not a man to be trifled with."

7

"The Chatts are bigger."

"The — who?"

"The Chatts — Germans. None of them under six feet, some nearer seven. They're good fighters. I've had to deal with them these last four years. I can't see Balbus standing up to them."

He did not see the warning in her eyes.

"What's that about me?" asked Marcus Balbus softly. He liked to amble from one table to the other to see that his guests had everything they wanted, and like many fat people he walked noiselessly. He was potbellied and almost bald, but the jutting chin spoke of energy, and the small eyes were cold and hard.

"We were speaking about fighting", Cassius said.

"Ah, were you? Of course, you've just come back from the German frontier. The Twenty-First Legion, I believe? I suppose he's been bragging a little about his military exploits, has he, Lady Claudia? Well, well. I bet you he's never seen a German near enough for real danger."

Cassius was too young to detect the angry undertone of jealousy. He heard only the challenge.

"It would be a difficult bet to take, sir, unless you can reach my commander, the Legate Cinna. He could decide it very quickly."

Balbus smiled. "Perhaps it's lucky that old Cinna has left Rome for a couple of weeks. Never mind, young man, I'm sure you did very well. And of course everyone knows Cinna flies into a rage at a breath of criticism against his legion. . . . If I were a German I would probably be deathly afraid of you. How many did you kill?"

"Only two", Cassius said quietly.

"Really? How interesting." Balbus grinned broadly. "With your own hand, too, I suppose. Strangled them, perhaps?"

"No." Cassius scowled. "I used my spear. You said something about bragging, didn't you? Well, I'll do just a little more bragging for you. I'll bet *you* I could hit you right in the middle of the stomach with a spear at a distance of fifty yards."

8

"Could you now?" Balbus snorted. "I'm almost inclined to take you on, you know."

"By all means do", Cassius said. "But it would be advisable to make your will first."

"Stop quarreling, you two", Claudia interposed. "Leave him alone, Balbus, he's only a child."

It was the worst thing she could have said.

"I'll bet anything you like", Cassius said hotly.

The fat man grinned. "I'm not accustomed to making an exhibition of myself. Will a small shield do, instead of your host's stomach?"

"By all means." Cassius shrugged.

"Very well, you have a bet", Balbus said. "But let's make it a *real* bet—nothing small. Say, twenty thousand sesterces. Agreed?"

Cassius hesitated. It was a large sum. If he lost, he would have to ask his father for the money. But since his return he had noticed, a little to his surprise, that his father seemed to be living in a far more luxurious style than Cassius remembered. And Claudia was looking at him.

"Agreed", he said.

Immediately Balbus produced his writing tablet and stylus. "Let's fix it up", he said crisply.

The bet was put in writing, and they both signed the document.

Balbus gave a low chuckle. "Wouldn't be fair to have the little matter settled at the end of the dinner. My wine is good and might make your hand unsteady. Better do it immediately. The banquet hall is large enough for our purpose."

"Anywhere and any time you like", Cassius said haughtily.

Balbus nodded contentedly. "Here", he said. "And now."

The guests were beginning to notice that something unusual was afoot.

Balbus whispered instructions to his majordomo, and soon two black slaves appeared with a small silver shield, a beautiful piece of work with the head of the Medusa in the center.

"Will that be satisfactory?" Balbus asked.

"Certainly", Cassius agreed. Under his breath he muttered to the girl, "It's not as big as his stomach, but it will do."

Claudia bit her lip.

"Very well, my witty young friend." Balbus had sharp ears. "Now let's measure the fifty yards—right along the main table. Fifty large steps. From here."

They measured the distance.

"Stand here, you two", Balbus snapped at the two slaves. "Hold this shield between you—yes, like that. And if you move an inch I'll have you whipped. Let's go back again, Cassius. I ordered a few spears to be brought up from the armory. You may take your choice."

There were three, and Cassius weighed each one very carefully before choosing a fairly heavy hunting spear. "Ready", he said then, and he smiled at Claudia.

Balbus glared at him. "Very well." He raised both arms. "Attention, friends. A little interlude for your pleasure. Young Cassius here has bet me twenty thousand sesterces that he can hit that shield with his spear from where he stands now. So keep your seats and don't move before he has thrown. Ready? Now! Throw, my boy!"

Cassius took a deep breath. He threw and then stood immobile, his right arm stretched out as if it were a prolongation of the missile.

Most of the guests ducked instinctively; they could feel the sudden gust of wind on their flushed faces. The two black slaves held the silver shield between them with forced equanimity. There was a shattering crash, and they both staggered and almost fell. The spear had gone right through the shield.

Everyone started shouting at once.

"Wonderful", gasped pretty little Nigidia.

The young lawyer Seneca on the couch beside her saw her nostrils flare. "The throw or the thrower?" he asked dryly.

"The man", was the frank reply. "Very handsome. Who is he?"

"By the biceps of Mars," interjected Tribune Caelius, "he's hit dead center — right through the mouth of the Medusa. Like father, like son."

"He's Cassius Longinus", explained the lawyer. "His father is a retired army commander who used to be one of the Emperor's best men in the German war. Incidentally, I'm his legal adviser."

"You know him well, then", said Nigidia. "Will you introduce him to me?"

"Old Longinus is not here tonight", teased Seneca.

"I mean his son, of course, silly."

"Careful now." Seneca smiled. "Can't you see that Claudia is taking a very lively interest in him?"

Nigidia gave the lady a cold, appraising stare. But there was nothing she could belittle. Claudia's figure was perfect, her face attractive in a provocative way, she was carefully made up, her jewelry matched her dress of peacock-blue silk, the new fashion, and her hair was sprinkled with gold dust.

"Who is she?"

"You mean to say that you don't know Claudia?"

Nigidia laughed a little harshly. "You forget that I've been away a long time."

Too late Seneca remembered that Nigidia's family had been exiled to some island in the Aegean Sea, because Nigidia's uncle had incurred imperial displeasure. "Claudia Procula", he said, tactfully glossing over the lady's remark, "is an orphan now but related to the divine Emperor."

"Your friend Cassius looks as if he were trying to hit two targets with the same spear." Nigidia sniffed.

Seneca nodded. "And both of them at the expense of our noble host."

Balbus waddled up to Cassius Longinus, a silk bag in his fleshy hand. "Twenty thousand", he said. "And I must admit it wasn't only luck, although luck seems to be with you, too."

Cassius Longinus laughed. "I can do it as often as you like. Want me to try again?"

Balbus smiled wryly. "Never cross the way of one whom Fortuna favors." It was the ancient proverb of the gambling table. "Twenty thousand is enough. And even Fortuna's favorite should content himself with one victory at a time." There was a hidden threat in the suave voice.

Cassius bowed mockingly. "As you wish."

"Where did you acquire such skill?" asked Claudia Procula quickly.

"It's a family trait", said Cassius. "We've always been good at it. There's a spear on our crest."

"You'd do well in the arena", growled Balbus. "You're built like a gladiator, too."

"Sorry that I can't return the compliment." Cassius smiled. "I shall send you Euphorus tomorrow—he's my masseur. He'll get you into shape."

A dull red rose in Balbus' massive face and darkened as Claudia laughed.

"He not only knows how to throw a spear", whispered Seneca to Nigidia, "but how to make enemies. . . . "

"Athletes", said Balbus, "have their drawbacks too. They're notoriously bad lovers."

Again Claudia laughed, and Cassius grinned broadly.

Balbus lost his patience. "You're very sure of yourself, aren't you? Well, that's usual before one reaches maturity and therefore pardonable. But some people don't learn caution even in their old age. How is your dear father, Cassius?"

The young man frowned. "My father is quite well. What makes you think of him?"

"Quite well, eh?" This time Balbus grinned. "I hope you're right. And I hope he'll remain well." He turned to his guests. "After this interesting little interlude I have a special treat for you. The best dancing troupe of the empire—the twelve Gaditan Fireflies."

The guests broke into tumultuous applause. Gaditan dancers were world famous, and the twelve Fireflies had taken Rome by storm.

Balbus clapped his hands. A curtain was drawn back, and the dancers appeared in a mad whirl of rose-colored transparent dresses.

"Do you want to watch?" asked Claudia lightly.

"Who wants the stars when the sun shines?" whispered Cassius.

"I feel tired", said Claudia, her eyes belying her words. "I think I shall order my litter."

"You need an escort", expostulated Cassius. "The streets are full of all kinds of rabble at this time of night and . . . "

" . . . and your spear will give me protection, I suppose." She smiled. "I have a strong guard indeed. But who will protect me against that guard?"

He raised his hands. "By the knees of Venus—"

"Definitely *not* a reliable goddess", she laughed.

"By Juno, then", swore Cassius.

She raised her beautifully penciled brows. "The goddess of marriage! Do you know what you are saying?"

"You're mocking me." He looked so hurt that she gave him her best smile. He was so young—twenty, perhaps twenty-one. She knew she could make him experience delight and despair between one breath and the next, and she felt touched—so much so that she seriously asked herself whether she was not in love with him. Perhaps she was. And anyway, it was ridiculous that people had started talking about her and Balbus, as if she could possibly care for the bloated toad, however rich he was.

She looked about her. All the others were concentrating on the dancers. "I'm going", she said. "Let's slip out this way—not through the atrium."

They passed a number of slaves, carrying heavy amphorae of snow-cooled wine and huge dishes of lark and nightingale tongues. Many thousands of the tiny birds had had to be caught to make a single one of these dishes.

"Balbus *is* rich", Claudia thought with a little sigh.

Cassius, his eyes fixed on the slender figure swaying gracefully ahead of him, bumped into one of the slaves, who managed, by desperate contortions, to keep his precious dish from spilling all over the mosaic floor, but Cassius did not even notice. They reached a small door leading to a court. Slave hands were raised in submissive salute.

"This is my litter", said Claudia, nodding toward one delicately designed of wood and ivory. The carriers were six Numidians, their bronze bodies gleaming in the torchlight, who jumped to their feet and bowed.

"My horse, quickly", ordered Cassius in a stentorian voice. What if Claudia decided to leave before they had brought his horse from the stables? Litters with their slaves were left here at the side door of the house, but horses had to be looked after, and the stables were at some distance. He did not know where Claudia lived. These Numidians were fast, and Rome was a rabbit warren. Once they were out of sight, it might well prove impossible to find them again.

He walked up to the litter. Claudia had just been helped in; he could see her profile, delicate and serene, in the dim light from the bronze torch on the wall. He ought now to say something amusing, but his brain was paralyzed. All he managed was a hoarse, "Wait for me, please."

Her smile reassured him a little, and then he heard Pluto's hooves clatter on the pavement. He jumped into the saddle without using the ready hands of the stable slave and rode up to the litter, but Claudia had drawn the curtains, and he could no longer see her face.

The Numidians ran swiftly past the Temple of Neptune and to

the left, past the Circus Maximus and left again, toward the slopes of the Aventine Hill, and stopped in front of a small villa in the Greek style. Cassius sprang from his horse, ready to help Claudia from her litter, so that no slave would touch her arm.

A torchbearer came to lead her up the stairs to the entrance.

"Domina Claudia," said Cassius hoarsely, "I beg of you, don't make me go back into a world that has no meaning without you—let me come with you."

"What, at this time of night?" She raised her brows in mock indignation.

"I assure you . . . "

"Almost all I know about you is your name and that you are a very courageous, determined, and self-assured young man."

"If only you knew how little self-assured I feel . . . "

"And I have neither parents nor brothers. I live alone here, with my old friend, the Lady Sabina."

"Remember, I swore by Juno . . . "

" 'Many a girl has been sadly deceived when a man swore an oath by the gods.' " She quoted a fashionable poet's epigram with a low chuckle.

"I mean it", he protested fiercely. "And in our family we do not swear lightly. Let your friend be present, if you like."

"You look like an honorable man", Claudia murmured, with a sidelong glance that made his heart pound.

The majordomo was now coming down the stairs, bowing.

As she swept past him she said casually, "Tell the lady Sabina I would like her to meet my guest—let someone look after his horse and bring wine and fruit."

Sabina was a stout little woman. Dressed in somber hues and sitting very erect, she gave an impression of dignity. A careful observer would have seen that her movements were perhaps a trifle too ladylike, that her eyes were shifty and her hands not those of a well-bred woman.

But Cassius saw her only as a dark blur.

Under other circumstances, Cassius, whose eyes were normally quick enough, might have noticed that the majordomo's tunic was shabby and that the beautiful myrrhine vase on the cypress wood table was chipped. But he saw nothing except Claudia.

"You are not drinking", said Claudia.

He raised the pretty cup and poured a few drops on the silver platter before him. "To Juno", he said.

"Evidently she is your favorite goddess", she mocked.

"It is the first libation she ever received from me", Cassius retorted. "But I hope I shall need her assistance soon."

"Listen to him, Sabina", laughed Claudia. "Do you think he can be believed?"

The stout lady emptied her goblet with amazing speed. "Young men will say much when they want to have things their way", she cackled, wagging her head. "They'll talk of Juno and mean . . . " She broke off as Claudia gave her a hard stare.

"I know I'm not worthy of you", admitted Cassius, deaf as well as blind to anything but Claudia. "But I—I'm not always so tongue-tied and stupid. You have bewitched me, Domina, and made me a little boy again."

The old woman giggled. "What a pity that would be."

"Sabina," said Claudia sweetly, "you must be tired. It was very inconsiderate of me to ask you to come down. Go now, my dear—I don't think any evil will come to me from the son of General Longinus."

Sabina rose with some reluctance—she had just poured herself another goblet of wine—but Claudia raised her head with an imperious little gesture, and she withdrew with an uneasy bow.

"She is not exactly a friend of mine", Claudia explained. "Only an old retainer to whom I give shelter and food because I am sorry for her—enough of her. I should be angry with you, you know! I told you Balbus is not a man to be trifled with, and you promptly challenged him."

"Yes, but I won, didn't I? And it was for your sake that I challenged him, though I prayed to all the gods that they might let me forget you for that one moment when I threw the spear so that I would not miss the target."

She smiled and let her eyes wander over his handsome young face with the broad forehead, the proud eyes, and the energetic, round chin. "You were heard, it seems."

"No, I wasn't, and I felt sure I would miss. But then I had an idea. I said to myself, 'Imagine to yourself that this throw is to save Claudia's life.' And suddenly I saw everything clear, and I knew I couldn't miss."

"What a strange boy you are", said Claudia, genuinely touched.

He took a deep breath. "I'll tell you something I never told anybody." He spoke with difficulty, his heavy brows drawn together. "I've always wanted to do something, something really big ... something important. But the thing I do best is what you saw tonight. I know I'm good at that. And the world is not yet entirely Roman. My father is a soldier, as you know. I was prepared for a career in the army. They say the time is past when a commander can strike or throw with his own hand—his cohorts and maniples are to be his hands. It's a long time since there has been single combat between leaders. But I have always had a feeling that there will be some great use to be made of my skill, some day."

"You are a strange boy", Claudia repeated. She did not want to show that she was amused, he was so deadly serious.

"Now it's different", he went on. "I have only one wish— Claudia. No, don't misunderstand me again, I beg of you. I shall speak to my father tonight. He'll go to the Emperor and ask for his consent. We are not one of the rich families in Rome; one doesn't get rich in the army. But we have some money and houses in Herculaneum and Agrigentum—you'll love the one near Herculaneum; it's just on the slopes of Mount Vesuvius. They say the god Vulcan used to have one of his smithies under it—like the one under Mount Etna—but I'm afraid that's just a fairy tale. It's such a lovely, peaceful mountain, and what a wine they grow on the slopes! You'll be happy there, Domina, *we* shall be. I'll do anything to make you happy."

"It sounds delightful," Claudia said softly, "and almost as if you really meant it. But", she shook her head, "we only met a short time ago. How can you possibly be certain?"

He sprang to his feet. "I've never been so certain of anything. But I know what you're thinking, Domina. Who is this Cassius Longinus? His father is a worthy man, no doubt. He has done well in his life, but what has the son done so far? Nothing—except dream about something big he might do some day. It is true, Claudia, but we are young, you and I, and . . . "

"How old are you?"

"I was twenty on the third day before the last calends."

"Then I'm a full two years older than you are", she exclaimed. "Aren't you afraid of marrying a woman so much older?"

"I'm afraid only of a life without you. I want to form my future with you at my side—and may the gods destroy me if I do not lay the world at your feet."

She stood up, feeling strangely unsure of herself under the impact of his emotion. "You must go home now", she told him.

"Very well, one kiss, but only one—Jupiter's lightning is slow in comparison to your courtship—one kiss only, I said. Talk to your father. And tomorrow or the day after, come and tell me what he said."

"I love you. Claudia—Claudilla—do you think you could love me, too?"

18

"I can try," she smiled, "and perhaps it won't be too difficult. No . . . No, Cassius—remember your oath."

"I do, I do. Tomorrow I shall be back—oh, gods, I never knew how beautiful the world could be."

When the door had closed, she sat down again, still smiling. She could hear him shout for his horse and then the sound of hoofbeats diminishing in the distance.

Was it foolishness? Twenty! She could pass for twenty-two; no man would doubt it and not many women.

A relative of the Emperor—it never failed, she thought, seeking refuge in cynicism. If they only knew how little Tiberius cared for his distant relatives. And now that the Emperor had withdrawn from political life any relationship meant less than ever. Sejanus was the real master of Rome.

But she did not really believe that meant much to Cassius. He was in love. And he did not have to think of security, of all the humiliating experiences one had to endure to keep up one's position in Roman society, short of funds as she was.

Sabina was impossible—she might have spoiled everything.

That gray-haired man, who had just been given some province or other—the one she met last week at Pomponia's party—she had thought seriously of him. She had to. She remembered his name but not which province he had been given. Nor did it matter. Any province would do. But he certainly was not an easy man to deal with; it was not likely to be fun. Cassius was fun. And he had a good chin and a good forehead. He might go far.

Villas in Herculaneum and Agrigentum . . .

Rome had changed; the very stones were changed tonight. Kissed by the silver light of the stars, they seemed to be stirring in a dream. The poet fellows said that love was like a dream. They all said it in one form or another. He had never cared much for poetry. A man must be practical and realistic, and if he dreamed at all, his dreams must be the seed of action. He used to laugh at the fellows who went about mooning about their love for some girl or other. And now he was as bad as they were and worse.

If only he had listened better when old Chrysogonus tried to teach him the art of poetry, Horace and Vergil and a little Catullus, the more decent bits, of course—he might have been able to spout quotations and make a better impression on Claudia. But all he remembered were a few rhymes from the *Aeneid* and a few of the less decent bits of Ovid. He should have read more.

She probably took him for a boor. He certainly felt like one when she looked at him out of those wonderful brown eyes, a boor and a fool and yet deliriously happy. "For the life of me I couldn't describe her to anybody", he thought.

"There, Pluto, steady now." Cassius tightened his grip on the reins as his horse stumbled. That came from looking for Claudia in the clouds. In the stars, rather. The sky was full of them, an army of enchanted gods and goddesses.

He turned into the dark channel of the Via Sempronia and chuckled, remembering that this was the street of the fortunetellers, the palmists and astrologers, Egyptians most of them, or Persians. It was a small, miserable, sour-smelling street, but powerful senators sent for some of these people to consult them on matters of importance. The horoscope sellers always said that things came in batches; one day was good, another bad. Perhaps they also were right, like the poets. This surely was a day when everything had gone on wings—steady, Pluto—and nothing could go wrong.

Father would be delighted, although he probably thought that a man must make a career first and then marry, because that was the way he had done it. But he had loved mother, and after she died, he had never thought of marrying again. He had loved—he would understand. "Right, Pluto—don't you know the way home?"

Past the Forum. The grim, forbidding halls and buildings were silent and deserted. Politics and business were dead, and love alone was reigning.

20

Today life started. What had he been doing, what had he been thinking all the years before?

The garden and the broad driveway, strewn with gravel—The house was in darkness. The slave who opened the door for him and took the reins of his horse had sleepy eyes.

"My father still up, Thrax?"

"No, master."

He might have been up; he often had businessmen at his house, to discuss things with them—boring things—till the small hours. But perhaps it was just as well there weren't any of them there now.

He walked in. There was no light in the library or in the small, oval room next to it, where father loved to browse over old documents; he hated to be disturbed then.

Should one postpone the vital talk till morning?

He knew he would not be able to sleep. But a man was not in his best mood when waked up in the middle of the night. It would have been different if father had met Claudia.

Surely it was better to wait until morning. Tullus never reported anything important to Father until after breakfast, and Tullus knew his master better than anyone else, having been his body servant for over thirty years, most of which had been spent in tents and camps.

What *would* Father say? Obviously he would congratulate him on being the luckiest man in the empire. At least that's what he would do if only he had met Claudia.

Cassius stood still, trying to make up his mind, and as he stood there, the silence in the dark corridor began to press against him, and with it came a sense of furtive unrest and even of fear. It was absurd, for what was there to fear?

Yet he felt as he had in his childhood, when in a dream he was walking through a dark room and suddenly knew that something monstrous and terrible was waiting for him in the murky blackness.

And, as he had then, he cried out, "Father!"

There was no answer.

But now he had made his decision. "Father! Wake up! I must talk to you."

Again no answer. He listened. From behind the heavy curtain of the bedroom he could hear a queer, dripping noise.

He tore the curtain aside, got enmeshed in its heavy folds, struggled free, and saw—his father was lying in his bed, sleeping peacefully, except...

For one breathless moment he stared without comprehension. Then he understood, he knew, and he leaped into action.

In half a dozen steps he reached the low table beside the bed, seized the small gong, and hit it several times in quick succession. The sound flooded the silent house. Before it had ebbed away, he had grasped his father's arm and pressed both his hands around it, just above the wrist and the terrible gashes.

Old Longinus groaned. The sound lifted Cassius' heart. Now *hurry*...

From outside came the tap-tap of heavy feet. The old servant appeared, bleary-eyed and disheveled. As he saw what had happened, his jaw dropped and he began to tremble.

"Pull yourself together", Cassius snapped. "Get Euphorus— and bandages! Get a lamp! Quick! And keep the others off. Not a word to anybody, except Euphorus. *Run, Tullus!*"

Tullus ran.

Once more Cassius was alone with the man who had given him life and whose own life was now flowing away, if his son's hands could not stop it, if Euphorus did not come in time... if he had not lost too much blood already.

There was a large pool of blood on the floor.

Why? Why had he done this frightful thing?

Only now did Cassius realize how little he knew about his father. He knew the strict, erect, stiffly courteous army officer who got up every morning at sunrise, however long he had been sitting up with his friends the night before, who went for a ride every morning after a frugal breakfast and talked of strategical and tactical problems and especially about his service years in Germany, Rhaetis, and Noricum. He knew him as the severe judge when something wrong had been done by his freedmen, his slaves, or his son. He was not a difficult master, although a stern one, and he was a good father, although he did not often permit himself to show affection.

It had never occurred to Cassius to wonder whether his father was happy or unhappy—he was simply himself. He did not seem to worry much about political issues and had never mixed in politics himself.

There was no doubt whatever that he had tried to kill himself—the instrument was on the low table beside the gong. Cassius had seen it immediately even in the dark room; it was his army dagger, sharp as a razor. Why, why?

Steps again at last, hasty ones this time, and here was Euphorus, also bleary-eyed but not disheveled: he was as bald as an egg. Behind him Tullus carried a lamp, and in the light Cassius could see that his father's face was the color of old parchment. Was it too late?

He looked at Euphorus. The slave was a good physician as well as masseur for whom Cassius' father had paid an enormous price at a sale, many years ago.

"Very good, young master", said Euphorus in a low voice. "Let me see now . . . bring the lamp close, Tullus. That's good. Right. Just hold on for one more moment, young master." He bent over the still body on the bed, opened the tunic, and pressed his ear against the general's chest. "Right", he said again. "Tullus, the bandages—you just hold on, young master, you're doing fine. Here, take that end, Tullus. We're making a tourniquet, young master, and then you can let go. There—and there—pass the end, Tullus. Now then: I need a brazier as quickly as you can get it here; yes, with a fire, of course. And a pot of water. And towels. And wine, Tullus, wine, honey, and a spoon."

Tullus was really Euphorus' superior in the hierarchy of the slaves, but now he obeyed without a murmur.

"You can stop holding him, young master", said Euphorus quietly. "There'll be no more loss of blood, except perhaps a few drops."

Cassius stared at him. "Do you think he'll . . . live?"

"Probably, young master, probably", was the cheerful reply. "He's been very lucky, you know."

"Lucky!"

"Yes, very lucky. See here—the blood has congealed; it often does, when there's some obstacle. That stopped the flow; otherwise he would have bled to death a good while ago. Ah, it's not so easy to do this sort of thing well, young master. Nature has many protective forces, even against our own stup—our own actions."

He began to adjust the position of the general's body.

"The head must be lower than the body", he explained. "That makes the blood go back to the brain. And now a little massage, till Tullus comes with the water and towels. Stir up the blood that is left." He worked away with a will. "Not so easy to do this sort of thing well", he repeated. "Now if he'd done it in his bath—a hot bath, of course—the flow wouldn't have stopped; it would have gone on and on. All over in a quarter of an hour, perhaps less. Now you know, young master, if ever you want to do the same thing, and may the gods prevent it. No congealing then, no clotting of the blood such as you see here—and here, too, see?"

Tullus came back, breathing hard, with brazier, water, and towels. "Wine and honey in a minute", he mumbled and made off again.

Euphorus stopped his massage and began to heat some of the water on the brazier. "Hot and cold compresses, alternating", he said crisply. "You can help me there, young master; I take the hot ones and you the cold ones. Just do what you see me doing. There now."

Hot and cold compresses. Before they were through with the second change of towels, Tullus came back again with a decanter, a goblet, and a jar of honey.

Euphorus filled the goblet with wine, poured a liberal amount of honey into it, stirred the mixture, and sat down beside the old man.

"Now then", he said. "Wake up, master, time for breakfast." He spoke in a strong voice. The general blinked but did not open his eyes. "You say it, Tullus", whispered Euphorus. "Say it as you do every morning when you bring in the tray—but loud. He's accustomed to your voice. Come on."

"Time to wake up, master. Here's breakfast", said Tullus in a thick voice.

"Once more", Euphorus whispered. "Louder."

Tullus obeyed, and—the general opened his eyes. At once Euphorus held the goblet to his lips. "Drink, master."

Instinctively, the old man drank.

III

It was almost midday when General Longinus awoke again from a leaden sleep, to find both Cassius and Euphorus sitting at his bedside. Once more he was given wine mixed with honey, and then Tullus brought a regular meal on a tray, oatmeal, milk, bread, olives, figs, and small slices of roast meat.

"Eat, master", said Euphorus quietly. "You need it."

The general frowned. There had been a time when a whole legion had trembled before his frown, but then it showed on a florid face with gimlet-sharp eyes and lips so grimly pressed together that they made a mere slit above the jutting chin. Now the face was waxen with heavy-lidded eyes twitching nervously and a sagging mouth, and not even his slave trembled.

25

"You must eat, Father", said Cassius. "No, don't explain anything now—just eat."

The old man obeyed. But at the second bite he dropped the meat and began to cry softly.

Euphorus gave Cassius a reassuring nod and tiptoed out of the room.

"Wish you hadn't stopped me", murmured the general. "Couldn't imagine anybody would come in before morning."

"Just as well I did, Father. But I wish you'd eat first—there's all the time in the world for talking it over."

"No, there isn't." Old Longinus grunted. "Think I did this for amusement? Had my reasons. It was foolish of you to interfere", he added wearily. "Now I must start all over again. Not pleasant. Rather that—than the Mamertinum."

"The Mamertinum? The jail? You?" Cassius was aghast. "What on earth for?"

Old Longinus shrugged his shoulders and winced. His arm ached, from the shoulder down to the heavily bandaged wrist. "Debts, son, debts. Had them before, but never like this. Most unfortunate. Debts. Always liked to gamble a little. Won many a good bet in my life."

Cassius gave him an encouraging grin. "Like father, like son. I won a bet yesterday evening. Twenty thousand sesterces. Against Balbus." He tried hard not to think of Claudia. That would have to be left for later.

"Balbus, eh?" Old Longinus growled something unintelligible. "Twenty thousand, eh?" He began to laugh, an old man's laugh, cackling and desperate. "Wish you had bet a million. That would have helped—if you'd won it. And it wouldn't have done any damage, if you had lost." He cackled again.

Startled, Cassius seriously wondered if his father had lost his reason. Perhaps the loss of blood . . .

"No, no," said the general, "you don't have to look at me like that. I'm as sane as you are—now. But I must have been mad to have tackled that wheat project. Fuscus suggested it to me. He's a sharp one, knows the grain business like no one else in Rome and has got his spies everywhere, Sicily, Cyprus, Egypt — the grain route to Rome. Always knows what's going on. Or so he says, and he's got a reputation for it; everybody admits that. He came to me — said he wanted to do me a favor. Should have made me suspicious, perhaps; why should Fuscus want to do me a favor? But I thought the real reason was that he didn't have enough capital, and he needed a great deal if his plan was to come off. Give me some more of that wine. Thanks. Now then. We became partners. We bought up wheat in Egypt, masses of it. It was going to be scarce; Fuscus knew all the reasons why. So, a few months later, we'd get a stiff price for it from the administration. It was all as clear as daylight, the way Fuscus put it. And of course, the more we bought, the bigger the profit." He sighed and sipped his wine. "So I borrowed money, altogether almost a million sesterces. Sounds like a great deal, but what is a sesterce nowadays? About enough for a plate of beans. There was a time when you could buy a full meal for it. Why, I remember . . . "

"What happened then, Father?"

"The money's all gone", said the general with a shrug and swore roundly in the language of the barracks. Cassius had never heard his father use it before.

"For once Fuscus was wrong", went on the general. "Something must have gone wrong with his communications. A whole fleet of grain ships arrived in Ostia, and he had known nothing about it. So of course there was a glut and prices were low, and when *our* ships came, there was no bidding — or very little. And we *had* to sell — I had used every ounce of my credit, and now everybody yelled for his money. We sold at a terrible loss. The money I got back was sucked up by my creditors, and that was only a small part of what I owed them. I'm — I'm not very good at calculations, but it was clear that I couldn't meet my debts even when I sold everything I had—this house and the villas in Herculaneum and Agrigentum— What is it?"

"Nothing, Father", said Cassius quietly. "Go on."

"Where was I? Oh, yes, the villas—and the little farm in the Alban hills, the horses and slaves. Do you know, I didn't mind losing the villas, never cared much for them since your dear mother died. She loved them, especially the one in Herculaneum. But the little farm . . . there's nothing to it, really, just a small house and a garden with some fruit trees—but it was thinking of that little place that hurt me more than anything else. I wanted to live there in the last years of my life. Well—I sold the house and the villas and the farm—everything. Yesterday, that was. And then I found I was still a hundred thousand short."

"But, Father, surely—that's not such a big sum. You have friends . . . "

"Friends?" The general grinned bitterly. "If you throw Venus you're welcome everywhere; if you lose . . . Any day now they'll come and take over. And they'll drag me away to the Mamertinum to rot there till the rest of the money's paid or till I've rotted completely. A few years ago I might have gone to the Emperor. Maybe he would have helped me—or maybe he would have kicked me out; you never knew with Tiberius. But now he's gone to Capri, and he won't see anyone, and I'm not going to run after that upstart Sejanus who lords it over us now. Not I. So I decided to foil those bloodsuckers at least about the Mamertinum. But of course, you had to drag me back, you and your precious Euphorus." He looked away. "Wasn't worried about you", he added harshly. "You're a stout lad, and the army's wide open to you. You could hew your own way and make your own fortune in your own good time. Didn't need me for it. Much better if I were out of the way."

Cassius had no knowledge of business matters, but he sensed that his father had been taken in somehow, somewhere, by that man Fuscus. His father was an army man and had all the army man's love of gambling, of taking a risk. He was meat for a fellow like Fuscus. And now all the family wealth was gone.

He grinned wryly. "I've heard better stories, Father. But if you want to give up fighting, I won't."

"Fight?" The general knitted his brows. "Fight whom? What for?"

"First of all we've got to find a businessman to advise us", declared Cassius. "I'm going to get your lawyer. Saw him at Balbus' dinner last night."

"Don't think he can do anything", growled his father. "Suave fellow, talks beautifully. Brains, too, I suppose. But lost is lost. Never mind. Do as you like. You'll probably find him at the courts."

"Oh, I'm not going myself", said Cassius firmly. "I'm not moving from your bedside till he comes. Got to make quite sure there won't be any more of this nonsense. And if anybody should come to talk about the Mamertinum, I'll run him through."

"Young lunatic", growled the general. But there was a gleam of pride in his tired eyes as Cassius caressed his thin twitching hand. Absurdly, he felt that his father, whom he had always regarded as a kind of demigod, was really a child.

Of course, there was no use talking to him about Claudia. He would have to talk to *her,* as soon as this matter was settled. True, his position was not what he had thought it. But did that matter, if two people really loved each other?

"Well, I made him swear that he won't do it again", said Seneca, entering Cassius' study with a smile. "And he's one of the few men in Rome who still believe in the sanctity of an oath. But you did very well, keeping an eye on him till I came."

"I'm most grateful to you." Cassius felt a load off his shoulders. "I only wish he had had your assistance earlier. May I offer you some wine?"

"No, thank you. I have another heavy dinner in front of

me, and I haven't got the capacity of Vitellius. Nice chair, this . . . "

"I suppose so. I wonder to whom it belongs—now."

Seneca gave the young man an appraising glance. "You are fond of taking risks, you of the Longinus family, aren't you? A spear's throw—a speculation in wheat . . . "

Cassius envied the young lawyer's calm, self-assured bearing. It was not only that everybody said Seneca would go far. With beautifully regular features, a melodious voice, and dignified movements he combined an excellent taste in dress and topped it all with a smooth-working, cool brain. What an elegant way of telling the son that he was as hotheaded and impulsive in his actions as his father! "How bad is it really, Seneca?"

"Oh, pretty bad—" The lawyer glanced at his fingernails. "As you said quite rightly, he ought to have called me in a little earlier. At the time when he made those contracts with Fuscus, for instance."

"You mean . . . it wasn't only bad luck?"

"My dear young man! Fuscus is one of the best wheat experts we have in Rome." He looked around to make sure the old man could not hear him. "It's no good telling that to your father, of course; it would only make him thoroughly miserable or so furious his convalescence would be retarded—but there is little doubt that Fuscus knew exactly what he was doing, which is more than can be said about the dear general. It was the oldest trick in the world. Fuscus probably never bought that Egyptian grain at all. And it's a million to one he had a finger in the Sicilian grain transport that is supposed to have spoiled the great transaction."

"You mean he simply cheated Father?" cried Cassius. "Can't we sue him and . . . "

"Hopeless, Cassius, hopeless. You don't think it would be possible to prove anything in court, do you? Fuscus is an excellent man at bookkeeping. The praetor and his officials could examine his books for months on end, without finding anything in the least irregular. Parchment is patient, you know. You'll find that the money went to Egypt, of course, and no doubt it really did, namely to Fuscus' agent there—who is also an excellent bookkeeper. And you could never prove that Fuscus knew anything about the Sicilian transport—that was all done by his middlemen, and they'd come forward and swear by all that's holy to them that Fuscus had nothing whatever to do with it. I wonder what *is* holy to them," he added as an afterthought, "unless it's their profits."

"So we won't get a sesterce back?"

Seneca smiled thinly. "I think you managed to get twenty thousand back."

"What do you mean? I got them from Balbus . . . "

" . . . who is a very close friend of Fuscus, yes."

Suddenly Cassius remembered how Balbus had inquired about his father that evening. "Some people don't learn caution even in their old age. How is your dear father, Cassius? . . . Quite well, eh? I hope you're right. And I hope he'll remain well." Balbus.

"He was angry with me yesterday, Seneca. And he did seem to have some grudge against my father. I have no idea why. They don't see much of each other."

"I don't understand it myself as yet", was the calm answer. "Maybe I shall know more when I discover who is behind those who bought your father's villas and all the rest."

"And is it true what father says—that they may come for him because he cannot pay those last hundred thousand sesterces to his creditors?"

"I'm afraid so. They won't come today, though. It's too late now—the courts are closed. But we must act quickly. I'll see what I can find out and whether it's possible to gain a few months' time, at least. That was an excellent throw of yours, yesterday."

"Oh, that—"

"But you couldn't very well miss, could you? Not with such lovely eyes watching you."

Cassius blushed furiously. "Seneca!"

"I'm not teasing you, my dear boy." The lawyer smiled. "I'm only drawing your attention to the fact that the little episode did not pass unnoticed. It didn't increase Balbus' goodwill toward the Longinus family, you know. I don't say that the lady is interested in him . . . "

"Claudia interested in that bladder of lard?"

" . . . but he is interested in her, I'm afraid. So are other people."

"I love her, Seneca", said Cassius vehemently.

"So I gathered, my dear boy, so I gathered. It doesn't exactly simplify matters." Seneca sighed. "Love . . . there is no word in our language with so many different meanings. Everybody thinks he knows what love is. And yet . . . does anybody?"

"I didn't know until I met Claudia", Cassius said simply.

"And now you think you do, because of what you are feeling."

Cassius frowned. "If you think that my love for Claudia is some shallow, superficial emotion . . . "

"I didn't mean that at all. But can you define it?"

"N-no, I don't think I could."

Seneca seemed to be concentrating on something beyond time and space. Suddenly he looked years older.

"Love is sevenfold", he began almost solemnly. "By definition it is an inclination of something toward something else. Take up a stone, and it will weigh heavily in your hand, because it is inclining toward, because it is drawn toward the earth, from which you have taken it. It is drawn toward its origin. It is longing for the earth, and you can feel its longing in the pressure on your hand. Drop it—and see how quickly it moves to meet the beloved—like a child running toward its mother's embrace. A mere stone, Cassius . . . For such is the first stage of love, and it is in everything on earth."

"You increase my respect for stones", joked Cassius.

32

"The next stage", Seneca continued quietly, "is the love of each creature for the self."

"Egoism, then."

"No. The urge for self-preservation, of which egoism is the perversion. And the third stage is the urge to preserve one's own kind—sexual love. The fourth is aesthetic love, the love of beauty. You find it in animals and birds as well as in man. See the peacock strutting, conscious of his beauty, see the playfulness of lambs or colts or cats, fully conscious of the capabilities of their bodies and exercising them with joy."

"That's true enough."

"With the fifth stage of love we leave the material field behind us. Here is the love of philosophy and of abstract thinking—the love we are indulging in at this moment, unless I am boring you . . . "

"That is almost an insult", Cassius parried. "Please go on."

"Here is the realm of exploration and speculation, of knowledge sought and found, and there are many who will prefer the searching to the finding, because finding puts an end to the search they love. Comes the sixth stage—the love of one person for another."

"Surely there can be nothing higher than that!"

"Here we find not only lovers but also philanthropists and all people concerned with the fate, destiny, and well-being of their fellowmen. Yet there is a step higher still, though only one: the urge that raises man above himself, the longing for things beyond the natural and finite. Plato knew about it. As we grow older we perceive that even the love of one person for another is imperfect, and there are whisperings in us that still more is required of man by the immortal gods. It is a longing that may take strange forms—like the attempt to placate the gods who despise our imperfections—the attempt to move in their direction, toward the stars on which they dwell."

"Religion, you mean?"

Seneca shrugged his shoulders. "Religion is one way of expressing it. All love is longing, even that of the stone longing for Mother Earth, the first stage of the sevenfold love. Much of it may be quite foolish—but then lovers will do foolish things and even revel in their foolishness. They will search for signs in the livers of geese and the kidneys of sheep, slaughtered in honor of this god or that; they will bribe their gods with money, flowers, or fruit. And yet their foolishness is better than the indifference of those who only seek material wealth or those who speak of love but mean only the quenching of their bodily desires."

Cassius looked at him in some astonishment. "This is an odd sort of conversation, under the circumstances. What—"

"For the first time in your life you will have to play your part in a personal crisis", Seneca interrupted unsmilingly. "It could easily lead you to hatred and bitterness, and that would be a pity. There are too many of those who go through life hating and being bitter. You are in love. I am not, but I believe in love . . . if one has the good fortune to find the right partner."

"You can't doubt that I have found her, can you?" asked Cassius.

"I know very little of Claudia", said Seneca slowly. "Perhaps no more than you do. But this I know: that I refuse to follow the fashion of our day, of marrying three, four, and five times in succession. When I marry it will be for life. It won't be easy in this society of ours."

He rose suddenly, as if he had said too much. "I must go. By tomorrow morning I think I shall know what is going on. Then I shall come back."

Cassius jumped to his feet. "What if they come and drag my father away to the Mamertinum? You don't expect me to look on and do nothing, do you?"

"First of all," said Seneca patiently, "it won't be the Mamertinum. That's only for political prisoners. Your dear father knows very little about Roman prisons, fortunately. It would be an ordinary jail. But that is not likely to happen before I return. I know the officials dealing with such matters, and I shall be in touch with them. Just leave it to me, and in the name of the sevenfold love don't do anything rash."

"I won't. And I'm most grateful to you."

Seneca shrugged his shoulders. "You might well be—if you have understood what I was trying to tell you", he said. "I believe in love—and I believe in Rome. We are no longer the city of Cincinnatus and of the Gracchi, but what good there is left in us is worth fighting for, I think. We still lead the world not only as soldiers but as legislators. There, you are calmer now, and I must go."

Cassius accompanied him to the door, where Seneca gave him the respectful greeting customary between equals in rank. It was most flattering and made one feel responsible and grave.

The sevenfold love—that was something not easily forgotten. But why talk to him about it now—was there any connection with Claudia? Seneca didn't seem to like Claudia much. He had hardly said a word in her praise, and part of that long talk had sounded rather like a warning.

It did not matter. It could not possibly matter. "I know very little of Claudia, perhaps no more than you do." That had been a jibe, of course, though it had taken a few minutes to recognize the fact. But with all Seneca's knowledge and erudition and elegant ways he was cold, cold as a dog's nose. He would probably work out a mathematical equation before admitting to himself that he was in love—in some one of the stages of his sevenfold love. He could never understand the feeling between Cassius and Claudia.

Back in his study, Cassius sat down and wrote a letter:

Cassius Longinus to Claudia Procula, to the loveliest of women and the heart of his heart:

"My father is ill, so very ill that I must stay at his bedside. I have not slept since I left you, and I am not likely to find sleep till I see you again. It will be tomorrow; it must be. You have taught me that the worst anguish in the world is called "waiting". I love you more than my own life, more than my honor. I love you.

He rolled the parchment up, tied it, and sealed it with his ring, on which was carved a strong, right arm holding a spear, the family coat of arms.

IV

Seneca returned about an hour before noon the next day.

"How is your father?"

"Much better. He wants to get up, and Euphorus says he may, for an hour or so. In a few days he should be entirely recovered."

"Very fortunate", murmured Seneca. "But I think it will be better if I talk to you."

"It's bad news, then", said Cassius calmly.

"Yes, I'm afraid so. You see, as long as you were up against ordinary creditors, something could be done. They would hardly dare ask the praetor for the arrest of a debtor of equestrian rank. But they have sold your father's debt to Balbus."

"That swine!"

"That, too, wouldn't have been so bad. Balbus is an important man in Rome, but a debt of a hundred thousand sesterces is not the world, and something might have been arranged. Unfortunately, however, Balbus also is only an agent in the matter, it seems."

"Who's behind him?"

"Sejanus."

Cassius turned white.

"You will understand now", Seneca went on sadly, "that you

won't find a man in Rome who will help you to pay the debt. Your poor father is a soldier and sometimes does not exactly mince his words. It seems he has made certain remarks about Sejanus' origin—true remarks, no doubt, but not exactly flattering—and they were reported. Sejanus was not yet the master of Rome at that time and could not act directly against a general who had fought with distinction under Tiberius while Sejanus was still in Sicily, making money by selling mules to the army. So he decided to ruin your father by making use of his weakness for gambling and speculation. He gave instructions to Balbus, who in turn told Fuscus what to do. The rest you know."

"Sejanus", Cassius repeated tonelessly. "Father is lost." He swung round so wildly that Seneca instinctively stepped back. "So this is the great Rome you were telling me about? The Rome that leads the world!"

"Control yourself, my dear boy. Your father will hear you if you shout like that."

"Forgive me." Cassius was fighting for breath. "Forgive me, Seneca. You haven't told me the whole story, I'm sure—you've found a way out. Perhaps you could raise the money somewhere, without saying what you need it for—perhaps..."

"I'm afraid that is out of question", Seneca told him. "They are keeping an eye on me anyway. They know I'm your father's legal adviser. If I raised the money, I'd soon be without a single client."

"I see." Cassius gave him a nod of bitter disappointment. "And what is the advice you can give to your client?"

Seneca bit his lip. "It is most unfortunate, but there is really nothing more I can do. Perhaps, if your father would try to see Sejanus..."

"And kiss his feet to be allowed to stay out of jail? Never."

"You have a very—blunt way of putting things, my dear boy."

Cassius gave a mirthless laugh. "You told me such beautiful things yesterday, Seneca. A mere stone is capable of love, you said. Now it seems that stones alone are capable of it. Rome, the city of soldiers and legislators! And her citizens tremble before a tyrant who entices a man into a speculation in order to cheat and ruin him and then uses his position to frighten off those who would come to his aid. The courage of Romans! The justice of Rome! And all you can give us as your last piece of advice is to become abject cowards like the rest and beg for mercy."

Seneca's lips tightened. "Your father acted very imprudently", he said sharply. "You can't expect me to imitate his example by openly offending the most powerful man in Rome."

"There are two Romes", Cassius said with disgust. "The one we dream about and the other, the real one. And the two have precious little in common with each other."

"Please give my respects to your father." Seneca bowed slightly, with cold courtesy. "And remember, when you have cooled off, how much easier it would have been for me to stay away, once I knew who your real enemy was. Misfortune has a habit of making us unjust, especially when we are young and inexperienced."

For a moment Cassius thought of imploring the lawyer to stay and help him think of some way to avoid disaster. But he could not bring himself to do it. He bowed and let Seneca walk away, composed and dignified as always.

"Better young and inexperienced than a coward and a hypocrite", he thought grimly. The idea of Father going to Sejanus, to grovel before that upstart . . .

A thought came on quiet wings, settled in his brain, and began to flutter excitedly. He paced up and down for a while. Then he shouted for Tullus.

The old majordomo looked pale and worried. He had not, of course, been told anything, but servants had their own way of finding out secrets, and he was bound to have drawn some conclusions from what had happened night before last.

"Go and get a travel carriage", ordered Cassius. "Not ours—a hired one. If it has no curtains, put some in. I want it ready at the back door in half an hour."

"Yes, young master." Tullus was much too well trained to appear bewildered.

Cassius went to see his father. The old general was struggling to get into a fresh tunic, with Euphorus dancing attendance.

"What is it now?" he asked gruffly. "Are they here to fetch me?"

Only yesterday Cassius had felt that his father had become a child. Today he was an old, old man, stiff limbed and helpless.

Perhaps Seneca would have said that human life was a circle and that we met our childhood again in old age. Curse Seneca and his philosophizings! Help was needed, practical help.

"Go, Euphorus", said Cassius. Until yesterday he had never dared give orders to the servants when the master of the house was present.

The physician obeyed.

"No one's here, Father, but I think I have found a solution."

"Eh? Solution? There is no solution. Even Seneca didn't find one. Talked a lot yesterday. Can't remember a single thing he said. All words. Lawyers. Pah."

"Exactly", Cassius agreed. "What we need is action."

"Action? I can't do anything. Creditors will do the acting. They'll come any moment now."

"Listen to me, Father. What you need is a few quiet weeks in the country. Go to your farm in the Alban hills."

For a moment the old man's face lighted up in sudden joy. Then he frowned. "Nonsense. Sold the farm. Told you so."

"I know. But you sold this house, too, and you're still in it. They'll probably come and take it over soon, I grant you that. But they won't be in such a hurry about the farm. It's forty miles away and not of much value to them. You go there and take a rest. In the meantime I'll try to raise the money you still owe them. It's not such a terribly large sum, after all. I have friends—I may easily get it together in a few weeks. Seneca will talk to the creditors and obtain time to pay. If I'm lucky I'll get a little more than the hundred thousand, and we'll buy the farm back and live there in peace."

"Nonsense", growled the general. But Cassius saw that the idea was working in him, was taking shape in his mind.

"All that's necessary is to gain time", said Cassius eagerly.

"It means running away", objected the old man. "Running away from the enemy. I was never good at that."

"It's a strategic withdrawal," was the quick reply, "and Caesar himself did that more than once. It's a ruse, too—you're withdrawing into enemy country. The farm is theirs now, but they won't know that you are secretly occupying it."

The old man began to chuckle. "Not bad. Not bad at all."

"Very well, then, Father. I've ordered a carriage. You'll take Tullus and Euphorus along with you."

"Ordered a carriage, eh? Before I had agreed, too. Rascal. But it's a good idea. Good idea."

Cassius beamed at him. If only the old man could stand the trip. Forty miles in a hired carriage, and most of the way uphill on bad roads. But it had to be risked.

He rushed out to get hold of Euphorus. The physician wagged his bald head at the idea of a journey but ran obediently to fetch his medicine chest and a few clothes. He was ready when Tullus arrived with the carriage.

Cassius looked at the driver, a large-boned man with gray hair. Two fingers of his left hand were missing.

"Old soldier?"

"Yes, sir. Pannonia under General Aemilianus, sir, Germany under General Drusus and General Tiberius—the divine Emperor Tiberius, I mean, sir."

"He wasn't divine then", Cassius grinned.

"Not so you could guess it, no, sir."

"Right. I'll charter you for a day's drive and back. Here's to start you off." It was a pleasure to see the man grin with delight at the sight of the coins. To this fellow one was still a power, a financial power. "Euphorus, go and fetch my father. Tullus, get a few clothes and the general's dark cloak. Don't let him start packing things. In five minutes you must be on your way."

They managed it. Euphorus had brought the general's traveling hat, too, and the old man was clutching a small leather bag, as well as a few script rolls.

"Mother's jewels", thought Cassius. They could not be worth much, not in money. That reminded him of something.

"You'd better take this purse, too, Father."

"What? What's in it?"

"The money I won from Balbus. It can serve a good purpose now."

"Not with me. You keep it. Then you'll have to find less. I won't need any money on the farm."

"As you wish, Father. The gods be with you."

"And with you."

They shook hands. They did not embrace. It would have been unbecoming before the servants. But as they shook hands, the old man looked straight into Cassius' eyes and gave a slight nod, and the pressure of his fingers was eloquent. A wounded commander was giving his staff to the next-ranking officer.

And suddenly Cassius knew that he had never been so near to the heart of the old man, and for the first time he felt his eyes grow moist.

The general turned away abruptly. "Help me in, Euphorus. Don't be so clumsy, man. There now."

The physician sat down next to him. Tullus joined the driver.

"Off with you!" Cassius nodded.

The clatter of hooves, the creaking of wheels grinding the gravel—then the carriage turned the corner, and soon there was silence.

Absurd ideas welled up. "I shall never see him again", and, "He is taking my youth with him", and, "All the rest is pain and bitterness."

The next thing really was an impossibility. It was quite childish to try it. Cassius did, nevertheless. He rode all across the city,
baking in the breathless midday sun, to the Viminal Gate.

At that gate was to be found the citadel of the Praetorian
guards. Rome commanded the world, but the Castra Praetoria
commanded Rome.

The great Augustus had never permitted more than three of
the nine Praetorian cohorts to stay in Rome at one time. The
other six had to remain in special quarters outside the city limits.
Cassius remembered his father's snorting contempt when the
new decree was published.

"Tiberius never needed nine cohorts around him even when he
was in enemy country. A guard of fifty men under a reliable
centurion sufficed."

However, everybody knew that it was not the Emperor's own
idea but that of the prefect of the Praetorian guards—Lucius
Aelius Sejanus. No one else knew so well how to make use of the
old Emperor's inveterate suspiciousness.

With the Emperor away in Capri for an unspecified length of
time, perhaps forever, the Palatine Hill had become a realm of
shadows, the Senate a futile assembly of uneasy, impotent figure-
heads, and the Castra Praetoria at the Viminal Gate the heart and
brain of the world.

Built like any other military camp in the empire, the praetorium
dominated the center; there were four spiked walls with turrets,
four main gates, and the parade field just outside. But, in addition,
there was a maze of auxiliary buildings, and in these the main
business of Rome was carried on.

The sentinel at the main gate on the right crashed his spearshaft
to the ground when he saw the equestrian ring on Cassius' finger,
but the man's face was a mask of frozen arrogance under the
gleaming golden helmet topped by a tuft of horsehair dyed the
Praetorian scarlet.

"Where do I find the prefect?" asked Cassius.

"You don't, sir."

"What do you mean?"

"The prefect only receives visitors he has invited to come. If you were one of them, you would have a tessera. If you had a tessera you would know where to go."

"A blacksmith could teach you politeness", snapped Cassius. "Call your officer."

A centurion came clanking, the long staff of his rank carried casually in his hand. He wore a wall-crown in silver on his gilded breastplate.

"Noble knight wants to see the prefect", said the sentinel crisply.

"Why didn't you tell him he can't?"

"I did, sir."

The centurion looked Cassius over. "Do you wish written testimony that the prefect can't see you?" he asked sarcastically.

"I'm the son of *General* Longinus", said Cassius ominously. "Where do I find the prefect?"

The centurion gave a supercilious salute. "Auxiliary building IV is the office where visitors can inscribe themselves."

"Thanks", said Cassius icily and rode off.

There was no sentinel at auxiliary building IV, a long, low barrack honeycombed with offices. Cassius left his horse in charge of an orderly and entered. The corridors were full of people waiting. To his surprise Cassius saw four senators among them, rubbing shoulders with the rest. No one so much as glanced at him. It was as if he were invisible.

Military secretaries in scarlet tunics without armor flitted to and fro with sheaves of papers, all wearing an identical expression of haughty insolence.

He stopped one of them. "Where can I see the prefect?"

The man stared at him. "Where is your tessera, sir?"

"I came here to get one."

"Room eleven."

43

The fellow who presided in room eleven was a secretary of higher rank. "Name, please."

Cassius gave it to him.

"Object of the visit?"

"I'll tell that to the prefect himself."

"Out of the question."

"When I was seventeen", said Cassius hotly, "I was presented to the divine Emperor on Palatine Hill. There was no need to announce the object of my visit then."

"Must do it now", said the secretary.

"Very well. Object of the visit: to see the prefect as the representative of my father, General Longinus, who is too ill to appear in person."

The secretary rose. "Just a moment", he said and went to the adjacent room. After a few minutes he came back. "The tessera will be sent to you in due course", he announced blandly.

"When will that be?"

"I should say in about three months' time."

Cassius bit his lip. "That is three months too late. It is a matter of life and death."

"Not to the prefect", said the secretary, smiling.

For a moment Cassius stood immobile.

"Next, please", barked the secretary, and one of the senators shuffled in, an ingratiatingly cheerful man, balding and paunchy.

Cassius turned and left. Outside he mounted Pluto again and walked him away, careful to show an absolutely impassive face.

He had not really expected to be received, had he? He simply wanted to try everything. What would he have said to Sejanus? It might easily have ended very badly.

A full cohort was marching across the parade ground, with an officer bellowing commands. The performance of the shiny men was excellent. They moved with the perfect accuracy of a single body, of one large, glittering arm, a Roman arm, but a Roman arm raised to protect the Emperor against the Romans.

They were trained to rule this vast city of bricks, tiles, marble, and smells, and they were hated by the people for their arrogance. And, as at least some of the secret police functions were taken over by them, they were feared. They, in turn, despised the people, citizens, freedmen, and slaves alike—and the regular army as well. Augustus had used them as his bodyguard, and according to the ancient laws the presence of three, even of a single cohort within the precincts of the city was a grave wrong. Now they were a state within a state, the haughty rivals of the three thousand policemen of the city prefect and at the same time brilliant showpieces of imperial strength and splendor.

When Cassius' father had old military friends as his guests, they invariably lamented that the empire was going to rack and ruin. Perhaps retired old officers always talked like that. But there were violent disagreements about the start of the downward trend. Some said it had started only lately—probably with their retirement; others accused Augustus or Caesar. What would Seneca say? To Hades with Seneca. It did not matter what he said about anything.

It was probably all nonsense, anyway. The empire was still the empire, and there was no power on earth that could replace it. The barbarians were beaten whenever they tried to rebel against Roman rule. The slaves? Many people were afraid of the slaves. There were so many of them—perhaps more than there were free men; in Rome alone there were half a million. Ever since the days of the slave revolt under Spartacus, nearly a hundred years ago, people had been afraid, although Crassus had vanquished the rebels easily and crucified them by the thousand. The story of the avenue of crosses from Naples to Rome, with slaves writhing on them at a distance of only a few yards from each other, was told to every child. And the law provided the sternest measures against another insurrection. But slaves came from half a hundred different countries; they had no organization; they had nothing in common at all, except their chains. Many of them were treated very well, too. Twice in the course of three years his father had had a slave whipped—seriously whipped, not just a few slaps in the face—and then sent to the ergastulum, the slave prison. Twice in three years, with almost forty slaves in the house. Besides, they had no spark in them: it was so much easier to do what one was told and receive food and shelter in exchange—just as in the army few men really wanted to be officers. No danger was likely to arise from the slaves.

Thus, unless the gods themselves brought about a change out of the clear sky, the empire was safe enough.

And here was the entrance to Claudia's house.

He had drifted there. He had been spinning thoughts about the Praetorian guard, the empire, and the slaves to hide from himself the fact that he was going to Claudia. It was stupid, of course, to see her so soon. What could he tell her? When he last saw her, he had been a victor; now he was—he didn't know what. Yet then he had been no more than an ignorant boy; today he was a man going to the woman he loved. How many hours since he had been free to dream of her? She would no longer be exiled. She had taken possession of him, filling his brain, firing his blood, and nothing was of any importance except seeing her again and seeing her at once.

He brushed past the majordomo who opened the door and rushed in, and there she was, alone and more beautiful than his dreams—he stopped and gazed at her, and words would not come.

She was impeccable and cool and aloof. She did not smile. He was still searching for words when she spoke: "It is not right to endanger one's friends."

He drew back a little, instinctively. "I don't understand."

"Oh, yes, you do. A man of breeding does not drag a defenseless woman into such affairs as yours!"

"But, Claudia . . ."

"I have nothing to do with such things. I live my own life,

46

and I will not be dragged into political affairs." Her voice rose shrilly.

"Claudia, listen to me, I beg you . . . "

"I've heard everything about you and your precious father. I suppose you staged that wonderful scene two days ago because you counted on my help. Well, I'm quite unable to do anything for you. The Emperor has a very numerous family, and he is too old now to remember them all. He certainly does not remember me."

"Claudia, it isn't you who is saying that! If you are referring to my father's present difficulties, I knew nothing about them myself two days ago, and anyone who tells you differently is lying."

"You seem to think I am very simple. I cannot help you with my imperial relative, and I cannot help you with money. I haven't got a hundred thousand sesterces to spare. Does that make it clear?"

"Balbus", he said hoarsely. His brain reeled. Balbus was speaking out of Claudia's mouth.

Somewhere in the back of his mind he heard Seneca's cool, suave voice: "I know very little of Claudia. Perhaps no more than you do."

"I shall thank you to refrain from writing to me again", said the pitiless mouth. "And I must ask you to leave me now."

"Claudia", he whispered. "Claudilla . . . "

She touched the lever of a small bronze group on the table beside her. The club of Hercules came crashing down on the shield of a frightened Titan.

The majordomo entered.

Slowly Cassius turned away and left the room and the house. His mouth was dry, and his knees were shaking. Only once before had he felt like this—the day when his mother died. He had been a child then, and he thought that life had come to an end. It had not. But now it had.

Nothing mattered any more.

47

Only after the third attempt did he manage to mount his horse.

He had not known that such pain could be, such searing, cruel, hopeless pain. He felt sick; he felt unclean, a leper whose touch must be avoided, whose very presence was shunned.

Pluto carried him through blurred streets, past blurred, meaningless faces.

"Claudilla", he thought. "Why did you do this to me, Claudilla, why?"

Was beauty nothing but skin over cowardice and evil, cracking at the first test?

"How can you ever be happy, if you destroy love, Claudilla?"

He should have asked her that. Now it was too late. He would never ask her anything again. She was dead.

"You are dead, Claudia, my life, my heart, you are dead."

Somehow Pluto found the way home.

At the gate Cassius suddenly awoke. It was closed.

The garden was deserted, and nothing stirred in the house.

Then he saw the large seal of the praetor affixed to the gate.

V

When Balbus' servant announced, "The noble Cassius Longinus", the fat man looked up sharply. "Alone?"

"Yes, master."

"Excited?"

"N-no, master."

Balbus whistled softly. "Nevertheless," he said, "I want the two Numidians there—" he nodded toward the heavy curtain behind him. "Armed, Firminus."

"Yes, master."

"When they are in place, let the young man come in—not before. Is that clear?"

48

"Yes, master."

A few moments later Cassius entered.

"By the gods, you are looking ill, my dear fellow", said Balbus cheerfully. "You haven't picked up a fever, I hope?"

"All that ails me is known to you", was the quiet answer.

"Is it? I don't know about that. And how is your dear father? *Still* well, I trust?"

Cassius bit his lip. He said gravely, "You've won this time, Balbus. And it's a greater victory than mine the other day. I am told you bought up my father's debts."

"Who told you that?" asked the fat man quickly. He was studying the face before him. Lack of sleep, but not only lack of sleep. Despair. And surrender.

"It doesn't matter who told me", Cassius said. "I know."

Balbus began to chuckle. "That's how it goes in love and in business—ups and downs, my dear fellow, ups and downs."

"My father owes you one hundred thousand sesterces over and above what you have already taken—is that right?"

"I suppose so", agreed Balbus lightly. "I have so many business affairs, I cannot possibly remember every detail. You haven't by any chance come to pay me, have you?"

"Yes."

Balbus jumped to his feet. "Who gave you the money?"

"It seems to annoy you that I want to pay my father's debts", said Cassius dryly.

Balbus' eyes narrowed to slits. "You must understand that I cannot take money without knowing where it comes from."

Cassius gave a harsh laugh. "Have you always followed that principle? But set your mind at rest. I haven't got the money." Cynically he watched Balbus' effort to conceal his relief. "But I have come to make you a proposition", he added.

"I'm afraid . . . " began Balbus.

"Don't worry", interrupted Cassius. "I shall not propose that you give us more time to pay."

Balbus raised his brows. "Then what *do* you propose?"

"First of all to give you back the twenty thousand I won from you."

"Eighty thousand remains."

"Yes. I have a horse outside, three years old, Spanish breed, a gelding. It is worth six thousand."

"Maybe."

"There remains seventy-four thousand", said Cassius. "And here is my proposition. I don't care about myself. But I cannot let my father at his age go to live in the Subura among dyers, barbers, and tavernkeepers. Now one item of the possessions you 'acquired' through your 'agents' is a small farm in the Alban hills. Father bought it for thirty thousand. I want you to give it back to him, so that he can live there quietly to the end of his days."

"That would increase the debt again to over a hundred thousand." Balbus shrugged. "You're mad. Why should I do that? I've been to see the praetor today, and he has made out an order for your father's arrest. It has probably been executed by now."

"I don't think so", was the icy reply. "And you did not let me finish. In full payment of the debt I offer you myself."

There was a pause.

"You mean—as—"

"As a slave, yes."

Another pause.

The fat man began to smile again. "This is not entirely uninteresting—on principle. But why do you want to do it?"

"I am worth nothing to myself", was the impassive answer. "And I want my father to live in peace."

"You are worth nothing to yourself—what makes you think that you are worth a hundred thousand sesterces to me?" Balbus was thoroughly enjoying himself. "What are your qualities and abilities, apart from the virtue of filial piety and some skill in throwing a spear?"

"You hate me, don't you?" Cassius smiled contemptuously. "If you were a patrician your hatred should be worth the money to you. As it is I must give you other reasons. Up to four times that amount has been paid for a slave of the first order, like the grammarian Thermonides or the physician Malik. I haven't got their erudition or knowledge, that is true. But there are other values. One is life expectancy. Thermonides was sixty when Sejanus bought him to teach his daughter. I am twenty, and you could keep me for fifty years or more, if your belly allows you to live that long."

"You impudent dog", snarled Balbus. "I might buy you and then have you whipped every day, and we'll see which of us lives longer."

"I'm not your slave yet, so you will have to control your temper", said Cassius icily. "Besides life expectancy I offer my abilities as a fighter. I could win a bet or two for you, Balbus—or be killed. A pleasant alternative for you, I'm sure."

"That's true", snapped Balbus. "Especially the latter."

"No doubt."

"Over a hundred thousand sesterces . . . " began the fat man.

"There's no use bargaining", Cassius interrupted. "No one can give more than he has, and what I have I give you—my money, my horse, my freedom, and my services. But I must know that my father is safe on his small farm."

Balbus thought it over for a while. "Very well", he said finally. "I shall take you to the praetor at once."

The praetor was a horse-faced man with an expression of permanent grief. "You have come a little too early", he told Balbus. "My men have sealed the house of your debtor, and we are holding his slaves, all but two—but he himself was not present, and the only thing we have found out so far is that he left in a hired carriage together with the two missing slaves. It may be a few more days before we get hold of him."

Balbus explained why they had come, and the praetor listened without a trace of emotion. "Very well", he said. "In that case the order to arrest the debtor will have to be withdrawn, of course."

"Well, yes", Balbus said reluctantly.

Cassius closed his eyes to hide his relief. But then he watched the proceedings with keen attentiveness. Document after document had to be drawn up. A deed giving back to his father the possession of the farm. A receipt for twenty thousand sesterces and a horse worth six thousand. When it came to the sale of his freedom the praetor glanced at him lugubriously and asked whether he had fully considered the matter. "After all, you are of equestrian rank."

Cassius took the ring off his finger. "I must pay my father's debts. My decision is made."

"Can the noble Balbus find no other way?" inquired the praetor, frowning.

"No", snapped the fat man. "There have been other cases of men of equestrian rank signing away their freedom and . . . "

"There is no need to teach me the law, noble Balbus", interrupted the praetor testily. "Will the noble Cassius Longinus answer my question?"

"There is no other way, sir", said Cassius bitterly. "Not with Rome what it is now."

The praetor frowned again and began to fill out the document.

"Sign here", he said to Balbus. "And here. Now the young man's signature."

Stylus in hand, Cassius looked up to the praetor. "May I ask you, sir, to have only these two documents sent to my father? The one about the farm and the one about the payment of the debt, but not the one by which I sell my freedom?"

The praetor cleared his throat. "I think I understand", he said. "Very well. But to what address shall I send them? Do you know where your father is?"

"Yes, sir", replied Cassius calmly. "He is on *his* farm." He signed. Balbus' face was contorted with anger.

The praetor gave the equestrian ring to an official. "To be destroyed at once", he said. "The metal goes to the treasury." He turned to Balbus. "The man is yours now. Do you wish to have his ear slit?"

"By all means", Balbus growled.

It was the ancient mark of servitude, though no longer obligatory, to ensure that a fugitive slave could not pose as a free citizen. The slit ear was the worry of all freedmen, who tried to hide it under a turban or earring or by wearing their hair long. Even so they could never be sure that they would not have to produce their document of manumission to any official who asked for it.

Cassius gritted his teeth. It was only the beginning, he knew, of a long series of humiliations to come. Balbus was not the man to renounce a single advantage the bargain gave him.

A subofficial performed the ritual in the simplest of ways with a military dagger. Knowing that Balbus was watching him, Cassius did not even wince. The subofficial stuck a little piece of cloth on the wound and withdrew.

Balbus and the praetor exchanged a few frosty courtesies. Then the fat man turned to Cassius: "Carry my cloak. And march before me."

The bracelet was huge, emeralds and gold, in the form of a snake. It was not the work of a great artist, but it certainly was expensive.

Claudia was trying it on.

"Wonderful", gasped Sabina. "You never had a more beautiful present. This Balbus must be as rich as the Grand King of Persia."

"He is rich enough", Claudia agreed. She was looking at herself in a large mirror of polished silver.

Sabina said, "I'd close my eyes and marry Balbus if I were Claudia Procula."

"So would I", Claudia drawled, "if I were Sabina." She took the bracelet off and dropped it on the small table inlaid with tortoise shell. "Put it into its box and send it back to him."

"Send it back?" Sabina was horrified. "You are out of your mind, child. Why, for this bracelet you'd get . . . "

"There are strings attached to it, Sabina. Balbus is the kind of man whose presents always find their way back to him, one way or the other. No, I don't want to hear any arguments. Did he pay you so well to plead for him? Send it back."

In the door the older woman turned round. "What tunic do you wish me to lay out for the dinner at Domina Pomponia's house tonight? The one with the golden fringe or the peacock blue?"

"Neither", Claudia said. "The amethyst-colored one. The new one."

Sabina raised her painted brows. "I hope it'll be worth it", she said and withdrew hastily.

Claudia sighed. It was time to get rid of that woman. But not today. There must be no upset today. She had to have her wits about her and look her best at Pomponia's dinner.

Pomponia had come to see her in the morning, just to make sure that she would come—Pomponia, who never rose before the early afternoon. "Claudia, dear, it is absolutely necessary that you come tonight. I *promised* a certain man who has just been given a province in the East that you would come. He's *madly* in love with you."

"Oh, come, Pomponia dear. I think I know whom you mean, but surely he is beyond the age when men are madly in love."

"You're quite wrong there, my dear. And besides . . . "

"Well?"

Pomponia's doll's face looked grave. "Besides, I have reason to believe that a—the most important man in Rome would be pleased if you could see your way to marry the man I mean."

"*Sejanus* told you that?"

"In so many words, Claudia."

Why should Sejanus want her to marry that man? But it was quite futile to try to understand what was going on in the great man's mind. And the last thing to do was to incur his enmity. Besides, the man he seemed to have chosen for her was neither ugly nor poor, and she would have an official position—a position many women would envy.

But one must not think of young Cassius.

She sighed again. "I wish I could afford to be foolish", she thought.

VI

Spurio was watching his men at work. There was not much fun nowadays even in being the lapista of one of Rome's four famous gladiators' schools—not with the scrofulous, spindle-legged weaklings that passed for gladiators because the provinces kept the best men for themselves instead of sending them to Rome, where they belonged. But to be the lapista of a private school was slow torture. You didn't have to play hide and seek with the aedil, who always expected first-rate material to grow out of nothing in a couple of months, and you didn't have to parley with the perfumed young nobles who pretended to be sports enthusiasts. But you got the scum of the earth because you could not make use of the officials who combed all incoming slave ships for potential material; you didn't get any of the fat bribes that came to the Big Four from the real sports enthusiasts or any of the hundred-sesterces pieces in gold even the perfumed little whippersnappers left for being allowed to admire their heroes, and you rarely got a whiff of the real thing at all. It was training puppies to perform at banquets for the amusement of a few hundred drunks, not preparing master fighters for a grand feast at the Circus Maximus, with all Rome yelling its head off over a man you had whipped into shape.

Twice in the course of four years he had been able to send a few men to an affair somewhat more substantial than a private banquet. One was a boxer, and *they* weren't worth much, except for the pleasure of the riffraff. Not one of them had ever made a real name for himself. Two of his men were "Gauls", and both had been slain on the same day by their net fighters. A Gaul had to be good to survive, and they weren't that good. The last was a net fighter, and he had won twice and then was finished because that stupid old idiot of an aedil had him matched against a boar. Fight a boar with net and trident . . .

This year's crop was one of the worst: of the sixteen men only one showed real promise, Polemon, the Thracian.

The men were training in pairs now, and Polemon had the new one. Light head protector, shield, and blunt sword. The Thracian couldn't stand the new one, and he was playing rough.

"Easy," roared Spurio, "don't kill him! The noble Balbus may want him again as a Gaditan dancer or something."

Polemon grinned. The new one went on fighting in his elegant little way as if he were not interested. He had had schooling, of course, but army schooling, officers' training, all perfectly neat and correct and clean and much too little weight behind it. There—down he went. No, he didn't. He wasn't bad. He wasn't raw either. But he wasn't the right stuff; how could he be? He didn't have the killer's spirit.

A visitor from the Castra Praetoria was shown into Balbus' study. He was Rufius, one of Sejanus' confidential secretaries, a lean, bony man with a pimpled face. He wore the scarlet tunic of the Praetorian guards without armor or badge of rank.

"A letter from the prefect to the noble Balbus", he announced, producing a wax tablet from a bag attached to his belt.

"Whatever the message, I send the great prefect my humble thanks", said Balbus.

Rufius, with insolent indifference, made no move to leave, and Balbus began to think that the letter required an immediate answer. He opened it.

Lucius Aelius Sejanus to the noble Marcus Balbus, greetings:

When I entrusted you with a financial transaction which in due course would cause a certain man to incur debts, I knew that it would enable you to make a good profit, and I regarded this as a just reward for an esteemed friend. I very much regret, however, that you have altered the original plan by accepting the annulment of the debt in exchange for the acquisition of a slave, although I quite understand your motive for doing so. The result is that the old viper may cause some annoyance, and I must now rely on you to see to it that this cannot possibly happen. Let me know when you are sure of that, and let it be soon. The fate of the young viper is of no interest to me, provided, of course, that no official law is violated. I am told that you are having him trained for the arena. By all means do that. There have been cases before, as you know, of well-born young men showing their skill in public. On the other hand, I cannot approve of merely social occasions in which a person formerly of equestrian rank is exhibited as a slave. It is not dignified, and I must rely on my friends to avoid anything that could foment a spirit of opposition to a government already in a delicate position due to the fact that the divine Emperor does not wish, for the time being, to be annoyed by state affairs.

"The prefect would like you to read his letter twice", said Rufius softly.

Balbus nodded and read again, trying in vain to understand what was going on in the prefect's mind. It was clear enough what he wanted done—but why, by all the furies, didn't he have it done himself? Why was he worried about Cassius being seen as a slave? Above all, how did he dare to write so openly?

"You have finished?" asked Rufius.

"Yes. And please tell the prefect I am as always his devoted servant and friend."

"The prefect will be pleased", said Rufius indifferently. He stretched out his bony arm, took the wax tablet from Balbus' fingers, and rubbed its surface smooth with a few strokes of his palm.

"What are you doing?" fumed Balbus. "That letter is mine."

"Order of the prefect", said Rufius lightly. "A little matter of economy." He put the wax tablet into his bag, gave a supercilious greeting, and left.

Balbus sat for a while, pondering. Why this bitter enmity of the most powerful man in Rome against a retired old general? The old man had said a few nasty things—but could that really be the whole reason? Surely nothing could be more humiliating for his enemy than to live like a small farmer in the Alban hills, away from everything that mattered, and with his only son, his proud son, sold into slavery? One might have thought that Sejanus would be pleased about a vengeance far more complete than the one he had planned originally. But apparently it had been his wish that old Longinus should die in jail. And that passage about the young viper? As if it had not been the perfect touch to let the fellow, dressed in a slave's tunic and with a huge earring in his slit ear, read out the names of entering guests, many of whom had known him in his former status, and above all with Claudia present. She had behaved very well. She had simply pretended not to see him at all. Who could have told Sejanus about it? The Tribune Caelius, perhaps, or Scaurus, or Apicius. No, Apicius was interested only in his new invention, to fatten the liver of pigs with a diet of figs, which made them twice as large and three times as delicious; he had talked about it for hours. Or Afranius, perhaps. It was futile to guess—Sejanus had informers everywhere. Caelius had looked displeased about the new slave, though he said nothing, and some of the women seemed to regret that a very eligible young man had become a thing instead of a man. Perhaps—perhaps Claudia has told Sejanus. In spite of her apparent indifference she was bound to have been impressed. Where was he now, the young hero of a few weeks earlier, the proud thrower of spears! She was much too intelligent and much too sensitive not to understand: this was what happened to those who crossed Balbus' will.

She was difficult to win. Yet Afranius, her banker, said she did not have more than a couple of hundred thousand to her name. She would have to make up her mind soon—and she knew now what might happen to one who paid her too much attention. Some women would find pleasure in such danger, but she was not the type. She needed security.

It was regrettable that the performance could not be repeated. But there was a definite meaning in Sejanus' sentence about Cassius Longinus. "The fate of the young viper does not interest me, provided, of course, that no official law is violated." In other words: don't kill the man just because you hate him, or I won't protect you against the praetor. Why did he want to kill the old viper but spare the young one?

It almost looked as if Sejanus were afraid of public opinion, as if he did not feel quite sure of himself.

Or was all this part of some larger plan? If so, what could it be?

Balbus took a beautiful piece of parchment, dipped the gold-mounted reed into purple ink. "No economy when Balbus writes to Sejanus", he thought grimly. He wrote:

Marcus Balbus to Lucius Aelius Sejanus, Prefect of the Praetorian Guards, Vice-Regent of the Empire:

"When I allowed the matter of the old viper to take a slightly different turn, I hoped to improve on the original idea, and nothing was farther away from my mind than to do anything against your wishes. I see now that I was wrong, and I shall endeavor to please you by speedy action. You who know everything are aware, I am sure, of my interest in the Lady Claudia Procula. May I hope that your magnanimity will see fit to give a hint to the noble lady that a union between herself and me would not be displeasing to you?

59

There. But now the great man's wish had to be complied with.

Balbus shouted for Firminus. "Send this to the Castra Praetoria. And I want Spurio here after the midday meal."

Three weeks. Three weeks among sweaty, muscle-proud oafs whose vocabulary consisted of a couple of hundred words, most of them filthy.

Up at sunrise, exercises on the bleak training court, a breakfast of pulsum, porridge with lemon juice, and watered wine. Huge quantities of pulsum. They attacked it with their dirty fingers and pushed each other out of the way, swine at the trough.

He had heard it said of Seneca that he liked to eat with his slaves. It could not be true, unless he was completely indifferent to manners, noises, and smells. The smells! There was something unhealthy about these men, who had been picked for their exceptional healthiness and strength. Life amongst simple men was nothing new to Cassius. But what a difference between regular soldiers, legionaries, and this motley crowd of muscular half-animals!

After breakfast, exercises. The net, the trident, the fight with blunt swords. The pleasure they took in playing crude tricks of the arena on unsuspecting newcomers. You lift your shield to block Spurio's view, and you bring up your knee hard into the opponent's groin; you hide a nail or a pointed stone in your fist; you tread on the other man's foot to immobilize him for the one short moment you need; dirty little tricks used by men continually boasting of their superiority. The German prisoner, Brinno, was the only one who did not make use of such methods. He despised them. But when you won your fight, you must be careful not to turn your back on him. He knew no tricks, but he could not bear to lose. The Thracian Polemon was the best man of the lot, and the worst lout.

The midday meal: pulsum again and a lot of vegetables. Very

60

rarely a little piece of fish or meat. An hour's rest followed, then training again, running, jumping, any kind of athletic games. The supper: vegetables and the inevitable pulsum—and lights out.

The four walls of the palaestra, the training school, the sand of the court: it was like living in prison.

But when night fell the prison became a hundred times more horrible.

In a dark room, just about large enough for five or six men, sixteen slept on cots so narrow and so close together that they seemed to overlap. Those disgusting bodies really did overlap in all directions. The air was dank and full of stertorous breathing. Sleep, no longer the gentle brother of Death, was an evil spirit, staring at you from red-rimmed eyes and mocking you. Thoughts, always the same thoughts, came like a ragged army, laying siege to a tired mind, all of them pitiless, jeering, unanswerable.

Fool. Stupid fool. You have thrown your life away, and what for? So that an old man can live on a little farm, get up, bathe, eat, sit in the sun, babble to neighbors about his strategic feats in the past, eat again, and sleep again. You are living in a horrible jail so that the old man can live in a comfortable jail.

Life itself was no better than a prison. You could be the jailer or the jailed, that was the whole difference.

Let the old man vegetate on his farm. Did he bother about where his son was? Probably not—or very little. And if he did, what difference would it make?

Fat swine Balbus never came to the palaestra. Since the day of the ear slitting Cassius had seen him only on two occasions. One was when he gave another banquet and paraded his new slave before his guests. It did not matter. It did not even matter that *she* was there.

A slave was not a man. A slave was not a person at all. He was an "it", a living mummy, a pair of hands, a kind of ghost.

61

He had found it curious to look at these people who were still alive. Curious and almost frightening. Ghosts, of course, could not be afraid for themselves. But those guzzling, laughing, talking people—they were in danger. Tomorrow, next week it could be their turn to be ruined or sold or to commit suicide. He knew that now.

And she? Perhaps Balbus would get her. What if he did? She was as rotten and cowardly as the rest. What did it matter whether one rotten coward consorted with another or not?

She ate Balbus' dainties and talked to her neighbors at table; she had no care in the world. But behind her face was a death's-head; beneath her flesh was a skeleton. There was a skeleton under Balbus' fat. He saw the entire hall peopled with skeletons clad in flesh, at a banquet in Hades.

That was the true picture, but only a slave could see it. If you were a philosopher, you might babble about the sevenfold love and then fade away as soon as things became dangerous.

A slave at least knew that he was a ghost. He had no pretenses. But he could still feel bodily pain—as on that second occasion when he had seen Balbus again.

The whipping hurt. The two Numidians—the same who had held a silver shield, some time in the far distant past—were strong and seemed to enjoy their task, though not as much as Balbus did.

There had been a time when a fool still believed in Rome and life and love, a day when one could send a spear whirring through the air and crashing through the mouth of the Medusa and feel jubilant about it. But the Medusa had hit back.

The whipping hurt abominably. There was no reason for it, except that Balbus wanted it done, which was as good a reason as any.

Some physician slave looked after his back and shoulders afterward. At first he thought he was to be strengthened for future whippings or other tortures, but nothing happened. Nor was he ordered to serve at another banquet. Instead he was sent here, to subsist among the muscle brutes.

Some day he would have to fight one of these brutes in some arena, or perhaps a four-legged brute instead, and if he won, he would have to fight another, and still another—until he lost. And then the ghost would be laid. At least there would be an end to stink and smell—unless the dead were perturbed by the stink of their own corruption.

It did not matter. In the first days he had raged and bitten into his hands because of the injustice. But now he knew there was no injustice. Not much. Just for a short, a very short, span of time, for a few thousand meals of pulsum and vegetables. Then they would all follow him. Balbus—that woman—the great Sejanus himself with all his sweet-mannered Praetorian guards—all of them would die and stink and be no more. They were all condemned to death, just as surely as the wretched net fighter or bestiarius. Jump about a little, preen yourself, sink, die, stink, be no more. It was only a question of a little time. "Life is a journey heading for death." Somebody had said that, but whoever said it went on living as if death would never come. They were mad. People were mad.

As a child he had been made to go to the temple of Jupiter and pray. He had gone a few times with his mother. She was religious— women often were. They always needed attention. When they did not receive enough of it, they pretended that the gods were interested in them. Later, when Mother fell ill, he had to go with old Turibia, and he hated it, but he did want to pray to the gods that they would make Mother well again. To Aesculapius, of course. And to Jupiter. There was a day when he prayed to all the gods he could think of. Aesculapius, god of health, came first; then Jupiter and Juno and Venus and Mars and Diana and Apollo and Bacchus and Ceres and Pluto ("You don't really want her, great Pluto, she is only a very small woman.") and Proserpina and Mercury; to Helios and Luna; to Neptune and Amphitrite and to the household gods. Still he had not been satisfied. There were temples of foreign gods in Rome, and perhaps they also had power. He prayed to Mithras, the Persian god, and to the Egyptian Isis of whom many people said that she could do quite incredible things. Those were all the gods he could think of; he hoped he had not forgotten any.

That day, when he came home, Mother seemed to be better. But in the evening she became worse again, and in the night she died. When Turibia told him, in the morning, her fat old face puffed up with crying, he had said, frowning, "I must have left out some god." Only later, when he saw his mother, white and strange and motionless on a bed of flowers, had he cried.

After that he had refused to go to the temple however much old Turibia pleaded with him. She had complained about him to his father, but apparently not very successfully, for she never bothered him about it again. Father never went to the temple himself.

Years later, when he was sixteen and about to join the army, his father suddenly returned to the subject. "You will have to swear the oath, son. By the Capitoline Jupiter and Mars and the Genius of the Emperor. I want no nonsense about that. They are sacred symbols, all of them, symbols of your city, your country, and the empire. The eagles of the legion are Jupiter's symbols, and any Roman who isn't ready to die for the eagle of his legion isn't a Roman at all. Think of that when you are throwing your bit of incense into the tripod."

"Yes, Father."

"Besides, we must give an example to the troops. Soldiers are simple people and believe in the gods. Rome has conquered the world—therefore Roman gods must be more powerful than any others. Gives them courage and strength. It's silly to discourage them. That clear?"

"Y-yes, Father. But why is there a temple of Isis in Rome? We defeated Egypt. Why do Romans worship Isis?"

64

"Because some Romans are fools, and worse than fools. Aping other people's customs is always the first sign of decadence. But some fools will fall for the mystery tricks of Egyptian charlatans and the like. Absurd."

"And—what about Roman charlatans, Father?"

The old general sniffed. "You're not exactly stupid. Must have drawn your conclusions from the fact that I keep away from the incense swingers and prayer sellers. And I didn't object when you refused to go to the moon sacrifice with old Turibia, eh? Remember your mathematics, son? Sometimes you have to draw auxiliary lines to solve your problem. Gods are auxiliary lines. *We* draw them to solve our problems. Difference is: we don't really solve them by that at all; we only think we do. We can't bear the idea that some problems just can't be solved, so we have to invent gods who alone know the solution, and so on. But all that is for the weak. To the strong it doesn't matter that certain problems can't be solved. They are their own authority. You go and serve Rome. That's all that really matters."

Was it? What was Rome? Bricks and marble, gold-plated temples for the "auxiliary lines", sweaty, cheating, pleasure-hunting masses, the Castra Praetoria, Sejanus and Balbus, faithless women, a horse-faced praetor, and an army of slit-ears, and all of them ghosts before they became putrefaction and nothingness.

Why serve that? Why serve anything or anybody?

VII

Spurio was away for two days, and in his absence Polemon became the overseer of the school.

It was a bad choice, as the Thracian was ill disciplined and given to bouts of black rage, but it was probably the only thing

Spurio could do in the circumstances. None of the other men would have been able to cope with Polemon. There were moments when even Spurio himself seemed to be on his guard against him, as a good tamer of wild animals will be when dealing with a moody, unpredictable beast.

Polemon's two-day rule went to show that even in the world of Hades things could become worse. Spurio at least had an aim: to make gladiators out of the raw material given into his care. Polemon only wanted to assert his own superiority. His way of supervising the training was to maul the men about and insult them in the grossest terms.

It might have been a good idea to teach him a lesson — why should he be the only one to profit from the lanista's absence?

But strangely enough the Thracian avoided Cassius Longinus. He did not even bother to address him. His favorite victim was the German, Brinno, whom he insisted on giving lessons with the cestus, the Thracian boxing glove, liberally studded with small pieces of lead. It cost the German two perfectly good teeth, quite senselessly, too, as Spurio had no intention of training Brinno as a boxer. Half insane with fury, Brinno hurled himself at his tormentor and was promptly knocked unconscious.

That night he kept tossing and squirming on his cot in the dormitory. "Lie still", whispered Cassius morosely. "Who can sleep if you insist on going on boxing here?"

"I wish I kill him", groaned the German. "Kill him, kill him."

He seemed to relish the word.

"It wouldn't help you any."

The German gritted his remaining teeth. "Dunno. Kill him. Run away. Quite away."

"Don't be a fool, man", Cassius said wearily. "You wouldn't get far. You'd be back in a few days, and Balbus would have you nailed to the cross. That's a little worse than taking a beating from Polemon."

"I want to go home", muttered the German. "I'm sick of it

here—of your sun and your palms and your pulsum. I want to see a forest again."

"What's so good about a forest?"

The German sighed. "Cool. Shadow. Clean water in the brooks. Smell of grass. Life. There, I used to live. This is no life at all. Just moving around. No life."

There was no answer to that. Perhaps even a barbarian's life in the wild forest was better than a gladiators' school in Rome.

"No life", came Brinno's thick voice through the darkness. "Just moving death."

So even a barbarian could feel it.

Everybody knew that Spurio had gone to Ostia to look for gladiator material. Ostia was the place to go; there the large ships arrived from all over the world, and if a man was lucky and knew his way around he might be able to snatch a few first-rate slaves from some owner who needed money urgently and did not want to wait for the ordinary sales in Rome. Besides, there was no need for middlemen, for the rapacious agents and professional dealers who claimed a juicy percentage of the sale just for exhibiting the wretches on their blocks and stands in the market. Balbus was a rich man; perhaps one of his friends had given him a hint that some suitable men were arriving at the port.

But the lanista came back alone. "Market's getting worse and worse", he said. "Nothing but sweet-faced little boys and old dodderers—haven't seen a body I couldn't have finished off with one hand tied behind my back. Why are you grinning at me like a hyena, you German scum?" Then he saw the two missing front teeth and understood that this was Brinno's way of making complaint.

"Who did this?"

Polemon shrugged his shoulders. "I told him seven times to keep his guard up, but you can't get anything into that wooden head of his."

"That didn't happen with a blunt sword", growled Spurio. "What did you do it with?"

"Well, I thought it might do him some good to learn a little boxing and . . . "

"You've been showing off your Thracian nonsense. Two weeks without wine—for damaging your master's goods. Any more complaints?"

But the men remained silent.

"I'm back now", said Spurio slowly. "There'll be no more nonsense." His little pig's eyes blinked evilly. "That goes for you, too", he added, stabbing his hard finger into Cassius' side.

The training square had three doors, one connecting it with the dormitory, another leading to the servants' quarters of Balbus' house, and a third to the street. The last was a narrow gate of heavy wood with an inset of iron bars. Spurio alone had the key. Sometimes street urchins or a few passersby stopped there to catch a glimpse of the men at training, but never for long. Spurio, who did not care for onlookers, had a habit of throwing at them the first thing he could lay his hands on, a few fistfuls of sand—if they were lucky—mud or even stones.

It was at that gate that the old seller of amulets appeared.

"Amulets—talismans—of unfailing effect", he whined. "Dead cheap, too."

"What's in this one?" asked a big, lumbering man curiously.

"Three threads of the cloak of Mars Repulsor, great Hercules, from the famous temple of the god in Puteoli. Wear it when you fight, and the iron of your enemy cannot touch you. Only seven sesterces, O mighty Achilles."

"Three threads of your own dirty cloak, more likely", laughed the man. "And the lanista won't let me fight yet, seller of rubbish."

Cassius Longinus, a few yards away, stood frowning at his toes. That voice—but it could not be, it was impossible. That voice . . .

"I have another one, O sturdy Atlas, a talisman to ward off all demons and witches, only three sesterces . . . "

Cassius Longinus whirled round. The old man at the gate was Euphorus.

News from his father. And Spurio was having a bout with his favorite Polemon at the other end of the square; they had eyes only for each other, slugging away and parrying. It was a good moment.

Cassius sauntered over to the gate, just as the man Euphorus had spoken to was walking away. "Euphorus", he whispered.

The old slave opened his mouth to speak and could not.

"Father", whispered Cassius fiercely. "Speak up, man—how is he?"

Euphorus made a short, violent gesture toward his own throat, as if he were slitting it with a knife. Then he began to sob.

"No!" said Cassius hoarsely. "No . . . no . . . "

"K-kk-killed!" gasped Euphorus. And as if the word had wrenched his tongue loose again, he went on. "Day before yesterday—evening—'twas one big brute of a man—his face blackened with soot—he got—Tullus first, then—the master—I escaped, ran for dear life—and then tried—to find you—somebody—told me—"

He broke off.

Spurio was approaching.

Euphorus' eyes widened in sudden terror. "T-there he is—I think", he gasped. "That's him—he looks exactly like—"

"Who?" asked Cassius mechanically.

Then Spurio was there, and in an instant the gate was open. The lanista grabbed the old man by the neck and pulled him inside. "I'll teach you to loiter here, you filthy tramp." He shook him a few times and then gave him a violent push that sent Euphorus flying. The old man crashed against the wall and crumpled up in a heap.

Spurio wheeled toward Cassius. "Do you know that man?" he asked, panting. His lips were white.

"He was selling amulets", said Cassius slowly. And he added in a low voice, "I think—you killed—him."

Spurio blinked. He turned away to the inert body of the old man. "Perhaps I was a little too rough", he said in an unnecessarily loud voice. "Better see to it that he gets looked after." He seized the frail body again and hoisted it on his shoulder. "Hey, Polemon!" The Thracian came running. "Here, take my key and lock that gate again. I'll be back in a few minutes." He stalked off toward the servants' quarters.

There he is, I think. There he is. He looks exactly like—

But Spurio had been in Ostia, to buy slaves. Or so he said.

Why—why should he have done this?

Killed. Day before yesterday evening. That was the first of the two days Spurio had been away. Day before yesterday evening. It was one big brute of a man. Face blackened with soot. He got Tullus first. Then the master. Tullus first, then the master.

Father was dead. Father was murdered. Father was murdered by Spurio. Spurio was sent by Balbus. Balbus had accepted him as his slave so that Father could live peacefully on his farm to the end of his days. Then he had sent Spurio to murder Father.

Why did not the earth vomit? Why did not the heavens fall at such a deed?

It *was* Spurio. He had knocked Euphorus out to prevent him from talking. He had thrown him against the wall *inside* the training square. He wanted to make sure of him. Now he was taking him—where? To some place where he could no longer talk. The slaves' prison in the house was safe enough. And Euphorus was not going to be missed. His master was dead. Tullus was dead. Euphorus could quietly disappear. Even if the fall had not killed him, he was not likely to live much longer.

Murder the old man on his farm. Send a great bully of an ex-gladiator to kill him. Why?

70

"I am a slave for all time," Cassius thought, "because I tried to give Father a few years in peace—which he never got."

Kill Spurio? Impossible. At the first attempt all the gladiators would rush to his help. They had to—or face crucifixion. And Spurio was only the fist anyway—not the mind that spawned the bestial thing. Perhaps not even Balbus—why should he hate Father so much? They had scarcely known each other. Sejanus? Sejanus again? Because of a few disparaging words?

"What's the matter with you—you sick?"

It was Aper, big, lumbering Aper.

"You're all white. Seen a ghost or something?"

"We're all ghosts", said Cassius, and Aper instinctively recoiled as he saw the look in his eyes. "Foul, evil ghosts. Mad ghosts."

Aper shook his head as Cassius turned away and went over to the place where the old man had fallen. Something was lying there in the sand—the amulet he had been trying to sell. Was it the one that helped against the steel of the enemy or the one to ward off demons? No matter. Three threads of the cloak of Mars Repulsor, wasn't that it? Swindle, most likely. But one couldn't be sure. He picked it up and hid it in his belt.

It was a full hour before Spurio came back.

"What do you think you're doing, standing around there and gaping? Get on with the training, you apes."

"How is the old man, lanista?" asked Aper.

Spurio glared at him. "Is he your uncle or your grandfather, you should be so concerned about him? He's all right. They gave him a goblet of wine, and he left singing. I'll make you sing too, if you don't go and do your stuff at once. You can pair with Polemon."

That was not true about Euphorus, of course. They had done something to him. They would not let him leave, even if he could. Most likely he was dead by now. Balbus had to be called in; that explained why Spurio had stayed away so long.

Cassius walked up to the lanista. "Just one question", he said in a low voice. "*Did* you kill my father?"

Spurio stared at him. "You crazy or something?"

"Did you kill my father?" asked Cassius again.

The lanista gave a short laugh. "Whoever your father is or was, I certainly wish I had killed him before he sired you." Then, in a louder voice, he added, "I've got news for you. The noble Balbus has decided that you are going to fight in the Plebeian games instead of Polemon."

The Thracian howled with fury. "He? That stupid monkey? Why, he isn't fit to fight a woman . . . "

"Shut up!" bellowed Spurio.

"I understand, I think", said Cassius, his eyes glittering. He turned abruptly and walked away.

"You promised me the fight, lanista!" shrieked Polemon. "You promised me the fight . . . "

"Stop yelling at me", Spurio gave him a mirthless grin. "You don't know how lucky you are."

"What do you mean?"

"The aedil's list has come through", said Spurio. "Do you know against whom you were paired?"

"Well?"

"Baculus."

The Thracian gulped. Baculus was Rome's most famous gladiator, a man with an unbroken chain of twenty-seven victories. And his victims never survived—no thumbs were raised for them. For the rabble loved the elegant way in which Baculus dispatched his opponents when thumbs went down and the master of the games gave him the nod.

"Better him than me", muttered Polemon.

"It so happens", said Spurio, "that you are not the only one to think so."

The Plebeian games were a success. Sejanus, sitting as the Emperor's representative on the throne of ivory and gold in the suggestum, the high loge, noted the fact with satisfaction.

He was a coldly good-looking man, tall and still slim, and the gala uniform of the Praetorian guards suited him to perfection. People who did not know him very well often thought that his good looks were the major cause of his rapid promotion. He looked the representative warrior; the warrior-courtier rather than the commander in the field, yet records showed that he had fought with great distinction and bravery both in Germany and in Pannonia. Tiberius, who trusted nobody, trusted Sejanus. It was an enigma, a riddle for which there seemed no answer.

What people frequently did not realize was that Sejanus had conceived a system of efficient government and put it into practice. In his younger years Tiberius had had the help of that amazing old lady, the Empress-Mother Livia. She had ruled her late husband, the divine Augustus, up to almost the very end, which according to some she brought about when he began to countermand some of her far-reaching plans. She had tried, then, to rule Tiberius as well, and for many long years he was obliged to tolerate her co-rulership. She was not easy to deal with—but when she died, Tiberius found his work almost doubled, so much had she taken on herself.

It was then that Sejanus stepped in, with his admirable system. He worked on it for a long time before showing it to his imperial master, who could then see how cleverly Sejanus had organized the business of the state in such a way that only the really important things would come before the Emperor. Tiberius tried it out and found it worked well. For years he made sudden investigations and examinations—always to discover that Sejanus had omitted nothing of importance and only shielded him against being flooded with immaterial business which could just as well be dealt with by underlings.

And to this day Sejanus' reports went daily to Capri, where the old man was now having a rest among the strange people whose company he enjoyed: Greek, Egyptian, and Persian physicians, philosophers, and astrologers, including his faithful Thrasyllus, who had shared his voluntary exile in Rhodes, where he had stayed for seven years. Some people said that the old man kept stranger company still—all kinds of degenerates—but then some people will always say that sort of thing.

Now Sejanus had to do all the work Tiberius and Livia had done together. But he had organized the Castra Praetoria as the nerve center of the empire, and at fifty he was still vigorous and energetic. Even so, he did not often manage to appear in person at public events. These were the first games over which he had presided and he was pleased that all so far had gone very well. The Plebeian games were not the most important—not like the games on great religious festivals, like the Saturnalia or Floralia, or the Roman games in honor of the city and its patron goddess. But they served to appease the population—especially when there had been a shortage of wheat or an increase of taxes.

As a matter of fact, the games were always important. They were the means by which a ruler could get into touch with the masses, and they could make or destroy a ruler's popularity. Here in the Circus—and perhaps here alone—the Roman people still had their say, and they watched over this privilege with jealous vigilance. Often a chorus of a few hundred would chant complaints or petitions up to the imperial loge—and then the ruler had to answer at once. Above all, it was the ruler's duty to see to it that the masses got everything they expected out of the games and if possible just a little more.

And they wanted a great deal. They wanted so much that many an organizer of games had been ruined in his attempt to provide what was necessary. The aedil had to bring wild animals of all kinds from all the countries and continents of the world: lions from North Africa; panthers and leopards from Ethiopia; tigers from the almost legendary land behind Persia, India they called it; and fierce buffaloes from Germany; gigantic Molossian dogs—an excellent match for wolf packs from the snowy country of the Sarmatians; bears and lynxes from Pannonia; from

74

Numidia elephants; from Egypt crocodiles and hippopotamuses. Every year large expeditions were sent out to catch the animals needed for the games. There was some talk in hunting circles about a fantastic creature, the unicorn—a large fierce animal with a single horn, not on his head but on his nose, though that was probably the invention of some smart joker.

Freaks were another necessity: dwarfs to be matched with dogs or with strong-armed German women; giants to fight between themselves or against buffaloes; and an army of misfits whose comical faces or figures would cause laughter, especially when they were dressed in extravagant costumes.

It was ridiculous, really, that one had to spend one's time bothering about such things, but it was necessary. Popularity was important for a ruler. And popularity greatly depended upon the games. All aedils were idiots—or disloyal. They'd sink millions into their own wide pockets and dress up some kind of a show, hoping no one would see the difference. You could not leave it to the aedils.

The crowd clapped enthusiastically as water poured into the arena from a dozen large pipes. A naumachia, or mock sea battle, was a favorite performance, and to have one at the Plebeian games was a novelty. Usually this kind of treat was reserved for the Circus Maximus, with its much greater technical facilities.

Two large, rather flat-bottomed boats were shoved into the water, one an exact replica of a Roman war bireme, the other a foreign-looking vessel. The official announcer proclaimed that the latter was an original Greek pirate ship, taken by a Roman squadron in the Aegean Sea and manned by its original crew, who would now fight for their lives against an equal number of Roman criminals, robbers, thieves, and no less than eleven genuine murderers, including one who had killed seven people before he was caught and who was now the "captain" of the Roman ship.

The crowd clapped enthusiastically, and Sejanus smiled.

The pirates appeared and were greeted with boos and catcalls; they manned their ship and began to hoist the sails. The "Romans" were accorded derisive applause. But when the noise died down, an irate voice could be heard: "Shame! Shame!" It came from the tribune reserved for officers of the army.

Sejanus recognized the belligerent face of old Cinna, commander of the Twenty-First Legion.

"Criminals, dressed as Roman soldiers!" Cinna shouted. "Shame!"

The crowd was amused by the incident, but Sejanus smiled uneasily and then frowned.

Old Cinna's face was brick red, and he bellowed some more, but his words were no longer audible, as the two ships were moving toward each other and the crowd was yelling, "Ram them, Romans, ram them!"

Balbus came up the stairs to Sejanus' loge. He was beaming. "The best games I ever saw, noble Sejanus."

"Nonsense, friend, but I will admit it's going nicely. Did you bet on one of the ships?"

"On the Romans, of course, and they'll win—there, there, look!"

With a resounding crash the long, iron beak of the Roman bireme penetrated the pirate ship, the Romans boarded, and the wholesale killing started. The crowd went raving mad with delight.

"Your man will be on after this", Sejanus said calmly.

Balbus nodded. "The young viper will go the way of the old one. You got my report about the old one, of course."

"Yes."

Eyes like those of a dead fish, Balbus thought. Perhaps it was the wrong moment to ask. But he had made up his mind; it was difficult enough to get hold of the man alone.

"If you will have the great kindness to remember, Sejanus, I asked for a small favor—for a word of yours on my behalf to the noble Lady Claudia Procula."

Fish eyes again. Dead fish eyes. Only the thin mouth smiled.

"I remember it well, Balbus. I do wish I could comply, but unfortunately I cannot."

"N-no?"

"Quite out of question, friend. You see, the Lady Claudia Procula is being married. May have been married today, or was it yesterday? One or the other, I don't remember which. But you won your bet on the Roman ship, I think."

So that was why it had proved impossible to get in touch with Claudia. Married. Balbus dug his nails into his palms.

The crowd yelled crazily. The Greek pirates were being slaughtered, down to the last man.

"Married to whom, noble Sejanus?"

"Eh? Oh, yes. She was to be here tonight, with her husband. Dining with me later on. They're leaving for overseas, you know. My old friend Gratus is coming back from Judaea; his time there is up, much to his relief. Claudia's husband is the new procurator. She'll be very decorative, I'm sure. Don't look so disappointed, old friend. I'm very sorry I couldn't help you there, but they had met, and I couldn't very well interfere, could I? Doesn't do any good to send a high official to his province with a grudge, does it? Perhaps if you had let me know your wish a few months earlier—but it's too late; the thing has happened. There she is, by the way; there they both are, just arriving. Pretty late in the day. Ah, well, newly married."

The water was running out of the arena, and fountain jets began playing, one fountain for each section of the amphitheater.

"Scented water", Sejanus said merrily. "Makes them feel as if they belonged to the upper classes and makes the upper classes suffer less from their stink. No, no, Balbus, don't go yet—let's watch the death of the young viper together. He's due any moment now. And don't fret, man—no woman is irreplaceable. When I married Apicata, I thought I'd never touch another woman again, and now I'm glad I'm rid of her; the very thought of her makes me shudder. That's the way it goes, man, that's the way it goes. You're not a boy of twenty, Balbus, you're a man of the world."

The smile was ingratiating now; even a Sejanus did not want the enmity of a millionaire. But the eyes remained cold as dead fish.

Balbus tried to smile back. Even a millionaire could not risk the enmity of Sejanus.

"You dine with me, too", said the great man. "Meet the lady and her new husband, wish them luck, show how little you care, and tomorrow I'll send you three girls I bought last week—you never saw anything like them, believe me. Phidias would have used them as models. Melissa trained them. You're a good friend, Balbus. I never forget good friends."

A little too gracious. A good deal too gracious. What was behind it?

"I shall have your name called out as the donor of the young viper, too", said Sejanus.

This was honor indeed, and Balbus bowed, and as he bowed he was thinking furiously. Sejanus talked to him as if they were equals, as if he wanted to make it quite clear that they were equals. You lost your woman, well, I also lost mine, got rid of her, rather—that's how it goes, man, that's how it goes, and we understand each other, you and I; can't offend a high official, can't let him go to—where was it?—to Judaea with a grudge—

Could he not? Of course he could.

"They had met. I couldn't very well interfere." Of course he could have—if he had wanted to. He did not want to. Why not? Because this marriage was his doing. He *wanted* Claudia to marry that man. Why?

Understanding came in a flash. Claudia was a relative of the old man in Capri. So he sent her to Judaea, about as far away from Rome as one could get. And old Longinus was one of the Emperor's generals, one of his faithful old guard, and so old

Longinus had to die. But Gratus had come back from Judaea, Sejanus' old friend Valerius Gratus. He was systematically sending away or finishing off those who would be absolutely faithful to Tiberius. He was putting his own creatures into the key positions.

He was out for the throne.

Out for the throne. That was it! Sejanus could easily encircle the island of Capri with his armed boats. So Tiberius would hear only what Sejanus wanted him to hear. The Emperor was very near his dotage. Lull him into security till the moment was ripe. Old men die; nothing suspicious about that. So that's why old Longinus had to be finished off. That's why a relative of Tiberius must not be allowed to marry a rich man called Balbus. That's why Marcus Messala, another Tiberian, was sent as ambassador to the Parthians, even farther away than Judaea.

But no one must guess what was in his mind. So he must be gracious to old friends, talk to them as to equals, let them think Claudia met her new husband without Sejanus' help, that important things could still happen in Rome in which Sejanus had no part, against which he was helpless.

Just as well Sejanus had turned away. Balbus needed a few moments to regain his self-control.

The throne, nothing less. And he might succeed, too.

Balbus began to perspire freely.

Down in the arena they had finished spreading a fresh floor of sand.

A lonely figure appeared, the figure of a very young man, a handsome young man, almost naked. A loincloth, helmet, the ornate shoulder plates, greaves, and leather gloves of the secutor — that was all. In his right hand he held the broadsword of the gladiator, in his left the helmet. The crowd looked at him indifferently.

A second figure appeared from another door, and at once many thousand voices shouted, shrieked, yelled, roared, "Baculus!"

The gladiator, whose elaborately decorated armor glittered in the sun, waved his hand almost contemptuously. Obviously he resented being matched against a mere beginner, a mere boy. A fight of this kind did his record no good. Tomorrow, in the *Acta Diurna,* there would be two lines about it, no more.

Baculus had tried to talk the aedil out of this impossible match. Apparently they wanted to be quite sure they got rid of the boy, the gods alone knew why. He was supposed to come from a good family. Infanticide, that's what it was.

He gave his opponent a perfunctory salute, and they both marched up to the imperial loge to greet the master of the games.

Sejanus beckoned the announcer, whose booming voice could be heard even in the most distant seats. "Quintus Baculus—against Cassius Longinus. The latter donated to the games by the noble Marcus Balbus."

Came a rough voice, with the broad accent of the Subura district: "Better send us his older brother, noble Balbus."

There was laughter. Balbus flushed. Sejanus smiled thinly. But from the seats occupied by the officers of the Twenty-First Legion came another shout: "Those criminals on the Roman galley should never have been dressed as Roman soldiers. *This* man should be."

"Old Cinna again", thought Sejanus. And indeed the stocky old man with the iron-gray hair had jumped to his feet and was continuing his protest. Of course, young Longinus had had a few years in Cinna's legion, chip of the old block—better not annoy the army. In any case, they did not enjoy having one of their men exhibited in the Circus. An idea came to him, and he gave the irate Cinna a nod. Then he whispered to the announcer.

The man with the big voice proclaimed, "In order to please the commander of the Twenty-First Legion, the master of the games has decided to let Longinus fight in the equipment of a regular soldier."

Old Cinna gave a dignified little bow and sat down, his officers applauded, but on the whole the masses were unimpressed. It took some time to get soldier's equipment from the Circus armory, which contained everything from the jeweled turban of an Indian to the furry tunics of German tribes beyond the Rhine — and more time was wasted while Longinus put it on.

The people were getting restless. Baculus grinned openly.

There was nothing ornate about the equipment of a Roman legionary. Regulation breastplate, shoulder plates, simple helmet, rectangular shield on the left arm, sword, short spear, and the pilum, the heavy spear with the long, iron head that made it topheavy.

"You've forgotten the palus", roared an irrepressible plebeian, and this time the whole Circus laughed. Part and parcel of the Roman legionary's equipment was a fairly heavy wooden stake, to be rammed into the ground as part of a palisade when the legion made camp.

Good humor was restored for the moment at least. And after all it was a novel fight — soldier against gladiator.

The outcome, of course, was inevitable; there were almost no bets, and the few made were twenty to one on Baculus. An experienced gladiator could finish off a soldier with ease, surely, and Baculus — why, the man could fight fifty legionaries single-handed. There was not only the difference in muscular strength and skill. There was such a thing as ringcraft, ring strategy. The whole thing was beyond dispute; it wasn't worth talking about. But at least it was novel. Soldier against gladiator.

"They should have taken a seasoned veteran —" shrilled a hunchback. "A man who knows all the tricks of the army just as Baculus knows all the tricks of the arena."

"Don't be stupid", growled his neighbor, a shoemaker. "The army knows nothing about tricks. Just a bunch of men used to fighting in a body. That's the trouble. They don't know how to fight singly."

The gray-haired man with the obstinate chin sitting next to Claudia Procula on the center tribune shook his head. "Cinna made a mistake", he said, frowning. "The army should never be made ridiculous."

"You don't think he has a chance, do you?" asked Claudia lightly. He *was* a handsome boy. The kind who isn't easy to forget. Family debts, Balbus said. And Sejanus hated the family. No one could afford to be hated by Sejanus. He had sent a magnificent wedding present, four fine myrrhine vases—she had spent hours in supervising the packing—it would be a real loss if they did not survive the sea voyage. She had not told Balbus, but by now he knew; she had seen him when he was talking to Sejanus in the loge. *He* would hate her too, of course, but it did not matter; Sejanus was for the marriage, so all was well, all was well. It was a pity about Cassius. Only twenty . . .

"Not a ghost of a chance", explained her husband indulgently. "He may last a little longer now that he has been given proper armor, but not much. I have seen mere barbarians deal with Roman armor in single fights—the Cheruscans, for instance, many years ago, when I was a tribune under Quintilius Varus. Poor man, he should have never been given a command in Germany. He came from Syria and Judaea—from where we are going, my dear; we are just doing it the other way round."

They were taking a long time to get young Cassius ready. He must have seen her. He was bound to have seen her. And he looked so calm, so defiant and proud. He knew she was watching him. He had imagined that he must save her life that evening when he threw his spear across all the people's heads into the silver shield. Couldn't he do it again?

"Well, maybe he'll give us all a surprise", she said aloud.

Her husband smiled indulgently and began to tell her about his experiences in Germany. "I shall never forget that endless march through the forest, always in darkness, rain, drizzle, and shouting and stones hurled from nowhere and Cheruscan archers picking out our officers. Poor old Varus—nothing but bad news coming in, losses in the vanguard, losses in the rear. I was a man in my prime then, just thirty-six. They shot my horse under me, twice. Trying to get me."

"Poor darling", said Claudia absentmindedly.

"We had a war council in the rain", he went on. "It was up to Varus to decide whether we should go on or turn back, but he wanted to hear our opinion first. He put up a bold front, trying to give the impression of being master of the situation, but I could see that he was wrestling with himself. He was thinking of the political implications, of course, at least as much as of the military ones. Here we were, sent out to punish rebellious tribes. If we were forced back, reports would go to certain quarters: incapability, inefficiency, lack of courage, all that kind of thing. Varus hadn't done so well in Syria; there was some rumor about extortions. This could be the end of his career. He must make a decision. Well, he made it—and signed his own death warrant and that of twenty thousand men. The trouble was that he allowed himself to be maneuvered into a situation where he *had* to make a decision. Great mistake. Fatal mistake. Couple of days later he was dead, suicide. Better than slow torture; they had a nasty way about them, those Cheruscans. I got away because I was with the rear guard. We broke through when the Germans thought it was all over." He sighed. "I was lucky to get out and thrice lucky not to have been in Varus' shoes. That decision—shocking responsibility . . . "

As his voice trailed off, Claudia patted his hand. She had not really listened, but she knew instinctively that he needed an expression of sympathy. The experience seemed to haunt him.

"They are ready now", she said. "Look!"

Down in the arena the two fighters stood, facing each other.

"All right, youngster", said Baculus amiably. "Took you longer to make yourself beautiful than most girls I know."

Cassius said nothing. He had been thinking. When he had first come out into the glaring sunlight, he had felt numbed and sluggish, and he did not care what happened. Somewhere up there Sejanus was sitting; he had to go up to him and salute, salute the swine, the murderer. He had rendered the salute. You got rid of us, Sejanus, of the father and of the son, though why you were so keen on that the gods alone know—if there are any gods. You got rid of us, fat Balbus. But first he had to exchange a few strokes and thrusts with someone called Baculus. He knew of him—who didn't! It wouldn't take Baculus long. He did not see or think of Claudia.

Then there was some shouting, and Sejanus gave an order, and they went to get army equipment for him. When they began to put it on—that was when he started thinking. Sword, spear, pilum, all three. Shield. From the officers' tiers they were shouting at him, "Come on, soldier!" "Show him what the army can do, soldier!"

He never had got accustomed to the gladiator's weapons. This outfit he knew. He had worn it for years. The pilum was always used in the same way, not to wound or kill the enemy but to throw it bang into his shield, where it stuck fast and made the shield unusable. There was nothing to do but drop the shield. Exactly for that a pilum was made; that was its function. And when the enemy dropped his shield, that was the moment for the short spear.

Baculus knew that, of course. He knew it even if he had never served in the army. He probably hadn't. He knew it, and he expected it. So what would he do? There were only two things he could do, of which one was obvious, easy, and natural and the other rather difficult and on the sensational side, the sort of thing that would please the onlookers. Therefore he would probably do *that*.

If so, there might be a chance—not much of a chance, but a chance all the same. Of course, if that were lost, it was the end.

This Baculus was not Spurio, not Balbus and not Sejanus. It

was not his fault that one had to fight him. But he was the uttermost end of Sejanus' arm. It would be fun to spoil the plan of the mighty lord.

Even ghosts could hate.

They faced each other at a distance of twenty yards. And Baculus—Baculus grinned and did not advance. He was waiting for the pilum, give the little soldier the opportunity to do his stuff.

Cassius' shield thudded on the sand as he let it drop off his left arm. An expression almost of pity flashed across the gladiator's face—so you know it's that first throw or nothing, it seemed to say.

Then Cassius threw the pilum. As he had guessed, Baculus didn't jump aside letting the pilum drop beside him, but with one lightning stroke of his sword the pilum was caught and deflected, and it fell . . .

Even as Baculus was watching the flight of the pilum toward him, Cassius threw the short spear with his left hand. Before Baculus was aware of the second throw, the spear had pierced that one inch of muscular throat between the upper rim of the shield and the metal flap of the gladiator's helmet, exposed as he turned his head to strike at the pilum. The gladiator fell.

It had all happened so fast that his body seemed to touch the sand of the arena at the same instant with the pilum, that innocent, treacherous decoy.

There was a spurt of blood, a fountain of blood. Baculus' feet beat a crazy tattoo in the sand and stopped, and for a breath there was complete silence.

Then came the roar. From a hundred thousand throats came howls, yells, shrieks. People were standing on their seats, jumping up and down like madmen.

Cassius stood in a daze. He had planned it, thought it all out, and now it had happened, and he did not understand it.

In his loge Sejanus hesitated. He knew they were going to yell for the young viper's freedom as soon as they finished yelling for yelling's sake. He knew that he could not afford to resist their wish. He would have to give in to them. It was unfortunate. He did so hate loose ends. One could not very well blame Balbus. It should have been a walkover for Baculus. Cunning fellow, that idea of throwing the pilum and the short spear almost simultaneously, using both hands. Old Cinna was shouting his head off, of course, and all his officers with him. And here they came, the cries for mercy, for freedom, for release.

But to have that young spear thrower running loose in Rome . . . He would be the hero of the populace, at least for some months to come. He would find support, money, perhaps power.

Balbus looked at Sejanus, his face contorted with fear and rage.

Sejanus smiled at him. "I hope you had a stiff bet on your man", he said, and Balbus. almost choked.

"Of course not—I hoped—I was sure he would . . . "

But Sejanus was scribbling a hasty note on his wax tablet. "At once", he said, as he handed it to an aide.

The people were still in a frenzy.

Claudia sat quite still, looking at the lonely figure down there on the sand. He had done it. He had imagined once again: I must save Claudia. And then he had done it. "I am not so stupid after all", she thought. "When I feel something for a man, he *is* a man. She looked at her husband triumphantly.

He nodded. "Quite amazing. Hope they'll set him free, whatever he's done. Silly of Baculus not to watch the other arm, of course. Just wanted to show off, hitting that pilum. Should have jumped aside, shield high up. Well, there it is."

A Praetorian guard gave him a wax tablet. He opened it and read. Then he began to chuckle. "Tell the noble Sejanus I shall be glad to comply with his wish", he said. The Praetorian guard saluted and withdrew. "Rather amusing, Claudilla—what is it?"

"Nothing. I don't like being called Claudilla. It reminds me of—of my childhood."

Her husband smiled indulgently. "Very well, my dear, I won't do it again. This was a message from Sejanus."

"Oh . . ."

"Yes. He wants me to take that young fellow with us to Judaea."

She stared at him with unbelieving eyes. "You're joking."

"No, no. It's true. See for yourself. Wants me to make him a soldier of our escort. We're taking about three hundred men with us. Mainly staff, of course, and a small escort."

"And . . . you accepted?"

"Certainly. Glad to do Sejanus a favor—myself, too, when I come to think of it. We can do with a few more good Roman soldiers there. There are five cohorts in Caesarea, where we shall reside, but from what I hear most of the men are Syrians, the sons of former veterans and their native wives and that sort of thing. Influx of pure Roman blood can only help. And the boy can fight—we've seen *that*. I'll take him gladly."

"You're right", said Claudia softly. "You are quite right. It *is* amusing."

The booming voice of the announcer could be heard above the din, and after a while he managed to get the crowd quiet.

The victor in the fight would be set free.

The thunderous applause brought a rather sour smile to Sejanus' thin lips.

Cassius, still dazed, was led away by a number of the officers of the Twenty-First who had jumped over the balustrade. They got him out of the arena. He was slapped on the shoulder, slapped on the back; men he had never seen before shook hands with him. Then a familiar figure appeared, the Tribune Caelius, whom he had seen a few times at the house of Senator Vatinius—and at Balbus' house, too.

"Splendid work", said Caelius grinning. "Make room, friends. I'm here officially, must talk to him. No, of course he won't be arrested; don't be ridiculous. Now, will you let me talk to him?

That's better." When they were out of earshot: "Listen. You've done very well. The army offers you a career. Will you take it?"

Cassius passed a weary hand over his forehead. The army . . .

"I would, if I were you, you know", said Caelius gruffly. "As a matter of fact it's practically the only thing you can do. Rome isn't too healthy for you, is it? The new procurator of Judaea is leaving for his province, wants to take you with him. Member of his personal escort. You know what that means. You'll be an officer in no time. Overseas service is just what you need. Right?"

A career in the army after all. Service overseas. Baculus was dead. But Spurio was not, and Balbus was not—and Sejanus was not.

He would have to let them live for a while, he thought coldly, until he had won sufficient rank and power to enter a different kind of arena with *them*.

He nodded, without speaking.

"Very good." Caelius hid his relief. "Better come with me. First we'll have a bite at my house. Then we'll go to the port. The galley is ready. The procurator leaves tomorrow morning."

The officers of the Twenty-First approached again. "Finished, tribune?"

"You come with me, all of you", said Caelius jovially. "We'll empty a couple of amphorae of Massic I have at home, and then we'll see this young hero off. He is rejoining the army."

The tribune's wine saved the situation. Without that it would have been unbearable. Unbearably cheerful, unbearably hearty.

They all tried to behave as if nothing had happened since the return of the legion from the frontier—nothing except the great and glorious victory over Baculus.

Their faces were familiar and awakened certain memories: this fellow with the large mouth was Minucius, with whom he had shared rations on patrol east of the Rhine on a day when they both thought they would never get back alive; the lanky one with the scar on his chin was Antonius Dolabella. Decius was there and Posthumus and Marcus Curio, the best rider of the legion, and many others. But they were children, cheerful puppies who did not know anything. Their ears had not been split. They hadn't been whipped. They hadn't been cheated out of honor, rank, and property. Above all, they could still believe in the nobility of sacrifice and in human decency.

Meanwhile they pretended that he still belonged to them, to the Twenty-First, and that he had added to their glory. But when young Decius asked why he didn't join the Twenty-First again, they changed the subject quickly.

Slit-ear Cassius had to start again from the ranks. It would have been too much of an embarrassment for the officers, to say nothing of the men themselves.

Slit-ear Cassius could do only one thing: he could get drunk. He did.

He woke up twice. The first time he found himself in a carriage, with the tribune sitting beside him, stiffly upright and stone sober.

"Where are we going?"

"To the port. To Ostia."

"Th-that's what I thought." He fell asleep again.

The second time he woke up was in the morning. He was lying on a hard cot, and somebody was shaking him. It was an orderly.

"Escort to assemble on the poop deck in half an hour. Procurator coming on board."

Unshaven faces were raised from half a dozen cots. There was a good deal of cursing, and the air was dank and musty.

The army again. There was worse. There was little that was better.

He rose, shaved. Somebody gave him a tunic, sandals, armor. Not the armor he had worn yesterday. Where was yesterday?

An orderly looked in, shouted, "Swords only!" and disappeared. So they did not have to get their shields and spears.

No one here seemed to know anything about what had happened in the Circus. That was all right. He knew he did not want to see a circus again as long as he lived.

A bugle call. They trooped out, along a narrow gangway, up still narrower stairs. The poop deck.

It was a fine morning. Gangs of workmen were busy on the wharves. He saw a couple of new galleys and a bireme in the new style, slanting a little. Farther out the sea was dotted with small craft, fishing boats, some of the sails shining golden in the early sun. The day was still cool.

A tribune appeared with a group of officers, all wearing the bluish armor they now produced at the factories in Gaul and Spain. Bluish armor; tunics of a dull red, like rust; and the horsehair tufts on their helmets dyed to match; nothing shiny or sparkling, nothing for parade; this was field service, the real thing.

A huge centurion began to bellow. The men formed up, stood to attention. Some commotion was going on ashore, people staring, a carriage, another one, a third and fourth and fifth. They stopped, and the slaves began to help the dignitaries out.

There he was, the great man, grayish, just a little paunchy, an obstinate chin, uniform of a full general, nothing bluish or rust-red about him. The new procurator. Who was he?

Cassius had been so drunk yesterday he had not even asked who his new chief was. He asked now, out of the corner of his mouth—every legionary learned how to do that.

The man next to him carefully refrained from changing his expression. "Don't you know? Pontius Pilatus. Just got married, too. This is his honeymoon. Wife coming with him. There she is. Whew—she's a beauty."

Cassius stared at Claudia. He did not believe his eyes.

Wife . . . honeymoon . . . Pontius Pilatus . . . wife . . .

It was a joke, a ghastly, ribald, horrible joke. A few minutes ago, when he saw the sea in its morning freshness and the golden sails of the fishing boats, he really believed that he had escaped into a new life. Now he knew there was no escape. The past would follow him wherever he went.

They were coming on board, Claudia, Pilatus, half a dozen women, a group of staff officers.

Bugle calls sounded. Solemn saluting. The tribune introduced himself and the other senior officers, the ship's captain and the flamen, the priest; of course, they would sacrifice to Neptune when they lifted anchor.

Claudia. Claudilla.

The flamen began the sacrifice on a small, portable altar, propped up amidships, chanting the invocation, the adoration, the imploration, the thanksgiving.

She looked on, cool and impeccable, flawless and serene.

Sold yourself quite well, haven't you, Claudilla?

She was looking around now; there, now she was looking straight at him. He could see her eyes—deep eyes, tilted at the corners—widen a little.

She smiled faintly. She knew then. It was no surprise to *her.*

He stared back at her with icy contempt.

The tribune bellowed a command. The gatherings began to break up. Claudia left with her ladies. The procurator left with his staff.

The big centurion rasped the dismissal. Another voice began to bark orders. As the troops were going below to their quarters, the clattering of the anchor chains filled the air.

There was no escape. There was no new life.

But a ghost could kill, he knew that now. That was something.

The ship began to move.

BOOK TWO

I

Boz bar Sebulun gave one last long look at his lovely garden. Palms and tamarisks filtered the sunlight to moderate and agreeable warmth, and the last roses were fully blown all around his favorite spot near the little pond, where he liked to doze in tranquillity and to calculate the likely profits of the next caravan he was sending to Egypt or Persia.

The comfortable house in the country was the result of a number of such caravans, and he hated the idea of leaving it, if only temporarily, to return to Jerusalem.

He turned away with a shrug, opened the entrance door, and crossed the hall. As he entered his study, he frowned. His desk was in disarray, covered with papers. Lists of what he had to take with him, lists of what remained here, the complete inventory — he had to check everything. Servants were empty-headed and unreliable nowadays, and honesty was rarer than rubies.

It would be better to take all really valuable things with him, the beautiful carpets from Susa, woven by masters of the craft, and the vases, although anything might happen to them on donkeyback. And the little collection of rare gems and the silver.

A journey meant nothing but discomfort and disorder.

But the Feast of the Tabernacles was imminent, and it must not be said that Boz bar Sebulun was lax in the fulfillment of his duty, not even at his age of three score and ten and a little over. He had a good name in Israel; he was related to the one who was wearing the holy vestments this year. His life must be exemplary.

He had told his wife so, severely, when she suggested that he should stay here and rest. Naomi liked life in the country herself, so maybe she only pretended to be worried about his health. Such was the nature of women, even of a woman not yet fifteen. They were all alike, always thinking of themselves. Leah had been no different. Perhaps he should not have married again, not at his age. Cousin Serubabel had practically said so, but then Serubabel was his closest relative and had reasons for not wanting him to marry again.

Boz sighed. He sighed again, when a servant announced that Zadoc bar Tubal had arrived and wished to see him. So inopportune, with all the preparations for the journey going on. Surely Zadoc also would go up to the city for the feast; they could meet there, if meet they must.

The servant shrugged, with an uncouth movement. "He says it is important."

What would be important to the mind of Zadoc? Most men were fools and spent their time on foolish things. Oh, well, let him come in since he is here. One never knows, even a fool might bring good, though it was not likely. They did not have a high regard for Zadoc at the Temple. They spoke of him as they did about one who has not yet lost all his money but may do so at any moment. An impulsive man, headstrong and not easily persuaded to see reason. As he entered the room Boz saw that he looked very much as he had two years ago: curly black hair and quick, black eyes that wanted to take in everything at once, too quick in his movements and no dignity. He was young, of course, going on forty. Now where was Naomi—

"Peace be with you, Boz bar Sebulun."

"And with you, Zadoc bar Tubal."

And Naomi came at long last to greet the guest, and Zadoc smiled at her and accepted the goblet of honey wine and the cake, and there was some empty talk as there is when a woman is present. Perhaps it would be better if she stayed on.

Boz had always been able to feel whether a man came with

something good and useful or not, and it had helped him greatly in making his fortune. Thus he had felt strongly that Simeon bar Judah was not the man one should have as a partner, and he said no to his offer though most men would have kissed their fingers and regarded themselves as very lucky. But he had had that feeling and had said no, and Simeon bar Judah took Aaron of Migdal as his partner instead, and two years later he had ruined Aaron, ruined him completely. There were many other occasions when his feelings had proved right. Of course Zadoc was not such an important figure; some might think that Boz was being kind in receiving him at all, but whatever he wanted it was not likely to be a good thing, he could feel that.

"I thought I would meet you here, before you went up to the city", said Zadoc, flashing his white teeth. Anybody could have white teeth at that age; wait till you are seventy.

"We are leaving tomorrow morning. This is our last day here."

"Yes, I calculated the time it would take you, and I said to myself, he is not going to leave before he has to, not when he has such a beautiful house in the country, but he will also not strain himself, and he cannot travel on the sabbath, so when will he leave? Tomorrow. So here I am."

"Surely you, too, are going to Jerusalem?"

"Certainly, certainly. But it is easier to talk here. I thought you might perhaps prefer our discussion to remain entirely between ourselves. You know how it is in Jerusalem. People gossip—now why did Zadoc bar Tubal go and see Boz bar Sebulun, what is going on between them . . . "

"I receive many people in Jerusalem", said Boz stiffly. But he knew that Zadoc was right. "Naomi, my child, you had better go and see that these fools do not forget everything. Servants nowadays, Zadoc, if you leave it to them, they will pack the stones of a house and leave behind the master's cloak and shoes."

The young girl who was his wife had not lifted her eyes. The long lashes lay on her cheeks like small, blue-black fans. Face and

95

hands emerging from the many folds of her wide, blue dress were the color of old ivory. She bowed to her husband, bowed to the guest, and left.

Zadoc waited until the door had closed behind her. Then he sat down.

Boz, facing him, gave him no encouragement.

"You are a very fortunate man, Boz bar Sebulun, a very fortunate man indeed, one to whom God has given out of the fullness of his riches ... "

He was bankrupt after all; he wanted to borrow money. Sooner or later it was bound to happen. He was that kind of a man, always headstrong and impulsive, never heeding the advice of the experienced.

" ... you have a lovely home in the country. You have a great house in the city, good enough for the High Priest himself. Your caravans are doing good trade with Persia, with Bactria, with Egypt and the provinces of Minor Asia ... "

"Son of Tubal, if you have come to make an inventory of my possessions ... "

"Bear with me, I beg of you." The younger man seemed in no way intimidated. There was even the shadow of a mocking smile on the full lips, bursting like ripe fruit through the curly black beard. "I have enumerated some of your possessions—only a few, as you know—which have made you the pride of some and the envy of many."

Perhaps he did not want to borrow money; perhaps he knew something or thought he knew something that he could use to exert pressure. A little blackmail? But what could he know? There was little now he could fasten on. You should have come twenty years ago, you fool, at the time when certain government contracts ...

"You are a rich man, Boz bar Sebulun," Zadoc went on, "and if there is anything certain in this world of ours it is that a rich man wishes to keep his riches, however much he may complain that the supervising of his estate is a burden to him and how much easier life is for those who have fewer responsibilities."

"First you count my possessions; now you tell me what I think and feel. Son of Tubal, I have many things to do before I leave here and . . . "

"By the vestments of the High Priest," said Zadoc, "if you were to do business to the tune of a million shekels it would be less important for you than to listen to what I have to say."

Boz blinked uneasily. It was wrong of Zadoc to pronounce so weighty an oath. But after that he could scarcely have in mind either borrowing money or blackmail.

"The time is coming", said Zadoc, "when Israel will shake off the yoke of the oppressor."

"Oh, no", exclaimed Boz in disgust. "Oh, no, no, no. Not that again. I've heard too much of that foolishness in my life."

"Foolishness?" Zadoc looked outraged. "The freedom of your people . . . "

"You are not altogether mad, son of Tubal; you have eyes in your head—and you are no longer a boy of twenty who thinks he can conquer the world because his blood is fermenting in his veins. Freedom! Freedom for what, son of Tubal? You want to get rid of the Roman occupation, perhaps? You want to fight the legions of Caesar, son of Tubal? You have come to me, perhaps, to ask me to give you the money for your helmet, shield, and sword?"

"The Caesar", said Zadoc, unruffled, "is a very old man—much older than you are, Boz bar Sebulun, so old that he has withdrawn from the business of the state and gone to some island to enjoy his last years in peace. The man who rules in his place is not likely to risk everything on a war in a far country."

"Even if that were true, there are troops in this country."

"Not even two full legions, and most of them stationed in Caesarea. We are—their movements are being watched constantly."

"By whom?"

"By those who are working for the freedom of Israel. By the Freedom Party."

Boz laughed contemptuously. "I knew it. The Freedom Party. Little bands of robbers, holding up caravans, looting, stealing, and all under the pretext of setting the country free."

"They have done a great deal of damage to Rome."

"They have done a great deal of damage to *me,* and to every other merchant in Judaea. They are a great nuisance to the country. Bands like the one led by Ephraim bar Saul or by the son of Abbas—Galilean bands more often than not, from the most backward places, disturbers of the peace. Are they the men who are to drive the legions out of Judaea? Does it tickle Bar Saul or Bar Abbas to match himself against the generalship of the procurator?"

Zadoc nodded calmly. "I have heard these views before. They always come from those who are living in prosperity and do not wish to be disturbed. If such had been the thoughts of the great men of our people, we would never have escaped from Egypt. We would have remained the captives of the Babylonians, Assyrians, and Persians. Always the thing looked impossible at first. Always the might of the oppressor seemed invincible, the rising of the people foolishness. I have not come to ask you to take up shield and sword. You are an old man, and you do not wish to encounter difficulties with certain people I could name. Be it so. But ... "

"What are you telling me, son of Tubal? How can you compare what happened in the past with what is going on now? God sent his prophet to deliver us from bondage in Egypt. But perhaps, God forbid, the little chieftains of the robber bands think that they are prophets and that it is pleasing to God when they loot the caravan of an honest merchant who is doing his duty, obeying the Law, and living in peace with everybody.... "

"And paying taxes to the Emperor, who uses the money to arm the soldiers who keep our country in servitude. As for the prophet—perhaps he will turn up when the hour demands it. I have heard strange tales lately. It will be well to be prepared for his coming. But I did not come here in the hope of winning you over to the cause of freedom. I know too well how the Sadducees feel about that."

"We feel that order—even Roman order—is better than disorder and lawlessness", said the old man stiffly.

"Yes, I know. But let me remind you once more that the seemingly impossible has happened before and can happen again. And *if* the Freedom Party should attain its goal, its leaders will have little sympathy for those who refused to help its cause."

A contribution. Pay, old man. Pay your taxes to the Romans, if you feel you have to, but pay us too—if you wish to keep your riches the day when we take over.

What chance of that could there be? It was absurd, ridiculous.

He rose. "Son of Tubal, if you wish to throw in your lot with the bandits of the highways, it is your affair, and I cannot stop you. But to suggest that I, who have suffered grave damage from them, should pay tribute to them or help their cause in any way is insulting to my intelligence, and I will hear no more about it."

Zadoc lifted both hands in protest. "Would I come to you if the cause were in the hands of bandits? Don't you understand that we are making deliberate use of bandits, men who have nothing to lose, but that behind them is the people as a whole, the people who cannot yet afford to show its hand?"

"The whole people?" Boz snapped his fingers. "The lestes! Bandits posing as patriots. All this has been tried before. Theodas tried it and Judah of Galilee. You were a little boy then, son of Tubal, and it seems to me that only your body has grown since those days and not your mind. Bandits, hotheads, malcontents, men who cannot make a success of their lives in a decent way and must put their hopes in bloody disorders and upheavals. Don't I know what the men of high position think of this Galilean nonsense? Have I not heard the members of the Sanhedrin speak of them as of so many rakas and shotim? Not half a shekel will you get from me for this brood of mischief makers and criminals."

"Is it wise—" asked Zadoc hoarsely, "is it wise to have all the mischief makers and criminals as enemies?"

Boz was very angry now. "Are you threatening me, son of Tubal? In my own house?" He stretched out a trembling finger. "Go—and be glad that in my patience and forbearance I will forget what you have said."

II

Boz was a man of regular habits; he always had been, and in his old age he was more precise than ever. The discussion with Zadoc bar Tubal had excited him, and excitement was bad for him. All the five physicians who were looking after his health agreed at least upon that, however much they differed about the medications they wanted him to use. He did not sleep well, and he felt nervous and worried in the morning. Nevertheless he insisted on the journey, and the caravan left at the hour he had fixed several days earlier.

First, six servants on donkeys, each leading two other donkeys with luggage. Then Boz himself on the handsome white camel he had bought two years ago from an Arab noble. Then Naomi in a litter slung between two swiftfooted donkeys from the Sindjar mountains, and behind the litter two maids and another six servants with donkeys and more luggage.

All the servants were armed, of course, the highways being what they were, although the road from here to Jerusalem was relatively safe, especially now, with so many people traveling to the city for the feast.

Even so it was better to be on guard. Boz had sent a runner to the inn where they would spend the night to make sure that they would spend it in comfort.

Boz was tired. He knew his legs would be badly swollen again tonight; Naomi would have to massage him. Her fingers were gentle, and old Levi had taught her how; she had picked it up quite easily. One could pick up anything easily at her age.

It was a long journey. Several times he thought he was going to have a cramp again, so painful. It was a little cooler when the sun began to sink. If only they could get to that inn before it was dark. He knew the way—but who could know any way when he could not see? One needed landmarks like those small oases on the left or that solitary hill over there.

Tomorrow it would be easier; they would soon enough come to the place where various roads converged and men, camels, and donkeys left a trail a mile wide.

No good trying to go faster; it was painful enough as it was. Camels were not what they used to be, nor were saddlemakers.

They met a Roman patrol, six men and a tall, sulky-looking leader, all on horseback. The Romans halted for a while, gazing at the caravan. Then they rode on, silently.

Boz raised his right hand to his heart and greeted them courteously. They took no notice whatever. Barbarians! But it was just as well that they were patrolling this part of the way, too, like every road in Judaea, Syria, Egypt, all along the African coast to the very end of the world, to Hibernia itself and the Britannic Isles and Gaul and the Rhine and the Danube. Oh, he knew all the names; his goods traveled on all the roads of the empire and everywhere there were patrols like these and the legions not far off.

Rome, Zadoc bar Tubal, son of calamity and ignorance—that is Rome. And you want my shekels to arm your miserable bandits; you really hope they will drive the Romans out. If it were not so sad, it would be laughable.

Sad. Sad indeed. They murder a patrol—and all the towns in the neighborhood and all the villages must pay a fine, and suspects are taken to the prisons by the dozen, and hostages are held—all for the sake of a gang of criminals and a few irresponsible hotheads, living in some filthy caves in the hills.

They should all be captured—but that was just what could not be done, not with a country like Galilee to offer them refuge, a country riddled with hills and caves and half the population at heart on their side. The Galileans didn't know any better; backward people that they were, they did not know the difference between a patriot and a bandit.

The caravan turned to the left, past a hill with a triple hump and through a small valley. A mounted party had been here, quite recently, for there was horse dung on the road.

Behind some thorny bushes a number of horses came in sight, six, eight, ten. Their riders leaped into their saddles, armed men, *not* Romans. They seemed to have been waiting here. Waiting for whom or what?

They came toward the caravan, walking their horses.

Boz tugged nervously at his gray beard. Ten. Now if they intended . . . His thoughts were interrupted by a piercing shriek from behind him, and he turned in the saddle. There was a commotion among the men in the rear—at first he saw only five, for the sixth man was writhing on the ground with an arrow sticking out of his chest, and his donkeys were loose and galloping away.

Boz wanted to shout to the men to stop the donkeys. He tried to order them to form a ring around him and the litter, but his camel kept turning nervously round and round, and he couldn't make it stop, and as it turned Boz saw the new group of riders coming as if out of the sun, a red sun, setting behind the bald hills. More than a dozen of them! He could hear the thunder of the hooves, and as his camel turned in crazy circles he saw still more riders galloping down the hill with the triple hump. A curse on Zadoc bar Tubal, may he be stricken with the unclean illness . . .

An arrow hissed past his face, and he raised both hands in protest; stop it, what good can the death of an old man be to you, stop it.

Giddily he saw that the first group of men was now in full gallop, and two more of the servants were on the ground, and the terrified donkeys were kicking up their hind legs.

Issachar next to him was drawing his sword, his eyes gleaming. "Put it down, Issachar. You'll have us all murdered; what can we do against so many? I'm a peaceful man. I . . . "

But Issachar was past hearing, brandishing his stupid sword. There was a flurry of horses and brown arms and glitter, and Issachar went down, with blood spurting out of his mouth, the stupid fool. Look at me, you men, I am holding up both arms, I have no weapons, I'm an old man, can't you see that?

They saw it. They surrounded him, a milling mass of men, their mouths open yelling, their swords and spears ready in their fists, but they did see that there was no enemy left to overcome.

They had seized the camel by the reins, and one of them made that guttural noise which tells a camel to kneel or get up as the case may be, and the camel knelt in its triple rhythm, fore, aft, fore, and now they towered over Boz bar Sebulun, wild-looking men with their swords ready, lestes, bandits, cave dwellers from the Galilean hills.

Greedy hands searched his coat, tore off his belt, and there were shouts of glee as they discovered the pieces of gold, but a tall, black-bearded man with a long scar over one eye shrugged his shoulders contemptuously. "That's nothing. There are many thousands more where these came from."

"Take everything", Boz said in a trembling voice. "Take everything. I am a man of peace. I have never harmed anybody. I'm an old man. Take it all and let me go."

"Let you go, eh? We'll see about that. Perhaps we will—when you've paid us the ransom we want from you."

Ransom! Were they going to take him with them, hold him for weeks, for months perhaps, in some cave till . . .

The man with the scar smiled thinly. "Eighty odd pieces of gold, a few dozen donkeys, and goods—precious little from a man as wealthy as Boz bar Sebulun."

They knew him. Zadoc bar Tubal, Zadoc bar Tubal . . .

"I will pay", Boz gasped. "I will pay anything—anything within reason—only let me go—I'm an old man. I couldn't possibly stand it, if— What good would I be to you dead? Let me go and . . . "

"And you will go to Jerusalem and laugh at us from behind the fat backs of the Temple guards, is that it?"

"Look, Bar Abbas", shouted a voice. "Look what we've got here . . . "

They had dragged Naomi out of the litter. Wide-eyed and with pale lips she stood between two grinning ruffians.

Bar Abbas, thought Boz, horrified. Bar Abbas himself . . .

"There are two more females", one of the ruffians reported. "But they aren't worth much."

"Oh, aren't they?" shrilled a voice behind him, and Abigail tore herself away from the man who held her. She was a woman in her late fifties, strong and bony, and the kitchen maids trembled when she raised her voice. "Even a female is worth more than a robber, they say where I come from."

A few of the men laughed, but Bar Abbas said angrily, "Can't you keep her loose mouth quiet, Dysmas?" He turned to Boz. "Who is the young one, your daughter?"

"My wife", said Boz, not without dignity.

The men laughed, and Boz shook with rage and humiliation.

"That will do", Bar Abbas said. "Get those donkeys ready; put the girl back into the litter. We must be off. Wait! One of the old man's servants was only wounded. Finish him off, Gestas. We can't have him telling the story to anyone who might find him."

"Some of the donkeys are wounded too", Dysmas told him. "What shall we do with their packs? Load them on the others?"

"No. The old miser has loaded them too heavily as it is. Leave the litter here. Let the girl ride. That gives us a donkey more."

There was a scream, long-drawn and horrible, and then Gestas came back, wiping his sword. "If one donkey isn't enough, I'll take the girl on my horse", he offered. "She doesn't weigh much."

"If one donkey isn't enough, I'll let the girl ride the camel, and you can take the old man on your horse," jeered Bar Abbas. "He doesn't weigh much either. Now get going, all of you. We've lost too much time as it is."

"Here, get on this donkey", Gestas ordered Naomi. "And keep it next to my horse if you know what's good for you."

She obeyed. She had never seen a man like this, flat faced, with long, yellow teeth and pale, restless eyes. His hand and forearm were spattered with blood. She shivered as he helped her into the saddle.

"We'll get along", Gestas said. "Don't you worry, little one, you'll see. And if you're nice to me I won't let any of the others touch you." She felt his greedy fingers on her shoulder and tried in vain to shake them off.

"If you're nice to me, I said", Gestas warned her. "You're much too good for that old bag of bones."

His face was suddenly quite near. It seemed enormously large; she could see the red veins in his eyes. She threw back her head to avoid his breath. The movement saved her life. There was a short hissing noise, followed by a scream.

"Baal-zebub!" Gestas roared. He released the girl. He stared at the man behind her, who was clutching his belly.

Naomi swayed in the saddle. She saw the horrible man running for his horse. He mounted it, and it reared as an arrow hit its shoulder. She saw her husband hastily taking cover behind his camel, as the big man with the scar rode up, shouting orders, his sword glittering in his hand. Everywhere men were mounting their horses; some had their bows ready and had begun shooting.

They were shooting at a cloud of sand, a cloud of sand moving toward them unbelievably fast. In the setting sun, it was all shimmery, bluish, and red. Naomi saw helmets and shields, the heads of horses.

She wanted to let herself slip off the donkey. She wanted to hide herself, and she could not; she could only stare at the blue-red monster as if she were under a spell.

"Stand! Fight!" yelled the man with the scar.

Then the monster was there, horses, helmets, shields, spears, and it really was like a monster, not a troup of soldiers, a monster with many heads and arms and legs, a single, huge animal, a brute of terrible strength, shaking the bandits in its awful fists, wheeling, coming on again with hideous sounds, wheeling again . . .

Sand splashed over her. She could not lift her trembling hands to brush it away. She saw the man with the scar gallop off toward the hills, his head low down on the neck of his horse, his shield wobbling on his back. Three, four other men raced after him. A large white horse, riderless, bleeding, fell just beside her, raised its head, and gave a long, long scream . . .

The next thing Naomi knew, Abigail was bending over her, rubbing her temples with essence. "It's all right, my lamb, it's all right now."

She struggled to sit up. "Where—where are they?"

"Who? The bandits?" Abigail snorted. "Most of them are dead. Some are prisoners. Over there, see?"

She saw a few wretched men, their hands tied behind their backs with leather thongs. One of them was the horrible one, the one they called Gestas. She shuddered and looked away.

Her husband was talking to the Roman leader, who seemed to be a young man. He wore the same uniform as his men, bluish armor and red-brown tunic, but he had a tuft of red horsehair on his helmet, marking him as a leader of one hundred men, a centurion.

Boz' gratitude was effusive, his attitude almost deferential.

Why, Naomi wondered, did all these Romans look so much alike, short-haired, clean-shaven, with curt, abrupt movements?

The centurion was haughty; he should be more polite to an old man, but they never were. Boz had explained it to her more than once. "Barbarians do not respect old age. It is the hallmark of barbarism."

Now they came up to her, the officer's small, round shield clanking against his shoulder plates, giving a merry sound, almost like the little bells of a leading camel. But there was a long smear of blood on the shield, and she closed her eyes in disgust.

"Naomi, my dove, say thanks to the noble Roman who saved our lives."

She forced herself to look up into the supercilious young face. She said, "I must thank you for having saved the life of my husband."

"Husband?" The Roman let his dark, cold eyes wander from her to Boz and back to her. He did not smile. It was good that he did not smile, but there was perpetual irony in the corners of his mouth. "Husband? I see. What about your own life, lady?"

His Aramaic was not bad, except for his inability to pronounce the guttural sounds; all Romans were alike in that, too—or rather the few who troubled to learn it at all.

"My life is of no value", Naomi said quietly.

"Do not mind her, noble Roman. She has been through much excitement and trouble, as indeed we all have. I am an old man and a man of peace—I shall need a long time to recover from what happened today."

The Roman continued to stare at her, coolly, appraisingly, as if she were a horse he might want to buy.

The small black fans came down to rest on her pale cheeks. She did not dare to frown.

"We are on our way to the city", Boz went on. "We hoped to reach the inn at Beth-horon tonight. If by any chance you could allow us to stay with you—the bandits might come back and . . ."

The Roman smiled. "The dead don't come back. Only five men have managed to escape. Eight are prisoners. The others are dead. Wait." His eyes were scanning the horizon.

Turning, Boz saw about a dozen men on horseback racing toward them. He began to tremble. "There . . . there . . . they're coming back."

The Roman did not bother to answer. He waited quietly. Soon Boz, too, saw that the riders were Romans, and he sighed with relief.

They stopped their horses before the officer, and one of them reported, "They got away. We had only their trail to go by, and the sun was sinking."

The officer gave a curt nod, and they rode on, to dismount at some distance. Boz could see that the officer was a little upset about something. Of course—Bar Abbas. Bar Abbas had escaped, one of the two most famous bandit leaders.

"We'll go on", said the Roman abruptly. "You can come with us, if you wish—we shall pass Beth-horon."

Boz gave another sigh of relief. Near Beth-horon several caravan roads converged, and it was only a few hours from Jerusalem. From Beth-horon they would be quite safe, even without a Roman escort. "We are most grateful", he said. "Will you tell us to whom we owe our lives? The name of Boz bar Sebulun is not unknown in Jerusalem, and there will be many who will wish to express their gratitude to the procurator for the help we have received."

The Roman gave him a dubious look. "As you wish", he drawled. "I'm Cassius Longinus, centurion in the Italican cohort."

The old man bowed. "Your name has a meaning in this country", he said. "At about the time I was born one Cassius Longinus was imperial Governor of Syria."

"A great-uncle of mine", the Roman nodded casually. "I never knew him, of course. He didn't stand much nonsense, I've been told."

"A stern man", affirmed Boz. His face was expressionless. The

Governor Cassius Longinus had oppressed Judaea, sucked it dry of money, and sold thirty thousand Jews into slavery. That was seventy years ago. But Rome and Jerusalem had good memories.

Cassius Longinus grinned. "Better get your servants together—or what's left of them. We shall leave at once." He walked away.

"We must get the donkeys ready", Boz tugged at his beard. "It will all be very difficult. Issachar is dead, and Gideon and at least two more. Are you all right, Naomi, my dove?"

"Yes", said Naomi quietly.

"Some of the donkeys are dead, too." Boz shook his head; he was thoroughly annoyed. "Bandits. Bandits and Gentiles. If they would only kill each other off, life would be worth living again."

III

Two days before the Feast of the Tabernacles the city of Jerusalem was almost surrounded by a huge crescent of many thousands of little huts, booths, and tents. The two horns of the crescent were separated only by the Valley of Hinnom, the desolate and accursed place of refuse and uncleanness, the burial place of criminals, inhabited only by outcasts, beggars, and lepers.

Two hundred thousand pilgrims had already arrived, and at least an equal number more were expected.

Fifteen men had gathered in a hut built for six or seven people. All of them were simply dressed. It would have been difficult to identify them in a crowd. But each one was a leader of many, and for the heads of most of them the Roman government would have paid a stiff price.

"Thirty-two dead, and nothing to show for it", said Ephraim bar Saul angrily. "Sheer madness."

Bar Abbas whirled around. "You'd have done better, would you? Against sixty cavalry, regulars—in the open!"

"I would have done better because I wouldn't have started on that absurd expedition", was the cold answer.

The scar on Bar Abbas' forehead turned livid. "True enough", he said. "If all we did was what you think is right, we'd never do anything."

"If you'd listen to me instead of this hothead we wouldn't be in this hut now, either", Ephraim bar Saul said to the room at large. "All the leaders of the party together, at the very gates of Jerusalem. If the Temple crowd or the Romans get to hear of it, our entire cause will be lost for years."

"There is no place in the country where we would be safer", snapped Bar Abbas. "With all those pilgrims camping around us, you might as well try to find a groat in a barn full of corn."

"If there is a traitor among us ... "

Bar Abbas stared at his rival. "There isn't", he said slowly. "Unless it's you."

Ephraim bar Saul jumped to his feet. Half a dozen men threw themselves between the two leaders.

"Be reasonable ... "

"This gets us nowhere."

"Peace", said Achim bar Simeon, a rugged Galilean. "Peace. Save your anger for the enemy."

Bar Abbas looked about him. "Sit down, all of you", he rasped.

They obeyed, even Ephraim bar Saul, after some show of hesitation.

"Never mind a skirmish I lost", Bar Abbas said. "There are greater things to be discussed tonight."

"You shouldn't have exposed yourself like this", Bar Saul insisted. "You're supposed to lead an army, not to go out on a small raid with a handful of men. No wonder they call us bandits."

Bar Abbas gave a short laugh. "I suppose I'd better tell you. You know how often we've tried to find out what the Temple crowd is planning. Caiphas is a very shrewd man, and his agents are everywhere—except in this hut. We know all the men around him and what their functions are. We know whom he visits and when and for how long. We have ears in his house and in the Temple. And yet we don't know from whom he gets some of his reports on—matters of importance. We can only surmise. Now I've found out that he sees one man a little more often than seems necessary, a relative it is true—Boz bar Sebulun."

"It is natural", said one of the men. "Boz married Leah, the sister of Caiphas. Why should he not visit his brother-in-law?"

"Leah died three years ago", Bar Abbas replied. "And Boz bar Sebulun has remarried despite his age. His new wife is little more than a child. It flatters the old man's vanity to have a young, beautiful wife. Caiphas was not pleased about that second marriage. Yet he visits his former brother-in-law. Perhaps the house of Boz is the place where Caiphas receives reports he wants to keep to himself. I wanted to make sure. So I sent an agent to Boz, to find out when the old man was leaving his country house for Jerusalem. I told him to try to win Boz over to our cause. It was a pretext, of course. I knew very well that the old man wouldn't do it, but why tell the agent more than was good for him? My plan was to catch Boz on the way and to take him to a safe place where I could question him. You know I always get them to talk."

A few of the men smiled.

"I wanted to search his luggage, too", Bar Abbas went on. "And everything went according to plan. I had him, wife, luggage, and all—and then the cursed Romans turned up. I should have had a report on their movements. The man responsible for that will be punished. So now you know that this little raid was not as senseless as it seemed. We lost thirty-two men, that's true—although some of them may be prisoners. We shall lose many more before we have driven the Romans out. And now, I hope, we can talk of something far more important. Yesterday afternoon the procurator arrived in Jerusalem."

Ephraim bar Saul nodded. "With twelve hundred men."

"That's right. A full cohort from the garrison in Caesarea and two hundred auxiliaries. With the regular garrison of Jerusalem that makes something over three thousand."

"We know that", said one of the men quietly. "The procurator always comes here for the great feasts."

"A little over three thousand men", repeated Bar Abbas gravely. "And we are two hundred thousand—and by day after tomorrow, when the feast starts, we shall be double that number."

There was a pause. From outside came the strains of a song; it was a very old song, one of the psalms of the great King David, but sung by a maudlin, drunken voice. Somebody shouted abuse, and the voice broke off. From farther away came the hum and buzz of camp life.

None of the fifteen men in the hut heard anything but his own breathing. They were like wanderers who turn a corner and suddenly stand in full view of the goal. But—was it the goal? Or was it a mirage?

Achim bar Simeon, the big Galilean, rose, and at the same time others, men from Hammon, from Chorazin, from Chinnereth and Caphernaum on the shores of the Sea of Chinnereth, which the Romans called the Lake of Tiberias.

"One of you at a time", Bar Abbas snapped. He knew what was coming. When these people spoke at all they spoke of only one thing.

"You want the great fight for freedom to come out into the open", he went on. "You want to make use of the Feast of the Tabernacles, of the procurator's presence in the city for the first big stroke.

"That is what I want. And the stroke may prove to be decisive. I've worked it all out. In two days the city can be ours . . . "

"The fortress, the Antonia . . . "

"With the Antonia. And with the procurator."

"The garrison in Caesarea . . . "

"They'll be troops without a commander. And there are good Jews in Caesarea too."

Achim bar Simeon nodded. "It will succeed—if the King Messiah is on our side. But only then."

There it was. And as always when that fateful title was named, there was a moment of silence.

"Last time I met you you said he had come, didn't you?" Bar Abbas sat down. He suddenly felt weary. "Or was it you, Oziah?"

Oziah of Hammon was a sturdy man in his forties, with deep-set eyes full of a dark fire. "I said so", he answered. "I believed it with perfect faith. I still believe it. It is he. It must be."

"Why?" asked Ephraim bar Saul sharply.

"Because there is no other. And because there has never been a time when the people have been so full of expectancy as they are now. Not here so much, perhaps, where they go on trading and collecting shekels and buying silk kerchiefs for their womenfolk and bangles and baubles of all kinds instead of thinking of what really matters. Their habits make them dull to what is in the very air around them. But we in Galilee—we know. We breathe it and eat it and drink it every day. He is here."

Bar Abbas put his hand over his eyes. He stifled a groan. Now they would go on prattling about their King Messiah for hours on end. Always waiting for the miracle worker from nowhere, for the one who would do for them what they ought to do for themselves, the Son of David, the Anointed One, the King Messiah who would liberate Israel and make it great, the One without whom they could no nothing, the One whom even the Gentiles would accept as their ruler. And so on and on interminably, and all anchored in Scripture, bits of this prophet and that. "It will succeed if the King Messiah is on our side. But only then."

"There is more", said Achim bar Simeon. "Oziah here believes that the King Messiah has come. But I—I know it."

"How?" asked Ephraim bar Saul.

"Because I have seen him do what is beyond man's power to do."

"There isn't much beyond man's power to do", growled Bar Abbas. "If only he would do it — instead of talking."

"Can you make blind men see?" asked Achim bar Simeon calmly. "Can you make deaf men hear?"

"I wish I could." Bar Abbas spat. "For then you would see that we must act if we want to succeed — and you would hear what my plan is. But you all are blind and deaf." He shook his head. "Did you see the man cure somebody who was blind?" he asked dryly. "With your own eyes, I mean?"

"No. But I spoke to three people who had seen it."

"There are no liars in Galilee, are there? And didn't you say *you* saw him do what is beyond man's power to do?"

Achim bar Simeon remained calm and unruffled.

"Yes. And it was a greater thing than giving a man back his eyesight. How many men can you feed on five barley loaves and two fishes, Bar Abbas?"

"What sort of a question is that?"

"The Rabbi Yeshua fed five thousand men on five barley loaves and two fishes", declared Bar Simeon. "I was there. I saw it. I ate. I ate half a loaf myself — and a piece of fish, as big as my hand. It was good fish", he added simply. "Everybody had enough to eat. And when we had finished, he ordered us to gather up the leftovers . . . "

"You aren't serious!"

"Leftovers. So we gathered them and filled twelve baskets."

Ephraim bar Saul leaned forward. "When was this?" he asked sharply. "And where?"

"It was only a week ago. On the east bank of the Sea of Chinnereth. He was sitting on a small hill; he likes doing that, they say. I had never seen him before. I was curious. He had crossed the lake in a small ship, but we had to walk a long way to get to the east bank, and we were tired and hungry. He has a number of disciples with him most of the time, and one of them discovered a boy who had those five loaves and the two fishes. He gave them to the Rabbi Yeshua. And he . . . "

"Well—what did he do? Go on!" Bar Abbas urged.

Achim took a deep breath. "He touched them", he said hoarsely. "All of them. And he prayed over them. Lifted up his eyes and prayed."

He broke off again.

"What is the matter with you, man?" asked Bar Abbas incredulously.

Achim scowled. "You haven't seen him", he said gruffly. "If you had, you'd know what praying means. I didn't know—till then." He looked up. "Laugh", he said. "Laugh—and I'll run you through."

"I'm not laughing", said Bar Abbas lightly. There was a new interest in his eyes. "Go on. What did he do then?"

"He gave a portion of bread and fish to everyone—as much as we wanted."

"Enough for five thousand, and twelve basketsful left", said Bar Abbas thoughtfully. "How do you account for it?"

"I don't", said Achim fiercely. "But he could have fed five million; he could have fed every man, woman and child in the world. And still he would have had twelve basketsful left. He gave us out of his fullness; he gave as the sun gives warmth. He is the One who comes from God. He is the King Messiah. We all knew it then. We talked about it, quite openly. I—I shouted to the others, 'This is he who is to be King in Israel—he is the Anointed One.' And a thousand voices shouted with me, and we went up the hill, to do homage to him as to the King."

Bar Abbas' eyes narrowed. "You did, eh? And he?"

"He was gone", said Achim dully. "Gone. We looked and looked and couldn't find him. I didn't see him again."

"But I did", interposed a thin, gray-haired man in a corner. "I saw him a little later in the synagogue of Caphernaum. And I tell you, he is not the King Messiah."

115

"How can you . . . "

"Quiet, Achim", Bar Abbas commanded. "Let Eliud have his say, too."

"Everybody in Caphernaum was talking about the loaves and the fishes", began Eliud. "So I heard about it, and when it was known that he had turned up in Caphernaum and would be in the synagogue, I went, to see the miracle worker." He smiled thinly. "I came late. And I found the synagogue in an uproar. The Rabbi Yeshua had told them things that shocked them to the very core. That he—he himself—was bread. The bread of life, he called it. That was the real bread, he said. Not like the manna that our fathers ate in the desert, but the real bread from heaven. I am the living bread that has come down from heaven, he said. Many of us knew him, of course. Yeshua bar Joseph, the son of the carpenter. Grew up in Nazareth. He couldn't very well tell *us* that he had come down from heaven. But that was nothing. He went on saying that the bread he had to give was his flesh—how did he put it?—his flesh, given 'for the life of the world'."

They looked at each other, dismayed.

Oziah shook his head. "How can he give us his flesh to eat?"

"That's exactly what I asked." Eliud nodded. "He heard me, too, and he answered. Know what he said? 'You can have no life in yourselves, unless you eat the flesh of the Son of Man and drink his blood. The man who eats my flesh and drinks my blood enjoys eternal life, and I will raise him up at the last day.'"

"He didn't mean it", objected Achim. "He was speaking in parables. He often does."

Eliud gave an angry laugh. "I wish you were right", he said. "But he seemed to know some of us thought that. He went on, 'My flesh is real food; my blood is real drink. He who eats my flesh and drinks my blood lives continually in me, and I in him.'"

"Strange", said Achim. He closed his eyes.

"Horrible." Eliud shrugged. "I left. Most of us left. Who can listen to such things? The King Messiah—he? Bah."

"I saw what I saw", said Achim obstinately.

Bar Abbas began to laugh. "Where did you say he grew up? In Nazareth? Fools that you are. I am not a learned man, God knows, but this much I do know—the King Messiah must be born in Bethlehem, not in Nazareth. How does it go, Ephraim? You are better versed in the Scriptures than I am."

Ephraim bar Saul was flattered. "The prophet Micheas says, 'And thou, Bethlehem Ephrata, art a little one among the thousands of Juda: out of thee shall he come forth unto me that is to be the ruler in Israel: and his going forth is from the beginning, from the days of eternity.'"

"There now", Bar Abbas said indulgently. "Bethlehem. Not Nazareth."

"They say the Rabbi Yeshua was born in Bethlehem", declared Oziah. "His parents had to go there just when his mother's time had come because of the census that Augustus ordered."

There was a pause.

"I remember that", said Ephraim pensively. "Cyrinus was Governor of Syria then. And the King Messiah must come from David's lineage. And Bethlehem is David's city in Judaea."

"There you are", said Achim. "I wish we could ask him. I wish I knew where he was."

"But you don't", said Bar Abbas acidly. "And time presses. If he wanted to be what you think he is, why didn't he allow you to do homage to him on that hill? Here we go, trying to solve riddles—when we should act."

"Perhaps I can help to solve the riddle", said a voice from another corner of the hut. They all turned toward the thickset, baldheaded man with the bushy eyebrows. It was Jaqob bar Mathan, one of the commanders in the north. He grinned cheerfully. "I let you all talk," he announced, "knowing that it would come to this. If this man Yeshua is the King Messiah, how is it that you haven't troubled to keep in constant touch with him? Well, don't worry about it. I did."

"You did? Where is he then?"

"Has he said who he is?"

"Have you got a message from him?"

They were all shouting at the same time. Bar Abbas alone remained silent.

"I have a message, yes", Jaqob bar Mathan told them. "It is not from him . . . "

"Oh . . . "

" . . . but from one of his disciples. A man called Judah. He comes from Kerioth. I have known him for some time. A man not without ambition, I believe." Jaqob darted a quick glance at Bar Abbas. "Well, according to Judah there is no doubt that the Rabbi Yeshua is the King Messiah."

"Of course", said Bar Abbas sarcastically.

"But, says Judah, he does not wish to disclose his hand too early. He will do so at the right time."

The room rustled with movement, but no one spoke.

"When?" Achim asked finally. It sounded like a groan, the groan of a long-suffering man who must know when the pain will stop. "When, Jaqob?"

Jaqob bar Mathan shrugged his shoulders. "Judah did not give me a date. He didn't say it would be on the first day of Nisan or the fifteenth day of Iyar. But he did say it would be soon. He was very emphatic about it. I think he himself is impatient for the King to act. But that is not all he said."

"What else is there?" urged Oziah. "Why do you keep us all on tenterhooks? In the Name of the Ineffable, speak up!"

Jaqob pursed his lips. "Rabbi Yeshua seems to be a cautious man", he said. "In any case, Judah said, there must be those who prepare the way of the King. It is not enough to fight little skirmishes here and there. 'When the King enters his city, it should be his city.' "

Bar Abbas snorted. "Not bad. Let us do the hard work—so that he can take over."

"May I be allowed to do hard work for the King as long as I live!" Achim said simply.

"If he is the King . . . " Eliud shrugged.

Bar Abbas' thoughts were racing. Most of the leaders seemed to believe that Rabbi Yeshua was the One who had been expected from generation to generation. They were looking askance at Eliud, and they could easily turn against him, Bar Abbas, too. He leaned forward. "Tell me, Jaqob, are *you* in constant touch with Rabbi Yeshua? Through this man Judah from Kerioth perhaps? Can you reach him anytime you want?"

"No, I can't", was the answer. "The Temple crowd has it in for him. That's why he remained in Galilee so long and didn't come to Judaea. Even in Galilee he never stays long in the same place; he moves around all the time."

"In other words," Bar Abbas went on, "you could not be sure that a letter of yours would be in his hands within two days—or three, shall we say?"

"It might not reach him for a week, or two weeks."

"And it might be intercepted by Caiphas' agents", Bar Abbas added. "Or by those of the procurator. No secret signs have been established, no passwords, nothing." He stood with his arms akimbo. "Very well then", he said. "Let's do what that man Judah suggested. Let's prepare the way for the King. We shall take the city—and invite him to enter it. Then we shall see whether he is the One we have been waiting for or not. And he will come, too—who wouldn't?"

He saw the flicker of enthusiasm brighten their faces. Why did most men need to find some reason, aside from their own advantage, before they would fight? As if the fighting itself was not a good enough reason, as if victory meant nothing by itself? As if it weren't enough to drive that arrogant, self-inflated crowd of Roman dogs out of the country, those self-styled demigods who thought they owned the world just because they were Romans. But all that wasn't enough. They must have their King

Messiah. No action without the King Messiah. And in the mean-time one had to do all the work.

Perhaps they would talk differently once Jerusalem was won. Perhaps *he* would talk differently then. Bar Abbas, the first Jew to defeat a Roman army — the first Jew to win a battle since the time of the Machabees . . .

Perhaps one day, one not very distant day, they would have to choose between Bar Abbas and their King Messiah.

"The time for action is now", he said loudly. "There are over six thousand of us here — some within the city, some outside, all of us armed. These six thousand are the nucleus of our army, the only ones we can count on in the initial stage. The others, the great masses of pilgrims, the hundreds of thousands, will come in only when they see that the fighting is going our way. Therefore everything depends upon immediate success. I have thought it all out. And now at long last perhaps you will listen to my plan . . . "

IV

Centurion Longinus, back from patrol, requests to report to the legate", Cassius said.

The officer on watch in the antechamber grinned. "You can't go in now. The procurator is with him and tribune Vindex."

Cassius nodded and sat down on one of the uncomfortable chairs. "Half a soldier's life is waiting", he quoted.

"And the less said about the other half, the better." The officer yawned. "Haven't had an hour's sleep", he complained. "They put me into Varro's room. I've never known a man snore as he does."

"What's wrong with your own room?" Cassius inquired.

"Don't you know? Of course you don't. You've been on patrol. The procurator brought his wife with him, and she needed three more rooms for herself and her maids. I had to give up mine, and so had Aufidius and Burrus."

Cassius frowned. "He brought his wife, did you say?"

The officer began to laugh. "Why not?" he asked. "Does he have to ask your permission first?"

Claudia here, in Jerusalem . . .

Cassius shrugged his shoulders. "We're cramped enough for space without the lady", he said to his sandals.

"True", the officer agreed. "But at least she's a pretty woman. Good-looking rather than pretty, I should say. Wait till you see her. Or have you met her before?"

"Yes", Cassius said curtly.

"Well, don't you think she's good-looking?"

"I'm glad they didn't take *my* room", Cassius said.

The officer gave him a quizzical look and resumed his desk work.

Cassius sank into a reverie.

Claudia in Jerusalem . . .

He had seen her last in Caesarea, almost four years ago. In the park of the procurator's residence. In front of the statue of Juno. It was several weeks after their arrival in Judaea.

He had avoided her as much as he could, almost to the point of rudeness. For a while she did not seem to notice. She was cool and aloof and formal with everyone, including her husband, who seemed to treat her with a kind of paternal courtesy.

But then, one afternoon, she managed to send Cassius a note, asking him to come to the park, to the statue of Juno, one hour before sunset. Pilatus was away at the time, on harbor inspection.

Cassius tore up the note and burned it. He was determined not to go.

He did not understand what made him change his mind at the last moment. She was waiting for him at the statue of Juno, looking rather pale and sad and as beautiful as ever.

She could no longer bear his enmity, she said, without preamble.

"I feel no enmity toward you, Lady Claudia."

She gave a nervous little laugh. "What is it then? Contempt?"

He said nothing.

"How easy life is for a man", she said with a bitter smile. "A man makes his own life, boldly and unafraid. Women are always afraid. A man has friends to help him, friends whom he can trust. A woman has no friends and can trust no one. I know you have suffered", she added quickly. "But you fought your way through, bravely. I wasn't made to fight, Cassius."

Still he said nothing.

"What did you know about me, Cassius? Almost nothing at all. But you had formed a picture of me in your mind, and you expected me to live up to it."

"Yes", he said, and for a fleeting moment he thought of Seneca's "I know very little of Claudia—perhaps no more than you do." "That's true, Claudia, and you didn't live up to it."

"I suppose not. But you never bothered to find out why!"

"It is fairly obvious, isn't it?" he said cuttingly. "I was ruined. My father was in trouble. So your feeling for me—if any—changed overnight."

"My feeling for you . . . " Claudia smiled. She looked so lovely that he ached to seize her in his arms, to kiss her until she had no breath left.

"So you married Pilatus", he said.

She looked past him at the statue of Juno. "I try to be a good wife to him", she said dully. "The kind of good wife he expects me to be. But I could not forget you. I shouldn't tell you that, I know, but there it is. I—I wasn't brave enough to keep it to myself. I love you, Cassius."

He took one step toward her. "Why did you marry him?" he demanded. "Why did you marry him, Claudilla?"

She leaned toward him, her eyes averted and half closed. "I had no choice", she whispered. "It was Sejanus' wish."

He recoiled, his face suddenly contorted with rage. "Sejanus!

Of course. Sejanus rules the earth. You had no choice. I understand. Good night, Lady Claudia."

"Cassius! What is the matter? Why . . . "

But he walked away, without turning his head.

The next day he had gone to his centurion and asked to be transferred to some garrison inland.

"Why?"

"Field service gives a better chance for promotion, centurion."

"True. All right, I'll take your request to the tribune."

The tribune granted it, and the transfer took place within a week.

To Jericho first, then to Jerusalem. Within six months he was a leader of ten. Six months later he became a centurion in the Italican cohort.

Why did the procurator have to bring Claudia along? He had never done so before. Perhaps he had learned not to trust her. Too many young officers in Caesarea.

The procurator hated Jerusalem; everybody knew that. Twice, in the course of the last four years or so, there had been serious trouble here.

The door of the legate's room opened, and both Cassius and the officer on watch rose and stood to attention.

The procurator came out, with the legate and Vindex, the head of Intelligence.

Cassius saluted stiffly.

"Yes, centurion?" Pilatus looked bored.

Cassius reported. A skirmish—four men dead, nine wounded. Loss of two horses. Seven horses temporarily incapacitated. Losses of the enemy: twenty-four dead, eight prisoners, including two who were on the special list—Dysmas and Gestas. The leader of the enemy escaped, unfortunately. His name was also on the special list: Bar Abbas.

"Who?" asked Pilatus sharply. "Did you say Bar Abbas? Where was that encounter?"

"Eight miles south of Beth-horon, procurator."

Pilatus looked questioningly at Vindex. There was a thin smile on the leathery face of the head of Intelligence. He nodded imperceptibly. "May I ask the centurion a few questions?"

"Go ahead", said Pilatus.

"Centurion, are you quite sure it was Bar Abbas?"

"I heard one of his men call him by name during the skirmish, and four of the prisoners surrendered only when they heard another man exclaim that Bar Abbas had fled."

"Did you see him yourself?"

"Yes, tribune, a tall man, reddish beard, deep scar over one eye."

"Was he wounded?"

"I don't think so, tribune. He had a very fast horse. I sent a patrol after him, but the men came back when it grew too dark to follow his trail."

The three senior commanders looked at each other.

"I think you did very well", said Pilatus. "Join us tonight at my table."

Cassius pressed his lips together. Then he said brusquely, "I'm on watch tonight, procurator. I beg to be excused."

"As you wish." The three commanders walked away.

Not at the same table with her, Cassius thought. Not unless I have to.

He went back to quarters.

"Well, how did it go?" asked First Centurion Abenadar. He had a long, melancholy face, sallow and wrinkled. Without armor, in his reddish brown tunic, his iron-gray hair always a little too long, he did not look like a fighting man. Yet he had probably seen and done more fighting than anybody in the Italican cohort within the last thirty years. He had come up from the ranks and was now in command of a thousand men, quite an achievement for someone not of Roman birth.

"I don't understand it", said Cassius. "They seemed to like it. It It was almost as if they were glad that I didn't catch Bar Abbas."

"Perhaps they were." Abenadar grinned shrewdly.

"But why should they be?"

"Vindex could tell you, I think."

"He was there, too."

"Oh, I knew that. In fact, that's why I thought it would be better if you made the report yourself. He would have only asked me to call you for personal questioning."

Cassius murmured something, sat down and shouted for an orderly. "Wine."

When the man had gone, Cassius said, "I still don't understand."

"I've known Vindex a long time", said Abenadar. "He's cut out for the kind of work he's doing. Intelligence. Bar Abbas is among the first two or three on the special list, isn't he? Well, there are times when it is better not to lay hands on a dangerous man but to let him run free. Then you always know that where he is, is the danger spot. You have something to go by. Take him away, and the lestes will choose somebody else whom you may not know. Then you will have to be on guard at many points at the same time."

"Perhaps you're right." Cassius drank. "The great man invited me to his table tonight, Abenadar. I told him I had the watch. You'll back me up, won't you?"

Abenadar looked at the list. "Aufidius, Varro, and Mela", he said. "You aren't on till next week. Why don't you want to enjoy yourself?"

"I'm no good at banquets."

"When I was your age . . . "

"Everybody must live his own cursed life, Abenadar."

"Maybe. But why should it be a cursed life?"

"Because it is."

"Well, it won't be much of a banquet anyway", said Abenadar. "The legate tried hard to get a sensation for it: the best singer and dancer this country ever produced. Saw her once myself, in Caesarea. Miriam of Migdal."

"I've seen the best Gaditan dancers in Rome", said Cassius contemptuously.

"You've seen nothing, my boy. This woman is a marvel. Your Gaditan girls may excite you, but they're crude, however beauriful they are. Miriam is a nymph and a nightingale, a goddess and a butterfly. She makes you laugh and cry at the same time— you feel that the world is a lovely place to live in and that you could fly like a bird if she whispered one magic word into your ear."

Cassius laughed. "Varro tells me that you're reading at night. Poetry, eh?"

"Miriam of Migdal herself is poetry", said Abenadar. "But she won't be here."

"Why not?"

"She doesn't dance any more. They say she's up north, in Galilee, following a certain miracle worker, a wandering rabbi . . . "

"Turned religious. Some of them do. Usually when they put on fat."

"You're a bitter man, Cassius."

Cassius grinned. "Feeling sorry for me?"

"I've been out here two years", said Abenadar. "And you almost four . . . you were transferred to Jerusalem almost as soon as you arrived, weren't you?"

"I didn't care for Caesarea."

"And in those two years I've heard every single young officer talk about his girls. Except you."

"What of it?"

"There are beautiful girls in this country."

"Yes, there are. I saw one the other day. A girl like a gazelle, like a young antelope. Eyes a man could dream of. And married to an old merchant of seventy. A very rich man, of course. There's a grinning skull under that lovely face, Abenadar—you couldn't tell it from the one under the spotty old face of her husband."

"How old was she, do you think?"

"Fifteen—sixteen. No more than that."

"She didn't choose him, you know", said Abenadar quietly.

"She didn't?"

"No. She was given in marriage. She had no say in it."

Cassius frowned. "That means she didn't sell herself—she was sold."

"Not necessarily. More likely it was an arranged marriage."

"Barbarians, these Jews."

Abenadar threw back his head to laugh. "What about Rome, Cassius? This Jewish girl of yours will honor her husband, even if he is seventy. How many Roman women would do the same? They're very severe in this country about a woman's behavior and morals. The Law of Moses is still obeyed: the adulteress is stoned to death."

"If they did that in Rome, it would decimate the female population." Cassius grinned. "Might even obliterate it."

"I wouldn't know", Abenadar said gravely. "I've never been in Rome. I was born in a mud hut in Syria. My father was a soldier in the Italican cohort. A Sebastene. There weren't many men of Roman birth in the cohort then. There aren't many now. Syrians, with a few drops of Roman blood picked up somewhere in the past. And my mother was Jewish."

"Jewish? I thought they never intermarried with non-Jews?"

"It doesn't happen often, no. She was my father's slave at first. A piece of loot. His share, dealt out to him by the quartermaster. When I was under way, he freed her. He wanted freeborn children. Mother just laughed at that. 'Jews are never slaves, whatever else you may call them', she used to say."

"They're a proud people." Think of old Abenadar, half Syrian, half Jewish—and in command of a Roman cohort! Of course, the Italican was Italican in name only; there weren't more than two hundred real Romans in it, though most of the officers were Romans, of course. Of course! Why of course?

127

"None prouder." Abenadar grinned cheerfully. "She and father often quarreled about that. She said, 'When Romulus was building the walls of Rome, Israel could look back on hundreds of years of glorious history.' And father hit back, 'Whenever Romans come to another country, they come as conquerors; whenever Jews come to another country, they come as captives.' And mother would snap at him, 'Who is more honorable: the robber or the one who is robbed?' And in the end she always said, 'Say what you like, we are the Chosen People of God', and he retorted, 'Chosen for what?' and then she would turn serious and say, 'Hear, O Israel, the Lord, our God is *one* Lord.'"

"They all pray like that, don't they?"

"Yes, they do. And they did, many hundreds of years before Rome was built. As far as I know they are the only people in the world who believe in one God. We have lots of gods in Syria, including all the Roman gods and goddesses."

"Gods", said Cassius. He shrugged.

"I know you're not exactly religious." Abenadar looked almost embarrassed. "I've seen your face when you put your handful of incense into the tripod before the statue of the divine Emperor. And your hands. You do it as if you were dishing out soup to the poor."

Cassius' eyes narrowed. "Sharp observer, aren't you? I suppose you reported it to old Vindex. For the record."

Abenadar stared at him. "It would be my duty, wouldn't it—as your superior?"

"Yes—commander", said Cassius.

"Ass", Abenadar said amiably.

For a while they sat silent.

"You're a good soldier", Abenadar said. "One of the best I've had. I wonder what you believe in."

"Nothing."

"Nonsense. Everybody believes in something. If it isn't gods, it's something else. Some men believe in their own prowess, or in a woman or in money or power. What are you living for?"

"My father believed in Rome", Cassius said.

"And do you?"

"Rome is a pigsty."

"And I won't report that one either", Abenadar said dryly. "There must be something you aim at—something you look forward to."

Cassius stared at the bleak, whitewashed wall. A row of helmets hung there, side by side, regulation helmets, nothing ornate. No fancy stuff, not like a gladiator's outfit.

"You've done a lot of fighting", he said. "Ever seen blood spurting out of a man's jugular vein? Like a fountain, a hot, red fountain. And he kicks the ground, half a dozen times. Then he's dead."

"I've seen that", Abenadar nodded. "What of it?"

"There are some men now alive whom I want to see end like that", said Cassius dreamily. "Just a few."

"Who are they?"

Cassius smiled.

"Meaning some people have done you wrong, I suppose. And what you want is justice."

"Maybe."

Abenadar shook his head. "Why should there be justice?" he asked. "I mean—if there is no God—or no gods? Why should there be any justice at all?"

"There isn't."

"So you tell me. But you demand that there should be. By what right do you demand such a thing—in a world that is no more than a mass of coincidences?"

"Philosopher, aren't you?"

"We all want it", Abenadar said thoughtfully. "We all want justice—and some of us think justice means the granting of all *our* wishes, and never mind the others. We want justice—yet we see injustice done every day. We demand it—in the face of reality, in the teeth of facts. Take the Jews: Do you know anything of their history?"

"Not much. Not much beyond the bit of history that I am trying to make."

"It's one long chain of suffering. Captives in Egypt, captives in Babylonia and Assyria and Persia, short periods of freedom and then captivity again—or the rule of foreigners anyway, as it is now again. And yet they believe in a just God."

"Fooling themselves."

"They've stuck to that God of theirs—that one God. All the other nations gladly accepted the gods of their conquerors. They must be powerful, obviously. They had vanquished the local ones. Not the Jews. Amazing loyalty, if you come to think of it. Ah, well, sometimes they strayed a little. But each time they did, up came one of their prophets and yanked them back again. *You* know what happened in the first year you came here—when Pilatus had the eagle of the First Legion carried into the city and the standards and vexilla with the picture of the Emperor and had them placed above the gallery overlooking the Temple! What a storm that raised!"

Cassius nodded. "Almost worse than the one a little later, when the old man st—er—took the money for the aqueduct. And *that* was bad enough. The Temple money! They were as mad as hornets. Fourteen attacks against us in three hours. I was thinking about the two incidents this morning while I was waiting in the legate's antechamber. Now the money—that I can understand. No one likes to be robbed, and their Temple money is sort of sacred to them, isn't it? But why did they have to kick up such a fuss about the vexilla?"

"Their God has forbidden the worship of images", Abenadar said.

"But who asked them to worship the vexilla?"

"No one did, true enough. But Jews go the whole way. If their God has something against images, there must be no images. They don't have any in their homes either. There are no Jewish painters or sculptors; you know that."

"Some of their dresses are ornate enough."

"Ah, yes, but even on them you won't find any semblance to man, animal, bird, or fish. Only designs, patterns. And then we come and carry our 'images' right into their holy of holies, the Temple precincts. Do you remember how many dead there were that day? I was in Caesarea at the time, as you know, and we never had the complete figures. They hushed it up, of course."

"Over six hundred, I think", Cassius said phlegmatically.

A couple of noisy young centurions entered, shed their armor, and went out again. Few officers would stay here at "quarters" during the day. The place was too bare: just four whitewashed walls and a minimum of ramshackle furniture. In the evening wine and dice helped them forget the meanness of what was supposed to be living quarters for twenty men.

Cassius thought of the terrible riot on Vexilla Day, as they called it afterward. The maddened Jews tried to climb the walls of the Antonia, but not like soldiers. They had no plan, no commanders, not even ladders. They came on in a wild rush; they climbed on top of each other, like insects, like locusts. Many were trampled to death by their own comrades, others crushed against the wall. There should have been no need to do more than push back the few who managed to get to the top, but the first centurion, in command, ordered a volley of arrows to be shot into the climbing, twitching, roaring mass of men. And still they came on.

The priests and the blackrobes whom they called Pharisees stopped them finally: beseeching, imploring, hustling forward and backward, negotiating with both sides and finally bringing about a truce. But the next day thousands and thousands of them streamed out of the city and marched to Caesarea.

Pilatus refused to receive their deputations. Instead he put the whole garrison on the alert.

But the Jews did not attack. They simply stayed there, clamoring for justice. It went on for days.

"I don't know how you got rid of them again", Cassius said aloud. "In Caesarea, I mean. I know there wasn't another massacre. What happened? There must have been forty thousand of them, at least."

"I know all about that", Abenadar said. "First the Legate Senecio talked to them. No good. Then Pilatus managed to have them all rounded up, and he told them to stop their nonsense and go home. Otherwise he'd have them all butchered by the First legion. I was there myself. We didn't like it much. They weren't even armed, and half of them were women, many of them with their children. Then they did a strange thing. Threw themselves on the ground and laid their necks bare. Said they would die rather than see their Law violated. So we looked at Pilatus, and for once he didn't know what to do, just sat there on his judgment seat, tugging at his chin. Then the blackrobes came and jabbered away at him, and the priests came, too, and with them the High Priest of the year, fellow called Annas or Hannas. In the end everybody had to step back, and Pilatus and Annas talked it over alone. A quarter of an hour later we were marched off, and the Jews marched off, too. The show was over."

"Money", said Cassius.

"Sure enough. It's always money with the priests. So a messenger went to Jerusalem, and you here had to take away the vexilla."

"And we didn't like *that*. The crowd stood there and jeered and screamed at us and laughed and threw dung and filth up the wall."

"Crowds are the same everywhere. But not all crowds will lie down and bare their necks rather than give in."

"That's true. You like them, don't you? Of course, your mother . . . "

"She was a very wonderful woman, Cassius. And a very wonderful mother. Syrians don't like Jews—as little or less than

Jews like Syrians. My father didn't like Jews. But he loved my mother. Me—what shall I say? Half Syrian, half Jew, a Roman citizen, the First Centurion of the Italican cohort. I read their Scriptures sometimes—learned it late in life. Mother couldn't read. They're extraordinary. At times you hate them, and then again you can't help loving them. All the same, if they didn't exist, something would be lacking. Something very important, I think. Maybe the world could do without the Syrians—or without the Sarmatians—or without the Ethiopians—I don't know. It would be difficult without the Greeks, I suppose. But it would be impossible without the Jews."

"You're joking. What's so important about them?"

"You've never read their sacred Scriptures, have you?"

"Certainly not."

"No good explaining it to you then. You couldn't possibly understand."

"A small, oriental people, an outpost of the empire—a people without art . . . "

"An ancient people that produced Scriptures as deep as the sea; the only people in the world who believe in one God. Perhaps someday they may bring forth what we are all looking for."

"What do you mean?"

"Justice", said Abenadar pensively. "Truth. Love. Mercy. Peace. Perhaps all these things are the same thing. Perhaps all these things are—never mind."

"You've been reading too much, I think. And I don't care about justice. All I want . . . "

" . . . is to cut a few jugular veins. I know. You told me. But you want to cut them because you feel that it would be justice. You don't want just anybody's jugular vein cut, or do you? If you do—your wish may soon enough come true."

"Not expecting trouble here, are you? Pilatus doesn't seem to be."

"What makes you think that?"

It was too late to back out now. "Well, he's brought his wife with him, hasn't he?"

He hates her, thought Abenadar. He really does. Suddenly he knew why Cassius did not want to go to the banquet tonight. Perhaps it was because of this hatred that he did not like Caesarea. He had been transferred to Jerusalem by his own wish. Young Mela thought he had had an affair with the old man's wife, back in Rome. Which was exactly what young Mela would think.

"I'm not so sure that's a good reason, Cassius. He may have brought her here because he wants to give the impression that he isn't expecting any trouble."

Cassius thought that over. "You may be right. It would be like him. Use her as a decoy, eh?" He gave a short laugh. "She'd be a very good decoy."

"Vindex has been working day and night", Abenadar went on. "Agents coming and going all the time. And their reaction to your report . . . "

"What do you think is going on?"

"I don't know. This festival, day after tomorrow . . . Goes on for days. Huge crowds of pilgrims. Atmosphere of tension, religious tension, national tension. Jews are inclined to mix those up. But the crowds are what matters. Crowds are always dangerous."

"They have several festivals every year, and there's usually no trouble or very little."

"There is always potential trouble. Why do you think the procurator comes here at all—with twelve hundred men? Because something might happen."

"Have you been talking to Vindex, by any chance?"

"No. Not my business. And Vindex wouldn't talk to me about his kind of work. You should know that. But I've been in this business for over thirty years. You get so you can smell it when something is in the air."

134

"And there is, is there?"

"Yes."

V

A visit from the reigning High Priest involved considerable ceremony. As custom and courtesy demanded, Boz bar Sebulun had been informed about it early in the morning so that due preparations could be made for the reception, the meal, the visit proper, and the leave-taking.

There was no need for rehearsals, as it had all happened before many a time. The head servant and his little army of trained men and women knew their duties. Even so, it meant a great deal of work, especially as the priest-messenger had announced that the visit was an official one, to felicitate the High Priest's venerable relative on his most fortunate escape from great personal danger.

It went very well, from the assembling of the household, all in clean linen clothes, all in the correct positions in accordance with their rank, to the presentation of the members of the family and the ceremonial washing of hands and the meal itself.

The High Priest, of course, took the elevated chair usually occupied by Boz. The High Priest could never be a guest. When he entered a house, he was the master of the house. Boz was careful never to give an order without first asking for permission.

Present also were the cousins Serubabel and Joab, two young nephews, eleven distant relatives, and the suite of the High Priest, consisting of two priests, the private secretary, Aza, two scribes, and the captain of the Temple guard, Malchus, who had left his six men in the outer court.

There was no woman at the meal, of course. The lady of the house and her attendants, having rendered their homage in the outer court, had withdrawn to their rooms.

The head servant noted with satisfaction that the High Priest deigned to take twice of the stuffed figs and that he praised the fish from the Sea of Chinnereth.

The High Priest, Joseph Caiphas, was a well-favored man in his late fifties. Both his dress and his beautifully kept beard were black and silver, but there was not a single silver hair in the strong, black eyebrows. Costly rings accentuated the white smoothness and elegance of his fingers. These hands seemed to be made to bless whatever they touched. Kohen Gadol was a man of commanding presence and obviously in a gracious mood on this occasion.

Only when the meal was over and incense in exquisitely carved vessels had been burned to overcome the smell of food did Caiphas ask Boz to tell in detail the story of his terrible adventure. Boz eagerly complied. He did not forget to mention the role of Zadoc bar Tubal, and he saw Caiphas nod to his private secretary, who at once made a note on his writing tablet.

After the story had been told, the High Priest found warm words of congratulation, followed by those of the members of the family. Cousin Serubabel was particularly effusive.

Caiphas then expressed the wish to talk to Boz about some matters of business, and they withdrew to the study. Once more the High Priest occupied the best chair, of cedar wood inlaid with mother-of-pearl. "I wonder why they did it", he said. "I wonder why they bothered."

"I do not understand . . . "

"Bar Abbas", said the High Priest thoughtfully. "As far as we know he's in charge of thousands of men. Why should he play the bandit, trying to rob a caravan — even one belonging to a man of your importance?"

A better observer than Boz bar Sebulun might well have missed the subtle irony.

"I am expecting Joram here", Caiphas went on. "Perhaps he will know more. I know he's back in the city, but he must not be seen anywhere near my house, obviously. It is getting more and more difficult. The lestes are everywhere; one can trust nobody. And the news is bad. Bad."

"The procurator?"

"Oh, no, no. No trouble with him at all. I paid my official visit, and I made my unofficial contribution—as usual. He is greedy. He lets me know what he wants each time he comes to the city—and each time he wants more. But it's worth it. At least I hope it is. No, it's the miracle man again."

"The Galilean?"

"Yes, of course, who else?"

"I don't know why you take him so seriously, my lord High Priest. We've had that sort of thing before, haven't we? There is scarcely a year when the rabble doesn't discover some strange and wonderful man who promises them the sun, the moon, and the stars. It lasts a while, and then it dries up."

"I know."

"And then of all people, a Galilean! As if anything good could ever come from Galilee—except fish, of course. The one we had today, for instance."

"Galileans", said Caiphas bitterly. "As if I hadn't enough trouble without them. The Essenes are bad enough, God knows, with their fantastic conceptions of what God wants of them, of each one of them privately and personally. The Pharisees rub everybody the wrong way with endless interpretations of the Law, and their attitude is becoming more and more supercilious. Life on earth is not good enough; they must go off to live in some shadowy beyond; you must have an immortal spark in you. If Rabbi Josephat is immortal, give me the peace of the tomb once and for all. They envy us and take comfort in the idea that theirs is the right teaching. Very well. But they insist on taking the attitude that they alone have the key to all the riddles and enigmas. And if it could be imagined, God forbid, I'd say they despise us. The lestes are growing in numbers as well as in impudence all over the country; my own relatives are not safe from their attacks, good Jews on the way to a good Jewish feast. Freedom! Freedom for them to loot and rob. As if we hadn't tyrants enough without them. The sons of Eli, they call us. And it's so easy for them to win over the ignorant. Follow us and you won't have to pay taxes to the priests—there could be no better incentive. All this—and now the miracle worker."

"I still don't see why you regard him as so dangerous."

"Because you're a political fool, my good Boz. That man is exactly what was missing. The man with the nimbus of the extraordinary, the miraculous. I've been getting reports about him for more than two years. His dossier is growing fatter and fatter. In the beginning it was all very innocent: friendly words for the poor, comforting words for the sick. But soon there was talk in a very different language, particularly against our friends, the Pharisees."

"Why should you mind that? If somebody takes them down a peg or two . . . "

"I do wish you weren't so shortsighted, my good Boz. Here was the first attempt to attack authority; can't you see that? The first attempt to make the people suspicious of those who are supposed to know better, the learned men, the men with the fringes on their robes, the men who formerly commanded respect and obedience. . . . He wouldn't start by attacking *us*. There is not a single report from my agents that says that he so much as mentions my name! He is shrewd, Boz, very shrewd. He knows his Law, too. Some time ago he allegedly cured some lepers. He quite properly ordered them to go and show themselves to the priests."

"He cured lepers?" asked Boz incredulously. "You don't believe that, do you?"

Caiphas sighed. "I'm not a physician, Boz. And I hadn't seen those men before he—cured them. I do know that an ignorant priest may pronounce a man unclean when he's only suffering from some ugly rash. But what if he did cure a leper or ten lepers or a hundred lepers? By all means, let him cure all the lepers in the country, so long as he does not interfere with the government."

"Does he?"

"He's not only going about curing people, you know. He teaches. The—healing is not his main purpose at all but an attempt to verify his teaching. If I can cure a leper, if I can make a blind man see—is that not proof that what I'm telling you is true? There are those who think of him only as a kind of physician, I suppose. But the great majority listens to his teaching and accepts his cures as the proof that he is what he thinks he is."

"And what does he think he is?"

"Ah, there is another point, Boz. He very, very rarely alludes to that. But there is little doubt that he regards himself as at least a prophet."

"At least", repeated Boz astonished. "At least?"

" 'There is a time for everything' ", quoted the High Priest. "But this is decidedly not the time for prophets. He should know that, too. He knew the most recent one, Jochanaan, whom they called the Baptist and whom the Idumean executed last year."

"I remember. He had some very nasty things to say about Herod's wife, I believe."

"Truth is a bitter root. But the end of Jochanaan does not seem to have deterred the Galilean. If only Herod would do something about him. But he is supposed to have been rather reluctant about the Baptist, and in this case he will not act at all."

"Did you want him to?"

"Galilee is Herod's legal realm. . . . I wish Joram would come. I hope nothing has happened to him. He is one of my best men and one of the few of whom the lestes know nothing. At least I hope they don't. Lately the Galilean has been uttering strange words, words emphasizing his own importance beyond anything he said before. I had a report from Caphernaum, where he preached in the synagogue."

"If his words were against the Law, why didn't you have him arrested?"

Caiphas shifted impatiently in the chair. "He said enough to warrant a dozen arrests, Boz. But I can't get hold of him. He comes and goes, and no one knows where he'll turn up tomorrow. He may come to Jerusalem for the feast, for all I know. I have tried to get him here, too. Not officially, of course. He is as elusive as a bird. And, of course, in Galilee it's very difficult to lay hands on him. He is surrounded by his faithful. But in Caphernaum he went a little too far. God has sent him, he said. And it is God's will that all those who believe in the Rabbi Yeshua bar Joseph should enjoy eternal life!"

Boz raised his hands. "The man is mad, my lord High Priest."

"The man is as sane as you and I. Oh, I wish you were right! How simple it would be to trap him. But have you ever known of a madman who defeated all the sane in argument? The Pharisees have been at him time and again—and time and again he made them look like fools. He turned their own words against them. He caught them in their own traps. Admirable work, Boz, admirable work. He is shrewd, I tell you. I've studied him. I read and read again what the reports say. And behind his teaching and curing and comforting there is something like a long-range policy. He is preparing the people for something. He is not rousing them as the ordinary rabble-rouser does. He is raising hopes, expectations—and he promises that he himself will be the fulfillment. He is driving at something, something very, very high. Need I say more?"

"You mean he thinks he is the . . . "

"Don't say it. But the answer is yes. That is what he thinks. He has not said so, mind you! And if I know anything about the man, he isn't going to say so either. He is waiting, till they, the masses, say so of their own accord! And then he won't deny it. And that, more than anything, proves that he is not mad. The madman who thinks he is a king, a prophet, anything you like,

140

will proclaim it aloud. Rabbi Yeshua does nothing of the sort. And in my opinion he is a far more dangerous man than Bar Abbas and Ephraim bar Saul and all the rest of the lestes leaders put together."

"Wandering about from place to place, in a backward province like Galilee . . . "

"And drawing crowds of thousands, yes. Why, the other day he is supposed to have performed another miracle, multiplying a few loaves of bread and a few fishes so that he could feed five thousand men."

"My lord High Priest! You cannot possibly believe that!"

"What does it matter whether I believe it or not?" snapped Caiphas. "What does it matter whether it is true or not? What matters is that there were five thousand people there who believed it. Five thousand! I doubt whether all the lestes together number that many. Now if they have brains in their heads, in the camp of Bar Abbas and the others—if they have brains in their heads instead of cow dung, they will combine with him. They will put themselves at his disposal. And then what will happen?"

"I—I don't know", stammered Boz, taken aback by the sudden vehemence of Caiphas' words.

"I'll tell you what will happen. They will strike together—first at Jerusalem, then at Caesarea. They'll butcher the garrisons in the smaller towns. They'll nominate a government of their own, with the Rabbi Yeshua the new High Priest and Bar Abbas the commander in the field. They'll take everything away from the wealthy and make a big show of dividing the money among the poor. They'll see to it that all enemies and all critics of the new regime disappear, and they'll call it the Kingdom of God!"

"But Rome." Boz was utterly bewildered now. "Rome! Surely you don't believe that these people can overcome Rome?"

"I don't. Neither does anybody who knows Rome. But how many of these people do? That Rabbi Yeshua—what has he seen of the world? A few villages and small towns in Galilee, and

Jerusalem, of course. Oh, yes, he'd been here several times before I realized that he was so dangerous. But of Rome he knows nothing. Neither does Bar Abbas. They'll think that when they have killed the Roman garrisons in Judaea and in Galilee, they will have liberated the country. That's what they are out for, aren't they? Of course, Rome will send her legions. Of course, all their heads will roll in the sand. But before that happens there will be several months for them to play, and what will happen to *us*? To you? To me?"

He broke off. Boz had laid a warning finger to his lips.

The head servant appeared in the doorway. He looked confused.

"There is a man here, my lord, who insists that he must see you at once. His name is Joram."

"Show him in", ordered the High Priest quickly. When the head servant had disappeared, Caiphas added, "I think it would be wise if you rejoined the others for a while, Boz."

Boz bowed and left. He was not offended at being ordered out of his own study. The High Priest was receiving a secret messenger here and wished to be alone with him. It was a great honor for the house of Boz bar Sebulun to be chosen for this meeting. It was proof that there was safety and loyalty to be found in his house when it could not be found elsewhere.

Joram entered, a small, bowlegged man. He looked ordinary in every sense of the word. It was one of his assets.

"No formalities", ordered Caiphas. "Talk, man."

"There has been a meeting of most of the leaders of the party", said Joram. "It was decided to attack the garrison of Jerusalem on the second day of the feast."

The High Priest paled. But his voice was quiet and controlled. "What details do you know?"

"Most of them, I think. I was very lucky. The leader of the contingent to which I belong is Ephraim bar Saul, and he and Bar Abbas do not see eye to eye. Bar Abbas won the day and was made the leader of the enterprise. Ephraim bar Saul was in a very bad mood and spoke louder than usual to his subleaders. I pretended to be drunk and asleep, and the sentinel at the tent did not bother to chase me away. He knew me as a comrade, and I think he was a little drunk, too. I had done my best to make him so."

"Never mind how clever you are. Give me the facts."

"They have about six thousand men, all armed. Many of them will be disguised as pilgrims, coming to sacrifice in the Temple. They will keep the peace on the first day because it is the sabbath. Bar Abbas wanted to fight immediately, saying that the Machabees also had fought on the sabbath, but here Ephraim bar Saul prevailed against him. There will be three main centers of attack. The first is the tribune of the procurator. The men there will raise a disturbance around the tribune and in the Temple square. When the sign is given, they will try to storm the tribune and the entrance to the Antonia."

"Go on", said Caiphas tonelessly.

"The second place is the Tower of Siloe. There won't be many of the lestes there, only about a hundred or so, but including their best speakers. They will try to rouse the people and arm them. They have started hiding arms in the tower itself. Once armed, the people are to join the others in the Temple square."

"And the third point?"

"The Temple itself, my lord High Priest."

There were beads of perspiration on Caiphas' forehead.

"The men will pretend to sacrifice", he said.

"Quite so, my lord. They are to close all the doors and gates and hold the Temple so that they can dominate the square."

"And get at the treasure", said Caiphas grimly.

Joram smiled. "They'll give out the word that the procurator intends to rob us of the corban again."

Caiphas groaned. It was clever tactics, of course. The corban, the Temple money . . . The masses would be inflamed as before, but this time priests and Pharisees would try to appease them in vain; this time they would not be irregular crowds without leaders. And it would give Pilatus the excuse he needed to do what they accused him of. Now he would take the corban—or rather the corban would disappear in the fighting. But there was one more thing he had to know.

"What did you hear about the movements of the Rabbi Yeshua bar Joseph of Galilee?"

"Some of his cousins are coming to the feast", said Joram. "I happen to know that because I came across one of my men who had come up from Nazareth. He told me that they wanted the rabbi to go with them but he refused."

"He did?" Caiphas closed his eyes, pondering. When he opened them again: "Any affiliations between that man and his relatives— and the leaders of the enterprise?"

"I have not been able to establish that", was the cautious answer.

There was a pause.

Caiphas drew one of his rings from his finger. "Take this", he said. "You have done very well. You must go back to your— comrades, of course."

Joram nodded, grinning. "They think I am visiting my mother. She has been dead eight years. Thank you, my lord."

He slipped out. Caiphas stood for a while, thinking. Then he walked to the door: "Aza!"

The secretary hastened up.

"Write, Aza."

When the letter was finished, Caiphas signed it.

"My lord has forgotten to dictate the name and address of him to whom the letter is to be sent", said the secretary respectfully, stretching out his hand for it.

Caiphas gave him a blank stare. "What letter?"

Aza bowed. He said nothing.

"You will forget what you have written", said the High Priest mildly. "And you will remember that only you and I were present in this room. Life is good for those who know how to obey. Now go and send me Boz bar Sebulun."

Half an hour later the High Priest and his host rejoined the guests, but only for a few minutes.

Guests, servants, and the entire household assembled for the official leave-taking.

Many of the passersby stared sullenly at the small procession: three guards, two priests, the High Priest, Aza, the two scribes, with Malchus and the other three guards bringing up the rear.

That evening the High Priest went to the Temple, where he spent two hours in prayer. He returned, pale and sad. His eyes were reddened and a little swollen as if he had been weeping.

VI

Naomi knew that she would never be able to finish the embroidery in time for the feast. Whenever she sat down to go on with it, something happened to interrupt her work. First the house was in a flurry because of the visit of Kohen Gadol with his attendants, and then there was the visit itself. She had had to supervise the meal, as far as the head servant would let her, but he was so busy he could not be everywhere at the same time, and there was much to be done. One of the kitchen girls had fainted for some reason, and Abigail was furious about it and would not say why, and Hanan had dropped a plate, one of the good ones with the gold rim. And then came the leave-taking, when they all had to be on hand again, even the girl who had fainted. Finally the other guests had gone, but now there were the first crowds of pilgrims outside, all merry and singing, the entire city transformed by them.

For weeks and months it was as if Jerusalem were asleep or only just waking up and in a sullen mood, like Boz before he had washed and dressed and partaken of the early meal, and people went about their daily business, buying and selling and shouting at each other, arguing and quarreling. But today they were full of laughter and joy and playfulness. She could watch them from her window, which was very small, not much larger than her head; even so, she really should not stand there. It was not seemly.

In the country it was different, although she could not quite understand why. But everything was easier and much more beautiful in the country. Jerusalem was so *small;* it was just one house, this house, and a tiny garden with a wall nine feet high around it.

She was still standing at the window when Boz came in, and the first thing she thought of was that he would scold her for not getting on with the shawl, which was silly, for he never bothered about such things. He never did bother much about her, except when she had done something wrong, like speaking out of turn or not being ready when her presence was required or . . .

Then she saw the basket he carried, and her eyes widened with surprise. She had never seen Boz carry anything; that was the servants' business. And this was a fairly big basket, filled with fruit.

"Where is Abigail?" asked Boz.

She made a move to fetch her, but he stopped her with an abrupt gesture. "Later", he said. "First I want to talk to you alone." He put aside the basket and sat down. He looked so weary and worried she felt sorry for him. "Sit beside me", he said, and he patted her hand. "Listen well to me, Naomi. It is important." He was perspiring. He dabbed his forehead with a handkerchief of Sidonian linen. "You and I, we were saved from a great danger the other day."

She nodded.

"We were saved, I am sorry to say, by the sons of Edom—and they who endangered our lives were men of our own people. Such are the times in which we live." Again he dabbed his forehead. "Gratitude", he went on, "is a virtue even when it is shown to the Gentiles. We must be grateful to the Roman commander, Cassius Longinus his name was, I think. Yes, yes, that's what it was, Cassius Longinus. Now this is what I want you to do. Take Abigail with you and go to the gate of Antonia—not the main gate, but the small side gate, just opposite the street of the coppersmiths. There is always a Roman sentinel there. Go right up to him and ask for the Centurion Longinus. He will not be able to leave his post, but he will shout for another man to fetch the commander. Don't let him tell you that you cannot speak to the commander for this reason or that—say that it's very important that you should see him. Say you cannot leave without having seen him. If they make you wait, wait. But ask to be let into the court so that you will not be stared at by passersby. Wait till the commander comes. When he comes, give him this basket of fruit. Tell him this—and I want you to learn it by heart: 'The best fruit is at the bottom of the basket. Look at it soon, commander.' Can you repeat that?"

She repeated it obediently like a child.

"Good", he said. "But I want you to say this sentence to him three times. Three times, do you hear? Then come back. Now get Abigail. I want you to go at once."

It was not a long way, no more than the fifth part of an hour, but it was the most exciting adventure.

The streets were full of people and full of animals, steers and sheep and lambs and doves in cages, brought by their owners to be sacrificed in the Temple.

Naomi heard a cheerful male voice say, "*Very* lovely . . . " and immediately Abigail snapped at her, "Draw your veil more over your face."

Naomi obeyed. She could still see what was going on, which was all she cared about.

A group of young girls came by, dancing together and clashing their cymbals. People laughed and applauded them, even old

147

people. It seemed that old people could have fun, too, instead of being dignified and ill-tempered and querulous. Perhaps the feast was making them younger. She wondered what Abigail would say if she suddenly thrust aside her veil and joined the girls in their dance, and the thought made her giggle.

"Behave yourself." Abigail was furious. Naomi, daughter of Amram bar Naasson, wife of Boz bar Sebulun, sent on an errand to a Gentile! By her own husband, too. Abigail had not dared say anything when Boz gave her his instructions, but she had oozed disapproval. She was carrying the fruit basket on her head, holding it in place with a stiff right arm and pushing people out of the way with her left.

Then they reached the small side gate of the Antonia, and Naomi took a deep breath and spoke to the sentinel. She had never done such a thing before in her life. As the crude alien face peered at her suspiciously, the words at first would not come. She pulled herself together. "I wish to speak to the Centurion Cassius Longinus."

The sentinel turned his head and shouted for the officer on duty.

The Centurion Mela was not feeling well. The official banquet the night before had ended at midnight, but only officially; the unofficial part of life was always the more enjoyable. Even so, he should not have tried to drink old Abenadar under the table. The confounded Syrian had the capacity of seven once he really set his mind to it.

He walked up to the gate. "What is it?" he barked.

However, when he saw Naomi, his handsome young face changed from sullenness to an expression of ingratiating charm. Whom did she want to see? The Centurion Cassius Longinus? He was not here at the moment. Most certainly the lady could come in. He himself opened the door for her; the heavy iron bars clanked as he threw it open.

148

Naomi and Abigail stepped in. They were in another world. Wherever they looked, cyclopean walls rose threateningly into the sky, topped by quadrangular towers so high that the spears of the soldiers up there seemed to be able to touch the sun.

Low barracks flanked the walls, each one a small fortress by itself with tiny windows set at regular intervals. Narrow stairs led up to the first, second, third, fourth, fifth, and sixth floors. Everything was gray, forbidding, warlike. Everything was gray stone and dully shimmering iron. Far at the back glowed the Insula, the castle where the commanders resided, an island of white marble, the citadel of alien gods, powerful and dangerous.

It was a strange and terrifying place. Trumpet signals came from afar and clipped commands and rhythmic noises, echoing between the towering walls.

The Centurion Mela smiled irresistibly. Cassius Longinus was not here, but he, the Centurion Mela, was at the young lady's service. It was refreshing to get a glimpse of Venus in the world of Mars. Whatever Longinus could do for the lady — he was sure he could just as well, *at least* as well. Perhaps the lady would tell him what she desired?

The lady desired to speak to the Centurion Cassius Longinus. The lady would wait here till he came. And that was all.

With the slight shrug of the man of the world, the Centurion Mela sent an orderly to fetch the enviable Longinus. In the meantime he tried to make conversation but found that the lady would not even look at him. The old harridan with her did all the looking, and she would have frightened the snakes out of the hair of the Medusa. Longinus, who pretended never to bother about anything in skirts! Well, well, this was a tidbit with which to sweeten the evening. Longinus and a little Jewish lady, married, too, from the way she dressed and obviously a lady with a certain background. How did he do it? There was no shortage of women in Jerusalem, but the accessible ones were either Syrian or

Phoenician or at best Greek, with few exceptions. How did he do it?

Before Mela could think of a new line of approach, Longinus arrived.

Mela saluted—Longinus was senior to him—and reported, "Beautiful young lady to see you, accompanied by somewhat less beautiful lady of more advanced age. Also: a basket of fruit."

"Less wine, less talk, and more sleep would do you good", growled Cassius. He turned to Naomi. "You're the wife of the old man whose caravan was attacked the other day, aren't you? What is it?"

Mela sauntered away. Trying to make it appear to be a service matter. Quite clever, but it didn't fool *him*.

"My husband, Boz bar Sebulun, sent me", said Naomi. "He wants me to give you this."

Cassius looked with amazement at the fruit basket. What was that supposed to be? A present from the grateful old vulture for having saved his life? There was no lack of fruit in the Antonia.

"The best fruit is at the bottom of the basket. Look at it soon, commander", said Naomi.

He looked up quickly, but in the lovely young face he could see no hint of any hidden meaning.

"Thank you", he said doubtfully.

"The best fruit is at the bottom of the basket. Look at it soon, commander", Naomi said again.

What a strange girl. Yes, girl. She certainly wasn't a woman. Or was she? Nonsense. It couldn't be. And she had the eyes of a child.

However, it was most unconventional for her to come here. If the old man wanted to show his gratitude, he could have sent his idiotic fruit basket by an ordinary messenger. He had servants enough, even if he had lost a few on his way to Jerusalem. Why send his wife?

"The best fruit is at the bottom of the basket. Look at it soon, commander", the girl repeated. She gave him a courteous little bow.

"Don't go," Cassius said quickly. It occurred to him that he had an entirely legitimate reason for asking her to stay. "Why did you say that— Why, you said it three times! Is there . . ." He broke off. He had seen the astonishment on the face of the old woman. She was surprised at the girl too, or seemed to be. What *was* going on? Did she have a personal message for him in that basket? Impossible. That's what Mela and his kind would think. She would never dare. That was Roman thinking, not Jewish thinking. He wondered what Abenadar would say to this.

Meanwhile she stood there, outwardly quite composed in a situation that—if he was right about her—must be unusual, to say the least. What was going on in that strange little mind of hers? She was not stupid. He was sure of that. She had said something that day, when she came to after her faint—something rather interesting. She hadn't been hysterical, not even excited. He had thought of that remark often since then. It puzzled him.

He turned sharply to Abigail. "I wish to talk to your mistress alone. Step back a little."

"It is not seemly", said Abigail acidly.

He walked up to her, quite close. "Step back, I say", he ordered menacingly.

She did not budge an inch. She said, "Shame on you for threatening an old woman."

He laughed. He unbuckled his sword. "Take it", he said, pressing it into her hand. "Now step back just a little. And if you find me in the least wanting in courtesy toward your mistress, you come and cut my head off. How is that?"

"Take that murderous thing away", Abigail said. "I will have nothing to do with it." She dropped it. He picked it up and turned back to Naomi. He laughed again.

"You are well guarded, lady", he said. "I begin to believe that my intervention the other day was quite unnecessary, as long as *she* was present."

For the first time he saw a smile brush over her little face; it was in a great hurry and disappeared quickly.

"So you *can* smile", he said. "But you don't believe in waste, do you? Well, I don't either. There is something you said the other day about your life. You said it was not worth much. Why did you say that?"

"A woman's life", she said, "is not worth much."

Perhaps that was what they taught them in this country.

"Neither is a man's", he answered lightly. "Men only think they are important. About this fruit . . . You said the best is at the bottom of the basket. What is it?"

"I don't know." The curtain was back over her face. "I told you what I was asked to tell you. I must go now."

"Right." He turned to the sentinel. "Open the door."

He lifted his hand courteously.

She had a curious dignity, despite her youth. So did old Cerberus, if it came to that. Strange people. He told an orderly to carry the basket to his quarters and went back with him. When the man had left he began to unpack the basket. Figs, dates, Persian apples, rare here: he had seen them only on the procurator's table, four years ago in Caesarea. The Lady Claudia was fond of them. He had seen her this morning when she came down to the swimming pool, a part of which had been partitioned off for her. She had aged. Perhaps women aged faster in this country. Perhaps this tiny, slender Jewess would be an old harridan in ten, fifteen years. It was difficult to imagine.

Oranges. What if the best fruit at the bottom of the basket was a scorpion? Burying a live scorpion under a mass of nicely arranged fruit would be a good way to get rid of a man. Wasn't that the way Cleopatra of Egypt had had the snake smuggled into her room when she was a prisoner?

Nonsense. Why should they want to kill him? Old Boz had no reason to do such a thing.

Cassius went on unpacking fruit. Here, a small bag. He opened it carefully. Gold. Coined gold. Quite a nice sum. Considerably more than a centurion's pay for a year. Not so mean after all, the old vulture. The best fruit is at the bottom of the basket, eh?

Then he found the letter. It was sealed, but a piece of parchment was on top. He read, "Keep the gold, but if you value your life deliver this letter to the procurator at once." There was no signature.

Cassius whistled softly.

"An interesting message?" asked a dry voice.

He turned on his heel.

The Tribune Vindex smiled. "Did you win all this gold at dice?"

One of the duties of the head of the Intelligence Department was to see everything that was out of the ordinary. Certainly it was something out of the ordinary for a Jewish woman of the aristocracy to visit a centurion in the Antonia. According to Centurion Mela a large basket, apparently of fruit, had changed hands. Well worth investigating. And what did the sender of this gold expect the Centurion Longinus to do for him?

Cassius grinned. "Not exactly at dice, tribune—no. Have a look at this." He showed Vindex the written message on top of the letter.

It was Vindex' turn to whistle. "Who gave you this and why?"

Cassius explained. Vindex watched him closely. The man was not embarrassed. His story sounded true, and it dovetailed with the report about the skirmish near Beth-horon. Should he open the letter here and now? It really was his duty. It was not an ordinary piece of mail sent to the procurator, for him alone to open. It seemed to be more in the nature of a secret document. But the sender was obviously that young woman's husband. Boz bar Sebulun was a very well-known man in Jerusalem. He was also a very rich man. It might be wiser to let Pilatus open it himself.

"Come with me to the procurator", he said, and as Cassius

took his helmet from the rack, he added, "Better put that gold away first." His mouth was a little sour. It was more gold than a tribune's pay for a year, too.

VII

Abigail was helping with the embroidery now, working on the other end of the shawl, but she was in one of her moods, and it was difficult to get more than an occasional growl out of her.

The streets outside were still merry, but in an hour or so the sabbath would commence.

How nervous Boz had been when she returned! Nervous and—unhappy. Had she seen the centurion? Had she given him the basket? Had she told him that the best fruit was at the bottom of the basket? That he should look at it soon? Had she said it three times as he had told her to? What did he say? Had anyone tried to stop her on the way there? Or on the way back? And all the time he was perspiring and dabbing his forehead, and his fingers trembled.

She had told Boz that everything had gone well, she had done everything he told her, she had said everything the way he wanted her to—and still he was not happy, muttering under his breath and staring at the wall as if the wall had a face and was staring at *him*.

And now Abigail was in one of her moods, too. Only the people in the streets were cheerful. Or did they only seem so? Could it be that if she were one of them she would see that they too were not happy, not really happy?

The Gentiles were not. The sentinel was not. The first officer, the one with the vain smile, he was not cheerful either behind that smile of his. And the commander himself was unhappy, a man of power and strong like the slayer of the Philistines.

"Why are men unhappy?" she asked.

Abigail looked up, but only for a moment. "It's not your business to bother about men", she said severely.

That was the sort of thing Abigail had been saying as long as Naomi could remember. It's not your business to understand what grownups say; a little girl must not speak unless she is spoken to; a little girl must not be greedy. From Naomi's observation and experience, it appeared that even when little girls grew up nothing changed very radically. And the Roman commander was surprised that she thought her life was not worth much.

But he said that men's lives were not important either, which was very strange. If Abigail were in a better mood, she would ask her what could be considered important. But even Mother had never been able to talk much to Abigail when she was in one of her moods. Mother never had any moods at all; she was always gentle and cheerful, until that last day, when she suddenly sat up in bed and said a very long prayer and then fell back breathing so strangely. She could not go to sleep alone, Naomi had been told, so Abigail had had to help her to close her eyes. But young as Naomi was, she had understood; they need not have tried to protect her by foolish stories.

Her father's death Naomi did not remember; she had been only two. An uncle took over the house after her mother's death, a very old man who regarded her only as a kind of minor disturbance, and he did not like disturbances. He knew Boz bar Sebulun and drew his attention to her, and they arranged the marriage. A year later the uncle also died, and Boz spoke of him rather severely as of a man who had not known how to keep his money together.

Now only Abigail was left. Naomi could not imagine life without Abigail.

Could it really be possible that the lives of *men* did not matter? Men *did* things. Boz sometimes told her about the many things he did. But Boz himself was often unhappy. Not just because this or that had gone wrong, or because he had pains in his chest or because his legs were swollen, but just unhappy for no apparent reason. And even Kohen Gadol, the High Priest . . .

Now Rachel, for instance, Cousin Serubabel's wife—when she lost her baby, two years ago, she screamed and howled and was half mad with grief. But Naomi suspected that Rachel had not been happy before.

"Abigail, why are the people in the streets happy, and we are not?" She forgot she had decided not to talk to Abigail.

Abigail frowned. "What have you got to complain about?"

"Nothing", said Naomi. "But I don't dance and sing, do I?"

"What next, I wonder?" Abigail said irritably. "You don't see them dance and sing every day, do you? There's a feast. You've seen it before. They sing and dance because they hope that the times will get better, poor fools."

The times. Boz was always complaining about "the times". The times, the Gentiles, the taxes, the servants. There were feasts every year, and always the people sang and danced and made merry and went to the Temple and prayed. Did they always hope that "the times" would get better?

"Is it foolish to hope for the times to get better?"

"Yes, it is", said Abigail grimly. "They never do."

"Why haven't they found that out yet?"

"Because they're looking in the wrong place. Because they are fools, fooling themselves."

Naomi listened attentively. "Where should they look, Abigail?"

"In a mirror", said Abigail promptly. "And start doing something about what they see there. But they won't. They'll tell you what's wrong with you and with anybody else. They won't look at their own faults. Times don't get better because people don't get better. You don't have to stop working just because I'm talking to you."

Perhaps the Roman commander was unhappy because he would not look at his own faults. It was a pity someone could not tell him. Now if her husband would—but she quickly put that thought out of her mind. "Will it always be so, Abigail?"

"No." Abigail bit her lip; she had not intended to give that answer. But it was too late.

"When will it change? How will it change, Abigail?"

Abigail looked over her shoulder. There was no one in the adjacent room. They could not be overheard. "You've never asked me such questions before, child", she murmured. "I don't think I can—I don't think I should . . ."

Naomi's eyes began to sparkle. "Tell me, Abigail dear, please tell me!"

"You'll tell . . ."

"Oh, no, no, no, I won't, I promise I won't. Do tell me, darling Abigail . . ."

"If *he* hears about it, I will be in trouble."

"I won't tell! I won't tell!"

"*They* don't believe in it", murmured Abigail, and the vehement little gesture of her head encompassed Boz bar Sebulun and all his kind. "But it's true just the same. My uncle was a rabbi, and *he* knew. Oh, I shouldn't say these things to you. What good can it do?"

"What did he know?" Naomi urged.

Once more Abigail looked around. Then she whispered, "The Messiah."

"Oh, *him?* I know all about him." Naomi was disappointed.

"What do you know?" Abigail asked sharply. "Who's told you?"

"Everybody knows." Naomi closed her eyes in order to remember better. "Rabbi Nathan told me when I was seven. He will be born in Bethlehem and come forth from eternity, and he will be a son of David, and when he becomes King he will rule not only Israel but the whole world, and his name will be God-with-us, and he will deliver his people from bondage and bring peace." She opened her eyes again. "I haven't thought of that for a long time", she added. "But I haven't forgotten, have I?"

To her surprise she saw that Abigail had tears in her eyes.

"Abigail! What have I done now?"

"You remembered", whispered Abigail. "My little one, my little lamb, you remembered. There are so many in Israel who have forgotten."

"I liked Rabbi Nathan", Naomi said thoughtfully. "His beard was all silver—not just sprinkled with silver like Kohen Gadol's."

"You are not to mention this to anybody else in this house."

"I promised I wouldn't, didn't I? But that's no secret. That's what we learn as children. Why, surely, my husband . . . "

"Hush", said Abigail. "He doesn't believe in the Messiah. Not really, I mean", she corrected herself hastily. "It's all very difficult, and I'm not good at explaining. There are some who think he is not a person at all, but just—just a feeling . . . "

Naomi giggled. "How can a feeling be born in Bethlehem? And how can a feeling be the son of David?"

"There now, you're talking like a Pharisee", mocked Abigail. "Like a learned man. What's come over you? I've heard people talk like that about the Messiah. It's foolish enough, I grant you, though it's not for ignorant women to say so. And there are others who say, what's the good, our forefathers hoped for the Messiah, and so did our fathers, and he didn't come, so why should he come now, and maybe another hundred or even a thousand years will pass before he comes. But how can that be, when the prophet Daniel said that it was near? Yet they still say we don't know when he will come and it is no good sitting back and waiting, we must go about our daily business and buy and sell, and all those who talk about him are just muddleheads or worse—people who stir up crowds and make mischief."

Naomi nodded. That was the way Boz so often talked with the men who came to the house: about muddleheads and mischief makers who interfered with business and the natural course of events.

"Abigail, do you think he will come in our time—the Messiah?"

From afar, from the Musach Sabbati, came the sound of the trumpet.

At once the two women put down their embroidery, and their lips moved in prayer: "Hear, O Israel, the Lord our God is one Lord."

VIII

The trouble started on the Temple square, in front of the Antonia.

In accordance with the rule on feast days, the tribune of the procurator had been erected in front of the lower fortifications. The procurator himself had arrived, surrounded by a group of officers and guarded by a detachment of five hundred men commanded by the Legate Sosius, oldish, bald, and looking very bored as usual.

The large middle gate had been opened wide, and behind it the military band played. No eagle, no standard, no vexillum, no statue of the divine Emperor was in sight. The procurator seemed to have learned his lesson. There was only this show of military power and not very much of that.

Even that little was irksome to many. The Jerusalemites had become accustomed to it, but of the hundreds of thousands of pilgrims many came from tiny villages in the north or east where one did not see a single Roman soldier from year's end to year's end, except when they accompanied a tax collector. These pilgrims— and many others—were deeply troubled by the presence of an alien citadel, guarded by alien soldiers, not only in the immediate neighborhood of the holy Temple, but actually looming over it. From the outer walls of the Antonia the Goyim could look down into the very court of the Temple. Israel was forced to worship God under the mocking eyes of the heathens.

And still the Temple remained what it was, a thing of sanctity and beauty, massive, and yet lightly striving to the heavens, a great and holy song in white marble and bronze and gold with curtains gently fluttering in the wind, clear blue and dark blue, brown and red, symbolizing air and water, earth and fire. There was no building like it in the whole world. It seemed to be the father and mother of all the styles known to men, combining them all in a strange, weird harmony of its own. Walls and towers and courts, and courts again, rows of pillars and columns and gateways and arcades, the court of women where thousands of women were pressed together in one mass of praying, adoring femininity, the court of men with small bands of white-clad priests walking about, Levites and Temple guards, musicians with their cymbals and harps.

And the pilgrims came with their sacrificial animals, with bullocks and rams and calves and lambs, with pigeons in cages, all without blemish, for they were carefully examined by the priests; only the best, the very best, was worthy to be given to the One whose holy Name must not be taken in vain.

And somewhere within the immense structure, invisible to the multitude and protected by the sacred curtain, was the inner chamber, the Holy of Holies, which no one but the High Priest ever entered and he only once a year, on the Day of Atonement, carefully guarded and dressed in vestments worn on that day alone.

There was no end to the stories among the Gentiles about what the inner chamber contained, although the Jews insisted that it was empty, except for the Presence of the One invisible God. That was too much for the Gentile mind to conceive. There had to be *something* in it; the statue of a calf, all of massive gold, some said, and others were sure that it was the withered head of a donkey, or a young girl destined to be sacrificed by the High Priest, a virgin, no more than twelve years old, one year of her life for each tribe of Israel; and many other lies.

As the pilgrims passed the Temple square, some spat or shouted insults at the foreign soldiers watching them: bloodhounds, wretched Edomites, dirty Syrians. And Syrians most of them were, who hated the Jews no less than they were hated by them, and many a mouth was pressed tightly together, and knuckles shone white on hands holding spear and shield, but none of the soldiers moved or replied with a single word or gesture. Discipline was the first thing a soldier learned in the Roman army, and he usually learned it the hard way, with the aid of the centurion's long stick.

Yet here in the Temple square the trouble started, in front of the Antonia. There was one pilgrim, a tall man and strongly built, who shouted, "Look at them—you have a right to! It was your money that got them their uniforms and arms."

Another, fifty yards away, howled, "He's right—and they are so dirty that Pilatus had to steal the corban to build a swimming pool for them."

And from another corner a voice rose shrilly: "He has come here to steal the corban again, the Roman thief—your half shekels, friends, your half shekels."

Now in the middle of the square a little group began to yell in chorus, "Thief! Thief! You won't have the corban again!"

Other scattered groups began to form, like small whirlpools in a pond. The shouting spread.

The Legate Sosius, still looking bored, waved his hand. At once the soldier standing beside him raised the tuba to his lips and blew it hard, just once. It was not a recognizable military signal but sounded almost as if the man were merely trying out his instrument. But the sound was still echoing across the square when somebody brandished a heavy stick and clubbed somebody else over the head. There was nothing to suggest any connection between the blowing of the tuba and the clubbing of the man.

The first man hit was Jaqob bar Mathan. Two of his men

161

nearby jumped to help him, but the assailant hit out against them too. There were thirty-odd men of the Freedom Party near enough to see quite clearly what happened, but they could not understand it at all, because the assailant was a Jew—or—or was he only dressed as a Jew? They had been waiting for Jaqob to give them the sign for the assault against the tribune—Jaqob was supposed to get it from Bar Abbas, farther back in the crowd—but now Jaqob was prostrate, and men were fighting over his body, perhaps he was no longer alive. The thirty-odd men howled with rage and tried to push through the half-hysterical crowd. But before they reached the spot where Jaqob had fallen they themselves were attacked. Six, ten, twenty sticks came crashing down on heads, backs, and shoulders. And, again, the assailants were in Jewish dress.

Bar Abbas, perched at the top of a narrow staircase, saw much more. He saw the first incident and knew it was in the sector under Jaqob bar Mathan, but before he could assess its meaning, two, three, ten, twenty such whirlpools appeared. Everywhere long sticks were being brought down on unsuspecting heads. A few moments more and he could not separate one vortex of fighting from another; they swirled and eddied from one side of the square to the other. And none of this was part of his plan. It was treachery. Treachery. Those men with the sticks were not Jews. They were Romans, Roman legionaries, disguised as Jews and planted in the crowd.

There was only one answer, and he gave it promptly. He drew a piece of red cloth from his coat, tied it to a long stick, and waved the stick, the signal for the general attack. That would wake his men out of their stupefaction and make them act as planned; it would give them back the initiative, and that was what mattered.

The red cloth on his stick was the sign not only for his men in the crowd below but also for seven hundred who were in the outer courts of the Temple, posing as pilgrims. A chain of picked men reached from the Temple square to the far-off Tower of Siloe, where wild-eyed speakers called their hearers to arms, and others began to distribute swords and spears that seemed to come from nowhere.

At the sight of Bar Abbas' improvised flag, the Freedom Party men in the center of the square disengaged themselves as best they could, drew close together, and went over to the attack, slashing their way toward the tribune.

The Legate Sosius gave a few clipped commands; the tuba sounded again; the five hundred uniformed Roman soldiers closed ranks and threw up their shields to form a living wall, protecting the officers, none of whom made the slightest movement.

The band of musicians vanished as a full cohort came streaming out of the main gate, split in two, and wheeled to right and left of the tribune. The living wall was now three times as strong as before, three hundred men long and five deep. Behind them the tubas of the Antonia sounded the general alarm.

Shields were raised in front of the procurator and his staff, and others were held over their helmets, to protect them from stones and other missiles.

The first waves of the Freedom Party men crashed against the living wall and fell back, leaving a ragged line of broken bodies. They attacked again, staggering over their own casualties.

At that moment an unheard of thing happened in the Temple.

Here the Freedom men had succeeded in acting according to plan, dropping the dove cages and the reins of bullocks and rams and lambs, drawing their swords, and forming a double line, while others began to close the gates of the Temple to secure it, to make it a counterfortress against the Antonia. As no Roman was within sight, they carried out their orders without difficulty.

But suddenly hundreds of Romans appeared on the gallery formed by the outer edge of the wall of the Antonia, overlooking the Temple. That was bad enough. What followed had a nightmare quality. The Romans *came down the wall.* Clinging to ropes, they slid downward with fearful speed, their armor clattering against the stones, jumped the last few feet, fell, sprang up, and immediately attacked.

"The Romans are in the Temple!" roared a bull-throated voice.

Even the fighters on the square could not resist turning their heads, and what they saw made them gasp with horror and dismay. A wholesale butchery was going on in the Temple precincts and in the outer courts of the Temple itself—a butchery that had nothing to do with the sacrifice of animals.

Small groups of Roman soldiers were clotting together and fighting as units, while more dropped from the gallery every moment. They did not seem human. They were like enormous metallic beetles, armored locusts.

Achim bar Simeon was in command here, with Oziah and the Galileans. He had rushed the nearest legionary, his sword crashing down on the Roman's helmet. The man, dazed, dropped his shield at Achim's second blow; he lost his footing and rolled down the broad stairway to the square.

Achim shouted triumphantly, "For the King Messiah!" But even as the cry rang out he was furiously attacked by a young centurion. The Roman was his superior in swordsmanship, and Achim was thankful when two of his Galileans came to his aid, though the centurion got rid of them with a double thrust so fast that they had no time to parry. Achim felt a searing pain run through his right shoulder. His knees buckled under him. "For the King Messiah!" he cried once more before he fell.

Cassius stepped over the body. "Come on!" he shouted to his men. "Don't give them time to regroup. Sections three and five, follow me!"

It was a dangerous moment; they were outnumbered ten to one. If Aufidius did not come in time . . .

Aufidius came in time.

Bar Abbas, from his vantage point, saw Roman soldiers bursting forth from the East Tower. How, by the power of Beelzebub, had they got there? Perhaps what people said was true, that bloody old Herod had had a secret corridor built from the Antonia to the tower. It meant that Achim's and Oziah's men were being attacked in the rear.

He prayed Ephraim bar Saul had got the masses at the Tower of Siloe in action by now and that he would have the sense to send them to the Temple square. Too late to send a messenger. His face contorted with rage, Bar Abbas looked back at the main gate of the Antonia. Eliud, Jonathan, Obed, and the others were leading their men in a second attack against the tight mass of Romans. If they were beaten back again there would be little hope for a third attempt. That bloated swine of a procurator would not wait; he'd give the signal to advance, and at the sight of a Roman advance most of the untrained men would panic, and that would be the end. This attack *must* succeed.

Once more Bar Abbas waved the long stick with the red cloth. It was the signal for his reserves, twelve hundred picked men, his own men, fully armed under their long coats. They shed the coats and moved forward, and Bar Abbas himself came down the staircase, with his bodyguard forming a living wall around him, to join the assault column.

The Legate Sosius signaled to the auxiliaries on the rampart behind the tribune, and a hail of arrows sped down into the mass of attackers. Many were killed, but the rest came on.

Again Sosius signaled. The disguised legionaries on the square dropped their sticks and drew their swords. They seemed to be everywhere. Some even seemed to be right in the middle of the assault column. As the legate signaled for a third time, the tight mass of soldiers advanced in front of the tribune. They did not wait for the attack to hit them; they marched straight into it, and the opposing fronts met with a crash that seemed to shake the walls of the square.

In his heart of hearts Bar Abbas knew that all was lost. At best, a frontal attack against regulars was a desperate measure. In addition, there was the danger of being outflanked by the troops occupying the Temple. Moreover, the enemy had already infiltrated the advancing men. But there was nothing else left to do—not after the pledge he had given to the other leaders that his plan would not fail, could not possibly fail. And there was still that unreasonable, absurd, passionate, ferocious hope that he could do it in spite of everything, that something would turn up to save the situation. If he could press those devils hard enough, if he could get through to the tribune, to that proud, erect group of officers, if he could bury his sword in the gullet of Pilatus himself!

He almost reached the procurator. He struck down two legionaries, ducked the attack of a third, and saw the haughty officers and the legate himself draw their swords. But then sudden pain shot through his right arm, and his weapon fell harmlessly, and he tried to retrieve it, and his arm would not obey his will. And something came crashing down on his head, and he fell and fell and fell into immeasurable depths of blackness.

He did not know that over eighty men had been killed all around him before that happened. He did not see his men fall back, slowly first, then faster and faster, with the Romans following inexorably, till everybody ran before them, ran for dear life.

In a few minutes the Temple square was empty, except for the Roman cohort called to a halt in the middle, and a few hundred dead and wounded.

IX

Few people slept that night in Jerusalem. Hundreds of wounded men had been smuggled into the houses of trustworthy families where they could be looked after. The physicians who came to these houses did so secretly or even in disguise. It was a grave crime to shelter a man who had raised arms against Rome, and strong Roman patrols—never less than twenty men—tramped through every street. The city was in a state of siege.

Rugged old Achim bar Simeon, with a broken arm and a deep wound in the shoulder, was nursed by faithful friends in a house only a stone's throw away from the Antonia. "I knew it", he repeated time and again. "I knew it. It could not succeed without the King Messiah. I knew it."

"He was not there, then?" his host asked sadly.

"I didn't see him. No one saw him. Jaqob bar Mathan told us—he had spoken to—one of the King's men—man called Judah—and *he* said—the King would come only when—we could give him—his city. That's why—I agreed to the plan. But it doesn't—work—without the King. Nothing is possible—without him."

The physician who had bandaged his wound shook his head. "We must give him wine with poppyseed in it, or he'll never be able to stand the pain when I set the bone."

There was wine in the house, but no poppyseed. No one dared try to get some, and not only because of the Roman patrols. Many of the Freedom Party men were out and about as well, trying to catch Roman stragglers or people known to be friendly toward Rome; they gave one very little time for explanations. There was talk that several houses had been burned in the street of the silversmiths, where many Greeks and Syrians had their shops.

The physician had to set Bar Simeon's bone without first dulling his senses. To his surprise the Galilean endured it quietly. But when the operation was over he began to talk excitedly.

"Why didn't he come to our help? We were waiting for him. He could multiply the bread and the fishes. . . . Why couldn't he multiply our number and our courage? What is he waiting for, I ask you, what is he waiting for?"

"Delirious", whispered the physician. "But he certainly isn't as feverish as he sounds. Who is he talking about?"

"The King Messiah", Bar Simeon's host replied tonelessly.

The physician drew up his hairless brows. "Foolishness", he muttered. "Why should he come in *our* time?"

"That is no valid argument; why not in our time? It must be at some time, mustn't it?"

"Now according to Isaias . . . "

"If you look up what Daniel said . . . "

They began to throw quotations at each other, neither listening to the other.

And in the background, unheeded, Achim bar Simeon repeated his lamentation. "What are you waiting for, O Lord? What are you waiting for? How long, O Lord, how long . . . ?"

"There are at least four hundred dead and over a thousand wounded", reported Secretary Aza. "Exact figures are still not obtainable. According to a usually reliable source the Romans have sixty-seven dead, and over a hundred and fifty wounded are lying in an emergency barrack in the Antonia. All that only on the Temple square and in the outer courts of the Temple itself."

"Desecration", murmured the High Priest. There were purple rings around his eyes. He had not slept at all. The beautifully kept, heavily ringed hands were shaking.

"At the Tower of Siloe things never got very far", Aza went on. "A number of speakers tried to incite the people to violence, and others distributed arms and tried to organize the men, but while they were doing that a strong Roman detachment appeared, fanned out, and began to butcher the crowd, armed and unarmed alike. After a few moments the crowd panicked and dispersed. I am told that the Romans did not pursue them but concentrated on a group of lestes who were trying to shield the speakers—their leaders, apparently."

"Of course", said Caiphas. "Go on."

"The lestes fled into the tower itself", Aza continued. "And the Romans tried in vain to break in. There are some who believe that the tower was full of arms."

The two men looked at each other blandly.

"Then what happened?" Caiphas asked coldly.

"The Romans sent a patrol to the Antonia. It came back with reinforcements and a battering ram. They used that, but not against the door — against the walls. They were in no mood to fight the desperate defenders inside. They just went on battering the walls with their machine till the tower came down, crushing the defenders inside." Aza gulped. "Eighteen corpses have been extricated so far", he added. "There may be many more, of course." His voice trailed off at the end. He was close to tears.

The High Priest bowed his head. "It was a tragic day", he said somberly. "Only one thing would have been worse — infinitely worse, Aza." He leaned forward. "If these foolish men had succeeded in their attempt, they would have lost three men for every one who fell yesterday. And six months later — perhaps sooner — the Romans would have destroyed the entire city, and the Temple with it. What is the death of four or five hundred lestes compared to such a catastrophe?" He broke off. There was no need to give many explanations. "Go and get some sleep", he added almost gently.

Sobbing, Aza kissed Kohen Gadol's hand and withdrew.

There was no need to give many explanations. Aza was young. He would not understand. He would not understand that the lestes needed yesterday's bloodletting, that it was a wholesome purge, medical treatment, the opening of an ulcer. And now the procurator had no excuse whatever to impose a fine on the Temple — to touch the corban again. He had never answered the letter, of course. But he had received it and acted on it. It would take a few more days before the city got back to normal again — that was only natural.

A servant at the door announced Joram's presence.

"Let him come in at once", Caiphas ordered. After the official report, the unofficial one.

The little man came in smiling, but he was very pale, and he carried one arm in a sling. "If my lord will kindly excuse me from bowing as I should," he began, "my back hurts, and there is this arm . . ."

"Of course", said Caiphas. "You may sit down. My physician will look you over as soon as you have made your report."

"There is nothing very much", Joram said. "One of those legionaries dressed as Jews hit me with his stick, and there was no room to duck the blow. I don't think my arm is broken—I can move my fingers."

"Where were you during the fighting? In the Temple square?"

"For a while, yes, my lord. I had to be very courageous, to avoid suspicion, but I didn't kill anybody—at least not that I know of. When the Romans advanced against us, my leader fled, so I could see no harm in following his example. After all, that is what a good soldier is supposed to do—follow his leader." He grinned but winced a little.

"I know how the fighting went", said Caiphas harshly. "And I know the approximate figures of the dead and wounded. Tell me what I do not know."

"Ephraim bar Saul is dead", said Joram quietly. "Oziah is dead. Jaqob bar Mathan is dead, too. Bar Abbas is probably alive—but a prisoner. In the Antonia. The Romans don't talk about it, but I know my way around that sort of thing and—"

"What else?" interrupted the High Priest. Joram was an excellent agent, but he had an irritating habit of praising his own abilities.

"The city is still very restless", Joram went on. "I have heard some talk that the houses of people known to be friends of Rome should be burned—the legionaries can't be everywhere at once."

Caiphas nodded. "That will be seen to", he said. "Will there be another attack?"

"No, my lord. There is no one left to organize it. Bar Simeon of Galilee is supposed to be alive but wounded. I could not find out where he is. There may be some sporadic action of little bands of twenty, thirty, perhaps fifty men, but no real attack is possible now."

"Good. Anything else?"

"Yes, my lord. That rabbi from Galilee you mentioned — Yeshua bar Joseph . . . "

The High Priest looked up sharply. "Yes? What about him?"

"He has come after all."

Caiphas rose. "He is here? In the city?"

"In the Temple, my lord. He entered it half an hour ago."

The High Priest seized a small silver bell and rang it so vehemently that all three servants waiting in the anteroom came rushing in. When they saw that the rough-looking visitor was standing at a deferential distance from the High Priest, they stopped in their tracks.

"The captain of the Temple guard — at once", ordered Caiphas. When they had left again he asked quickly, "Has he communicated with any of the lestes leaders? How many men are with him?"

"I don't know, my lord. He came with a group of men. Some looked like Galileans; some didn't. There were about twenty or so, and as for the lestes leaders, those who escaped are in hiding, and I very much doubt that he could find them so quickly. I couldn't say for sure, of course . . . "

"There never seems to be anything sure about that man", sighed Caiphas. "But I'll know soon enough."

Captain Malchus entered, a large, fleshy man with sad eyes.

"You will go at once to the Temple", ordered the High Priest. "You will find a rabbi there called Yeshua bar Joseph. Arrest him and bring him here."

"It may create trouble", warned Joram. "The Temple is full of people again. And I have heard a good many of them whisper that this man is none less than . . . "

"Be still", Caiphas interposed quickly. "We have gone far — but not so far, I trust, that Jews will fight Jews in the Temple. Take two other officers with you, Malchus, and as many men as you think you need. Joram, go with him. You can rest later. Off with you."

As soon as they had gone, the High Priest sent out messengers to summon both Sadducee and Pharisee leaders.

X

The street from the High Priest's house on Mount Zion to the Temple was fairly broad and well kept, but Malchus took a shortcut. He had chosen his two officers, picked up ten guards at the barracks, and now they went down the steep hillside in a brisk trot.

Joram felt sorry for himself. "Not so fast, captain, I beg of you. I'm a weary man this morning, and my back hurts abominably."

"Kohen Gadol is in a hurry."

Joram sighed. That ox of a legionary who had clubbed him had a heavy hand. What he needed was a couple of days in bed, with somebody putting salve on his back and changing the dressing on his arm, and he said so. Kohen Gadol might have spared him this. But the great man did not bother about Joram's back. The great man was worried. It was almost as if he were afraid of the wonder worker from Galilee. What was there about the man to make such an impression on the High Priest who had never seen him?

They hastened through a dirty street. Curious, hostile faces peered at them from tiny windows. The Temple guards were not popular. At last they reached the huge accumulation of buildings that was the Temple.

"Now then", Malchus grunted. "As soon as I've got the fellow, you can scurry off and nurse your back as much as you like. Which court is he in?"

"I'll show you."

"What does he look like?"

Joram shrugged his shoulders—the movement hurt badly. "I don't know, captain. Only had a very brief glimpse of him. Too many people around. Tall, I should say. Dressed in white."

Malchus gave an impatient snort. "You've been asked to come with me to point him out to me, but you don't know what he looks like?"

Joram laughed angrily. "You won't find it difficult to recognize him. He's the one they're all staring at. Come on, follow me."

A few minutes later Malchus had to admit to himself that Joram was right. The huge quadrangular court with its pillars of black marble was packed, but all eyes were on a tall man dressed in white and sitting in the chair usually occupied by the judge when a trial was held. The man was preaching.

Malchus frowned. A preacher had no business to sit in the judge's chair. A preacher was supposed to stand up. He turned to his men. "Follow me slowly", he muttered. "Don't push anybody. If there's a commotion, he'll slip through our fingers." It was the one thing that must not happen. There were still hundreds of thousands of pilgrims in the city; it would be impossible to find the man again.

Malchus had been made captain of the guards a year ago, the first office he had held which carried a decent salary, and he had a wife and three children to provide for. He could not afford to take risks, and it certainly would be a risk if he had to tell Kohen Gadol that he had failed in his mission. "Slowly", he repeated. "And mind, be polite to them, you—" He broke off. After all, they were in the Temple now.

But the people were packed so tightly that he could not help pushing some of them out of his way. He did it as gently as possible, muttering apologies and smiling at them ingratiatingly. They did not seem either to hear him or see him. Their eyes were fixed on the man in white, and they suffered being pushed and pressed as if they were completely unaware of it.

Malchus inched his way forward, his men close behind him. He tried to see whether that rogue of a Joram was still with him, but there was not enough room to turn around.

And then he got stuck. The backs of the men in front of him seemed to be made of stone. He strained to see how far he still was from his quarry, and all he could see were more backs and heads and beyond, a little higher up, still more. The steps, of course, the steps leading up to the platform with the judge's chair.

But now for the first time he could hear the Galilean's words clearly.

"I am the light of the world. He who follows me can never walk in darkness; he will possess the light which is life."

There was stillness. A voice cut through it: "Thou art testifying on thy own behalf; thy testimony is worth nothing."

Malchus recognized the speaker: Rabbi Mordecai, one of the finest minds of the rabbinical school, a man who could argue on fair terms with Gamaliel and even with Hillel.

The Galilean's voice came again: "My testimony is trustworthy, even when I testify on my own behalf; I know whence I have come and where I am going. You do not know whence I have come; you do not know where I am going. You set yourselves up to judge, after your earthly fashion; I do not set myself up to judge anybody. And what if I should judge? My judgment is judgment indeed; it is not I alone; my Father who sent me is with me. Just so it is prescribed in your Law: The testimony of two men is trustworthy; well, one is myself, testifying in my own behalf, and my Father who sent me testifies in my behalf too."

"Who is this father of his?" Malchus thought, and just as he was thinking it, someone asked, "Where is this father of thine?" and back came the answer: "You have no knowledge, either of me or of my Father; had you knowledge of me, you would have knowledge of my Father as well."

174

"I think this is pretty near blasphemy", said a thickset man next to Malchus. The captain of the guards did not answer.

"For a little while I am still with you", said the Galilean, "and then I am to go back to him who sent me. You will look for me, but you will not be able to find me; you cannot reach the place where I am."

A fine sweat broke out on Malchus' forehead. That rabbi or miracle worker or prophet or whatever he was seemed to read his thoughts. It was just what he was afraid of—that he would not be able to reach the place where he was. Or—or did he mean something else? And that voice rose again: "I am going away, and you will look for me, but you will have to die with your sins upon you; where I am going is where you cannot come."

The thickset man wore the fringed robe of a Pharisee. He said ironically, "Sounds almost as if our friend intended to kill himself, doesn't it?"

But it did not. There was some meaning in what this Yeshua said, something that he alone knew, something great and terrible that he could only allude to but not disclose. Malchus felt his hair stand up under his leather cap like the hackles of a dog. He summoned all his willpower to overcome this—fear. Yes, it was fear. He was afraid of a man, afraid of a voice, afraid like a child in the dark, like a stupid woman.

"Let me pass", he said to the thickset man. "I am here officially. Let me pass."

But the Pharisee did not hear him. He was listening to that voice again.

"You belong to earth, I to heaven; you to this world, I to another."

"I can't do it", Malchus thought desperately. "I can't go on with this. Perhaps it's true what he says. Perhaps he is not human at all. A demon, maybe, or a devil—but if that's what he is, why . . . "

175

"That is why I have been telling you that you will die with your sins upon you; you will die with your sins upon you unless you come to believe that it is myself you look for."

A sort of groan went through the multitude, drowning a voice asking a question and drowning the answer. Then the voice swelled up again to terrible strength: "When you have lifted up the Son of Man, you will recognize that it is myself you look for, and that I do not do anything on my own authority, but speak as my Father has instructed me to speak. And he who sent me is with me; he has not left me all alone, since what I do is always what pleases him."

It was then that the terrible thing happened. One single, thin voice started it, and ten, fifty, a hundred, and more took it up, the cry echoed from the walls: "The Messiah! He is the King Messiah!"

The court was in an uproar. There were cries of "Blasphemy!" "Kill anybody who says that!" "Deny it! Deny it!" and the thickset Pharisee looked as if he had swallowed vinegar.

Yeshua's voice rang out: "If you continue faithful to my word, you are my disciples in earnest; so you will come to know the truth, and the truth will set you free."

And Rabbi Mordecai's voice, acidly indignant: "We are of Abraham's breed; nobody ever enslaved us yet. What dost thou mean by saying, 'You shall become free'?"

"Excellent question", whispered Joram. "Now he must show his hand. Does he agree with the Freedom Party, or doesn't he? He's a sharp one, is Rabbi Mordecai."

Yeshua's answer came as clear and calm as before: "Believe me when I tell you this: everyone who acts sinfully is the slave of sin, and the slave cannot make his home in the house forever. To make his home in the house forever is for the Son. Why then, if it is the Son who makes you free men, you will have freedom in earnest. Yes, I know you are of Abraham's breed; yet you design to kill me, because my word does not find any place in you."

176

To kill him, Malchus repeated to himself. Was that what Kohen Gadol intended? Was that why he had to arrest this man? Arrest him—how? What if he was the Messiah? What if he was a demon? A man couldn't be expected to lay his hands on either, could he?

"My words are what I have learned in the house of my Father, and your actions, it seems, are what you have learned in the school of *your* father."

"Our father?" shrilled Rabbi Mordecai. "Abraham is our father."

There was a tumult of voices now, till somebody shouted over the din, "We are no bastard children; God and he only is the Father we recognize."

"If you were children of God, you would welcome me gladly; it was from God I took my origin; from him I have come."

"Blasphemer!" roared the Pharisee, and the tumult became general.

"The man's a Samaritan, surely."

"He's possessed, that's all."

It was incredible how the Galilean managed to make himself heard. "Believe me when I tell you this: if a man is true to my word, to all eternity he will never see death."

It was too much. "Now we are certain that thou art possessed."

"What of Abraham and the prophets?" screamed Rabbi Mordecai. "They are dead; and thou sayest a man will never taste death to all eternity, if he is true to thy word. Art thou greater than our father Abraham? He is dead, and the prophets are dead. What dost thou claim to be?"

Yes, what was he? Joram said something, but it was lost in the clamor. And still Yeshua could be heard:

"Honor must come to me from my Father, from him whom you claim as your God, although you cannot recognize him. But I have knowledge of him; if I should say I have not, I should be what you are, a liar. Yes, I have knowledge of him, and I am true

177

to his word. As for your father Abraham, his heart was proud to see the day of my coming; he saw and rejoiced to see it."

Rabbi Mordecai became visible for a moment, as those around him clotted together in their excitement; he was as white as a grave cloth and trembling visibly. "Hast thou seen Abraham, thou, who art not yet fifty years old?"

The answer came, loud and clear: "Believe me, before ever Abraham came to be, I AM."

There was a sudden hush, all breath suspended. The Word had been uttered, the one that must never be uttered in vain, the dreaded Word that first entered human consciousness when God spoke to Moses on Sinai. The Word that was God's answer to the prophet's question: "Lo, I shall go to the children of Israel, and say to them, 'The God of your fathers hath sent me to you.' If they should say to me, 'What is his name?' what shall I say to them?" God said to Moses, "I AM WHO AM." He said, "Thus shalt thou say to the children of Israel, 'HE WHO IS hath sent me to you.'"

There was no Jew alive who had not been taught that. There was no Jew who had forgotten it.

And now a man had uttered the Word, a man of flesh and blood, born of a woman.

Rabbi Mordecai lifted up his trembling arms. "He has blasphemed!"

"Sacrilege!"

"Here in the Temple!"

"Death to the blasphemer! Stone him!"

Where a moment ago no one had seemed able to move an inch, men now rushed about waving their arms, shrieking, roaring. Four or five men tried to speak, but no one would listen.

"Stones!" yelled a high-pitched voice. "Get stones from the outer court."

Ten, twenty, thirty men ran for stones.

"Seize the blasphemer!" shouted Rabbi Mordecai. "Seize him first, you fools."

But Yeshua was no longer in his seat.

"He has vanished!" somebody screamed. "He is gone."

"Wouldn't you go, if you were insulted like this?"

"Are you trying to defend him?"

Malchus looked about him. One of his officers had buried his face in his hands; the other was swaying as if he were in ecstasy. The guards looked utterly bewildered. Ten men. He needed an army to stop this riot. And where was the man they were to take prisoner?

Several excited men had come to blows. People screamed words which no one heard.

"The Messiah has the right . . . "

"Shut up, blasphemer, or I'll kill you."

"Stones . . . get stones . . . "

A few elderly scholars fled, their eyes glazed with terror.

"Stone a man in the Temple, God forbid!"

Suddenly a tall man in a white robe passed by, calmly and without unseemly haste.

Malchus stared at him, blinked, stared again. Instinctively he raised his hand as he would before giving an order to the guards. But he gave no order, and his hand dropped.

The man in the white robe slipped round the next pillar and was gone.

Somebody said, "I couldn't have done it either."

Joram. Joram, smiling an uneasy, frightened smile. Malchus wondered why he had always disliked Joram. He was a good man, a good man, a friend.

The fighting had stopped, but people were still arguing, heads shaking, arms flailing.

There were some who had stones in their hands. They must have picked them up in the courtyard outside, and now there was no one at whom to throw them. They looked absurdly, stupidly, disappointed and yet somehow relieved.

Little Joram was saying something.

"I'm not coming with you, Malchus. But you can give Kohen Gadol a message for me."

A message. "What is it, Joram?"

The little man gave him a strange look. "Tell him he won't see me again."

"What? What do you mean?"

Joram looked over his shoulder toward the pillar behind which the man in the white robe had disappeared. "I'm not working against *him*", he said.

Malchus nodded. He said nothing. It was easy for Joram, he thought. Joram did not have a wife and three children.

He braced himself, cleared his throat, and marched his men off.

Back at the High Priest's house, he left the guards outside and walked in with his two officers.

A secretary—not Aza—told him that Kohen Gadol was expecting him in the councilroom and led him there. The two officers followed in uneasy silence.

The sound of many voices came from the councilroom. The secretary went in to announce them.

" . . . I know whence I have come and where I am going. You do not know whence I have come; you do not know where I am going. . . . You belong to earth, I to heaven. . . . You will die with your sins upon you unless you come to believe that it is myself you look for. . . . "

The secretary was back and beckoned them to enter. They marched in like good soldiers.

A dull council: the chief priests and a number of Pharisee rabbis. Kohen Gadol in his high-backed chair in the middle of them.

"Have you left your prisoner outside?"

Malchus' eyes were fixed on the ground. "We have made no arrest, my lord High Priest."

He could hear the rustle of their robes.

"Did they defend him so well? None of you seems to be hurt. Speak up, man—how could he escape you?"

Malchus looked up. "We could not do it, my lord High Priest", he said simply. "Nobody has ever spoken as this man speaks."

Caiphas bit his lip. Then he looked significantly at the others.

Rabbi Josaphat, a Pharisee leader, spoke up with angry condescension: "Have you, too, let yourselves be deceived? Have any of the rulers come to believe in him yet—or of the Pharisees?"

Malchus gulped. "There were many present who did believe in him."

Rabbi Josaphat gave a contemptuous laugh. "Common folk who have no knowledge of the Law. A curse is on them."

Caiphas said bitterly, "We don't seem to get much sense out of you, Malchus. Tell Joram to come in."

The captain took a deep breath. "He is not here, my lord High Priest. He—he begs to be excused. He says . . ."

Caiphas rapped the table. "Out with it. What does he say?"

"He says he won't come any more, because—because he does not wish to work against the Rabbi Yeshua."

There was a long pause. Then Caiphas said very softly, "You may go."

The three officers marched out. When the door had closed behind them, the High Priest said, "Do you see now what I mean? This man is more dangerous than all the lestes put together. You may imagine what will happen when he becomes their leader—if he is not already their leader."

"It is an outrage." Rabbi Josaphat was pale with anger. "The man must be arrested at all costs. He ought to be in jail now—should have been there long ago."

A grave-faced, gray-haired Pharisee rose.

"Yes, Rabbi Nicodemus?" asked Caiphas.

"My lord High Priest, is it the way of our Law to judge a man without giving him a hearing first and finding out what he is about?"

"Are you from Galilee also?" jeered Rabbi Josaphat. "Look in the Scriptures; you will find that Galilee does not breed prophets."

"The Rabbi Yeshua bar Joseph will get his hearing as soon as I have got hold of him", said Caiphas again very softly. "But I don't think that time is yet. You have seen that we cannot rely on our own guards when it is a question of arresting the man. That alone shows that he is building up his own authority against the established rulers."

"True. Very true." Several voices spoke at the same time.

"I need not tell you in what danger we would all have been if this insane riot had succeeded." The High Priest looked about him. "It would have been a very good pretext for the procurator to hold us responsible and to impose a fine, since he no longer dares to commit open robbery—knowing that we would bring it to Caesar's attention, as we did the last time and the time before that. I have good reason to believe, however, that this time the corban will not be touched, or any other fine imposed upon us."

There was obvious relief on many faces. But Rabbi Nicodemus said stubbornly, "I have seen no evidence that the lamentable events referred to have any connection with Rabbi Yeshua bar Joseph."

Caiphas gave him a wintry smile. "The Rabbi Yeshua has a warm defender in you, Rabbi Nicodemus. There is no direct evidence so far—no. But we do know, do we not, that he is constantly undermining our authority and especially that of the Pharisees. He has found very unkind words for them. Ill-doers, liars, whited sepulchres, wolves in sheep's clothing—I could prolong the list."

Nicodemus looked down. "Would that none of us deserved such harsh words, my lord High Priest."

But the irascible Rabbi Josaphat banged the table. "Anybody following this man should be forbidden the synagogue."

Caiphas raised his bushy eyebrows. "It would not prevent him from speaking to the masses under the open sky, as he has done before. He spoke to five thousand men in Galilee, not long ago. There are few synagogues in the country that could hold so many. But there is nothing to prevent you from making a motion at the next plenary sitting of the Sanhedrin."

XI

"You did very well at the Temple", said Abenadar. "I saw you jump, and I saw you tackle them when they came streaming out. Very pretty. You killed one of their leaders, didn't you?"

"Wounded him", Cassius said. "They carried him off, and I think I saw him move."

"You didn't lose your head." Abenadar gave a nod of satisfaction. "Saw you rally sections three and five and lead them where they were needed most. You're a soldier all right, my boy."

"Did you report it?" asked Cassius crisply.

Abenadar laughed and stretched his limbs. They were lying on couches on the gallery of the Insula, munching figs and drinking Greek wine. An awning protected them against the sun, still strong in midafternoon. Half the officers' corps was up here, and there was fruit and meat and wine for all of them, an extra meal at the expense of a grateful procurator.

"You're ambitious, boy. Well, the answer is yes. And I think they'll give you a cohort within a year or so."

Cassius murmured something unintelligible.

"Not enough, eh?" Abenadar grinned. "Took me twelve years before I got my cohort. You'll do it in five. What do you want, a legion right away?"

"One legion is not enough", Cassius said.

Abenadar was enjoying himself. "An army. He wants a whole army. Those fellows whose jugular veins you want to see spouting must be pretty high up, if you won't settle for less."

Cassius emptied his goblet. "They killed my father", he said quickly.

Abenadar's long face became serious. "Who were they? Barbarians?"

"Romans."

"And you received no justice. They must be high up. This is where I stop asking questions. Wouldn't do either of us any good. And if I were you I'd keep my mouth shut."

Cassius looked at him. "You're the only man I have ever talked to about it. Was I wrong?"

"Sure you were. I might talk in my sleep." Abenadar chose another fig. "Well, I hope you get what you hope to get. But I doubt it."

"I must. There is no other purpose in my life."

Abenadar grinned again. "At least we agree that life should have a purpose. That's something."

"You and your damned philosophy." Cassius grinned too. "Whatever I say you seem to make something out of it."

"Yes, but you won't, I'm afraid. Next year a cohort—in five years; in eight, perhaps, a legion. Another ten years before you'll have a higher command, if you get one at all. You won't get it on military merits alone, you know. You'll have to know the right people and make yourself liked, and they must think you will be able to ward off Persians or Picts or Germans without getting too highhanded about it, if you see what I mean. Takes a lot of diplomacy, they say. All right, say you can do it. So after another five or six years you come home and you are a powerful man and you look about for those fellows with the jugular veins. It's odds on they're no longer alive. Maybe you're not the only one who had a grudge against them. Maybe they died from a surfeit of nightingale tongues or Falernian or simply from a stroke. And if they aren't dead, you'll find them poor, old, wretched, toothless, mumbling, and just waiting for death to take pity on them. Then you come, spear in hand, and do your stuff, or you look on while your men are doing it. I'm telling you here and now, Cassius, you won't find it half as enjoyable as you think. It will all be flat, like yesterday's wine."

"A beautiful speech", Cassius jeered. "But it won't be flat. Curse you, what do you think you're doing, spoiling the only fun I have?"

"You're a crazy one", growled Abenadar. "But at least you're a soldier. Well, you have to be, in this part of the world. Some of those young good-for-nothings they're sending us from Rome seem to think it's an easy job dealing with Jews. Orientals, they say. You should see the Germans, they say. Maybe the Jews they met in Rome or Milan are soft—but not here. Your Jew is a fighter, as good as they come. Everybody gets soft, living in big cities and doing some fancy bit of trading with the patricians. But not here. Almost got it myself, on the Temple square."

"Seems to me that spying is at least as important as fighting in this place", Cassius said. "If old Pilatus hadn't known their plan beforehand . . . "

"Think he did, eh?" Abenadar blinked a few times. "I heard something about that. Somebody found a letter in a fruit basket."

"That's right", Cassius said.

"It was quite a good plan, as far as it went", Abenadar declared. "But not good enough. Didn't provide for treachery. One must always provide for that."

"I wonder who wrote that letter, Abenadar."

"Well, you should know. It was given to you."

"Mela told you, I suppose. He told Vindex, too."

"Somebody told me", Abenadar said. "I can't remember names, these days. Must be old age creeping on. It was a girl who gave you the letter, wasn't it?"

Cassius frowned. "Yes. But I don't think she knew about the letter. Perhaps the old woman who was with her knew. I'm sure she didn't."

"What makes you think so? Was she that pretty?"

The frown deepened. "What's that got to do with it? She told me the best fruit was on the bottom of the basket and I should look for it soon. She said that three times. Sounded as if she had learned it by heart. Perhaps her old man taught her."

Abenadar poured himself some wine. "I thought you said he was her husband."

"So he is. He's old enough to be her grandfather, though. Man called Boz bar something—Sabulo or Sebulus or something like that."

"Boz bar Sebulun." Abenadar whistled through his teeth. "He's a relative of the High Priest, I think."

"Is he? I don't know."

"Now that explains a lot", Abenadar said. "The High Priest. The Pontifex Maximus himself, Kohen Gadol, they call him."

"You think he was behind it?"

"Of course. Boz bar Sebulun would never dare to send such a message on his own authority."

Cassius wrinkled his nose. "Their Pontifex Maximus giving away the plan of his own countrymen, eh?"

"Somebody once told me that Rome was a pigsty", Abenadar reminded him dryly. "Why are you so surprised that Jerusalem has its shady side, too? Besides, the poor man has long-range policy to consider."

"How's that?"

"Well, suppose the lestes had succeeded. How long do you think they could have kept it up? The High Priest is a man of fifty-seven or eight. He hopes to live another twenty years—he wouldn't particularly want to be butchered by our legions from Syria and Egypt and Greece, when they landed here six months later to set things right again. So he prefers to sacrifice the bunch of hotheads and rabble-rousers and lestes. He isn't a bad man, I suppose, or a good one either. If he had been born in Rome, he'd probably be in charge of a province now. He and his set—they're just out to keep what they've got. He's the top man, and he wants to remain top man. Can you blame him? It's not nice, perhaps, but it's understandable. The Pharisees, now, that's an entirely different proposition."

"The fellows with the fringed black robes? What about them?"

Abenadar rubbed his nose. "I've listened to some of their debates, and, believe me, they can argue. A school of Greek sophists is a bunch of lapdogs in comparison to them. The trouble with them is that they are always right. Every one of them is right every time. Usually they and the Temple set stick to our side, as you know, but they don't like the procurator much."

"No? If what you say is right, he's done good work for them lately."

"They've never forgotten the aqueduct and the images. They came to terms with him, but the terms were stiff, and they secretly sent an embassy to Rome to complain about the procurator. They have influence there, more than one might think."

"What's the latest news from the pigsty?"

"Ask Vindex. He gets all the reports, I don't. On second thought better not ask him. It's funny, but people who ask questions all the time hate nothing more than to be questioned. Somebody mentioned that the Emperor is in bad shape and won't last long."

"Who do you think will succeed him? Sejanus?" It sounded just a little too casual.

"How do *I* know? And if I were you ... "

"I haven't said anything." Cassius rose and walked to the rampart. For a while he stood there staring into space. Then he saw clouds of smoke rising, two, three, four, six ... "Houses on fire to the north", he reported. "The city isn't quiet yet. Think they'll try again?" He stepped back and resumed his place on the couch.

"I doubt it. We took over their arsenal in the tower. Seems we got the head of the movement, too, or one of the heads. The man you let escape in that little skirmish of yours, remember?"

"The one with the scar, Bar Abbas?"

"Yes—and he's the one who almost nicked me, curse him."

"Sorry I let him escape", said Cassius apologetically. "Is he dead?"

"No such luck for him, poor devil. He's up there in the west tower."

"What's going to happen to him?"

"Pilatus hasn't decided yet, as far as I know. He's being nursed back to health again—gets more care than you or I would. Means that the procurator wants him strong enough to suffer sufficiently before he dies. Probably the cross, as a warning to others."

Cassius winced a little. After a while he asked, "What do you think those burning houses mean?"

"They're turning against each other. It's like a man biting his finger because he can't bear his toothache. Also they've lost most of their leaders—the Freedom Party people, I mean. Means their men are turning into a mob—into a hundred mobs. Bar Abbas was the man who could make them march together, at least for a while. But he couldn't have got far with them either. No one could, really."

"Why not?"

"Because they are too small a nation."

"Macedonia was a small nation, too. Yet under Alexander they conquered the world."

"How long did they keep it?"

"Till he died. He was thirty-three then."

"What's the good of conquering the world just for a few measly years?"

"Fun while it lasted, I suppose. And he might have lived to eighty—no one could have taken the world away from him. He was a genius."

Abenadar shook his head. "What happened when he died?"

"Oh, it all broke apart, of course. Lots of generals all fighting each other, but none of *them* was a genius."

"Genius", said Abenadar thoughtfully. "Genius. What is that?"

Cassius shrugged his shoulders. "I was taught that a genius was a man whose mind could give form and content to the time in which he lived. As Alexander did. As Caesar did, too, till my venerable great-uncle stabbed him — very clumsily — in the Senate."

"Did he do that?" Abenadar did not seem to be very impressed. "And when Caesar died, what did he leave? A beautiful theater for civil war."

"He couldn't help that, could he? He was dead."

"The real genius would be he who went on living after his death", Abenadar said in a low voice.

Cassius shook his head. "That is either nonsense or metaphysics — which amounts to the same thing, I suppose."

Abenadar took no notice. "It wouldn't matter when he died, whether at the age of eighty or of thirty-three, but he must live on in people's hearts. They would go on doing certain things because he did them and avoid doing others because he avoided them, and they would do so because they loved him, even if they had never set eyes on him."

"What's the matter with you? I've never heard such — "

"I'll tell you what is the decisive test", Abenadar interrupted him. "No one would die today for Alexander or for Caesar, not one single soul. But for the man I'm thinking of, people would go on being glad to die, for generation after generation. But maybe that's more than any man can hope to achieve. Maybe he would have to be a god."

"There never was such a man, and there never will be", said Cassius. "How many goblets have you had?"

"Don't be ridiculous, boy." Abenadar was outraged. "Want to challenge me? Young Mela did, the other day. Ask him what happened after the tenth goblet."

"All right, all right. I take it back. How did we come to talk of all this? Oh, yes — Bar Abbas. Well, you're right there. He's no genius, neither according to my definition or yours."

"He isn't", assented Abenadar. "And old Caiphas isn't either. But there's a man in the city whom I would like to meet. Makes me feel curious, that one."

"Who is he?"

"A Jew. A rabbi. Remember the girl I told you about, the singer and dancer, whom the legate tried to get for the banquet when the procurator arrived?"

"The one you said was better than the best Gaditan girls?"

"That's right. Miriam of Migdal. I'd give a month's pay if I could see her dance again."

"You said she had turned religious, didn't you?"

"Yes. And it was that rabbi who made her do it. Seems to be an extraordinary man. The Lady Claudia went to see him today."

Cassius yawned ostentatiously. "Don't tell me she's turning religious, too."

"You never know, boy, you never know. All kinds of strange things can happen, apparently. She came back, swearing she saw the rabbi cure a man who had been blind from birth."

"What next! Wait a minute—did you say she saw him today? Today? Where?"

"In the old city—some suburb. I wish I knew exactly where it was, but my source wouldn't or couldn't tell me more."

"And the procurator let her go there? With the city in the state it is? I don't understand it."

"He didn't know. She slipped out, with one of her maids—a Jewess. Veiled, of course. The maid must have told her about the rabbi. Pilatus was furious when he heard about it."

Cassius gave a short laugh.

"Look here", Abenadar said, "I know what you're thinking. But she really went to see that man. It was nothing else, I know."

"How can you possibly know that?"

"Because she repeated some of the things she heard the rabbi say, and it's the kind of thing she couldn't have invented. Neither could you or I or anybody I know."

"What kind of thing?"

The Centurion Mela walked up to them. He wore armor and carried some official-looking papers.

"What's up now?" Abenadar wondered. "Too many houses burning, I suppose."

The young centurion saluted stiffly. "Field order for the First Cohort."

Abenadar nodded. "Show me." He looked at the papers.

"A list of people we must protect against the rioters. Friends of Rome", drawled Mela. "We are to send out patrols at regular intervals."

"I see." Abenadar studied the list. "Never knew we had so many friends here." He rose. "Better do something about this."

"May I have a look?" Cassius asked suddenly.

"By all means. Here's the list. There's a plan of the city, too. They must have been busy in the office. Boz bar Sebulun is on the list. Of course he would be."

"I've heard that name before somewhere", Mela said. "Where was it, I wonder? Ah, yes, of course—that's the man who sent you your pretty girl friend the other day, isn't it? I heard her mention his name just as I left you two together . . . "

" . . . to report to Tribune Vindex that I had received a fruit basket and you hadn't." Cassius' tone was downright aggressive.

"I don't know what makes you think so", drawled Mela. "I only wished to be discreet. I thought she was *very* pretty. Congratulations."

"Idiot", said Cassius.

Mela registered surprise. "You mean to say you are not personally interested in the girl? Well, that's different, of course. Then you won't object, I suppose, if I take over sector twenty-three, the one in which their house is?"

"You can take over any sector you like, as long as you leave me in peace", Cassius growled.

"That's fine then." Mela grinned. "Commander, please, mark me down for sector twenty-three, will you?"

Abenadar waited for a moment or two, but Cassius said nothing. "All right then", he said, marking the sector on the plan. "Ten men for each patrol, fifty for each sector. Day and night patrols every hour. And remember, Mela, no one is to enter a Jewish house unless he is called in by the owner."

Mela's face fell. "Why not? That business of uncleanness again, is it? We pollute their wonderful houses, do we? If we are good enough to protect them . . . "

"A dog is good enough to protect me", Abenadar smiled. "But that's no reason for me to take him into my bed."

"Of all the ungrateful, mangy rascals!"

"Oh, shut up, Mela." Cassius shrugged. "We don't protect them from the rabble because we like them, do we? Even you can't be naïve enough to believe that. We protect them because we need them — they're our mainstay in the country, the priests, the Temple set, the Pharisees, the wealthy. We need them. And they know it. So don't expect them to overwhelm you with gratitude. Give me any sector you like, commander. I don't care which it is."

"Take twenty-two, then", Abenadar said dryly. "Here — these twelve streets up to the small bridge."

Cassius nodded and strolled away. One of these days some one would have to teach young Mela a lesson. He felt thoroughly irritated. He knew there was really no reason for it. Which made it worse.

XII

Achim bar Simeon seemed to be sinking fast. Jonah, his host, felt obliged to send for the physician again, although the streets were still far from safe. Twice the man had been stopped on his way to Jonah's house, once by a Roman patrol, the other time by three Freedom men who had seen the Romans talk to him. He explained to the Romans that he was going to a woman whose hour had come; to the Freedom men he whispered the name of Achim bar Simeon.

He felt the wounded man's pulse and frowned. He changed the dressings on the wound, and he did not like what he saw there either. Perhaps one day a physician would know why some wounds healed well and without complications, while others, apparently no worse, did not. It had little to do with the man's age. Achim bar Simeon was only sixty; often men much older than he got well again. No good bleeding the man—he had lost too much blood as it was. There seemed to be an accumulation of fluid in his chest, for he was breathing with considerable difficulty.

"Not so good, physician, eh?" croaked Achim bar Simeon.

"All life comes from God", was the answer. All devout physicians used the phrase, whatever the malady, but in this case it sounded somewhat ambiguous.

"He giveth, and he taketh away", murmured Achim, closing his eyes. "But I wish—I wish he couldn't take my life yet. Jonah—where are you, good Jonah? I can't see you."

"Here I am, Achim." The good-natured man tried to sound as cheerful as he could.

"Has Benjamin not come back yet?"

"No, Achim."

"Perhaps he is late because he has found him", murmured the wounded man enigmatically. "If only—he—comes back—in time to tell me."

"Yes, Achim. I'm sure he will." This time it was the physician who asked a silent question and Jonah who answered it with a shrug. Achim had sent one of his men on some errand—a young man, almost a boy—and he had been gone for many hours. The streets were dangerous, but it served no purpose to say that now.

What a feast this was! Why couldn't they all be peaceful and quiet instead of going about murdering each other? Rabbi Josaphat had warned him more than once to keep away from the Freedom people, to refuse to have any dealings with them. They would only bring bloodshed and misery on Israel and gain nothing in exchange; the Edomites were too powerful. But then when one listened to Ephraim bar Saul, it seemed wrong to sit back and do nothing to free the country from its oppressors, who sat up there in the Antonia spitting down on the very Temple of the Most High. But Ephraim bar Saul was dead, and it looked very much as if Rabbi Josaphat had been right. Was it surprising? He was a learned man; he had studied the Law; everyone said he had a wonderful mind.

Jonah should have listened to him. It would have saved him many shekels he had given to the Freedom men, and he would not now have a dying man in his house: during the Feast of the Tabernacles, a dying man.

Achim bar Simeon was good and pious, no doubt, even if he was a Galilean and perhaps a little coarse in his speech; they would never learn how to speak properly in Galilee. But it would have been better for him, too, if he had looked after his trade and spent his time working, instead of running about with a sword—a man of his age. What had he gained by it? A hole in his shoulder and a broken arm, and now it seemed he was dying. He could have lived out his life peaceably as a man respected by his neighbors and an elder in the synagogue.

Somebody scratched at the door, and Jonah went and looked cautiously through the slit, his heart thumping, but it was Benjamin after all. Of course. The Romans did not bother to scratch. They simply banged their spearshafts against the door and broke it down, if it were not opened quickly enough.

The boy was excited and out of breath; he rushed past Jonah into the sickroom, and Achim bar Simeon sat up straight, as the physician stared at him astonished.

"Report", barked Achim bar Simeon.

Young Benjamin forced himself to speak coherently. "He has been in the city for more than a day. He was in the Temple — preaching. That is not where I saw him; I only heard about it from somebody. He caused an uproar there and there were some who wanted to stone him — "

Achim bar Simeon gave a hoarse chuckle. "Stone him — him! What did he do? What did he say?"

"I know little of what he said in the Temple — "

"Did he not — reveal himself? Not even — now?"

"He said he was the light of the world."

Achim bar Simeon's eyes were burning. The physician leaned forward in protest but was waved aside. "What else is he? Go on."

"He said he came from God — he said he had known Abraham. . . . "

"Go on — go on — there has never been a song like this — you said they wanted — to stone him."

"Yes, but he vanished before they could do anything. He was not hurt."

"If only he had come earlier. We would have — won the battle."

"The man who told me about it wanted to find him, to hear him speak again, and so we both went and searched for him. We looked into four synagogues, and in the fifth we found him; it was the one in the street of the dyers. He was speaking. . . . "

"What did he say? What did he say? Did he mention the battle?"

"Only once — when they asked him some question about the eighteen men who had died under the Tower of Siloe."

"The Tower of Siloe — where Ephraim bar Saul fell."

"He said, 'You will all perish as they did if you do not repent. What of these eighteen men on whom the tower fell in Siloe and killed them? Do you suppose that there was a heavier account against them than against any others who then dwelt at Jerusalem? I tell you it was not so; you will all perish as they did if you do not repent.' These were his words. I have a good memory."

There was a puzzled expression on Achim bar Simeon's face. His gnarled hands twitched nervously. "Go on, boy."

"Then he told us a parable, about 'a man that had a fig tree planted in his vineyard, but when he came and looked for fruit on it, he could find none'."

Achim was listening with sharp attention. Jonah shook his head disapprovingly. Hundreds of dead, the houses full of wounded, the city a battleground and here a dying man was listening to a tale about a fig tree as if nothing else mattered.

Benjamin went on, "So the man said to his vine-dresser, 'Cut it down; why should it be a useless charge upon the land?'"

There was such fear in Achim's face that the boy stopped short, but at a vehement gesture he continued, "But the vine-dresser said, 'Sir, let it stand this year too, so that I may have time to dig and put dung around it; perhaps it will bear fruit; if not, it will be time to cut it down then.'"

Achim bar Simeon took a deep breath. "More—more . . . This is not all of it. The King is angry with his people, as well he might be. But it is not all of it."

"No, sir, it isn't. There was another parable. There were two, I think, but I could not hear much of the first, there was so much shouting going on, but this I heard him say: 'It is I who am the door of the sheepfold. Those others who have found their way in are all thieves and robbers'—and then again: 'I am the door; a man will find salvation if he makes his way in through me'—and then again: 'The thief only comes to steal, to slaughter, to destroy; I have come so that they may have life, and have it more abundantly.' That's what he said, sir."

Achim bar Simeon sat very straight and very still for a long time, but when the physician, alarmed, reached out to touch him, he brushed the man's hand away. "Thieves and robbers", he repeated slowly. "Slaughter. And destroy. We all did, we all did. The sons of Eli did—they stole the money of the poor in unjust taxes. We did—we killed and destroyed, and what did it avail us?

May God have mercy on us. We all went the wrong way—all of us." Tears welled up in his eyes. "He gave us bread, that day on the mountain, bread—not swords, and when we would have hailed him King, he left and hid himself from our eyes. . . . But even now he will not cut down the fig tree—not even now."

"He said still more, sir." Benjamin was worried, the old man looked so strange. "I could only hear some of it. He said, 'I am the good shepherd. The good shepherd lays down his life for his sheep, whereas the hireling, who is no shepherd and does not claim the sheep as his own, abandons the sheep and takes to flight as soon as he sees the wolf coming, and so the wolf harries the sheep and scatters them."

"Kohen Gadol", gasped Achim bar Simeon. "Kohen Gadol. He is—the hireling . . . "

"Yes, sir, there were many who understood it that way and said so, some agreeing and others very angry about it, but he said, 'My sheep listen to my voice, and I know them, and they follow me. And I give them everlasting life.' "

"Everlasting . . . "

"Yes, and he said, 'This trust which my Father has committed to me is more precious than all else', and he said"—Benjamin hesitated, for these were the most difficult words to repeat—"he said, 'My Father and I are one.' "

Achim bar Simeon's eyes shone brightly. "One", he said. And again, "One." He was unaware that the physician was supporting his trembling body. He said almost in a whisper, "Tell me, son, was there—no sign? Did he not—do anything—in the city—that was a—sign for us?"

"No, sir, nothing. Nothing except—he cured a man who had been blind all his life."

The wounded man smiled radiantly. "Not only one man", he said. "Many men. And I—am one of them. I—have been blind— all my life. But at last—I see. Bread—not swords. Sheep—not wolves. O God, forgive me, I've been such a fool. . . . You alone—can give us sight. To see the kingdom—not without but within. . . . That's where it is—within us . . . "

He went limp in the physician's arms.

Benjamin gulped. "Is he . . . is he . . . ?"

"No, he isn't dead", comforted the physician. "But he is delirious. He doesn't really know what he is saying. He may go on talking like this for hours."

The young man hung his head. Jonah put his pudgy arm around him and led him away. "What you need is something to eat", he said.

"I couldn't eat anything now."

"Nonsense. At your age one can always eat. It's not so long ago that I can't remember." Jonah closed the door of the sickroom behind them. "Besides, you heard what the learned physician said."

But the learned physician proved to be wrong. Achim bar Simeon did not speak again. In a few moments he died, with a strangely happy smile on his rugged old face.

XIII

Sector twenty-two proved to be routine work, nothing more. The Freedom men had attacked one of the houses—that of the rich Sadducee Elias bar Levi—a few hours before the first Roman patrol tramped through the streets, but they had not got very far. Elias bar Levi was not the kind of man who could be easily intimidated. He had armed himself and twenty of his servants and made a spirited defense against the attackers, who, having expected an easy victim, showed little taste for battle. When Cassius arrived with his men, Elias was standing in front of his door, leaning on a long, curved Persian sword, and told him all about it. "I made my fortune trading with Bactria and Persia, centurion—took me the better part of thirty years, and during the first half I always led my caravans myself. What with Arabs, Kurds, and the like a man gets accustomed to fighting."

"What did you trade in?" Cassius asked.

"Wool, silk, spices."

Cassius pointed to the Persian sword. "To which of these articles does this belong?"

Elias bar Levi smiled. "It belonged once to a man who tried to use it for the acquisition of wool, silk, and spices which belonged to me."

"If there were many more like you, we wouldn't have to patrol the streets", Cassius said.

Elias bar Levi's smile broadened. "If there were many more like me, there would be no Romans in the country—except of course as welcome guests. Unfortunately, there aren't many."

Cassius grinned, gave him an almost respectful salute, and went on. So that notion existed too—a wealthy Sadducee who thought he could do without Rome. Perhaps some day one might find a Pharisee who was not sure that he was always right. It would amuse Abenadar to hear about this. But it might be worth while to comb the city for arms.

At the next crossing he met the second and third patrol, who had nothing to report, and a few streets farther down they picked up the fourth, who had settled a small street brawl without loss.

The fifth and last he found waiting for him at the sector boundary. Their leader reported they had found about a dozen bandits trying to throw torches into a house. "When they saw us coming, they fled. We caught these two." He pointed to a couple of sullen young men whose hands were tied behind their backs.

Cassius nodded. "Anything else?"

"Not in our sector, sir. But there is something burning over there. It's pretty dark now, but you can still see it."

Sector twenty-three. Mela's sector. Well, that was his business. And their time was up—his men were hungry by now.

199

Sector twenty-three.

"Calvus, march the men to the barracks."

They clanked away with their prisoners.

It was silly, of course. Mela had fifty men, more than enough to take care of whatever was burning. If he really wanted to do something about it, he ought to take ten or twenty of the men with him. The sensible thing to do was to follow his men back to the Antonia. He had no business in another officer's sector.

By then he was in it. The third street to the left. And by the cold snout of Cerberus, it was the house, the old man's house, the girl's house, and there was a cloud of smoke hanging over it.

He began to run, and soon tendrils of smoke reached him, making him cough. As he came nearer he saw in the light of the fire the dull bluish sheen of Roman armor. Mela and his men were there. Of course. But he hardly slackened his pace.

No fighting. The soldiers were merely trying to put the fire out. Mela had made them form a chain along which they were passing pails of water. They were getting the better of the fire, too. Mela, blackened, perspiring, and grinning, walked up to Cassius.

"Bandits fled when I came", he reported, rubbing his eyes. "All we have to do now is to put the flames out."

Cassius nodded.

"The old miser should do it himself, really, he and his slaves", Mela said. "He's sitting over there, counting his possessions. I hope *I'll* get a fruit basket this time."

When Cassius walked over to Boz bar Sebulun he heard him shriek at his servants, who were bringing out cupboards, chests, carpets, and silver.

"Faster, you wretches, faster—or the water's going to spoil what the fire has left."

"Where is your wife?" barked Cassius.

Boz looked up, but only for a moment. "Who is . . . Ah, it's you, centurion. The women's quarters are untouched. Easy with that chest now, you imbeciles! Do you want to ruin me? It's full of glass! Phoenician glass, one piece worth more than all of you bundled together. Be careful, you sons of mangy mules!"

The women's quarters were untouched. And the wind was blowing the smoke away from that part of the house.

Cassius walked around the walled garden. The night was dark, but he thought the back door seemed to be slightly ajar.

Striding toward it, he stumbled over something—over somebody.

He bent down. It was a woman. It was the old woman who had come to the Antonia. She was lying on her back in a pool of blood. There was a deep wound in her chest and she was moaning softly. He knelt down. She was still conscious, but very weak. And in her eyes was hatred.

"What has happened?" he demanded. "Where is she? Where is your mistress?"

Abigail stared at him. "Nothing . . . good . . . ever comes from . . . dealing with . . . Romans . . . "

"Where is she? Is she safe?"

"They came in . . . back door . . . they carried us out. I screamed . . . so they stabbed me . . . took her away . . . "

"Where did they take her? Speak up, woman!"

But she was past answering. Cursing, Cassius jumped to his feet. And then he saw the little group of men huddled together close to the house. They did not move.

He drew his sword and approached them. They were holding somebody. A girl. The girl.

Suddenly he understood. Mela and his men were on the other side of the building, but the fire lit up the whole street. The bandits were apparently afraid they could not get her away without being seen. They were waiting till the flames had died down. But when they saw him they started running in the direction of the street of the coppersmiths.

Cassius raced after them. Glancing back, he saw Mela gesticulating to his men, curse him! They were paying no attention to anyone else. And Boz was still busy with his servants. It seemed to Cassius they were all making a lot of noise. No good shouting. And a waste of time, running to Mela for help; the bandits could vanish so quickly in the maze of small streets.

He ran on alone. The moment of indecision had made him lose a dozen yards. The bandits were perhaps forty yards ahead of him, rather more than less. But if he was slowed down by his armor, they were hampered by the girl. If only she would struggle . . .

Eyes gleamed at him in the darkness; someone spat curses at him.

In the dim light of a lantern he could see them more clearly. Three. Only three and the girl. And he was overtaking them.

They became aware of it, too, and Cassius could have shouted with joy when they stopped. He did not shout. He had to save his breath for what came next. They were not stopping for nothing. They stopped because—ah, there it was, just as he had thought. One of them was dragging the girl on while the other two planted themselves in his path.

It had to be quick work, Cassius thought, or the game was lost.

As usual when he fought, he fell into a strange state of clear-headed fury. The two men were standing at a distance of about a yard from each other. He rushed the man on the left and at the last moment threw up his shield and turned against the one on the right. The man had his dagger ready to stab Cassius in the neck, but the attack was unexpected, and Cassius' sword went clear into his chest, the orthodox three inches, so that there was no trouble about withdrawing the blade.

A quick step aside and a half turn—but the second opponent was already running, disappearing down a side street. There remained only the third man, the one carrying the girl, who seemed to have fainted.

Cassius raced to the corner as the man skittered around it. He spurted ahead with such impetus that he shot past them and had to turn back. The man dropped the girl like a log and fled.

She was unconscious, and he lifted her up. She was light; he could easily carry her home, he thought.

And then he saw that this was not the end of the matter after all. Several doors had opened, and there were shadowy figures bunching together in the doorways and more coming out of the shadows.

Twelve, fifteen, perhaps twenty men. Too many for him to handle alone. And with the girl . . . Something had to be done, and quickly.

"Rush him", shouted a voice. "Hold him."

It was too late. The Roman had turned toward the nearest house and pushed open the door, the girl over his shoulder. There was a shriek and the noise of heavy objects falling.

When the men entered the house, they found its owner, a trembling old man, half paralyzed by fright, but no one else.

"Where are they?" bellowed the leader of the Freedom men.

The old man pointed dumbly to a hatch with a heavy wooden cover.

"What is this, a cellar? Anyone down there beside the Roman and the girl?"

"N-no." The old man caught his breath. "She looked like a Jewish woman. Has he stolen her from you?"

The Freedom man frowned. This was not going to be easy.

"How many steps are there?"

"Six. And all my wine and oil is down there. Why couldn't he find another place?"

Six steps into a cellar, through an opening only large enough for one man, who would have his feet hacked off as soon as they showed on the first step. Of course, a man might slide down, head forward and protected by a shield, but nobody could fight in such a position, and the Roman would finish him off with a single stab or blow.

"There is no second entrance to the cellar, by any chance?"

"No, only this one. All my wine and my oil is down there . . . "

"You told us that before. What else is there?"

"Nothing. Only old furniture. I am not a wealthy man."

"No use trying to get in there", one of the others said sullenly. "He's just waiting for us."

"True." The leader scowled. "We can't get in. But there is at least one good thing about it. He can't get out either."

XIV

It was so obviously a dream, she did not even bother to think about it. She was lying on an old couch in a room she had never seen before. What little light there was came from a small oil lamp, and the place smelled musty like a cellar. The Roman commander was sitting on a rickety chair, fully armed and with his helmet on.

"This is the second time you've done this to me", she told him gravely.

He gave her a look of surprise. "The second time? Oh, I see, you mean getting you out of trouble. We're not out of it yet, lady."

"I mean it's the second time that I've dreamed of you", she declared reproachfully. "Shoo—go away."

He shrugged. "I wish we could go away, little lady. Afraid we can't. But at least we're safe here—for the time being. What's that about a dream? Your Aramaic is a little too quick for me. How do you feel?"

"I—I—" She stopped. A strange idea occurred to her. That smell in the room—musty and dank—she had seen and heard many things in her dreams, but— She rose. She walked over to touch the Roman breastplate with one finger. She could feel the cold iron.

He began to smile, and for some reason that frightened her. She quickly pinched her arm, and it hurt. "No", she said breathlessly. "No. No, no—"

By now he understood. "Steady, lady", he said. "You're not dreaming."

"But—but—what happened?" She put her hands to her head, suddenly aware that it ached terribly. "Where am I? Why—"

He saw memory flooding back into her eyes. "Steady", he repeated. "Sit down again. That's it. Now tell me what you remember. Then I'll go on from there."

"I—I—"

"Steady, I said. The bandits set fire to your husband's house, remember that?"

"Y-yes. Oh, there was such excitement. He called all the servants, and some of them ran for arms, and then he said, 'Leave it; the Edomites have chased them away.'"

"The what?"

"He meant the Romans", she said, a little embarrassed. "Then he told us to go to our rooms, Abigail and me. There was no fire there, not even smoke."

He nodded. "Quite right. But then the bandits came into the house, through the back door, is that right? Three men?"

She shuddered. "Yes, they were horrible. They clapped their hands over our faces and dragged us away—"

"Did they say why?"

"One of them said something. Abigail was struggling and—but where are we now? And where is Abigail?"

"Slowly", Cassius said. "Let's take things in order. First you tell your story . . . Just a moment: be quiet, please."

He listened intently, as if he were expecting a noise to come from the ceiling, no, from the top of a small staircase, leading up to—where?

But there was no noise, and he turned back. "You can go on now. You said somebody was struggling with Abbi—Abi—"

"Abigail. She is my maid. She used to be my nurse. Where is she? It is not fitting that I should be here alone with you, you know—she will be very angry when she comes."

"That's the old woman who came with you to the Antonia, isn't it?"

"Yes, but she's not so very old. She wouldn't like you to say that."

"Probably not. Anyway, she was struggling, and one of the bandits said something to her, right?"

She stared at him, bewildered. "You're a dream after all. Please, say that you are a dream, please!"

"What *did* the bandit say to her?" Cassius asked firmly, and the terror came back in her eyes.

"He said, 'We want you two, and you are going to tell us what kind of business you were carrying on at the Antonia.' "

He whistled through his teeth. "Now we know", he said dryly. "I wondered about that. Might have been just ransom, of course. So they wanted to interrogate you and your maid. Then what happened?"

"They dragged us out by the back door, and I kicked the one who held me as hard as I could, and I am sure Abigail did, too; she is very strong, you know. She can lift me up easily."

"You don't weigh very much." His smile died quickly. "Go on."

"I don't really know what happened then. I think I screamed, but I couldn't scream very loud, because that man was holding his hand over my face." She shook her head with disgust. "And Abigail screamed, but only once, but then I suppose they stopped her, too."

"They did", Cassius said. "What else do you know?"

"N-nothing. Yes—they held us behind the house for a while, and one of them said, 'It won't be long now before the fire is out.' "

"Then they saw me coming and ran away with you."

"I didn't see you at all. That man's hand was so big, I couldn't see anything. They made me run, and I lost my breath and—I know nothing more, really I don't."

"Very well", he said. "Now here is my part. You fainted. I caught up with you and the bandits and took you away from them. Then some more of their friends turned up, and I got you into the nearest house and down into the cellar. And that's where we are now."

Suddenly her eyes widened. "You are wounded; you are bleeding."

He looked where she was pointing and shook his head. "No, lady." He threw the piece of cloth into a dusty corner. "One of the bandits got too near my sword. I had to clean it with that rag. A soldier must keep his arms clean, you know. Forgot to put it away before you came to."

To his astonishment she looked at him with something very much like compassion. "It must be very terrible to be a soldier", she said.

"Not really." He grinned. "And we have our uses sometimes—it seems."

She blushed. "I am very ungrateful", she said in a choked voice. "You did it to help me, didn't you?"

"As it happened, I did, yes."

"I am stupid", she said, "I cannot think right. My thoughts all run about in my mind like ants."

"You should lie down a little and close your eyes. You've had a rough time, little lady."

"I think you are a good man", she said in a trembling voice. "Please let me go home now. I—I think I can walk."

"Of course you can." He scratched his head under the helmet. "But I'm afraid we can't go home just yet."

"Why not?"

"Because they're waiting for us up there." He pointed with his head. "I told you before—the trouble is not over yet."

"But—Abigail will be so worried! My husband will be worried, too. And it is—it is *not* right that I should be sitting here alone with you. Really, it isn't. You must understand that. It—it is important."

"Oh, certainly", he nodded. "I am fully aware of it."

She looked at him doubtfully. She knew that it was hopeless to try to understand an Edomite. They had nothing in common with Jewish people. Most of the men drank a lot and sometimes got terribly drunk, and then they beat their wives; she had always heard that. She had often felt sorry for Edomite wives: the procurator's wife, for instance. It was impossible to know whether this Roman commander meant what he said or whether he was mocking her.

"Then we must do something at once", she said resolutely.

He folded his arms around his knee and began to swing his leg back and forth. "You're a hopelessly spoiled brat, aren't you?"

She lifted her chin. "That is not a courteous thing to say."

He was exasperated now. "Look, lady, you seem to be sufficiently awake to understand what I'm telling you. There are at least half a dozen bandits sitting up there, waiting for an opportunity to kill me and to drag you away again and do their—interrogating. Which I think you will not enjoy. There were about a dozen more outside a short while ago, and I have no reason whatever to believe that they have gone. Will you tell me what you want me to do about it? Shall I ask them to come down and join us here—as it is unfitting for you to be alone with me?"

"You are a commander", she answered promptly. "Tell them to go away. Then we can go home."

He glared at her. Was this as naïve as it sounded? Or did it not rather signify the deep contempt these people had in their hearts for everything that was not Jewish? Perhaps she was really saying, "You are an officer of the occupation forces, aren't you? Very well then, show it, if you can. Get a perfectly innocent lady of good family and breeding out of an impossible situation and be quick about it—lest it be said that Roman protection is worth nothing."

For a moment he seriously thought of going up the staircase and fighting it out. But that was sheer bravado, madness. To hold this one-man fortress was the only chance he had. And it irked him that her words should have such an effect on him.

"Perhaps you don't take these bandits very seriously", he said sharply. "You'd better, though. I'd hate to see you end up like your maid or nurse or whatever she was."

"Abigail? What do you mean?"

"They killed her." He had tried to avoid telling her; now it gave him a kind of ugly satisfaction, but the instant the words were spoken, he regretted them.

"Oh, no", she said. And suddenly she looked again like a little girl, a child. "You don't mean that, please say you don't, please . . ."

He looked away. "I'm sorry, but it's true. They stabbed her when she screamed. I found her."

She broke down completely. She hid her face in the dirty rug on the couch and sobbed convulsively.

He felt desperately uncomfortable. He felt, as a matter of fact, unhappier than he had ever been before, but a new sort of unhappiness that was in some queer way sweet, and good to feel. He was ashamed—a strange sensation. The girl was too lovely to be hurt.

He turned away, walked to the staircase, went up a couple of steps, and listened. Nothing. The only sound was her sobbing, half stifled by the rug on the couch.

He tried to concentrate. What would he do, if he were in command of the bandits outside? Open the door of the hatch and throw down a few burning torches to smoke the enemy out? Nonsense. Of course not. That would be the best way to bring a Roman patrol in no time. If he were alone, he might consider this as a way to escape from this trap. Set the cursed place afire. Give the Antonia a fire signal. But not with the girl. If he were a bandit leader he might try to flood the cellar, flush the enemy out instead of smoking him out. But water was scarce in Jerusalem; they would not be able to get enough.

The poor little thing was still sobbing her heart out. He walked back and sat down next to her. "I know it's sad", he said gruffly. "She was a good soul, I suppose. But she wasn't a close relative...."

She looked up, her face stained with tears. "You don't understand. She was the only friend I had in the world...."

He would have to do something.

He looked around him. Then he walked to the other end of the cellar, where pitchers and jugs were stacked against the wall. Oil, oil again and again, but this one looked like wine. He took off the straw ring, unwound the bark, and poured away the thin layer of oil on top that prevented the wine from going bad. He tasted it. It was not very good, but good enough to serve its purpose. He took a few more sips and walked back to the girl. Gently he lifted her head. "Drink", he said. "No nonsense now; do as you're told."

She obeyed instinctively and gasped.

"More", he ordered severely. "Come on, that's better." The things a man had to do, he thought, determinedly sardonic. Her nursemaid having got herself killed, he had to replace her. "A little more ..."

But she had had enough. He took a deep draught himself. It was coarse wine, but not too bad. "Tell me about the poor old girl", he said. He had heard somewhere that it was a relief to talk about someone one had lost. "Abigail, her name was, wasn't that what you said? I'm sure she was a kindly woman even if she did not like us Romans very much."

"How do you know that?"

He grinned awkwardly. "Well, she still had the strength to tell me that nothing good ever came from dealing with Romans."

"Yes. Yes, that's what she would say . . . " Suddenly the girl sat bolt upright, her eyes aflame. "You—you didn't do anything to her, did you?"

He flushed angrily. "No good may come from dealing with us, but we do not go about stabbing women. We leave that to bandits posing as the liberators of their country."

She hung her head. "I'm sorry", she said wearily. "Of course you didn't harm her. Why should you?"

Now why did he have to make a pompous little speech in defense of great and noble Rome, he of all people? There were a hundred thousand men in Rome who would stab an old woman for a handful of sesterces, or slit an old man's throat, an old man who had gone gray under the helmet, who had been a general.

"Have a little more wine", he said. "Give you strength. Sorry you have to drink straight from the pitcher. No goblets or glasses in this place. Not in the cellar anyway."

She drank a little and then said, "I suppose we shouldn't do that. It's somebody else's wine." She was making a valiant attempt to regain her composure.

Cassius was amused. "Our host won't grudge it to us, I hope. I could always leave him a couple of coins to make up for the loss of property, if you are so much concerned."

This time she knew he was mocking her a little, but it did not hurt. "If he is our host, he should offer us some", she said primly.

"Quite right, lady—look, I'm getting tired of calling you that. This is the third time we have met, and I still don't know your name."

"Naomi."

As she looked down, the little black fans came to rest on her cheeks again. She began to smooth her dress; it was badly mussed, and no wonder.

She looked like a very young Jewish goddess who had come down into a shabby, hostile world. But there was no such thing as a Jewish goddess, of course. Only the one, invisible God in the

Temple with the subterranean corridor leading to barrack number four of the Antonia.

"It's a pity you don't have a Jewish goddess", he said. "You'd fill the part admirably."

"You always mock me when you speak", said Naomi acidly. "And there is no such thing as a goddess."

"Not in your religion there isn't", he replied. "But we have a lot of them. Venus—I wonder what makes me think of her first—and Minerva and Diana, and Juno . . . "

"Do you believe in them all?"

"No."

"In which of them then?"

"In none of them."

It was not possible to understand Gentiles. One might as well try and understand what birds were saying to each other. But perhaps . . .

"Is that why you are so unhappy?" she asked.

"Unhappy? What makes you think I am?"

"You must be. Even when you smile, you make a face as if you had a bitter taste in your mouth."

"Oh . . . "

"Yes. And you said your life was not worth much. Don't you remember?"

"No life is worth much." He shrugged his shoulders. "I don't know that I am particularly unhappy."

"Life can end very suddenly", she said, and her eyes were filling again. "I know that now. Ever since I met you I have known it."

"Ever since you met *me?*"

"Yes. The first time I met you was also the first time that I saw people die quite suddenly. Poor Issachar, and the others. And now Abigail. I don't know how I shall live without her."

"You'll live all right", he said gruffly. "If we get out of here alive, that is."

She said nothing.

"We shall have to wait until morning." He was thinking aloud now. "There will be patrols in the streets again an hour after sunrise. Then we can try to get out."

She looked at him horrified. "We must stay here all night?"

"Life may not be worth much, but there is no need to shorten it unnecessarily."

She rose. "This is quite impossible", she said. "What will my husband say! I can't . . ."

"Your husband would have done better to watch over your safety", he replied grimly, "instead of counting his Phoenician glass and all the other nice things his slaves carried out of the house. Serves him quite right if he is worried about you now. He doesn't deserve any better. How did you come to marry him?"

"I was given in marriage by my relatives."

"Not by your parents?"

"They were both dead by then."

"I see. And did you want to marry him?"

"I was not asked that question then, and I should not be asked now."

The dignity of a princess. He nodded. "You're right, Naomi." He took off his helmet. "But I still think it was a wicked thing to do to you."

He looked much younger without his helmet, that terrible metal thing with the tuft of horsehair on top. Almost like a boy. He *was* unhappy.

"Wicked? Why wicked?"

"How old are you, Naomi?"

"Going on to sixteen. Well, past fifteen anyway. And you?"

"Nearly twenty-five. And your husband?"

"Oh, he is very old. He was married before, but his first wife died. She was a wonderful woman, much better and wiser and more gentle and skillful than I am."

"How do you know? Did you ever meet her?"

"No. Boz, my husband, told me."

"He would. And you would believe him, of course."

"Why, yes, I'm sure I'm not much of a wife. If it weren't for our head servant, everything would be wrong in the house."

"I didn't mean that. What kind of a husband is he to you?"

A sudden angry impatience choked him. She *could* not be so much of a child. After all, a Roman girl of her age would know her way about — would have her third or fourth or seventh lover now, even if her senile husband watched her day and night. Girls always found ways and means. And they matured fast in this country. Was it Abenadar who had said that? Of course, Abenadar believed in Jewish marriage customs. But then he had had a Jewish mother. Anyway, she must know what he was talking about.

Perhaps she did. She made that haughty little princess face again and said, "It is not fitting that I should talk about my husband."

He walked over to her, shaken by the pounding of his heart. "You don't know what life is, do you, little one? All you know is what they taught you when you were a child — this isn't fitting and that isn't fitting. But life is not like that, Naomi." Big eyes, the eyes of a frightened child. The texture of her skin was finer than a Roman girl's, like ivory. Her mouth . . .

"I'll teach you what life is", he muttered.

She struggled in his arms. As his lips sought hers, she turned her head away, only to feel his kisses on her throat, her neck, her burning cheeks. It was wrong; it was forbidden; it must not be. But sweetness welled up in her, a thousand voices whispered that this was the fulfillment of all unspoken wishes, wishes never fully realized, longings never quite conceded. She felt his powerful hands holding her, and she knew that not only she could not escape from him but that she, that something in her, did not want to escape but to surrender, and that surrender was happiness. And now her lips were caught and began to burn and were hungry for more, hungry to give as well as to receive, and all was flame, and with a little cry she yielded.

When she awoke she saw her lover's face above her. He was looking at her intently, as if he were searching for something.

"I dreamed of you again", she said very gravely. "You are here, whether my eyes are open or closed."

"Keep them open then", he said. "I want to see them. I have never seen eyes like yours before. They are real."

"They are yours", she murmured humbly.

"They are real", he repeated. Almost harshly he added, "You are not a ghost. You are wonderfully real. I didn't know I would ever . . ." His voice trailed off. He smiled at her. He looked happy and very young.

She felt deeply moved because he looked so happy. He is changed, she thought. I have changed him. But then she was afraid. The oil lamp was still burning. Impossible to say whether it was still night outside. But the day would come and then — what then?

He kissed her, and she forgot night and day.

She could feel him stir at her side. When she looked up, she saw him standing at the foot of the staircase, listening. And shield and sword were in his hands.

Swiftly she rose too. Her hands busied themselves with dress and hair, but her heart hammered, and for the first time she really felt trapped, trapped like an animal.

There was a faint noise from above, and at once he raced up several steps, his sword ready to strike.

The door of the hatch was lifted. A face appeared in the opening, and with a sudden stab of fear she recognized it.

The face withdrew at once.

"It is Serubabel", she whispered. "My husband's cousin."

Her face was ashen. He saw it and bit his lip. There was a

terrible stillness in the room. The walls stared at her mutely. She put her hands before her face. She heard Serubabel say, "There is no further need to hide", with no expression whatever in his voice.

The man she loved put on his armor and his helmet. He whispered something to her, but she did not hear the words. She felt icy cold. He went up the staircase, and she followed, and every step was a step nearer to something indescribably horrible. If only she could have stayed forever in the gray musty cellar. But even that was no longer friendly.

The man she loved was speaking to Serubabel. It was quite a lengthy explanation, and Serubabel listened very carefully, his eyes fixed on her all the time. There were four servants with him, servants of his own; she did not know any of them.

"We had to use the cellar as a fortress. It was the only thing we could do and the only way to keep the bandits out."

Serubabel nodded somberly. "Most unfortunate", he said, still looking at her. "I have a litter outside", he added.

"How did you find the place?"

For the first time Serubabel looked at Cassius. "There are several searching parties", he said. "And people will talk. There are Roman patrols looking for you, too, commander. The streets are quiet at present. So, if you will permit me, I shall escort the Lady Naomi home to her husband."

"Of course. I shall come with you and report to him what happened."

"There is no need for that", said Serubabel tonelessly. "I shall pass on everything you have told me, word for word."

Cassius looked at him sharply. "I do not doubt that in the least. Nevertheless I shall come with you."

Serubabel shrugged his lean shoulders. "As you wish, commander."

The way back was short. No further word was spoken. When they arrived at the house, Serubabel helped Naomi to descend from the litter. His hands were clammy.

One wing of the house was burned badly; it looked black and threatening.

She stumbled over some rubble, and Serubabel held her up quickly, before Cassius could reach over to her. She did not dare to look at him.

She was led, past gaping servants, to her rooms. There she was left alone.

Cassius waited outside in the courtyard. To force one's way into the house would have made matters worse. It was bad luck. If they had left an hour earlier—but they would still have had to explain. Same thing, more or less. Curse it, it was not their fault that they had had to take refuge from those rioting rascals! If it were anyone's fault at all, it was that of the old man for paying more attention to his possessions than to his wife. His wife! His showpiece, the symbol of his senile vanity, not his wife!

Cassius had good reasons for insisting on seeing Boz in person.

First of all he would not sneak away. Moreover he did not trust that sinister-looking cousin. And finally it might be a good thing to ram the point home that the girl had been under the protection of a Roman officer—just in case they had any funny ideas.

If only little Naomi kept her head. He had told her to, of course, but he doubted if she had heard what he said.

Boz bar Sebulun stepped out, leaning heavily on his cousin's shoulder.

Cassius remembered him as an excited old man. Now he was quiet, but he seemed to have aged twenty years. His eyes had sunk in; his jaw and his hands were trembling. He was a pitiful sight.

"I crave the commander's pardon for not asking him to enter my poor house." The voice seemed to come from out of a tomb. "The fire has done much damage, and I am ill."

Cassius gave him a courteous bow. "I hope your health will soon be restored. It gives me pleasure at least to be able to reassure you about your lady's safety. No doubt your cousin has already told you that she was attacked by bandits and that I succeeded in freeing her, but that . . . "

"He has told me all this, commander, and I am quite satisfied that you did everything in your power to protect her against — the bandits. I shall write to the procurator accordingly. Now if you will forgive me . . . "

More bows. And the door closed behind Boz and his cousin.

All one could do for the moment, Cassius thought. An absurd situation. But it would have been the same even if nothing had happened between them. Her family's sense of decorum would have been outraged; they would have made the same remarks and the same speeches. It was only because he knew what he knew that he worried. If Naomi kept her head, all would be well, for the time being. Later — he could not think of that yet.

Then a Roman patrol came from the direction of the Antonia, with Calvus in command. There was some back slapping and joking, and they returned together to the Antonia, where Cassius also had to make a report and give an explanation for his absence.

It was ridiculous to feel so worried.

An hour after Naomi's return the family council was in session. Boz bar Sebulun was huddled in the high-backed chair. The physician who had been with him most of the night entreated him to go to bed, but the old man stubbornly refused.

Many of his relatives had never approved of his second marriage, although few of them had dared to say so, and none of them directly to his face. It was not only that the girl was too young. She did not come from their set, although her family was quite respectable. There were also those to whom the marriage meant a very definite disappointment materially. She could not legally inherit his fortune, but she would have to be provided for in accordance with her rank.

But unsuitable as the marriage undoubtedly was, no one could have expected *this* to happen. What "this" meant was clear enough to anyone who had listened to cousin Serubabel's terse, factual report. First the report of how he had found Naomi, where and with whom. Then the explanatory report of the Roman officer, as given to cousin Serubabel. There was a slight edge to his tone that detached him from that second report.

Cousin Joab was not satisfied. He suggested that the whole story of bandits and kidnapping was pure invention and that the Edomite probably broke into the house himself.

Serubabel disagreed sharply. Roman officers were under orders of their High Command to protect the houses of those who preferred to live in peace with the Roman authorities rather than make common cause with highway robbers. Did cousin Joab suggest that the Roman officer had acted in open rebellion against his own superiors? No, *that* part of the Roman's story was undoubtedly quite true.

Cousin Joab stuck to his opinion. They had only the Edomite's word. He saw no reason for believing it. Surely such a man was quite capable of an act of violence? And why should Freedom Party men, or highway robbers, as cousin Serubabel preferred to call them, steal a woman? What good would it do them? Hold her for ransom, by any chance? Here, in the heart of Jerusalem?

For a moment Serubabel was nonplused. He mentioned, somewhat lamely, that according to the Roman Naomi had been kidnapped by the bandits because they wished to interrogate her about an alleged visit to the Antonia, but he himself did not feel that this sounded like the truth, and cousin Joab gave a snort and said that it was obviously a lie. Why should the wife of Boz bar Sebulun pay a visit to the Antonia?

Here Boz himself interfered. "The visit took place. We sent some presents to the Roman officer as a token of our gratitude for his intervention when my caravan was attacked."

"If that is so," said cousin Joab, hastily concealing his astonishment, "it seems that the Roman thought these presents not enough, and so he took that which was not given him."

Cousin Serubabel said that such a remark was uncalled for and that the situation was not one that could be dealt with in a spirit of levity, at which cousin Joab protested angrily.

Boz cut them both short. "The visit to the Antonia was an official visit to express our thanks. It may have been wrongly interpreted by the bandits. Conspirators always think that everybody must be conspiring all the time. And I wish you would stop speculating and arguing about things that do not concern you. I begin to think that I should have dealt with the matter alone."

The two cousins had black looks for each other. The worst thing that could happen was for Boz to divert his wrath to the family.

Suddenly the old man burst into tears. All he wanted was peace and quiet for what little span of life was still allowed to him. If Naomi was guilty he would divorce her at once, of course. But she should not go unheard. He himself would ask her the questions. He needed no guardian. After all, perhaps the Roman had forced himself upon her.

Serubabel bit his lip. All the girl had to do was to deny any guilt, and the matter would be closed. If only cousin Joab had kept his stupid mouth shut. She was guilty, of course, and if he had been allowed to go on in his own way, he could have made it clear to everybody, even to the old dodderer, that Boz bar Sebulun would be the laughingstock of the whole city if he did not rid himself of her. Now Boz would put the right defense into her mouth by the way he questioned her.

Naomi was called in.

Boz did not look at her. He asked her whether the Roman officer had forced himself upon her against her will.

She said no.

Boz, still looking away from her, asked his next question: "Are you innocent?"

There was a breathless silence. Then she lifted her head and said in a very low voice, but quite clearly, "I love him."

XV

Rabbi Josaphat and some of his learned friends were watching the crowd in the Temple court.

"At least five hundred of them", said Ruben, the chief scribe of the treasury. "And all around him like moths around a candle."

"Common folk, as usual." Rabbi Josaphat nodded. "Listening to another of his little parables, no doubt. They are clay in his hands. None of them knows anything about the Law. He can tell them what he likes; they will swallow it whole. There—still more are joining them."

"Why, the man behaves as if he owned the Temple! And his statements are becoming intolerable. I cannot understand why Kohen Gadol still hesitates . . . "

"We've been through all that before, Ruben. There is a time for everything. His time will come, believe me. Moths will fly around a candle, but every candle burns itself out—or it is snuffed out. I am collecting material . . . "

But the chief scribe was not listening. He was looking toward a small group of well-dressed men who were entering the gate escorting a prisoner. And the prisoner was a woman.

"Isn't that Serubabel?" Rabbi Josaphat asked. "Boz bar Sebulun's cousin? And Joab, too?" He pursed his lips. "I think I must find out a little more about this. It may be interesting. Come with me, Ruben? Wait for us here, friends."

They sauntered over. "I find it hard to believe," Rabbi Josaphat muttered under his breath, "but the prisoner is Boz bar Sebulun's wife."

"But why? What can she have done?"

"In the case of a woman," said Rabbi Josaphat, "the possibilities are fairly limited." He gave the Sadducee's formal greeting. "You are going to see the judge in a legal matter, no doubt?"

Serubabel agreed coldly. Meeting some of the Pharisee crowd here was unavoidable, but he did not relish their ways.

"And the lady?" asked Rabbi Josaphat politely.

No use trying to hide the shame. It would be talked about in the city in any case. Serubabel said brusquely, "This woman was caught in adultery."

Rabbi Josaphat arched his eyebrows. "A grave accusation. Is the evidence complete? Two witnesses?"

"She has admitted the crime", Serubabel said pointedly. He would not have any hairsplitting on this issue. This thing had to be finished and finished quickly, lest Boz change his mind despite the woman's admission.

Rabbi Josaphat's eyes shifted from Serubabel to the courtyard of the Temple, now more crowded than ever, and back again.

"You are fortunate, if I may be allowed to say so on such an unhappy occasion", he remarked. "A learned rabbi is teaching here, and I am told that he has great authority with many people. You can take your case before him at once instead of waiting for the ordinary court."

Serubabel looked doubtful, the more so as Chief Scribe Ruben seemed to be a little surprised at the suggestion. "Are we to rely on the decision of just any rabbi?" he asked. "Who is he?"

Rabbi Josaphat smiled. "I'll come with you," he said, "and so will friend Ruben here, I'm sure. If the man's judgment is not according to the Law, we shall be quick to set things right."

"Oh, very well then." Serubabel agreed with bad grace; he was not anxious to antagonize a man of Rabbi Josaphat's standing.

So Serubabel and Joab, holding Naomi between them, two cousins of the second degree who had taken part in the family meeting, Rabbi Josaphat, and the chief scribe walked together toward the court.

"Why did you do this?" murmured Ruben. "It will look as if we believed in the man's authority."

Rabbi Josaphat had little patience with a slow-thinking man. "Don't you understand?" His voice sank to a whisper. "You know as well as I do what the Law is and . . . "

He had to break off, as Serubabel was looking at them. They reached the outer edge of the crowd.

"Make room", said the chief scribe aloud.

Before the voice of authority and the fringed robes the people recoiled right and left, letting the group pass through their midst.

Now the teaching rabbi's voice could be heard: "Believe me, the time is coming, nay, has already come, when the dead will listen to the voice of the Son of God, and those who listen to it will live. As the Father has within him the gift of life, so he has granted to the Son that he too should have within him the gift of life, and has also granted him powers to execute judgment, since he is the Son of Man."

Rabbi Josaphat sucked in his breath sharply. A wave of astonishment swept over the crowd.

"Do not be surprised at that", came the voice of the teaching rabbi. "The time is coming when all those who are in their graves will hear his voice and will come out of them, those whose actions have been good, rising to new life, and those whose doings have been evil, rising to meet their sentence."

The little group had pierced the center of the crowd and stood in full view of the teacher. Rabbi Josaphat smiled, as if to say, "We do not wish to interrupt, but if you have a moment for us . . . "

The teaching rabbi looked at him questioningly and at the woman prisoner and the two men holding her wrists and again at him.

Rabbi Josaphat cleared his throat. "Master, this woman has been caught in the act of adultery."

A whisper passed between the people. Some faces became dark and angry, but most seemed frightened more than anything else, and many looked with pity at the forlorn little figure held by two strong men.

Rabbi Josaphat took it all in. It was exactly the reaction he expected. He waited for a little while and then continued, "Moses, in his Law, prescribed that such persons should be stoned to death. What of thee? What is thy sentence?"

And now at last Rabbi Josaphat saw a flicker of understanding on the chief scribe's face, and he suppressed a smile of triumph. The great demagogue, the great rabble-rouser — this time he was caught and caught properly. If he dared speak for mercy, he thereby acted openly against the Law of Moses. If he acknowledged the Law, most of these people would think him a harsh and unbending judge who clung to the letter of the Law. In short, they would say of him what he had so often said about the Pharisees.

The Rabbi Yeshua said nothing. The people stared at him, silent now and waiting. He leaned down and began writing on the ground with his finger. There were some who craned their necks to see what he was writing, but they were not near enough.

Rabbi Josaphat gave the chief scribe a quick glance, and Ruben answered with a little nod of profound admiration. The miracle man was trapped. And Rabbi Josaphat had thought of all this in one short minute, when he saw the Sadducees with their prisoner. What a brain he had!

Still the Galilean said nothing.

"We are all awaiting your sentence", cried Rabbi Josaphat, and this time he did not even try to keep the triumph out of his voice. "What is it to be?"

The Rabbi Yeshua looked up at last, first at his interrogator, then at the chief scribe, at Serubabel and Joab and the other cousins and at the crowd around him. He said aloud, "Whichever of you is free from sin shall cast the first stone at her."

And he leaned down again and went on writing on the ground as before.

It was then really that Rabbi Josaphat showed the quickness of his perception. He had asked for a sentence, and it had been given. But it had been given in such a way that everyone now had to pass sentence on himself. He turned away abruptly, his lips pressed tightly together, and pushed his way out of the crowd. It was rare for him to be the loser in an argument, too rare for him not to be aware of it when it happened. He went so quickly that the crowd had no time to react to his flight. But as the chief scribe also slipped away, there was a rustle as of leaves dancing joyfully in the wind. Some faces looked sheepish, others sullen, but most broke into smiles. Some men even dared to laugh, but not for long—only until it dawned on them that they also must answer to their consciences. A steadily growing trickle of men followed in the wake of the chief scribe. Soon the trickle became a flood.

Serubabel, bewildered, looked about him. Joab murmured something unintelligible and turned away.

"Wait!" Serubabel fairly ran after him. "Wait for me, cousin."

Naomi stood alone in front of the judge.

From the moment when they had seized her at the house of her husband and led her through the streets, she had never looked up. She had seen nothing but the ground under her feet.

But now the judge addressed her: "Woman, where are thy accusers?"

She was forced to look up now as the sunflower looks up at the sun. She looked straight into the judge's eyes, and at once her world dissolved.

"Has no one condemned thee?" asked the judge.

She heard herself say, as from afar, "No one—Lord."

The judge said, "I will not condemn thee either."

225

She stood, gazing into his face.

Once more the judge spoke: "Go, and do not sin again henceforward."

She fell on her knees and bowed her head to the ground. Then she rose in obedience and walked away into a new world.

The Rabbi Yeshua remained alone. The wind blew across the wide Temple yard, carrying grains of sand, blotting out what a finger had written on the ground.

Naomi walked through the new streets of the new city. Neither the longing of her heart nor a thought in her mind told her where to go. He had not told her where to go. He had simply said, "Go." So she had gone. "Go, and do not sin again. . . . Go."

Somebody addressed her, a woman, an elderly woman. She knew her, but she could not remember who she was. The woman spoke kindly to her and began to walk beside her. It was only when she found herself standing before a door she knew, before the door of her husband's house, that she realized the good woman had taken her there, believing that she was ill and in her illness had lost her way.

She did not knock at the door. She sat down on the doorstep and waited. She could think of nothing else to do.

After a while the door opened, and somebody looked at her.

She rose and turned. It was the head servant. He said, "The master says you are not to enter his house again." The door closed.

She stood there for a while. Then she left.

She walked a long time before it occurred to her that it was necessary to ask someone where she would find the judge again. That was all that mattered now, finding him again.

He was no longer in the Temple. She knew that, although she could not have explained how she knew it.

He was the house she had to go to. And where he was was the Temple.

226

She asked a passerby, "Where do I find the Rabbi Yeshua?" He gave no answer and hurried on.

She asked another man. "I don't know, lady. I wish I could find him myself."

She asked a woman, who looked at her and said sharply, "Oh, it's you, is it? Must you go and parade your shame in front of everybody? Be glad your sentence was so light and go home and hide that face of yours that tempted a man who was not your husband."

Her words fell on the ground like little stones thrown by children in a childish game. She talked of things that no longer existed, things of a life sunk into the past, forgiven and gone irretrievably.

Naomi walked on. She came to the Eye of the Needle, the narrowest gate of the city. A baker passed her with a load of freshly baked bread, and she smelled the fragrance of it and knew that she was very hungry. She was so hungry that she felt faint. She had to sit down. She drew an end of her veil across her face so that people could pass by without being scandalized by the woman who no longer existed.

When she felt that she could walk again, she went up to the gate and asked the guard, "Do you know where the Rabbi Yeshua is?"

The guard towered over her. He was one of the city guards, a Jerusalemite, not a Roman. High above her head he said, "Are you one of his people?"

"Yes", Naomi said.

"He passed through here, not so long ago", said the guard. "Only a few men with him. I don't know where he has gone."

She thanked him and started walking again. When she was halfway through the gate, she heard the guard's voice behind her: "Try Bethany."

She gave a little bow and went on. Bethany was not very far.

Bethany was not very far when one was fresh and rested or

being carried in a litter. It was immensely far when every step was an effort, when one's knees were wobbly and one's throat parched.

Twice on her way she stopped to rest. After the second time she did not dare stop again because she knew she would not be able to get up again.

Once more she saw nothing but the ground under her aching feet, stone and twigs and earth and dried seeds.

Bethany was a village of few houses. She did not pause at the first house, or at the second or third, but went straight on, past a group of old men sitting together on a wooden bench, past a number of children playing in the street. She was covered with dust and perspiration; her eyes were smarting. At the fourth house, the door opened.

She stopped then.

There was a woman standing in the door. She was tall, and though her face was in the shadow of the doorway, she seemed to be young. She asked, "Are you looking for someone?" Her voice was deep and smooth, a golden voice.

Naomi said, "I am looking for Rabbi Yeshua."

Her heart beat many times before the woman spoke again.

"What do you want of him?"

What did she want of him?

"I have nowhere else to go", she said.

The woman stepped out of the shadow. She was very beautiful, so incredibly beautiful that Naomi gazed at her open-mouthed.

"You look very tired", said the woman. She put her arm over Naomi's shoulder. "Come into the house and rest."

The few steps were agony. But the house was cool inside. With a little sigh Naomi sank into the chair she was led to. "You are very good", she murmured.

"Only God is good", the woman answered cheerfully. "That is what *he* says when people call him good. What is your name?"

"Naomi. I am . . . I used to be . . . "

"None of us here is what we used to be. He changes us. I think he has changed you. I am Miriam. They used to call me Miriam of Migdal. Rabbi Yeshua is not here at present. I don't know when he will come."

He was not here. She did not know when he would come.

"You said you had nowhere to go. Stay with us, then", Miriam said. "This house belongs to my brother Eleazar and my sister Martha. They will be glad to have you here."

"I don't know", whispered Naomi. "They may not want me to stay. I—I am . . . "

"I know who you are." Miriam of Migdal smiled. "You are a woman he did not condemn. And so am I. You and I, we are sisters. Stay here, little sister, and be happy."

"I am happy", said Naomi. She smiled too. "I have never been so happy. Why is that?" Then she fainted.

BOOK THREE

I

The weeks following the Feast of Tabernacles were very quiet. The pilgrims had left the city to spread the tale all over Judaea, Galilee, and beyond—a tale of bloodshed and calamity, of death and the invincible power of Rome.

There were many who asked whether Rabbi Yeshua had been there and what he had said and whether he had been fighting in the forefront of those who struggled against the iron wall of the legions, and they were told that he had appeared only when the battle was over and lost and that he seemed sad and also strangely impatient about it; also that he told them to repent—not of having fought or of having lost the fight, but of their sins. Some thought they grasped the meaning of his words: they ought to have purified themselves before the battle.

And Ephraim bar Saul was dead, and so were Eliud and Achim bar Simeon—and Bar Abbas was a prisoner of the Romans, as were Gestas and Dysmas. Who would lead the Freedom Party into battle now?

There was a rumor that the High Priest himself would do so in person and another that Kohen Gadol was a traitor and in the pay of the Romans and a third that he himself had spread the rumor of his leadership in order to bring the Freedom Party under his control.

The Pharisees, as always, spoke for peace: sensible, reasonable men, exasperated by the kind of talk that would lead only to more bloodshed and more calamity. The Pharisees, of course, were for cowardly submission, for licking the boots of the alien conqueror, for keeping Israel in Roman captivity.

What was a man to believe? What was a man to do?

Old men sat in front of their little houses in Moreshethgath and Gedor, in Anaharath and Megiddo, in Rimmon and Chorazin, gravely discussing it with their neighbors. Farmers talked about it across their fields; men shouted at each other in the courts of the synagogues; they quarreled in barns and argued with red faces in fishing boats. The dyers and the weavers talked about it, the carpenters and the sandalmakers, the water carriers and the shepherds, even the beggars, even the pickpockets in Caesarea, Joppa, Gaza, Jericho, and Migdal. And as usual, the great majority of the people said, "Let the hotheads and firebrands kill themselves if they want to. All I want is a good harvest this year and no increase in taxation."

The Messiah? He would come some day, without doubt he would, was it not written so in Scripture? But why should he come now?

Most of the hotheads as well as the peaceful people could not read or write; they had to rely on the learned men and on the interpretation they gave to this passage or that. Now it seemed that these learned men, Pharisees first and foremost, and Scribes, did not think that the Messiah was likely to appear in the foreseeable future. Surely they ought to know? Who could possibly know, if they did not?

And deep down in their hearts many hoped that he would not come within their lifetime. However glorious the age he would herald and indeed create, it was bound to mean a great upheaval and a great disturbance of their peaceful life, however burdened that life might be . . .

Cassius came up the stairs to the gallery of the Antonia. Just as he had expected, he found Abenadar in his favorite spot, having a sunbath. There was no celebration this time, no wine and no figs, only a couple of hours' rest on a routine day.

They nodded to each other, and Cassius sat down wearily.

"You ill, son?" asked Abenadar.

"No."

"You don't look too good, you know."

"Tired, that's all. Been on patrol."

"What, again? It wasn't your turn, it was..."

"I know. Mela's turn. I asked him to give it to me."

"You've been doing that often lately", Abenadar said. "Why?"

Cassius smiled wanly. "Mere boredom, I suppose. I—I like having a look around. You never know what you may find."

"Well, and did you find anything?"

"No. Let's change the subject, shall we? Is there any news?"

Abenadar stretched himself in the sun. "Well, yes, there is. The procurator is leaving at last."

"Is he! That'll make Sosius happy. He can get his rooms back. Probably take him some months to get the lady's scent out of them, though. I don't know why the old man stayed on so long, do you? Everybody knows he hates Jerusalem, and if I know anything about her she hates it even more."

"I don't know about that", said Abenadar. "But I have an idea that the procurator wanted *all* the reports to go off to Rome before he left—if you see what I mean."

"No, I don't see what you mean. Stop talking like the Delphic oracle and give it to me straight."

Abenadar glanced about. Then he said, "While the procurator is here, he has to see every report that leaves headquarters— including those of the legate."

"Ah. And Sosius?"

"Is probably not exactly happy about the fact that Pilatus made very little of the battle during the feast and did not mention the admirable leadership of the Legate Sosius at all."

"I see—but why didn't he?"

"Because it never pays a procurator to boast about quelling a revolution or rebellion or whatever you want to call it. The kind of procurator they like in Rome is the one in whose province

233

everything is nice and quiet. Shows he is doing good work. So it's no laurels for Sosius. And if the procurator had left, say, a week ago, Sosius could have written a little report of his own—it would have just reached the mail ship in time. Of course he thinks he saved the day and feels cheated."

"The man who saved the day was a centurion by the name of Cassius Longinus", said Cassius. "If it hadn't been for the arrival of a certain fruit basket, both the old man and Sosius would have been taken by surprise, and that might have made quite a difference."

"The old man was furious with Vindex", Abenadar said thoughtfully. "He thinks Vindex should have known something at least about a plan of such dimensions. But he is even more furious against the Jews. And he's the sort of man who never forgets. So he's going to give the Jews a little memento during his next visit here."

"That would be the Passover, in the spring, I suppose."

"That's right. The Feast of the Unleavened Bread. And that is when he will have Bar Abbas and his two henchmen crucified."

"Did he say that?"

"Yes. I was there, and so were Sosius and Vindex. The old man was in a bad mood. I always know. He's got a trick of speaking out of the corner of his mouth when he is. 'Rome is very lenient', he said, meaning himself. 'Rome will not interfere with the religious customs of the nations she rules over. But Rome will see to it that no one else interferes either. It will be a good thing to remind some people of what happens to those who disturb a feast.' "

"Bar Abbas was popular", Cassius said. "Probably still is. The Jews won't like it."

"They're not expected to like it."

"The Passover is one of their greatest feasts, isn't it?"

"Yes. Thanksgiving for having been liberated from bondage in Egypt. Well, Pilatus is going to make quite sure that there will be no confusion between Pharaoh and Caesar."

Cassius stared into space. He said nothing.

Abenadar shook his head. "My dear boy, there is something wrong with you. You've lost weight. You say you're not ill. If it weren't you, I'd say you're in love."

"To Hades with you", said Cassius.

"Seriously, son," Abenadar put his hand on Cassius' shoulder, "why don't you tell me what it's all about? Maybe I could help you."

"You can't help me", Cassius said tonelessly. Then he began to talk, quickly, almost breathlessly, as if he wanted to get it all out before his pride got the better of him again: the whole story, from his first meeting with Naomi to the moment when he last saw Boz bar Sebulun.

Abenadar listened quietly. "Then what did you do?"

"I knew it would be dangerous for her if I tried to get in touch with her, so I had the house kept under constant surveillance under the pretext that there might be another attack."

"When did you do that?"

"The very next day. None of my men saw her leave the house."

"Jewish women don't go out much", Abenadar said. "On the other hand she may have left the house the day before your men started watching it. Go on."

"I wrote a letter to the old man, inquiring about his precious health and, by-the-by, also about that of his lady."

"No answer", Abenadar said.

"None. So I got really worried. I thought of trying to bribe one of the servants with Boz' own gold, but the fellow could have told me a bunch of lies and then reported it to Boz, so I didn't do it. After a week I was so worried, I went straight to the house and asked for Boz. They made me wait outside again, curse them, and then the head servant came and told me his master regretted very much that he was too ill to see me. I asked whether the lady had recovered, and the fellow said with a sneer, 'The lady is not here anymore.' I asked, 'What do you mean? Where is she? And he closed the door in my face. Then I thought of what you told me about the Jews, and the stiff views they have about everything concerning their womenfolk . . . "

"It was a little late in the day to think of that", Abenadar said curtly.

"D-do you think they've done something to her?"

The stark terror in Cassius' eyes made Abenadar relent. "I don't know, son. I hope not."

"I tried all sorts of idiotic things, joined patrols or led them, searched houses for arms—all the time looking for a trace of her. No result, of course. Abenadar, is there anything I can do, anything . . . ?"

"No, son", Abenadar said gently. "You've done far too much as it is. You can't change what happened. Leave it alone."

"I love her", Cassius blurted out. "She—is real. I don't know how to explain what I mean. . . . "

Abenadar nodded. "I think I know."

Cassius was on his way to his quarters when he heard the voice behind him: "Centurion Longinus!"

He turned round and stiffened. It was the procurator's wife. Behind her was one of her maids, a young Jewess—he had seen her before.

"A word with you, Centurion Longinus", Claudia said quietly.

There was no escape. She walked ahead of him to the small terrace in front of the legate's, now the procurator's, series of rooms. She sat down on a couch and beckoned him to a chair. "You may go now, Judith."

Cassius sat stiffly, as if awaiting some official instructions. He refused to give her the satisfaction of looking angry or even tense. He was both. She certainly knew, she was bound to know that he avoided her, yet she had chosen to force this meeting. She would not get any pleasure out of it.

"The procurator and I are leaving this afternoon for Caesarea", said Claudia Procula. "Perhaps you have heard."

"Yes, noble lady."

She sighed. "I hate leaving here."

He saw that she had aged, aged beyond her years. There was a network of small wrinkles around her eyes, and the corners of her mouth were beginning to droop. A few more years and it would be the mouth of a resigned old woman, he thought. Yet she could still be called a beautiful woman. It was quite incomprehensible that he had been in love with her only four years ago.

"Surely Caesarea offers you a far more congenial atmosphere", he said coldly. "There is not a single theater in Jerusalem.... "

"A theater ... " She gave him a tired smile. "Yes, I suppose there was a time when that might have made a difference—perhaps to both of us? We change, but it is difficult for us to conceive that other people change, too. I am no longer what I was in Rome."

"No", said Cassius dryly. "You are the wife of the procurator of Judaea."

"Yes. Instead of being that most vulnerable, that most pitiful creature, a young unmarried woman, living alone in Rome and trying to put up a brave front and worrying day after day how long I would be able to go on. But then, you have been through much worse. We were both children then—although I remember I lied to you about my age." That tired smile again.

I don't hate her any longer, he thought, and was mildly surprised. She is not worth hating. Fleetingly he thought of old Abenadar and what he said about meeting enemies again after many years. But Claudia was only Claudia: she was not Spurio—not Balbus—not Sejanus. She was hardly even Claudia.

"I did not call you to talk about myself", Claudia said. "I want to talk about you."

"About me?" He was too surprised not to show it.

"At least about something that concerns you. You must admit

that I've never made use of my—position, so far as you are concerned."

"Not until now", he said.

She looked past him toward the roof of the Temple. "You may go at once, if you wish. But I hope you will bear with me a few more moments. I want to ask you a question first. It is about the young woman you saved from the bandits."

He stared at her. "What do you know about that?" His voice was dangerously steady.

"Ordinarily I would know little or nothing", she replied. "But here in Jerusalem it is different. We are very much cramped for space; conferences and meetings and discussions of all kinds go on in front of my door and even in my rooms, and so I hear a good deal, whether I want to or not. Besides, my husband trusts me, I think."

"So did I—once." He could not hold it back.

She frowned. "My good Cassius, I ceased being important to you a long time ago. And surely you also are no longer the child you were in Rome. You can't be."

"Maybe not. But you were not a child then, noble lady. You knew exactly what you were doing."

"Did I? Does anybody? Perhaps that's the only thing that will save us all one day—that we do not know what we do." There was no bitterness in her tone. He could not make her out. But she had mentioned Naomi. Perhaps—it was just an off chance—perhaps she did know something. Vindex was in and out of these rooms, and he got all the agents' reports. The Centurion Cassius Longinus could not ask the Tribune Vindex about the reports—certainly not without giving himself away. The Centurion Cassius Longinus could only try to ferret out things on his own.

He asked point blank: "Do you know anything about the young woman you mentioned? Anything at all?"

"I know that she is alive", said Claudia Procula softly. Poor Cassius, sitting there, rigid as a statue while his eyes revealed everything.

"How do you know?" he asked after a moment.

"I will tell you", she said. "You saved her. You were unable to leave the place you took her to. In the morning you were found together. She was taken back to her husband's house. You went with her but could not enter the house. In ordinary circumstances an important person like her husband would have sent a letter of thanks to the procurator for the intervention of his troops. No such letter came. Then Vindex mentioned a report that the man had his wife taken to the Temple, charging her with something that Jews regard as a very grave crime and for which their Law prescribes a very cruel death."

"You said she was alive", stammered Cassius. "You said she was alive."

"The judge acquitted her", Claudia said quietly. "Although she admitted the charge."

He jumped up. "Where is she?"

"That I don't know. Her husband divorced her. She is no longer in his house, of course."

All his defenses crashed. "I tried and tried and could not find her anywhere . . . "

"I know, Cassius, I know."

"And Vindex told you all that?"

"He didn't exactly tell me. He reported while I was present. I should not really repeat this, of course. But I felt it must mean a great deal to you. And I had a debt to pay."

He saw the tears in her eyes. "If all this is true," he said harshly, "it is good of you to tell me. But there is one thing I don't understand. You say she admitted the charge. Then how could the judge acquit her?"

"He could. He is the only one who could."

"You know him?"

"I have seen him, yes."

"Who is he?"

"I wish I knew."

He shook his head. "You don't know his name?"

"They call him Rabbi Yeshua."

Suddenly she began to speak very rapidly, as if all the thoughts dammed up in her wanted to flow over at once and scarcely had the time to dress themselves in words.

"I saw him only once—during that awful feast when they had tried to murder each other—very soon after the battle on the Temple square. And there he was, calm and serene and talking of things so simple and so high, you had to be a sage to understand him—or a child. And I saw him cure a blind man—don't smile, curse you, no, no, I don't mean that, but I beg of you, don't smile, that's what Pontius did when I told him. I saw it, I tell you. . . ."

She was ill. She must be. Unhinged by something. Some of the younger officers were sure that the old man was brutal to her, but perhaps that was because they would have liked an opportunity to comfort her.

She went on, "That's why I hate leaving, don't you see? He may come here again, and I want to see him. . . . He lives in Galilee, they say. I always wanted to see Galilee, but Pontius doesn't want me to go there without him, and if he went with me it would be a state affair, because Galilee is not under his jurisdiction but under that of the tetrarch, that awful, slimy little man." She shuddered. "He is horrible. And his wife is worse. Even to look at her made me feel quite ill, and her daughter is no better. They are like poisonous mushrooms." She made a vehement little gesture, as if to push all these people out of her mind. "So I can't go to Galilee", she concluded. "I wish I could."

"Just to see that man again?"

"Yes."

Strange creatures, women. Suddenly he remembered what Abenadar had told him about that girl from Migdal, the great dancer and singer who became so impressed by some rabbi that she gave up her profession and followed him on his wanderings—

something like that. Abenadar had mentioned the man again quite recently, that he was in Jerusalem, that he wanted to see him. Perhaps it was the same man?

"Pontius was angry with me for going to see Rabbi Yeshua", Claudia said. "I didn't ask for his permission. I knew he wouldn't grant it. The city was still restless. Little Judith led me to him. It was she who talked to me about him in the first place. I went out of sheer curiosity, you know, sheer, stupid curiosity—like going to see a magician or a soothsayer. What a fool I was."

"What does Tribune Vindex think of the man?"

"Vindex?" Claudia shrugged her shoulders contemptuously. "Vindex is a policeman. He thinks in terms of crime, rebellion, unrest, and that kind of thing. He's about the last person to understand such a man. I tell you, Cassius, if I hadn't listened to Rabbi Yeshua, I would not have spoken to you today at all."

"Did he ask you to talk to me?"

"No, it wasn't like that. But he made me want to talk to you."

"I don't understand."

"It isn't an easy thing to explain, Cassius. He is a *just* man. You feel that so strongly that you know how unjust you are yourself. He is a compassionate man, so compassionate that you come away from him filled with the wish to help others. And yet his justice and his compassion are one and the same thing. Perhaps that is why he acquitted the young woman who said she was guilty. I don't know."

"And do you think Naomi may have joined that rabbi of yours?"

Claudia looked away at something he could not see. "That is what I would have done", she said.

Naomi's new life had nothing to do with anything that had happened before, with the exception of that one moment in the court of the Temple when her old life was unmade. There were no servants in the house, and there was work for each member of the household. Martha was teaching her how to cook; she knew how to make fourteen different dishes, even the seasoned lamb that Eleazar—Lazarus—liked so much, with six different kinds of spices in just the right quantities added at just the right moment. But of course that was a dish for great occasions; lambs were fearfully expensive this year, and they would never eat one of their own, because they knew them by name.

Martha was so different from Miriam that it was hard to believe they were real sisters and not half-sisters. Miriam was tall and slim; Martha was round and bouncing and almost as cheerful as Eleazar, who went around singing all day. But Miriam was often sad.

At first Naomi had asked every day when he would come back, but they were never impatient with her. Miriam would smile and say nothing, but Martha usually said, "Perhaps tomorrow", and Eleazar corrected her gravely. "It might be this afternoon", and finally Naomi realized that they were not trying to tease her; they really lived as if he might come back at any moment to stay with them again. Then after a while she began to understand that, in some way, he had never quite left them.

The house belonged to Eleazar—he had inherited it from his father many years ago—but the best room was never used by the family but held in readiness for *him,* as a great noble may keep a special room in his palace for the time when the King may spend a night under his roof.

He was the head of the family.

Naomi said so one day, and Miriam smiled at her. "Of course he is. That is why you are happy here."

It was true. He belonged to them all, and they belonged to him. They had him in common, and that was why they were happy. It was as impossible to think of him as away as to think of a rose without color or scent.

One day, when Naomi was cleaning the main room and Martha was preparing the midday meal, a stranger arrived from Jerusalem and Eleazar talked to him in the dooryard. It was odd that Eleazar did not ask him to come in, Naomi thought. Then she heard a slight rustle and saw Miriam, with her hand pressed to her heart and looking very pale. Though the men's voices were inaudible to anyone in the house, yet somehow Miriam seemed to know that it was bad news, and a moment later Martha came from the kitchen, and the two sisters looked at each other as if they were sharing a secret, a sad secret. After a while Eleazar came in. He was pale, and his large eyes were strangely luminous. He closed the door behind him. He said, "He has been forbidden the synagogue. He and all those who believe in him. It is official now."

"So it has come to that." Martha gave an angry laugh. "The master must not enter his own house."

"They have forbidden the sun to shine", said Miriam. "Soon they will gnash their teeth because it is so dark." She turned abruptly and went into her room.

Eleazar dropped into a chair and stared out the window, and suddenly Naomi realized how much his profile resembled Miriam's. The same high forehead, the same finely chiseled nose and chin. Martha had come to stand behind him, gently stroking his head, sharing his suffering. Quietly Naomi slipped out of the room.

Later in the evening, she saw Miriam alone in the garden, gazing across plain and hills toward Jerusalem. Naomi stood still, uncertain whether she should go to her, much as she wanted to, but Miriam turned and nodded, and she ran to her eagerly. The two women stood together in silence, the two who had so much, and so little, in common.

243

"He loves that cruel city", Miriam said at last. "He loves us, and we are like the city, full of crime and lies and vice. Because of his love, he is bound to suffer. I am afraid—that it condemns him to death, Naomi."

"May it please God you are wrong", said Naomi. She shivered involuntarily.

"You are fortunate", said Miriam. "I cannot even pray for that, because I know nothing. But it seems to me—there must be a plan. I have watched it, ever since the day he made me clean—yes, me too, just as he made you clean when he acquitted you. But not even those closest to him see it. They tell him he is a good man, and he answers that only God is good, and they do not understand what he means—yet I think it would change the world from one moment to the next, if they did. And still he loves them. I can understand his enemies—that is easy. Look at this rose, Naomi—if its root could think and feel, what would it think and feel when the stem grows out of the dark earth into the sight of the sun? A good root would feel delighted and grateful that part of itself should see the new kingdom above the earth. But a bad root would hate the stem—why could it not stay down under the earth like the rest? And then the stem—what would it feel when a bud forms and opens and becomes a rose, a joy to everyone who sees it? If it is a good stem, it will praise God for the miracle and be proud of having brought forth a rose. But if it is bad, it would feel that a stem should remain a stem always and that a rose should never have grown out of it. But all of it, root and stem and rose, was God's plan from the beginning."

"He is the Messiah", said Naomi dreamily. "That is what you mean, isn't it?"

"He is the Messiah. Many people believe that now. But what does that word mean to them?"

"The King of Israel, the Anointed One . . . The son of David who will rule the world and deliver us from bondage and bring peace."

There was a time when she had answered that question before. Yes—when Abigail asked her what she knew about him. Abigail . . .

"Yes", Miriam said. "And born in Bethlehem. Yet he will come forth . . ."

" . . . from eternity."

"Yes. Yes. From our midst he is born—to rule not only us, but the world. By force, Naomi? Shall he be a great soldier, a general, to lead the young men from Jerusalem and Jericho, from Gaza and Caesarea, from Migdal and the villages of Judaea and Galilee against the Gentiles all over the world? To kill and conquer?"

"I—I don't know. I have never thought of that."

"There have been so many conquerors. I learned about them from my Greek friends, and from the Romans. Some of them came from small nations, like ours. Alexander did, whom they still call the Great; even the Romans call him that. He conquered Greece and Asia Minor and Phoenicia and Egypt and Persia; he even invaded India. And what is left of all his conquests? And Cyrus the great Persian, and Hannibal the Carthaginian, and Caesar, the first Caesar, they came and went. But are we not the Chosen People of God? Is there not something that makes us different from all the nations on earth? When the Messiah, the King of Israel, comes forth, the Anointed One for whom we have been waiting century after century, of whom the prophets spoke with such yearning and such love—can it be that the Messiah is to be just another conqueror, killing and looting and winning battles and making thousands and thousands of women unhappy? If it were so, in what would we be different? And if we were not different, why should we be the Chosen People?"

"I don't know", repeated Naomi.

"When the conqueror is born from the root of Israel, he will be no ordinary man", Miriam said. "For the prophet says that he will come from eternity. And he will not be just another conqueror—he will conquer singly, one by one, for he will conquer the heart, and his weapon will be his Love."

If only Abigail had lived to hear this, to see *him!*

"But then I read in Isaias," Miriam went on, "so wild and sad—about the coming of him whom the Lord sent and about his death. The thorns of the rose, Naomi. And I struggled against Isaias, who would lead the Messiah like a lamb to the slaughter and kill him. Kill him! Though he was killed for our sins, and we were healed by his bruises . . . "

Naomi knew she was remembering—this was the wild, desperate language of the ancient prophecies, yet in Miriam's magical voice the words took on a personal, tragic meaning.

"And David", said Miriam. "Shall I sing you the song of David, Naomi? He sang, I do not know how many hundred years ago, the fate of his son, of his son whom he called his Lord! I will sing it to you. Not many people hear my voice now, but I will sing it to you, because you are my sister." And she lifted her glorious face up to heaven and sang, "My God, my God, look upon me: Why hast thou forsaken me? Far from my salvation . . . "

A psalm of David, a sacred psalm, sung time and again throughout the centuries in hope and despair, in sadness and in joy. The song of a nation and the song of a man, both in anguish, both besieged by the enemy, jeered at and mocked in misfortune. "I am poured out like water . . . " cried Israel. "My heart is become like wax . . . My strength is dried up", cried the Messiah. "The council of the malignant hath besieged me; they have dug my hands and feet—they parted my garments amongst them, and upon my vesture they cast lots." But from lamentation and despair the song went on into triumph. "The poor shall eat and shall be filled: and they shall praise the Lord that seek him; their heart shall live forever and ever. All the ends of the world shall remember and shall be converted to the Lord, and all the kindreds of the Gentiles shall adore in his sight. For the kingdom is the Lord's . . . "

There was no harp, no lyre, no cymbal to accompany the sweetest voice in Israel, but none was needed. People appeared in the doors of their houses, or leaned out of their windows, for they all knew the singer who now sang so seldom.

Naomi felt tears rise in her throat. It was impossible to tell her how beautiful it was; it was impossible to thank her. No voice should be heard after that voice for a long, long time. Naomi caressed Miriam's hand—it was cold, cold as ice.

A shadow fell across them, and Martha said in a frightened whisper, "Miriam, come at once. I think Eleazar is very ill."

Naomi was not allowed to enter the sickroom, but once, bringing up clean towels for Martha, who was constantly making fresh compresses, she saw Eleazar toss and turn on his bed, his face contorted with pain. And each time she came near to the door she could hear him breathe in a strange, desperate way, as if he could not get enough air into his lungs.

They had sent to Jerusalem for a physician, and when the learned man came he prescribed a bleeding and more compresses. He did not seem too pleased with the state of the patient but promised that he would be much better in the morning.

Both sisters stayed up all night but insisted that Naomi go to bed. She obeyed, but she could not sleep. Long before the dawn came she was back at the door of the sickroom, just in case she might be needed for something, for whatever she could do.

Martha passed her on her way out for fresh water "You ought to be in bed", she said crisply and walked on. Then Miriam came out of the sickroom, and at the sight of her white, anguished face, Naomi caught her breath to keep from crying out.

Miriam did not speak. They waited in silence for Martha to come back. "What is it?" she demanded.

"We must send for *him*", Miriam whispered.

"We can't." Martha's voice shook. "You know as well as I do he must not risk coming to Judaea now."

"I know, I know. But he's so near; he could be here in a day. And the fever is rising again."

He. They knew where he was. They had known all the time but had kept it a secret, because he was in danger. And now they were torn between their love for Eleazar and their fear of endangering *him*.

Naomi said quietly, "Why don't you just tell him and leave it to him. Surely he knows best."

They stared at her. Then Miriam kissed her. "You are right, my sweet, dear child. You are quite right."

And Martha, usually so undemonstrative, gave her a hug. "Blessed be the day we took you into this house", she said. "I'll go and fetch Jared. He's got a good horse." She hurried out.

A quarter of an hour later a seventeen-year-old boy, still half asleep, was galloping away toward the north, repeating again and again the message entrusted to him: "Lord, he whom thou lovest lies here sick."

The dawn changed to midday and midday to dusk.

The physician from Jerusalem did not come again. Eleazar was worse.

Late in the evening Jared came back. Yes, he had found him and the Twelve who were always with him. No, he had not spoken to him, only to Simon, but Simon had promised to give him the message at once: "Lord, he whom thou lovest lies here sick." He had not forgotten.

Was there no message from him?

No. No message. "I didn't wait too long there. I had to get back, and it's a long ride. Mother needs me."

That was all. The two sisters looked at each other.

"Miriam! Martha!" It was Naomi's voice, and the urgency in it made them run back into the house.

Naomi was standing at the door of the sickroom.

"What is it? What's happened, child?"

"I—I don't know. I can't hear him breathe."

III

"A sad bereavement", said Baruch bar Obed gravely. "Don't you agree—errh—I don't think I know your name."

"Joram", said the bow-legged little man walking beside him. "The best man in Jerusalem to find anything for you that you may want. Your servant."

"All I want at the moment is to get to Bethany without breaking a leg on this rubble field they call a road", said Baruch bar Obed. "It's a disgrace." He was an obese man and perspiring freely.

"There's no hurry", Joram said. "The burial was four days ago, I'm told."

"Yes, I was out of town when it happened. But I knew the father of the family, and I'm going to pay them a visit. I hope I know what is the right thing to do. Are you in any way related to them?"

"No. Didn't know their father either, if that's any comfort to you."

"It is not I who needs comforting", said Baruch solemnly. "You're a friend of the family, then?"

"One of many", Joram answered evasively. "They seem to have friends everywhere. Look, there must be at least twenty people going our way, and as I said, the burial was four days ago, and most of their friends must have visited them before. I wonder whether Rabbi Yeshua bar Joseph has been to see them. Also a friend of theirs, I'm told. Perhaps you know him too?"

"That man?" Baruch gave a snort. "He wouldn't dare to show himself so near the city. He's been forbidden the synagogue, you know. No one can go nearer to him than four cubits. He's forbidden to preach. About time, too."

"You do know him, then?"

"No, indeed, I don't, and I hope I never shall. A man in my position cannot be too careful. One of my cousins is Rabbi Josaphat, you've heard of him, surely, and he is most indignant about that man and his ways. Undermining the authority of scholars! Going about with the lowest of the low, including quite notorious persons. Now they say—" he lowered his voice, "they say that one of poor Eleazar's sisters did not always lead an exemplary life; but she doesn't live here, and it wouldn't be right to hold the other sister responsible, I feel. Nevertheless, I hope she won't be there, the one with the past, I mean. As I said, one cannot be too careful." He wiped his forehead with a silk handkerchief.

"I have never spoken to Rabbi Yeshua," said Joram, "but I heard him speak some months ago. And then I heard that he cured a man who was born blind."

"What next, I wonder!" Baruch snorted again. "You didn't see it happen, did you? No? I thought not."

"I've spoken to people who know the blind man, though", Joram said. "Known him for years. He was a well-known beggar."

"Beggars, lepers, tax collectors—it's always that kind of people one hears about when that man is mentioned."

"I should think", Joram said innocently, "it would be just as difficult to make a blind beggar see as a blind Pharisee. But I may be wrong. In any case the neighbors were surprised, of course, and they dragged him to the Pharisees to get an explanation. So the Pharisees questioned the beggar for hours on end, how it happened and when it happened and what Rabbi Yeshua had said and what he had done, and he answered their questions, and then the Pharisees began to argue among themselves about it, some saying that rabbi could not possibly be a messenger from God because the healing took place on the sabbath . . . "

"On the sabbath!" Baruch lifted his chubby hands. "There you are. Breaking the sabbath! What did I tell you?"

" . . . and others saying that a man could not very well be a sinner and yet do miracles."

Baruch wagged his head. "That is logical", he said regretfully. "Either way it is logical. So what did they do?"

"They questioned the beggar again and asked him what he thought Rabbi Yeshua was. So he said, 'Why, he must be a prophet.' Then the Pharisees sent for the man's parents, because they didn't believe the story that he had been born blind. Up came the parents and were confronted with their son. Was it true that he was born blind? It was true? Then how did they account for the fact that he could now see?" Joram grinned broadly. "The old people were pretty worried, you may imagine. They knew that Rabbi Yeshua had been forbidden the synagogue and that anyone who acknowledged him would share his fate. So they said, 'We can tell you that this is our son, and that he was blind when he was born; we cannot tell how he is able to see now; we have no means of knowing who opened his eyes for him. Ask the man himself. He is of age! Let him tell you his own story.' "

Baruch could not suppress a chuckle. "Go on", he said. "What did they do then?"

"Summoned the beggar again and told him to be grateful to God, who had cured him. It could not be Rabbi Yeshua because he was a sinner. So the beggar shrugged his shoulders and said, 'Sinner or not—I cannot tell. All I know is that once I was blind and now I can see.' So they started questioning him anew, what had Rabbi Yeshua done to him—what had he done to open his eyes—and finally he became a little impatient, and he said, 'I have told you already, and you would not listen to me. Why must you hear it over again? Would you too become his disciples?' "

Baruch began to laugh. He broke off and looked about. When he saw that there was no one within earshot he laughed again.

"You can imagine what they told him then," Joram continued. "They were furious. They yelled at him, 'Keep his discipleship for thyself; we are disciples of Moses. We know for certain that God spoke to Moses. We know nothing of this man or whence he comes.' But the beggar was not so easily intimidated. 'Why,' he said, 'here is matter for astonishment. Here is a man that comes you cannot tell whence, and he has opened my eyes. And yet we know for certain that God does not answer the prayers of sinners; it is only when a man is devout and does his will that his prayer is answered. That a man should open the eyes of one born blind is something unheard of since the world began. No, if this man did not come from God, he would have no powers at all!' Phew! How they flared up. 'What? Are we to have lessons from thee, all steeped in sin from thy birth?' And they chucked him out."

Baruch bar Obed wiped his eyes. "I wish I'd been there," he said. "No, I don't. Anyway, it's a remarkable story; it certainly helped to shorten this tedious walk, with nothing to see but dust, rubble, and shrubs."

"If you were blind," Joram said lightly, "would you go up to the Rabbi Yeshua and let him touch your eyes to give you sight—or would you keep off at least four cubits, as the Sanhedrin ordered?"

"It is fortunate", Baruch said, "that I am not blind."

"Yes, but if you were?" Joram persisted.

Baruch squirmed a little. Then he gave Joram a shrewd look. "If the rabbi has such powers, I'm sure he could cure me also at a distance of four cubits."

Joram nodded. "You did say that some rabbi of the Pharisees was your cousin, didn't you? Rabbi Josaphat, was it? I can well believe it."

Baruch bristled. "Are you trying to be rude? Errh—I mean to say—"

"Don't worry, I know what you mean", Joram said soothingly.

They had reached the first houses of Bethany, and through the spring air drifted the thin wailing of female voices—the sound known so well all over Judaea, Samaria, and Galilee, high-pitched and monotonous—making the lamentation for the dead.

A group of men was approaching the village from the north. A tall man dressed in white led twelve who followed at a little distance. They had come a long way, and they were tired.

The children saw them first and ran to tell Martha, who was standing at the door of the house. Her sad face lighted, and she ran.

She found him at the entrance of the village, and she stopped and raised her folded hands. "O Lord," she gasped, "if thou hadst been here, my brother would not have died."

Rabbi Yeshua said very quietly, "Thy brother will rise again."

She wiped away her tears. "I know well enough that he will rise again at the resurrection, when the last day comes."

Yeshua said, "I am the resurrection and life; he who believes in me, though he is dead, will live on, and whoever has life, and has faith in me, to all eternity cannot die. Dost thou believe this?"

She bowed her head. "Yes, Lord. I have learned to believe that thou art the Christ; thou art the Son of the living God; it is for thy coming the world has waited."

He looked at her without speaking, but she knew that he wanted to talk to Miriam, and she turned and ran back to the house.

There were a good many people there, some from Bethany, but most of them from Jerusalem. She made her way to her sister and whispered in her ear. Miriam rose at once and left.

Word went round that she was going to visit the grave, and the mourners followed her. At that moment Joram and Baruch bar Obed arrived at the house and quietly joined the others.

When they came to the entrance of the village, they stopped. A few of them had seen the tall man in white before, and they murmured his name to the others. Miriam was at his feet.

I should tell Baruch to keep at four cubits' distance, thought Joram, but the thought only flashed angrily through his mind and was gone, and he looked at Yeshua as they all did. At last, he thought. At last he is back. It makes all the difference in the world, where he is.

Naomi was at the back of the throng. She could only catch a glimpse of him, but she did not dare come nearer.

Yeshua asked, "Where have you buried him?"

"Lord, come and see", Martha sobbed.

"He is crying", thought Joram. "He is crying. He is crying."

"See how he loved him", someone whispered.

Baruch gulped. He murmured to Joram, "Could not he, who opened the blind man's eyes, have prevented this man's death?"

But Joram moved away. Yeshua, the men with him, and the mourners were all following the two sisters walking toward a small cave, a distance of only thirty paces.

A heavy stone had been put over the mouth of the cave.

"Take away the stone", Yeshua said.

Martha looked up at him uneasily. "Lord, the air is foul by now; he has been four days dead."

Yeshua said sternly, "Why, have I not told thee that if thou hast faith thou wilt see God glorified?"

"Come, Baruch", Joram muttered. "There is work to be done." He walked straight up to the grave. Baruch bar Obed held back, but three other men stepped forward, and the four rolled the stone aside. They moved away hastily, holding their breath.

But Yeshua remained where he was, nearest of them all to the tomb. Raising his eyes he said, "Father, I thank thee for hearing my prayer. For myself, I know that thou hearest me at all times, but I say this for the sake of the multitude which is standing round, that they may learn to believe it is thou who hast sent me."

And he cried in a loud voice, "Come out, Lazarus, to my side!"

The veiled head of the dead man appeared from the mouth of the cave, his shoulders, his arms.

"Oh, no", whimpered Baruch bar Obed, shaking from head to foot. "Oh, no, no—no—"

"The glory of it", Joram thought. "God of my fathers, the glory of it."

Slowly, clumsily, the terrible apparition emerged in its grave clothes, feet and hands tied loosely with linen strips, until he was fully out of the cave.

Yeshua said, "Loose him and let him go free."

A time passed—it seemed long—before some of the men dared to approach and touch the apparition, and it was a great act of faith, so great that none of them was afterward what he had been before. They removed the linen strips and touched warm flesh. They took the veil from the man's face, and it was Eleazar's face, and he opened his eyes.

"Come away", said Joram, and he took Baruch bar Obed's arm.

They walked in a dream. After a while Baruch began to mutter to himself. "Terrible—terrible—never thought that I would live to see it." Suddenly he stopped. "I must go back", he said. "I was so excited, I completely forgot to speak to them and tell them how sorry I am that their brother—" He broke off, then seeing Joram smile at him, clapped his hand against his forehead and shouted, "What have I to be sorry for? He's alive! By the vestments of the High Priest this is beyond belief. It *upsets* everything."

"Yes, it does", Joram said. "Nothing will be quite the same after this."

"Wait till I tell Rabbi Josaphat about it." Baruch's voice was still blurred with excitement. "I wonder whether he will have an explanation for it. But think of it, man, think of it! Now a man isn't safe even when he is dead! What if my father comes back or my brother Jonathan who died five years ago, what if he comes back and claims—"

"Steady now", Joram said. "Pull yourself together. It won't happen every day. I don't think you'll ever see it happen again."

"I hope not, I hope not. Maybe—maybe it didn't happen at all. Maybe I just imagined—"

"Yes", said Joram disgustedly. "You imagined it. And so did I, and so did twenty-odd people. Want to go back and have a look?"

"God forbid—"

"Then don't talk rubbish. Tomorrow it will be all over Jerusalem. It'll be hard for some people I could name to swallow it, but that can't be helped."

"Rabbi Josaphat—why, he'll *prove* to me that it can't have happened."

"I wouldn't be surprised", Joram said. Then an idea struck him, and he became very thoughtful and said nothing more, although Baruch bar Obed went on prattling excitedly the rest of the way.

IV

The session of the Sanhedrin had gone on for more than an hour before the High Priest said a word. He was in the chair, as usual, nodding to this or that man who signed that he wished to speak, but he himself said nothing. At times it seemed as if he were not even listening.

The waves of anger and excitement rose high, with Rabbi Josaphat demanding again and again the arrest of Rabbi Yeshua bar Joseph and all his followers and Rabbi Nicodemus answering ironically, "When you have arrested ten or twelve thousand people, where are you going to put them? Are they to build their own jails?"

"Ten or twelve thousand? You are raving!"

"There are rather more than less."

"Of course, ever since that incident at Bethany . . ."

"How often must I repeat, no learned men were present at the incident. Nothing about it can be regarded as definite."

"Maybe not. But that man Eleazar is alive."

"That is no proof that he was dead."

"You can't go against the evidence of so many witnesses . . . "

"Does not the quality of the witnesses matter? Besides, even assuming that the man was dead and did come to life again when the Galilean conjured him up, there is still the possibility that he invoked a demon—"

"We've had all that out before when that accursed beggar was giving evidence about his alleged blindness, and it did us no good at all. Do you want us to become the laughing stock of the people?"

"When will you understand that we have to *do* something about it?" That was Rabbi Josaphat again. "They are streaming out to Bethany, day after day to stare at a dead man who is alive, to talk to a man who was four days in his grave. The Galilean is gaining new disciples every hour. We can't afford to let this go on. We should have acted months ago, perhaps years ago."

"Yes, and the Freedom Party men are beginning to close their ranks again. If they get hold of him ... "

"Bah, most of these hotheads never think of the Mes— of that side. All they are out for is their own power."

"Today, perhaps. But tomorrow? And when *that* happens ... the battle on the Temple square will seem like nothing in comparison."

"I think we can safely assume that Pilatus only waits for such an opportunity."

"Now if Rome ... "

The High Priest stretched out both hands, and the speaker broke off. Everybody looked at the imposing figure that suddenly had come to life.

Caiphas shivered. His voice was surprisingly low as he said, "You have no perception at all; you do not reflect that it is best for us if one man is put to death for the sake of the people, to save a whole nation from destruction."

There was silence.

Beyond all impulse, all emotion, they felt that Caiphas had not said that of his own accord. He was Kohen Gadol, and over that tremendous office hovered the spirit of prophecy.

Little Joram was watching. He saw the fringed robes go in, Pharisee rabbis, Sadducee nobles, lawyers, and scribes. He knew

257

almost all of them by sight, but they, of course, did not know him. They were respectable people and had no dealing with those who reported the less obvious things, the real things, the things that might make a difference, not between this or that interpretation of the Law but between life and death. None of them had risked his life by joining up with the Freedom Party to find out what was going on and to report it to Kohen Gadol, and none of them would be so stupid as to walk out of a well-paid job for no better reason than that he did not like working against a certain man. Well, at least not many of them.

Joram settled himself as comfortably as possible behind the broad back of a camel by the wall of a house across the road from the High Priest's palace—not directly opposite, but near enough to keep the entrance under surveillance.

He was not particularly interested in what they were discussing in there; he had a fair idea of what it was. A dead man called back to life was bad enough. But when that sort of thing happened at the very gates of the city, it could not be endured because it could no longer be denied. The subtle lifting of erudite eyebrows was no longer effective.

What mattered was what Kohen Gadol was going to *do*. "It upsets everything!" Baruch bar Obed was quite right. It was certainly bound to upset the assembly. They would be arguing now, but that was not interesting. The next stage was what mattered. For the next stage might be action.

Joram produced a handful of figs from one of his many pockets and began to eat. He had been an agent for many years, first for some of the big merchants who were always in need of private information, then for the High Priest, and lately he had been doing a little work for the merchants again. A man had to live. If the most important of his assets was that he looked inconspicuous, the next most important one was his patience. Half, three-quarters of an agent's work was waiting for something or somebody to turn up.

He had counted the men who went in—twenty-three of them, not a full session of the Sanhedrin, of course, just a council held in an emergency situation. After about an hour and a half they came out again, all twenty-three.

Joram did not budge. He made a mental note of the fact that some of the most highly respected members had not been present—like Joseph of Arimathea, member of the Committee of Ten, and the great teachers and scholars. Gamaliel was not present either. Was it because this was not a matter to which such men cared to attend? Or—more likely perhaps—had someone "forgotten" to invite them?

So much for the twenty-three; here came the one for whom he had been waiting. The twenty-fourth. Aza, the confidential secretary.

Joram let him go up the road a way. Then he rose and followed.

Only when he knew for certain where Aza was going, and not two hundred yards away from the side gate of the Antonia, he walked up to him and greeted him. Joram was very submissive, very deferential to the young man, far more so than he had been in the past. He would like to ask for a favor; he had never done that before, had he? Was there any chance, in Aza's opinion, that Kohen Gadol might employ him again?

Aza was a little embarrassed. A quick glance showed him that there was no one near enough to overhear them, but even so . . .

"Things are not going too well with me", whined Joram.

"You left of your own accord, I believe", Aza said. "And you were not too successful before you left, were you?"

"It wasn't my fault", pleaded Joram. "It wasn't I who was supposed to arrest—well, you know whom I mean, I never mention names in the street. It was up to Malchus, and he failed. He's still captain of the guard, though, isn't he?"

"Well, yes, but . . . "

Joram waited a little, but as Aza did not continue, he said, "There you are. It wasn't really Malchus' fault either, you know.

What could he do? We were crammed in there; you couldn't lift an arm if you tried. It isn't so easy to arrest—that man. Have you got hold of him yet?"

"N-no, not yet", Aza said. "But it's only a matter of hours. Why, I'm just—" He broke off.

"Oh, well, there will be other tasks for me", Joram said casually. "You will put a word in for me with Kohen Gadol, won't you? I'll come to his house one of these days, and then you can tell me what he said and whether he will receive me."

He bowed most courteously to the young man's curt nod and sauntered off, a man of no occupation, a man with only too much time on his hands.

He changed his manner abruptly as soon as he had turned the next corner. He rushed across the street, passed a doorway, crossed again, and walked up to Jaqob bar Nahum, the dealer in donkeys and camels. He hired a strong, young donkey, paid, mounted, and rode off. A few minutes later he reached the gate, and then he made the donkey trot as fast as it could. A quarter of an hour later he was in Bethany. There were at least a hundred people in front of Eleazar's house. He jumped off the donkey, gave the reins to a surprised youngster, and pressed his way through the throng till he reached the entrance, where Martha was trying to ward the people off. He managed to wriggle through in spite of her and found another thirty people crowding around a pale young man who was quietly eating a piece of fish. They did not talk to him; they just stared. Neither Rabbi Yeshua nor any of his followers was in sight. Joram swore softly under his breath. Then he recognized Miriam. He made his way to her, and whispered, "Message for Rabbi Yeshua."

"He has left", Miriam said.

"When? Is he coming back soon?"

"He left this morning, early. He won't come back soon."

Joram grinned. "I might have known that he didn't need me to warn him", he said.

"Why? What do you mean?"

"The Romans may send for him."

"But why? He has nothing to do with . . . "

"Lady, I've been riding a donkey as fast as I could to tell him this. The Romans will be on horseback. I hope you are quite sure that he has gone. Don't tell me where to; it is better for me not to know. I might fall under suspicion, and they have ways of making a man talk however little he wants to. He is safe, I take it. I don't know about your brother . . . "

"Eleazar? You don't think they . . . "

"I don't know, lady. I hope not. I'd better go now. Peace be with you."

"And with you. But I wish . . . "

He did not hear the rest. Better not stay a moment longer. If Aza was riding with them, or any of the Temple guards, he would have some difficulty explaining why he was here. Again he pushed through the crowd, reached his donkey, gave the boy who held it two mites, mounted, and rode off, not back to the city but in the opposite direction. Stupid to ride straight into them. Behind Mount Oliver he could cross over to another gate.

Rabbi Yeshua had gone, that was the main thing. It had been silly to think that he needed Joram. "I'm not sorry I tried, though", he thought. "Maybe he knows it. Wouldn't put it past him. But even if he doesn't, I'm not sorry. That fool Aza—" He chuckled. He wondered a little on what pretext the Romans would be persuaded to take action. And where Rabbi Yeshua might be now. Crossing the Jordan, perhaps, or on his way to some place near the desert. There they could search for weeks without finding him. Samaria was another possibility.

He patted his donkey's neck. "Easy now," he said. "No more hurry for you and me. And what we did was quite unnecessary. But it doesn't matter. We tried. A man can do no more than that."

"Order from the tribune", the Centurion Mela announced.

261

Abenadar was dicing with the Centurion Calvus while Cassius looked on. All three had been drinking steadily for the last hour or so, and none of them liked the interruption.

"What's he want now?" Abenadar said grumpily. "No wait, Calvus, it's my turn. Yours was a five, keep it in mind if you've got a mind. Well, Mela?"

"Somebody's been here from the High Priest's palace. The old Pontifex wants us to arrest two fellows at a place called Bethany."

Cassius looked over the rim of his goblet. "Why's he got to send for us, curse him? He's got his own guards, hasn't he? They may not be worth much as a fighting force, but they should be good enough to arrest two men."

"Orders are orders", Mela remarked.

"I heard that one before." Cassius emptied his goblet. "Most hackneyed remark there is in the army. Bet they were tired of it in the Trojan War. Orders are orders."

"No good snapping at me." Mela was indignant. "I didn't give the order. I don't care whether . . . "

"Just a moment", Abenadar interrupted. "Who are the two men?"

"Members of the Freedom Party, the fellow said. Bandits I suppose."

Abenadar nodded. "Then it's clear enough."

"Not to me", Mela said.

"Because you're a blockhead. The procurator will be back in a few weeks, when the Jews have their Passover. The tribune wants to make sure there won't be any surprises like last time. That's why he falls in with the High Priest's suggestion. What are the names of the two?"

Mela glanced at his notebook. "I wrote them down as best I could when the tribune mentioned them. One is called something like E–Lazarus. And the other—wait a moment—Jesus or Jesua. Who can remember the names of these people!"

Abenadar rose heavily. "I think I'd better go myself", he said in a strangely muffled voice. "I think—no! I won't. Anybody who wants to go?"

"I've drunk too much." Calvus belched heartily.

Abenadar looked straight at the blank wall.

"I'll go", Cassius said. "Somebody's got to do it. I'm drunk, too, but not that much. How many men do I take?"

"Take the whole Roman army, son." Abenadar sat down again. "Take all the thirty legions from Britain to Persia. But the best thing would be to go alone."

Calvus grinned. He had never seen Abenadar drunk before; usually the old man could carry his wine better than anybody else in the Antonia. "That's settled, then. I threw a five. Your turn."

Cassius took his helmet off the rack and put it on. He reached for his sword and fastened it on his belt.

Abenadar rattled the dice. "Dog or Venus", he shouted. He did not seem to see Cassius wave at him as he walked out.

V

Riding out of the main gate of the Antonia at the head of four men, Cassius wondered how much Abenadar knew or guessed. He had never told him what Claudia said the day she left for Caesarea, but you could not be sure with Abenadar. And this Jesua or Yeshua probably was the man Claudia had told him about—and perhaps also the man Abenadar had mentioned. The man who had saved Naomi. The man for whose sake that dancing girl gave up her career. The man who perhaps knew where Naomi was.

He grinned. Abenadar was quite right; it would have been best to go alone. But it would not look well, if Vindex asked questions, and Vindex always did. Four men were enough, though. The four most stupid men in the entire cohort. He had chosen them with care.

He felt a twinge of excitement as they clattered over the wooden bridge beyond the gate and took the road to Bethany. Part of it was due to the wine, he knew, but not all. There was just a chance, just a ghost of a chance, that this man would know where she was, and if he did, Cassius could strike a bargain with him. Pilatus would hardly mind much if the man escaped—and Claudia would be glad. He was not likely to be a man of much consequence, despite the High Priest's personal interest in him. If he were, he would have taken a stand in the rebellion at the last feast, instead of merely making a brief appearance, preaching, and curing a blind man. Always assuming, of course, that he was identical with the fellow both Claudia and Abenadar had been talking about. Which was probable, on the whole.

One could always pick up the other fellow, of course, that Lazarus or Elazarus.

Bethany. One of those mud-house villages, palm trees, fences, sheep, coal fires; if you had seen one of them, you had seen them all.

Nobody paid much attention to the patrol. They never did, unless the patrol was riding at a gallop. Except that occasionally somebody spat.

Cassius raised his hand, and the men stopped their horses. "Dismount and wait for me here", he ordered. He had seen a group of people bunched together before one of the houses. Perhaps that rabbi was speaking to them. He approached. They also ignored him. However, when he walked right into the throng, they opened up nicely for him. But perhaps that was because they regarded him as unclean.

A woman in the door looked worried at the sight of his uniform, but before she could slip back inside the house he had his foot in the door.

"What is it you want?" she asked.

"I'll tell you that inside", he answered. He walked past her and closed the door behind him, in the face of the group outside. A number of men and women in the room stared at him.

"Which of you is called Je-sus or Jesua or Yeshua?" he asked. "And which is E-Lazarus?"

The woman who had first spoken to him replied, "The Rabbi Yeshua left here long ago."

He frowned and looked around. But none of the faces he saw was likely to have impressed Claudia. None—except perhaps that of a young man, sitting in a corner and looking at him with quiet eyes. But he was too young, surely.

Then he saw her.

She was standing at the foot of the small staircase leading to the upper floor. She was as pale as when he had seen her last, stumbling beside that coldly polite, soft-spoken man who led her back into the old man's house—as pale as the heart of a seashell.

He had thought so often of her face and her body and her tiny, slender hands, and a few times he had jeered at himself for believing her to have a beauty that could exist only in a dream, for exaggerating absurdly under the spur of his desire and his longing. Now, as she stood before him, she was all he had dreamed of and more—despite the utter simplicity, the poverty of her dress. Or was it that silk and jewels only deflected the eye from absorbing her beauty?

"Little goddess," he whispered, "I've been searching for you everywhere."

"Martha", Naomi said breathlessly. "This is the Centurion Cassius Longinus."

"Peace be with you", said Martha. She turned to the people in the room. "Go home now, friends. You see that we have an official visitor. Go then—*all* of you." She gave the dreamy-looking young man in the corner a friendly shove, and he rose and sauntered to the door with the others. Martha let them out. But she remained in the room.

"Little goddess," said Cassius, "this is the best day of my life. I thought I'd never find you again. The gods know how I tried. Then I found out what you had to go through—" His voice broke. He did not recognize himself. He felt lightened of a burden too heavy to carry—all because he had found a little Jewish girl again. In a sky bereft of all other gods there was still Venus.

"It does not matter now", said Naomi. She smiled at him, and his heart leaped with joy. He stepped forward.

"Don't", Naomi said. Her smile vanished.

For a moment, he stopped. Then he laughed. "It is not fitting", he said. "Is that it? I thought I had taught you what life is?"

He took off his helmet and put it on the nearest chair. Then he saw Martha standing in the doorway, and he frowned. "I want to speak to the lady alone", he said.

"This is Martha's house", said Naomi quietly.

He became angry. "I've had far too much respect for this kind of thing in the past, and it caused you a great deal of trouble."

"I shall go, if Naomi wishes", said Martha.

"Don't go", Naomi said at once.

Cassius made a gesture of irritation. "My good woman," he said to Martha, "I've come here to take two men into custody—both members of the so-called Freedom Party—the Rabbi Yeshua and a man called E–Lazarus."

"I told you Rabbi Yeshua left long ago", said Martha. "Eleazar is my brother. He—he isn't here either. And neither the rabbi nor my brother belong to any party. Whoever told you they did spoke a lie."

"Maybe", Cassius said. "And I am willing to believe you—if you will let me talk to Naomi alone. I won't search the house, and I shall report that the two men are no longer here. Now go."

"Search the house", said Martha coldly. "Search the whole village. Do whatever you regard as your duty. I shall leave this room only if Naomi wishes me to."

He stared at her. "I have four men outside", he said. "What stops me from having you thrown out?"

"Nothing", Martha replied. "Unless a Roman officer has a sense of honor."

For a moment his eyes narrowed. Then, surprisingly, he laughed. "You are right. You have a good friend here, Naomi."

"I know it, Cassius."

"Very well then." He turned back to Martha. "Forget what I said and listen to me. I love her. I would kill, and gladly, to have five minutes with her alone. You are a woman and her friend. I beg of you to give me these five minutes. And I swear to you by all that is holy to me she will be safe with me."

Martha hesitated. "What is holy to you?" she asked severely.

"Nothing much", he admitted, after a moment of stupefaction. "But she is. I—I have caused her much pain. But I too have suffered."

She looked at him, then at Naomi. "So be it", she said. When the door closed behind her, Naomi said, "Do you know who saved me?"

"That man Yeshua, I heard."

"Yes—he, whom you wanted to arrest."

"Those are my orders." He nodded. "And I brought four men with me to carry them out, the stupidest men I could find in the whole cohort. Too bad we didn't find him—or your friend's brother." He grinned. "It seems that your High Priest doesn't like either of them very much. It was he who told us they were members of the Freedom Party. But never mind all that, little goddess . . . "

"Please, do not call me that. The other man you want to arrest is my host; he has given me shelter all these months."

Cassius nodded. "I think he was here up to a few moments ago—a dreamy-looking young man. Your friend was in a great hurry to get him out of the room. I let him go, didn't I? These people helped you, and I am trying to show my gratitude. But look, little—look, Naomi . . . "

267

"Do you know that Rabbi Yeshua raised Eleazar from the dead?"

"Naomi, I don't want to talk about—*what* did you say?"

"Eleazar died. I was here when it happened. He was buried. Rabbi Yeshua arrived after four days and brought him to life again."

He stared at her in dismay. For the first time he began to understand why the High Priest wanted that man taken into custody.

Raised from the dead. It was absurd, of course. There was a trick here somewhere. Women never could investigate such matters properly and were only too ready to believe anything. It had been the same way with Claudia. But a man who managed to spread such a belief was certainly dangerous.

He remembered Claudia's words: "You come away from him filled with the wish to help others . . . his justice and his compassion are one and the same thing. Perhaps that is why he acquitted the young woman who said she was guilty."

Perhaps Naomi had been bewitched by that man too, like that Jewish dancer Abenadar told him about.

"He must be an extraordinary man." As Cassius said it he felt the inadequacy of the remark.

"He is the Son of God", said Naomi. "He is the Resurrection and the Life."

Everybody who came in contact with that man lost their mind. Against his better judgment he tried to reason with her.

"I thought you believed in only one God! And surely . . . "

"He and the Father are One. He said so."

"Ah, he did. And therefore it must be true?"

"Yes", said Naomi simply.

It was exasperating. "Look, Naomi, I have heard about him. I know he has a strange influence on people, especially on women. I was told about some wonderful dancer who came under his influence and gave up her career and followed him around. I can understand that—up to a point. When a woman is no longer as beautiful as she was and no longer so much desired by men, she may turn to religion and wish to follow a god or the Son of God or whatever deity it may be." He stopped. "What are you laughing about?"

"I'm sorry, Cassius, but it's because you talk such nonsense."

"Nonsense?"

"The woman you mentioned is Miriam, Miriam of Migdal. She is Martha's sister and the most beautiful woman I have ever seen."

"The most beautiful woman I have ever seen is Naomi," he said, "and I love you. We stand here talking about other people . . . Naomi, you and I are the only important people to me." He stepped toward her, his arms open.

She said nothing, and he was never sure that she actually retreated from him. But he felt an invisible wall between them. There had been such a wall when they first met, and he had broken it down. He could do it again. As he thought that . . .

"You gave your word", Naomi said.

"You doubt me—and you doubt that I love you, do you?" He stood rigidly, tense with determination to break down the wall. "I didn't know, myself, right away. I didn't even know, I didn't realize it—that night. Only when I thought I had lost you— when I could not find a trail, a sign of life even—then I knew. I told you once that life was not worth much. I believed it. I still would—except for you. And the one thing I dread is that you may tell me that I mean nothing to you now."

"When I stood before the council of the family and they asked me whether I was innocent, I told them that I loved you", Naomi said gravely.

His eyes blazed with admiration. "Lying is for the lowborn. You are a queen", he said breathlessly.

"Now I know that it is not enough."

"Not enough? We love each other. What could be added to that and not make it less?"

"Nothing is possible without *him*", she said.

"Without your husband, you mean? He—he divorced you, didn't he? Surely, you are free!"

"I was not speaking of Boz bar Sebulun. You—you won't understand, Cassius, you won't understand. And I want you to. I want you to . . . Look, Rabbi Yeshua raised Eleazar from the dead . . . "

"So you told me. What's that got to do with it?"

"He has given him a new life. But I also was dead—sentenced to death by the Law of Moses—and he gave me a new life, too."

"And in that new life you love him instead of me, is that it?" he burst out.

"Of course I love him", she said joyfully. "How could I not love him? He is the Son of God, and he and the Father are One. To God I owe my life and my soul and my body and my love for you—everything."

"You are right. I cannot understand." He shrugged his shoulders. "A god is not a man, and a man is not a god. And either you love me or this miracle man. I shall put that to the test here and now. Will you come with me?"

She said soberly, "I will—if he permits it. And I wish he were here. Then you would soon understand that . . . "

"If he were here, he would be my prisoner", Cassius said. "And I would take good care to see that he did not escape. I was quite wrong about him—he is a very dangerous man. Very well then. I gave your friend my word, and I'm going to keep it—this time. But I tell you this: I took you away from the old vulture who pretended to be your husband. I shall also know how to take you away from this magician who pretends to be your god."

He took his helmet, saluted her ironically, and stormed out.

Back at the Antonia with his four men, he went to see Tribune Vindex and reported that he had not encountered the two Freedom Party men in Bethany. "From what I have seen and heard, I very much doubt that they really are Freedom Party men", he added. "But they may be dangerous in a different sense. One is a rabbi of some standing with a strong personal influence on people and especially on women. People in Bethany seem to believe that he can raise people from the dead, cure the blind . . . "

"And so on", said Tribune Vindex. "And the other?"

"Is supposed to be the man who was raised from the dead. As far as I could make out that is the only remarkable thing about him."

The two Romans smiled.

"We had a famous priest of Isis in Rome", said Vindex. "He was a great success with the ladies, curing them of all kinds of ailments and performing quite admirable feats of magic. I was at a banquet when the old Pontifex of the temple of the Capitoline Jupiter was present — I forget his name now — and for two hours he could speak of nothing but the infamous magic tricks of the Isis priest. I suppose the good High Priest has not got a lucky hand with *his* dead and blind, so it is necessary for the two men to be lestes. Well — you couldn't find them, that's all."

Later, in Abenadar's company, Cassius drank a good deal. In the end he told him what happened. He had to tell somebody. "I didn't make much of the matter in my report to Vindex", he concluded. "But I shall certainly look for that miracle worker myself, and when I get hold of him, we shall see!"

"I think you were very foolish", said Abenadar wearily.

"Why? Because I didn't put the girl across the saddle and take her with me?"

"That", said Abenadar, "was one of the few foolish things you did *not* do. Part of this is my own fault. I should have gone to Bethany myself."

"You? Why, in the name of Hades?"

"To interrogate that young man whom this Yeshua raised from the dead."

"Ye gods! You don't believe that story, do you?"

271

Abenadar shrugged his shoulders. "What does it matter what I believe? A great many people do believe it. There have been hundreds going out to see the man day after day."

"How do you know?"

"Because I have spoken to some of them. Because such a story interests me. Vindex knew all that, of course."

"He didn't seem to know when I told him."

Abenadar sighed. "It doesn't happen every day, does it? Hundreds have been there. Thousands are talking about it. Of course Vindex gets to hear of it. That's what he's paid for—hearing things. You didn't make much of it, in your report to him! He made light of it himself. But neither you nor he are making light of it in your minds. And both of you are thinking only of one thing in regard to this man: of the damage he may do to you personally. Vindex worries about some disturbance at the Passover feast and a rebuke from the procurator. You worry about the influence the man has on the girl you love. Neither of you has the slightest idea of what the man is really like, and neither of you is interested in that in the least."

"Why should I be?"

"Because your girl is, obviously. He saved her life, didn't he? So perhaps she sees him as a bigger person than he is. It would be natural. If that is so you can regain your position in due course. But the one thing not to do was to drag the whole thing down to the level of jealousy. Yes, jealousy, you fool. I'm not at all sure whether I understand her, but it seems to me that what she was trying to tell you was this: she loves you as a man. She owned up to her love when her very life was at stake. But she knew that she had done a forbidden thing and that she would have been killed but for the justice or mercy of that rabbi. She had a spiritual experience through him. She still loves you—but she cannot love you fully so long as you do not share her experience with her. It would not be enough. It would not really be love as she sees it now. It would again be a forbidden thing."

"You're making her out to be a metaphysical sage like yourself", Cassius jeered.

"She is a thoroughbred Jewess; she belongs to the Jewish aristocracy", said Abenadar calmly. "That's the most ancient aristocracy in the world, my boy. And from what you've told me today, her little finger is worth more than the Centurion Cassius Longinus."

"Thank you."

"Particularly," went on Abenadar, "as the Centurion Cassius Longinus is no more than a clumsy boy who hasn't grown up but sees himself as a great avenger of wrongs . . . "

"Thank you again." Cassius' lips had turned white. "I'll remember that."

"Let's hope so." Abenadar emptied his goblet. "But I wish I had gone to Bethany myself."

"Well, why didn't you?"

"Because I was afraid of what I might find there", Abenadar said.

"Meaning that Rabbi Yeshua?"

"Yes."

Cassius threw his goblet on the floor. "I'll meet him one day", he said. "And when I do, he'd better perform a very fast miracle—if he wants to stay alive."

VI

"This is a state of siege", thought Caiphas. He was a born leader and he knew his strength. Yet never before had he felt so alone.

Something spectral and uncanny was approaching the city, converging on it from all sides, just as the pilgrims were coming again from all sides; and it hovered over the pilgrims and came down upon them and filled them with that strange spirit, at once anxious and joyful, a spirit of mystical expectation.

They built their booths and tents again all around a city too small to take in a third, a fifth, of them, and a wave of anxious and joyful expectation circled the walls. The old, old story of ancient longings and hopes filled them once more with exhilaration and excitement. It was in the very air they breathed; it was in the water of their ablutions and the wine they drank; it came out of the very soil like an invisible mist. And it would become bloodshed and fire and destruction unless he stopped it.

Unless he stopped it. And he was alone. Today, this unheard-of, this most terrible day showed clearly that he was alone, with no one to rely on.

They came in here, agents, servants, scribes, rabbis, guards— Aza had orders to let them come in freely—but all they did was to stammer their news and look to him for help, all of them, not excluding the Pharisees, who had formerly been so sure that they could drive away any danger with a few clever arguments.

He could not help them. He could only listen to their reports and wait.

The lightning had struck early in the morning, on the tenth day of Nisan, the very day on which the procurator returned to the city for his usual stay during the Passover. Not unheralded— for some days past the clouds had been gathering. Agents reported a growing feeling of unrest among the early pilgrims, a few rumors, many rumors, a sea of rumors that "he" was coming, that this time "he" would declare himself openly for what he was, that nothing and nobody would be able to stop the beginning of the "new time", that the events at the Feast of Tabernacles were no more than a prelude, that no other day but the Passover feast could usher in the coming of the Messiah, the day commemorating Israel's delivery from bondage.

The old quotations ran from mouth to mouth again, about the "Son of David", the Anointed One, who would bring peace and happiness to the world, the one of whom Jaqob spoke in the forty-ninth chapter of Genesis: "The scepter shall not be taken away from Judah, or a ruler from his thigh, till he come that is to be sent, and he shall be the expectation of nations"; quotations from the psalms of David foretelling the coming of the Messiah and Isaias' dark cry, "Prepare ye the way of the Lord; make straight in the wilderness the paths of our God." And they were talking of Jochanaan, the Baptist, as the forerunner Isaias mentioned. They called up the prophets one by one, Jeremias and Ezechiel, Amos and Zacharias and Daniel—but they meant that the day was approaching when the Messiah would scatter the Romans and make an end to their rule.

Then suddenly somebody spread the news that "he" had arrived, that "he" was in Bethany and preparing to enter "his" city, and the news raced across Jerusalem like wildfire, and everywhere people bunched together and shouted with excitement and broke off palm branches and streamed out to receive the King Messiah.

And from then on the messengers came in wild-eyed, spluttering and stammering, scarcely any one of them able to deliver a cold, clear report. And no wonder.

It was incredible but true. He really dared to come out in the open. He came riding on a donkey. Of course! He knew his Scripture. He had read his Zacharias: "Rejoice greatly, O daughter of Sion, shout for joy, O daughter of Jerusalem; Behold thy King will come to thee, the just and Savior; he is poor, and riding upon an ass, and upon a colt the foal of an ass."

Many hundreds of people came with him. They had gone out to Bethany to fetch him in state, and they found him, of course, as the Romans did not, the Romans who could have prevented all this so easily, if only they had acted at once when the High Priest sent them the message.

That man Eleazar was with the Nazarene, telling everyone that he had been raised from the dead, and a number of witnesses cried that they had seen it with their own eyes, and the crowd swelled bigger and bigger, and they shouted, "Hosannah!" "Save . . . ", and "Blessed be he who cometh in the Name of the Lord!" The priest who came to tell the High Priest about it could scarcely articulate for anger against such blasphemy.

Another messenger: the two processions, that of the procurator entering the city with fifteen hundred soldiers and that of the prophet from Nazareth, were going to meet in the heart of the city.

The High Priest did not know what to wish for. A few Roman swords could of course put a swift end to the Nazarene and his friend, but what then of the hundreds of thousands of pilgrims? What would they do if they heard that their precious prophet had been slain by the Romans?

The moment had passed. The Galilean's procession turned off the road on which it would inevitably have clashed with the soldiers, going instead through the street of the coppersmiths, and soon the next messenger came in, an irate Pharisee. "I have spoken to that man! I could no longer listen to the blasphemous shouting. They called him the Son of David, the ignorant fools, and they shouted, 'Blessed is the King!' and I said to him, lifting my hands in reproach, 'Rebuke thy disciples?' and he replied as serenely as if it were all his due and no more, 'I tell you, if they should keep silence, the stones will cry out instead.' "

And reports came that people were saying eternal spring had now come and peace on earth and glory in the heavens, and other reports, more important, that the Freedom Party was rallying everywhere and ready to make common cause with the prophet from Nazareth. Many of the loudest criers of Hosannah were said to be former followers of Bar Abbas and of Ephraim bar Saul and Achim bar Simeon and Eliud and Oziah and other leaders of the Freedom men.

The city was in turmoil. And the Romans in their gross ignorance accepted the excitement as the usual rejoicing at the time of a great feast, looking on with their usual condescending indulgence.

All the responsibility was his, Caiphas', alone. And he could rely on no one. The Temple guard? They had failed to arrest that man during the last feast. He could still hear Malchus apologizing. "No one has ever spoken like this man." So he had been unable to perform his duty.

The Sadducee members of the Sanhedrin? The Pharisee rabble? When things came to such a pass, their weapons, dialectics, and learned arguments were like blunt arrows shot at a tiger.

Caiphas had always been sure that Rabbi Yeshua was the real danger, not that stupid brawler Bar Abbas. But he had failed to carry out the only practical plan. He had waited too long. Now he was under siege in his own house, in his own city.

He could still find men to kill the Nazarene. But if they failed, it would make things worse. Half an hour later a mob would tear down the walls of the house and murder everybody inside it. And if they succeeded? The Nazarene had disciples enough who would lay the deed at the door of Kohen Gadol. Besides, how could an assassin get at the man now? The Nazarene was surrounded, no longer by a few disciples but by thousands of enthusiastic followers, ready to tear into pieces anyone who tried to harm him.

Impossible to make the attempt anywhere near the Temple or in the streets of the city.

At night? So far, no one seemed to know where he would spend the night. Probably in Bethany. But Bethany also was swarming with his friends. Or he might stay among the pilgrims, which meant that he could not be found at all, certainly not within a few hours.

It was hopeless.

There was a small thunderstorm in the afternoon—just one clap of thunder—into which the people read a myriad signs and portents: they believed that an angel had spoken to the prophet;

according to one report he had said something about sentence being passed on this world and that the prince of the world was being cast out and that he himself would be lifted up from the earth and then would attract all men to himself.

On the following day the reports continued to pour in as fast as before.

The first act of violence was committed by Yeshua himself, and, of all places, in the Temple. He bodily attacked the officials who changed the people's money into the right currency, laying about him with a whip, overturning their tables, while coins rolled all over the place, kicking the chairs of the pigeon sellers away, and shouting, "It is written: 'My house shall be known for a house of prayer.' And you have made it into a den of thieves." After all, the money changers were licensed, as were the pigeon sellers. Naked violence! And worse than that. The bystanders might not understand, nor might most of the people, but it was clear to Caiphas what the Nazarene meant and whom he meant.

Caiphas sat motionless. He understood. Perhaps he alone understood. This blow was not struck merely against those little men, but against the entire established priesthood and its laws.

This was the first act of dispossession by him who regarded himself as the Messiah and therefore as the highest priest of Israel, the first overt blow in the battle against Kohen Gadol.

With the people in their present mood, nothing decisive could be done—unless the man committed a blunder of the first magnitude.

Yet something *had* to be done. For at least two reports indicated that some of the erudite men had begun to waver, perhaps were even past wavering.

Caiphas had had his suspicions about a few of them before: Rabbi Nicodemus, for instance, and possibly also the Arimathean, although he was very wealthy and the Galilean had pointed out more than once that rich men would not easily enter the kingdom of heaven.

Now suddenly there seemed to be more. Certainly some of them were *thinking* of changing sides, trying to ingratiate themselves with the man who might be the power of tomorrow. After all, if he took over, he had to have some erudite people on his side. He could scarcely hope to run the country with the help of fishermen and peasants alone. This was the time to approach him, to make sure one would get a good job under the new government.

Something had to be done, and quickly.

Caiphas gave careful instructions to a number of priests.

They did not have to wait long for the man's next appearance in the Temple. Everything went according to plan. The Nazarene was met by an imposing array of priests and elders and formally asked by whose authority he was acting.

Caiphas hoped to surprise from him some wild or at least carelessly phrased statement. Then the cry of blasphemy could be raised in earnest. That would not defeat him permanently—things had progressed too far—but it might well split his followers into factions, which was the best result to be hoped for at the moment.

The report of the confrontation in the Temple reached Caiphas by midday. The Galilean had turned the tables on his interrogators: "Whence did Jochanaan's baptism come—from heaven or from men?" He would answer their question, he said, when they had answered his. He knew, of course, that they could not answer it. If they said, "From heaven", he would retort, "Then why did you not believe him?" If they said, "From men", they would have against them the people who believed so firmly in Jochanaan whom they called the Baptist that many thought he was the prophet Elias come back to earth. The priests could only say that they did not know, and the Galilean promptly refused to answer their own question. It was as if he had said pointblank, "I do not feel required to answer you because you are not sincere—as you have just proved."

Not content with that, he then regaled them with one of those little parables of his, about a rich man who had let his vineyard and wine press and the storage tower to some vinedressers, who promptly killed or stoned or beat his servants when he sent them to claim his revenues. The rich man sent other servants, who fared no better. Then he sent his own son—surely they would have reverence for him. But they said to themselves, "This is the heir—come, let us kill him and seize upon the inheritance." And they killed him.

The Galilean asked very slowly, very gravely, "What will the owner of the vineyard do to those vinedressers when he returns?"

He quoted David—the 117th psalm—about the very stone that the builders rejected becoming the chief stone at the corner. And, rising, he said, "I tell you, then, that the kingdom of God will be taken away from you and given to a people which yields the revenues that belong to it."

So fell the second blow against the established priesthood.

Not only did the Galilean disclose that he knew his life was in danger; he also made it very clear who was endangering it. He made it so clear that the people were bound to understand. If anything happened to him now, the mob would raze the High Priest's palace to the ground.

Only Rabbi Mordecai had a partial success. At least it was to be hoped it would turn out that way. He and a few Pharisee rabbis approached the Galilean with a courteously phrased question of utter simplicity.

Was it right to pay tribute to Caesar or not?

It was a deadly question. Of the people standing around, at least some were bound to be Freedom Party men. If the Rabbi Yeshua said yes, they would know that they could not expect liberation from him. If he said no, it was incitement to rebellion, and the procurator would be informed at once.

The Nazarene saw the trap, called the rabble hypocrites, and asked for a coin. Whose likeness was it? Whose name was on it? Caesar's? Then they should give Caesar what was Caesar's—and God what was God's.

The deputation withdrew. Rabbi Mordecai did not regard it as a success and was even heard expressing a grudging admiration for the adroitness of the answer. Still, it might have a cooling effect on some of the Freedom hotheads.

Caiphas groaned. He knew only too well that all these attacks were needle pricks and no more, that the influence of the terrible man was steadily growing.

The reports on the next day amply confirmed his fears. The man had won over one of the finest lawyers in the city with a single sentence of praise. He had launched a sermon of unsurpassed vehemence and directness against the Pharisees. It seemed quite clear that he was preparing the way for his common Galilean followers to take over. He made a—still careful—allusion to his own exalted position. Whose son was the Messiah, he asked? David's? How then was it that David called the Christ, the Messiah, his Master, when he said, "The Lord said to my Master, Sit on my right hand while I make thy enemies a footstool under thy feet?" Then he had asked into an awed silence, "David calls Christ his Master; how can he be also his son?"

Preparing them, preparing them all the time.

But then came a strange report about something he said when standing in front of the Temple. "Believe me, there will not be a stone left on another in this place; it will all be thrown down."

Why should he talk like that, in the hour of his imminent triumph? It was—perhaps—the first real blunder. If he had really said it. If he had not added, "*Unless* you acknowledge me, unless I rule over you ... "

There was little new on the fourth day after his entry into the city. He had been in Bethany. A feast had been given in his honor—whatever kind of feast they could afford in Bethany.

Caiphas paced up and down in his room. Was this the calm before the storm? Did the man intend to wait until the feast itself? Or—or was he losing his grip a little?

Would *I* wait? Would I not try to hammer the iron while it

was hot? Or did his mind work along different lines from mine? Surely all men were driven by the same urges! But if he hesitated too long . . .

Aza came in, looking pale and excited.

"What is it, Aza?"

"My lord High Priest, there is a man outside . . . "

"There have been men outside all day. Who is it? What does he want?"

Aza gulped. "His name is Judah. He is from Kerioth."

Caiphas passed a weary hand over his forehead. Judah—from Kerioth. He had heard the name before. Judah. From Kerioth.

But Aza spoke again. "He says he is one of those very near to Rabbi Yeshua."

The High Priest controlled himself with an effort. This could mean anything. It could be the last message before open warfare, and it could be . . . "Show him in."

When he entered, Caiphas looked at him keenly. The man was excited, overwrought. Intelligent face. Bloodless lips, eyes shifty.

The man from Kerioth looked past the High Priest at the blank wall. He said, "What will you pay me, if I deliver him into your hands?"

When Rabbi Yeshua had returned to Bethany, some days ago, Naomi's first thought had been to fall at his feet and ask him what she should do, what he would permit her to do about her love.

It did not discourage her that all kinds of people were around him all the time, talking, arguing, asking questions, kissing the hem of his robe, that there were councils—in which many spoke while he said nothing—and that the richest man in Bethany, Simon, gave a feast for him with many notables present.

She knew he would listen to her if she went to him.

But she would not do that before she had spoken to Miriam first.

282

Many a time she thought of what might have happened if only Miriam had been in the house when Cassius arrived. Miriam could have explained things so much better. She could have said that one sentence, that one word which might have made all the difference. Miriam understood her.

Perhaps—perhaps Miriam even understood *him*.

But Miriam had been at the cave where Eleazar had lain under the heavy stone and where he had returned to life. Martha never went there, and Eleazar did not even look at it when he walked by. Miriam spent hours there every day. "It is a glorious place", she said when both sister and brother asked her why. "It is the most glorious place I know. It is the battlefield on which the King vanquished the most terrible enemy of man."

Martha said it was not healthy. Eleazar said nothing. He did not speak much nowadays, nor had he regained his usual cheerfulness. After Cassius' departure his sisters made him stay at a neighboring village for a while, to make sure that he was safe in case the Romans sent out another patrol, or if the Temple guards came to look for him. After a week he came back, and now that Rabbi Yeshua had returned, too, he never left his side.

But recently something seemed to be very wrong with Miriam. She, who had longed more than anyone else for her King, did not enter into the joy of the others. Just once, on the first day, when he set out to ride into Jerusalem and they all followed on foot and the people rejoiced and sang and lifted their palm branches, she had cried with joy.

"At last, Naomi, at last they give him welcome as they should. May God give me the grace not to forget it in the dark hours. However little his people understand him, once at least they give him due honor, and they give it when he comes to them as the King of Peace and not as a conqueror. Look, he is riding on a donkey, not on a charger. He is without a single weapon. Yet they greet him as their King. No one can take away this hour from Israel."

But on the return to Bethany, she was very quiet and sad and absentminded and did not answer when Naomi asked her what to do about Cassius.

When Martha mentioned that Yeshua had cured several people in the Temple, she said, "He touches them, and they are whole again. But who will touch him to make him whole again? He comforts them when they are weary and oppressed. But who will comfort him? He raised my brother from the dead. But who will raise him from the dead when his hour comes? He takes our suffering on his shoulders, but we cannot ease his pain. He is always the Giver. No one gives to him. . . . "

A very short while afterward she seemed to have forgotten what she had said about the King of Peace. When Martha asked her why she looked so worried she suddenly jumped up. "Don't you understand that the King is at war? At war, I say. They are waiting for him in a thousand ambushes; they watch him all the time. Ruses, traps, lying, yapping at his heels—and no one to help him. Where are his friends? Are they fighting for his glory or for their own? All they can think of is what place they will have in the kingdom. When he talks to them, they listen only to the words about themselves, all of them, all of them. . . . "

"Just the same, they love him", Martha said staunchly. "Simon loves him. Jochanaan loves him—they all do. You know that."

"Reeds", Miriam said tonelessly. "Reeds—broken reeds. Oh, why am I a woman?"

"Now you know better than that", Martha said reproachfully.

Miriam hugged her and burst into tears. "You are right, you are right, I lost faith, for a little while I lost faith, but only because I love him."

Was it the thought that he was always the Giver while no one ever gave him anything that made Miriam appear, unexpectedly, at the feast in his honor, to anoint his head and feet with spikenard?

Naomi and Martha were helping serve and were in the banquet room only for short moments, but when they heard Rabbi

Yeshua say that she had prepared his body for burial they both fled into the kitchen and wept, feeling helpless and confused. For burial?

Did Miriam know something she had not told them?

They saw her later for a brief moment, back at the house. Her glorious long hair was still loose; she had not bound it up again after wiping Yeshua's feet, and it was full of scent.

"I gave him a present," she said, "and there was one who begrudged it to him. The one from Kerioth. Did you see his face? Did you? The King gave us the world, and we begrudge him a poor little gift, his own gift."

On the first day of the unleavened bread Martha wanted her sister to help with the preparation of the meal, the paschal lamb. She found Miriam sitting at her window, her face drawn, her eyes half-closed. She looked years older.

Martha spoke to her, but she would not answer.

VII

The atmosphere within the Antonia was one of extreme irritation.

The arrival of the procurator with his wife, his staff, and almost fifteen hundred men had cramped everybody for space again.

There was a persistent rumor that the procurator had clashed with the legate and another that he had threatened physical violence to Vindex.

Certain it was that he had imposed a strict curfew on the entire garrison a few hours after his arrival. They had to stay in their quarters, without enough room for games, with the swimming pool sadly overcrowded, and snobbish officers from Caesarea talking as if Jerusalem were a third-rate provincial town with third-rate officers and troops.

The curfew was imposed to prevent friction between the soldiers and the pilgrims outside; but the confinement created so much friction inside the Antonia that a number of brawls took place, both among the troops and in the officers' quarters.

The procurator's remedy was to keep the men occupied with training exercises.

After four hours on the training ground Cassius came back to the officers' quarters in a vile temper. He got rid of his armor and then found that he could not bathe, as the swimming pool was occupied by the procurator's ladies. He had a perfunctory wash instead and went to dinner.

The dining hall too was overcrowded, although the procurator and his staff were having dinner in their private suite.

Cassius found a seat only by pushing a chair between two Caesarean tribunes. One of them asked him whether the meat was always as rotten as it was today.

"Complaints should go to the quartermaster", Cassius said curtly.

The other tribune inquired whether anything nice and lively could be expected to happen again during the feast, "to justify the temporary presence of experienced soldiers in the city".

"The experience of the Caesarean troops is sadly wasted here", Cassius replied. "There are no theaters in Jerusalem."

An open quarrel might have followed if old Abenadar had not broken in to say that three bandits, members of the so-called Freedom Party, would be crucified tomorrow: a fellow called Bar Abbas and his two henchmen, Gestas and Dysmas, all of them rather popular with the hotheads—so there might well be a bit of rioting.

Tribune Vindex remarked sharply that the execution of the three bandits was taking place precisely in order to deter the hotheads from any further nonsense and that a detachment of sixty men was leaving the Antonia this evening to secure another arrest.

One of the two tribunes from Caesarea still glowered at Cassius, but the other inquired about the potential strength of the Freedom Party, and Vindex told him that practically all the leaders had been killed during the last rising and that there was now no real coordination and a good deal of bickering between small groups. "The best man they have is a fellow called Zakkai, who used to be one of Bar Abbas' men."

Showing off how efficiently his agents operate, thought Cassius. He left the stale, sticky air of the dining hall early and went back to his quarters for a game of dice with Calvus, Aufidius, Mela, and Varro. But Varro was absent—he had been ordered to make an arrest outside the city, Calvus said. That was, of course, the matter to which Vindex had referred.

Cassius would have liked to ask the tribune what it was all about, but as Vindex always loved to be secretive he would probably not have answered. Abenadar, as Varro's direct superior officer, was bound to know all about it, but Cassius and Abenadar had been talking very little to each other lately, and he was not going to invite a snub.

Abenadar came in half an hour later and sat down in a corner by himself. He, also, did not seem to be in a good mood.

The game went on. Cassius lost, won again, and lost again. Even dice were no fun tonight.

Abenadar had ordered wine and was drinking heavily.

After another hour the game broke up. Aufidius and Mela turned in. Best thing to do, really. But Cassius knew he would not be able to sleep, and he did not want to think. There was something about tonight that reminded him of the time in Spurio's school, a sense of death and ghosts. After a while Calvus left, too.

Cassius stayed. And for the better part of half an hour he and Abenadar sat alone, each in his corner of the room, without exchanging a word. Then Varro came back, big, hulking Varro. He muttered a greeting that sounded almost like a curse, hung his helmet on the rack, and began to take his armor off. He was about forty and getting pretty bald.

"Well?" Abenadar asked. "All over?"

Varro nodded.

"Did you report to the tribune?"

"Yes."

"Sit down and have some wine."

Varro sat down heavily and drank. "It was queer", he said.

"Any fighting?"

"Nothing to speak of."

"No one dead, then?"

"No."

"Wounded?"

"No. Yes. N-no."

Cassius began to laugh. "Quite a report, Varro. Vindex must have been pleased."

"I said it was queer", Varro grunted.

"Seems to have been."

"All right", said Abenadar sharply. "Let's have it. From the beginning."

Varro drank again. "All Vindex told me was that I was to take sixty men as soon as it was dark and march them off to the Temple. There I would meet the chief officer of the Temple guards, who was supposed to make the arrest. The men were to be fully armed, and we were to take torches and signals, but no light was to be shown before it was absolutely necessary. The whole thing was to be done as quietly as possible."

Abenadar nodded. "Obvious. Go on."

"Well, we found the chief officer—fellow called Malchus—and with him were thirty guards, a few civilians who looked like learned men to me, and a guide who was supposed to know exactly where this Jesus could be found."

Cassius sat up with a jerk. He said nothing, but his eyes gleamed.

Varro did not see it. Abenadar saw but took no notice.

"Just as well we had that guide", Varro went on. "Without him there wouldn't have been a ghost of a chance of finding the man. I've never seen such crowds of people as there are camping outside the gates. That man Malchus was in a state! Would I tell the men to make as little noise as possible—would I keep close to the guards! Then he muttered curses or prayers or both, all the way. The guide was excited too. Once the whole column stopped, because the guide had stopped, and he had stopped because he was vomiting."

Varro shook his head and drank again. "Well, we got out of the city and crossed that little brook, Cedron they call it, and stumbled along as best we could in the darkness. You know what it's like there, all full of little gardens and fences before you get to the olive groves, and then the hill, Olivet, and that big garden to the north of it, Gethsemani. We bypassed the hill and got to Gethsemani, and the guide whispered to poor old Malchus, and he told us to keep *very* quiet."

Varro emptied his goblet. "By now I thought we would have to deal with a whole band of lestes. I couldn't get a sensible word out of that guide, neither how many men this Jesus would have with him nor whether there was a way to surround the place—he kept shaking all over and repeating, 'I'll show you, I'll show you.' Well, he showed us all right. We came to a little clearing, and the guide nodded to us, and I ordered a number of torches to be lit and kept two signiferi at my side with their lanterns lit, in case of a pursuit when we'd have to signal to each other. The guide walked on with the Temple guards behind him, and there was a cluster of men in the clearing, perhaps a dozen, certainly not many more, and the guide went straight up to one of them and kissed him—have you ever heard of such a thing? I found out afterward, he told the men in front he'd point out the right man to them that way so there would be no misunderstanding. As if there could have been! They were clustering around him like chicks around a hen! And that is where the funny business began." Varro helped himself to some more wine. "I'm going to get good and drunk tonight", he said. "Got a funny taste in my mouth. Must get rid of it."

"What happened?" Abenadar asked. His voice was thick. If he was not drunk, he ought to be, Cassius thought, after hours of solid drinking.

"The man didn't try to escape", Varro said. "Mind you, he couldn't have escaped if he'd tried—I had my men ready for him. But *he* didn't know that. He couldn't possibly see them—not yet. We were hidden in the bushes. All he could see were the guide and the Temple guards. He could have fled over to Olivet. But he didn't make the slightest effort. Instead he said something to the guide, but I couldn't hear what it was. I know what I would have told that treacherous, kissing swine, but I don't think he said anything like that at all. He looked sad. Not a bit surprised; not angry, just sad. And I couldn't help thinking how silly we all looked setting out a hundred strong against that one man with a fistful of followers and they unarmed. He stood there, looking at the guards with their swords drawn and their clubs ready, and he asked, 'Who is it you are looking for?' I heard him quite clearly this time. Somebody answered, 'Jesus of Nazareth', and he said, 'I am Jesus of Nazareth.' He didn't roar at them, just said it quietly. And, believe it or not, they recoiled as if he had hit them. A dozen or more of them fell flat on the ground, and for the first time I began to think he must have some kind of magic or something."

"Maybe he has", Abenadar said. "Go on."

"Well, I was thinking of marching my men up, as the guards didn't seem to be getting anywhere, but to tell you the truth, I felt a bit queer myself, and it *did* look strange to see them all rolling on the ground, and I know my men felt it too. Told you, it was queer."

Cassius opened his mouth for a sneering remark.

"Keep quiet", Abenadar ordered. "Go on, Varro."

"The next thing that was funny was the face of the guide. He was watching it all, and he looked intensely pleased, as if everything was going just as he hoped it would. I couldn't make him out at all. First he leads us to the man whom we would never have found without him—then he looks pleased when the guards roll on the ground. However, they picked themselves up again, looking a bit dazed, and he asked them again, 'Who is it you are looking for?' sort of patiently, as if he were trying to tell them that there was no reason to be frightened. And finally the captain of the guards, that Malchus, stepped forward—not too quickly though—and said again, 'Jesus of Nazareth.' Mind you, they have their own way of pronouncing that name. I can't imitate it. And the man said, perfectly calmly, 'I have told you already that I am Jesus. If I am the man you are looking for, let these others go free.' So finally they had the courage to seize him, and when they did, some spark of life came into one of his followers, and he actually drew a sword and hit out against the good captain. It was quite a nice stroke, and it might have split his skull, but Malchus jerked his head aside and caught it good and proper on the right ear, and then I did give the signal, and my men marched forward. But there was no more fighting. This Nazarene man told off his own follower and made him put his sword back into the sheath. He—he touched Malchus' ear—it was hanging loose; I told you, it was a good blow. Touched the ear and—well—by that time I was so near him, I could have touched him—and . . ."

Abenadar shouted, "*Will you go on?*"

Varro shrugged his shoulders. "Malchus was all bloody, of course, you know how it is with head wounds, and his ear was almost off. Then all of a sudden—it wasn't. It was back in place, and Malchus wiped the blood away with his forearm."

"You were mistaken, perhaps; the light must have been bad", Abenadar said gruffly.

"That's what I thought." Varro nodded noncommittally. "Then the Nazarene man spoke again. He had said something to his followers before, but I missed that, wondering about Malchus' ear. Anyway, now he saw the civilian fellows who had come with us. They had come up, seeing there wasn't any danger of a fight starting. And he said to them, 'You have come out to my arrest with swords and clubs, as if I were a robber, and yet I used to sit teaching in the Temple close to you, day after day, and you never laid hands on me.' And he added that it was ordained that way and that some prophecy must be fulfilled, and then when they saw that he wasn't going to offer any resistance, his followers suddenly broke and ran. One of the civilian fellows screamed, 'Hold them, hold them, too!' but by then they were swallowed up in the dark, and I certainly wasn't going to send any of my men after them to please those gentry. My orders were to get that Nazarene man, and we got him. They had tied his hands by then, and we started marching back. Our torches were still burning, and I saw the face of the guide who was coming back with us. He was trotting along as if he were drunk, and he looked to be the most miserable man I've ever seen, eyes popping out of his head, mouth twisted, and muttering to himself all the time. The man must be mad, I thought, but then almost everything seemed crazy. Well, Malchus said he had orders to take the prisoner first to the house of old Annas or Hannas or Hanaan, who was the former Pontifex here and happens to be the father-in-law of the present one, and I said you take him wherever you like, my orders were to see to it that you got him and came back safely, but will you please let me have a look at that ear of yours? And he said, 'What for?' and I said, 'Curiosity', and I looked closely before he stepped back. There was no scar." Varro poured himself more wine. His hand was not quite steady. "No scar", he repeated. "That Nazarene is a magician or something. But if he is, why did he allow them to arrest him? He could have vanished or used some other trick." He drank noisily. "That's what baffles me", he added almost in a whisper. "It's queer. And all the time . . . "

292

"Yes—all the time?" Abenadar urged him eagerly.

"Oh, I don't know—I couldn't help feeling that the whole thing was a mistake somehow. They'd got hold of the wrong man—no, it isn't that. They had the wrong idea about the man, perhaps. Maybe it's that. I don't think he is a lestes."

"He said he wasn't", said Abenadar. "Did you mention that when you reported to Vindex? Clearly? Oh, well, it probably doesn't matter. Nothing to do with Vindex."

"Nothing to do with us at all", Varro said. "I don't know why we were asked to send troops."

"You say he had only a dozen men with him", Cassius interposed. He could not remain silent any longer. "But the man has literally thousands of followers, and if it hadn't been for that guide and for the fact that it was dark, there could easily have been a clash that would have cost more than an ear, healed or not healed. Why, that man has a tremendous influence. He had his captors rolling on the ground, and he made you feel damned funny, too, Varro."

Varro nodded. "I did feel funny, and that's a fact. And I wish you hadn't sent me, commander. What do you think they'll do to him? Kill him?"

Abenadar shook his head. "They can't do that. Certainly not during the feast. They'd become unclean if they did, according to their Law."

"I'd risk that danger", Cassius said coldly.

"I wouldn't", said Varro sullenly. "I don't feel clean now, if you ask me. And if he is a magician, it's very unlucky. I think I'll make a sacrifice to Jupiter tomorrow. I suppose it's all nonsense and I'm drunk, of course. Well, I'd better go to bed. There's nothing left in the damned pitcher anyway. Good night." He stalked away, not too steadily.

Cassius glared at Abenadar. "You knew I wanted to meet that man, and you sent that idiot instead."

Abenadar rose heavily. "I sent him because I thought he was

the right man for the task", he said coldly. "And after him I would have chosen Aufidus or Calvus or Mela, and if none of them had been available, I would have gone myself. But I wouldn't have chosen you. Not a word out of you, now. Just in case you've forgotten—I am still in charge of the cohort."

VIII

There were many who did not sleep that night.

Old Annas did not, the former High Priest. His son-in-law had sent a messenger just as the old man was getting ready to go to bed. The messenger brought a letter. Annas read it, grunted, and ordered his servant to dress him again. "No, no, no, not this. The ceremonial robe, the purple robe." It took the better part of an hour to get the old man ready, and he shuffled over to the hall and sat down on the ornate chair as if he were to receive official guests. His two secretaries had to be fetched. All this on the eve of the Passover. The servants looked at each other, shaking their heads. But they knew, and some of them from bitter experience, that the old man was still in full control of his mental faculties, and so did his son-in-law.

After waiting another hour, a prisoner was brought in by ten Temple guards under the command of the captain of the guards himself. It was clear that the man had been taken only after some fighting, for the captain's uniform was spattered with blood. It was clear also that the captain had been fighting valiantly, for he himself was not wounded, so the blood must have been that of an enemy. The prisoner also appeared to be unharmed.

What followed then was very strange. The old man in his chair began to ask the prisoner questions. Simple questions. What was his name? What was his age? Where was he born? Who had been his teachers?

294

To none of these questions did the prisoner give an answer. He simply stood there with his hands tied before him and said nothing.

It did not seem to upset the old man in the least. He went on asking questions, always leaving long pauses after each one, and never seemed disappointed when the man said nothing. He asked when the prisoner had come to Jerusalem—what exactly he was doing here—whether he had been preaching at the Temple—what was his knowledge of the Torah?

And still the man said nothing, nothing at all. When after a long while Annas ran out of questions, he began again from the beginning. He had a soft, gentle voice, and he showed a patience that surprised all his listeners, and especially those who knew him well. It did not seem to surprise the prisoner, who stood quietly as if it were not he who was being addressed and indeed as if the whole matter were of no concern to him.

At last another messenger arrived and was led in: Aza, the reigning High Priest's confidential secretary. He carried no letter but bowed deeply to the former ruler, and Annas immediately broke off his questioning and ordered his litter, a present of honor given him by the Emperor during the time of his reign. "To the House on the Mount", he said. It was what most people called the High Priest's palace on Mount Zion. "And let the prisoner march ahead of me."

Twenty more guards had been waiting in front of the old man's house. They led the way. The prisoner followed, with the ten men who had been in the house around him. The litter and Annas' two secretaries brought up the rear.

At the House on the Mount they found more men who would not sleep that night.

Some were in the inner court—servants and minor officials—conversing in subdued voices. They had lit a fire. It was getting on to midnight now and fairly cold.

A number of priests, including several former high priests, had arrived within the last hour or so and were now in secret council in the house. Every one of them had been summoned by special messenger, and all of them were Sadducees. Others were still arriving.

Inside the palace Kohen Gadol was presiding over the meeting of the Small Sanhedrin, or Sanhedrin of Priests, without the presence of the heads of the rabbinical schools, without the presence of the great leaders of the Pharisees.

This was his hour, and he knew it. Never would it be said of him, as of so many spinners of political webs, that he lacked the courage for decisive action. He also was taking risks. Thousands of pilgrims had formed a ring around Jerusalem, of whom at least ten thousand were potential followers of his enemy.

Yet Kohen Gadol had clawed him out of their midst, and now he would deal with him before the sleeping world around him awoke.

He had to confer with his colleagues before the trial, and above all he had to get witnesses together. That was why Annas had been given the task of "interrogating" the prisoner till all was ready.

All was ready now.

There was a good reason for the absence of the Pharisees. They were first and foremost sticklers for the letter of the Law and only too fond of formalities and of accuracy, at least as they saw it. Much as they hated the prisoner, they were certain to come up with a hundred questions about the legality of the proceedings; and it was not lawful, really, to summon the Sanhedrin at night, worse still the eve of a great feast. Besides, there was no telling what stand Rabbi Nicodemus, for instance, might take, or the Arimathean and some others of the same ilk. Nicodemus had been seen sneaking off to Bethany to visit the Nazarene in the middle of the night, despite the official anathema. At the very best they would vote for a postponement of the trial until after the feast. And tomorrow the Nazarene's many followers would rally at the story of his arrest and perhaps try to liberate him by force.

There was no time to be lost.

For many of the priests present it meant the hour of retaliation. Time and again this so-called prophet had shamed them before the people, had exposed them as greedy and money grabbing. What if they did wax rich on the sacrificial gifts the people gave to the Temple? Why should wealth not be pleasing to God? What could be done with the carcasses of oxen, sheep, and other animals, killed at the altar, but to sell them to those who wanted the meat? Was it better to let the meat go bad? Just because this Galilean nobody had no money of his own, was it right for him to condemn his betters? Listening to him, one might have thought that—God forbid—he regarded himself as the supreme authority in sacred matters.

To Caiphas most of these arguments meant little or nothing. What mattered was the elimination from their midst of a man who had the power to endanger the peace. What mattered was to preserve Kohen Gadol's power over Israel. He and his house alone had the political experience to cope with the extremely difficult situation and to avoid a war that the hotheads of the Freedom Party were sure to bring about if the man at the helm was a religious fanatic, blind to the implications of his own mouthings.

And here again it was just as well that the Pharisees should not take part in this session of the Sanhedrin. For after all they still believed in the coming of the Messiah, in the immortality of the individual soul and all the rest of the claptrap; unfortunately there were passages in Scripture which could be interpreted in their way, especially if one laid aside one's common sense. And as any learned Jew had the right to interpret the Law as he saw it, it was not possible, alas, to accuse them officially of misleading the people.

If they had been present, there would have been an endless discussion about who could or could not be the Messiah.

Grimly Caiphas watched the procession bringing in the prisoner. He was going to get this over with. When everything was finished and done, then the Pharisees or anybody else could launch their protest. Most likely, almost certainly, they would do exactly that—and at the same time rejoice secretly that a Sadducee assembly had done the work for them.

He had never seen the Nazarene before—perhaps for the simple reason that neither of them was particularly anxious to meet the other.

Well, they were meeting now in the only possible way: one as the judge, the other a prisoner. He had never heard the Nazarene say, "Judge not so that you may not be judged", and if he had heard it, he would not have known that judging others *was* judgment of the self. He was acting under political necessity and could justify every . . .

Kohen Gadol froze. Something utterly unforeseen was happening. First one witness weakened—one might not be too important—then another. And another. Their stories did not tally. Thus one declared that the accused had boasted that he had the power to destroy the Temple and build it up again in three days, while the other maintained that the accused had only said the Temple would be destroyed with no stone left upon another.

It was found that the two remarks were made on two different occasions, one several years ago, and that the two witnesses were not attesting to the same fact. Caiphas remembered a report he had received about the second of the two stories, but not about the first. A definite impasse. The Torah prescribed explicitly that there must be two witnesses for one and the same incident and that their evidence must agree.

He would have liked to call in that man Judah from Kerioth, but that again was impossible according to law. The informer could not be a witness at the trial.

From the corner of his eyes Caiphas saw the worried faces of the chief priests and elders. Was this trial to be no more successful than so many attempts to catch this formidable man? He had gone to the extreme in every way, even to asking the Roman authorities for military help. Was he now to be beaten by this Nazarene who had not even opened his mouth? He could hear the mocking laughter of Rabbi Josaphat of the Pharisees when he came to hear about it: "Many a time that man has beaten us by his eloquence and his arguments; for the High Priest his silence sufficed."

Caiphas did not look at the prisoner. There was no need to do so, and indeed it might have been tactically quite wrong. He could afford no mistakes. What he had decided to do was so dangerous that he had to brace himself to speak with a clear and steady voice, the voice of a judge, determined to break a recalcitrant prisoner's sullen silence.

He knew this was the decisive moment, not only of this trial but of his long, long struggle against the Nazarene: the moment, therefore, to say that most terrible thing and to say it in such a way that there could be no possible escape, nothing to do but to answer yes or no.

He was the High Priest, Kohen Gadol. Let the people mutter and grumble that an alien power, that Rome had put him into office, that he and his house had secured their position only by paying huge sums to Rome and continuing to pay in one form or the other. He still was the High Priest.

And his voice was clear and steady and sonorous as he said solemnly, "I adjure thee by the living God to tell us whether thou art the Christ, the Son of God."

"Thine own lips have said it."

And as if that was not enough, the prisoner spoke again: "Moreover I tell you this: you will see the Son of Man again, when he is seated at the right hand of God's power and comes on the clouds of heaven."

The High Priest rose. His strong hands tore his costly mantle, the sign of deepest mourning. Into the awed hush of the assembly he spoke with deadly finality: "What further need have we of witnesses? Mark well, you have heard his blasphemy for yourselves. What is your finding?"

One after the other they gave it, and it was death.

Judah of Kerioth did not sleep that night. One of the priests of the treasury had paid him a sum of money, carefully counting piece for piece up to thirty. It was the usual amount due an informer, and he put it into his purse, the same that had served as the community purse for the Rabbi Yeshua and his twelve closest followers during these last three years. He wandered through the streets, a little unsteadily. He was trying to think, to grasp what had happened, and what he could say, now, to Zakkai when they met. He must go to see Zakkai. Zakkai was waiting for him at—where was it?—at the Dung Gate, at the place where the camel drivers met. Zakkai felt safe there. "The Romans don't like to go there unless they have to. It stinks too badly." He must go there now. But what could he tell Zakkai?

He groaned. "I am the only one who is trying to do something", he thought. "Even now. Even now, though he failed me completely." The others were fools. He had known all the time that they were fools. Rabbi Yeshua had picked them up at the beginning, and he had never got rid of them. Some false feeling of loyalty, probably. Or lack of judgment. He *did* lack judgment, and he wouldn't listen to anyone. No man was perfect, and undoubtedly he had all the other great qualities of leadership. There was no man to match him in eloquence, and he had his own inimitable way of gaining influence over other men—even over Judah of Kerioth, with his great gift for seeing right through people. Besides, Yeshua had the ancestry a man needed if he wanted to be the Messiah. He did descend from David; he had been born at the right place, too, in Bethlehem, although that was not known widely enough so that many people thought he had been born in Nazareth in Galilee, and therefore they could not believe that he was the Messiah.

But his lack of judgment spoiled everything; that is, it would have spoiled everything but for Judah of Kerioth. Nothing could be expected from the others, dumb sheep following their leader with no ideas of their own. Yet they wanted the first places in the kingdom! As if they were capable of filling them.

That evening at Bethany, with that idiotic woman coming in with her ointment. What a travesty of the anointing of a king—performed by a woman, instead of by the High Priest, and by a woman who had been no better than a slut. And Yeshua let her go on with it; he protected her when the only man who understood the situation protested against it. A former slut, a former fisherman, a former tax collector—that was the sort of cattle he tolerated around him. He should have won over Rabbi Josaphat, and with him the entire erudite clan of the Pharisees. Made use of the rift between them and the Sadducee priests to explode the whole rotten top layer. But no. Lack of judgment all the way through. And he would not even listen when one suggested that he should receive the heads of the Freedom Party. Of course, for a while that had looked like an extremely shrewd maneuver. An open alliance with those men might have enabled the rulers to have him arrested. It was sensible to wait for the right moment before taking over the army. But then they had attacked without him, that day of the Feast of Tabernacles, and they failed, and *that* had been the time to tell them, "Without me you *must* fail. Now rally under me, and I shall lead you to victory." He did nothing of the kind. He went on curing sick wretches. But, ah, the glorious moment when he raised that man Eleazar! It was all over the city, all over the country in no time. And then—instead of following it up, of making use of the opportunity, he withdrew again.

And that wonderful entry into the city—why, they had been all ready for him. He had had only to say one word. . . . Instead of that he told them parables. Too fond of talking. And so he had missed the decisive hour.

One had to do something. One had to force *him* to do something.

He knew so many things about God, but he did not understand the mentality of men. Men wanted action. Not only words. Action.

Zakkai was clamoring for action. Zakkai's men were champing at the bit. Something had to happen.

The Dung Gate. The second house on the left. But what was he going to tell Zakkai?

It—it was so difficult to think after that look, that one look of—contempt. Or was it worse still, was it—pity?

Pity for what? For an intelligent action, a courageous action, taken by the only one of all his followers with a brain in his head. All Simon could do was brandish his silly sword. The fool. The fools.

Someone spoke to him, and he heard himself answer and was dragged into the house and into a dirty room, and the door banged behind him, and there was Zakkai, grinning. "You don't have to say anything. I know. Nothing has happened. Right?"

"It isn't over yet, Zakkai."

"No?"

"There is still some hope." Was there? There must be. There had to be. He could not have wasted three whole years on a dreamer of dreams. He pulled himself together. "I know how much you expect, Zakkai, and you'll see it will all come right—you *must* have the Messiah to lead you—you'll never get the factions of the party together without him and—"

"You've told me that a dozen times—and many other things. Yet I have never even met that Messiah of yours. Where is he? We joined those crowds hailing him when he came into the city a few days ago, but there was no possibility of getting at him to fix a plan for action. And all he did was preach in the Temple! There was a moment when I believed everything you told me—when he laid about, driving out those bloodsuckers. Good, I said to myself, he's a man of action after all. But then? Sweet nothings. Talk, talk, talk. If only Bar Abbas had not been captured! He and not this lily-mouthed fellow of yours was the man to unite the party, as he did in the past. He was all action, that one. I should know—I served under him long enough. And now? What is going to happen now?"

Zakkai's large face almost touched the face of the man of Kerioth, and a thick, blue vein showed on his forehead, swollen with his excitement and anger. "I'll tell you what is going to happen. The Romans are going to crucify Bar Abbas. Tomorrow! Just before the feast, on the first day of the feast. Crucify him! And who is going to stop that? Not you—and not that rabbi of yours who can do nothing but talk."

"But, Zakkai—"

"Today he will act, you told me. Today you can be sure he will act. I'll make him act, you said. Well—what has happened? Nothing, nothing, nothing."

"Liar! Ignorant liar!" shrilled Judah. There was desperation in his voice, and Zakkai felt it.

He stepped back. "What do you mean?"

Judah's hands clenched. "I forced his hand", he shouted. "I myself went to the High Priest and told him where my rabbi was. I myself led the guards there. Roman troops went with them. They arrested him in Gethsemani. I did it, I!"

Zakkai stared at him, open-mouthed. "I don't believe it", he gasped. "*You* went . . ."

"I am telling you—I forced him to act. But—but he would not. He would not even then. . . ."

Zakkai stepped back still farther. "Four cubits", he said hoarsely. "Four cubits' distance between me and you—between every son of Israel and you."

"But don't you understand?" Judah's voice trembled with

excitement. "I had to do it to get him to move. And it's not over yet. I told you it isn't. They have taken him to the House on the Mount and there ... "

"There Kohen Gadol will anoint him and crown him, of course, and all the little Romans will applaud. And you will become the King's first minister." Zakkai spat. "They'll kill him!"

"Absurd," cried Judah. "How could they kill him? They have no power to do that, in the first place. And the feast ... "

"They'll find a way, they or the sons of Edom—or both. And you delivered him into their power. He wasn't worth much, being no more than a talker. As far as I and the party are concerned it's good riddance. But you—he was your rabbi. Go, Judah, go quickly. This place is rotten with the dung of camels, but it will be a scented paradise when you have left. Go!"

At dawn a young man called Jochanaan bar Zebedee knocked at the door of a small house in Jerusalem. It was his mother's house: she opened the door and let him in.

He tried to tell her what had happened during the night. He was a strong and impulsive youth, but now his jaw was trembling, and his voice shook, and she had to wait as patiently as she could until he could speak coherently.

She was frightened and sorry and upset. The new kingdom, in which her sons were to be great, seemed suddenly far away, and she could not help feeling a twinge of bitterness as she pressed her son's beautiful face to her heart and caressed his long hair, the color of dark honey.

She was so proud of him—of both her sons. They were courageous, strong, and noble—everybody said so. They were so clearly cut out to be the closest companions of the King. She was terrified by the thought of what this disappointment might mean.

"Don't, Mother", said Jochanaan without looking up.

"What do you mean, son?"

"Don't be bitter about what you can't understand."

"Can you understand it, son?"

"No, and there is in me also something that would like to be bitter, and if you add your bitterness to that, it may be strong enough to take full possession—and that must not be. I must not fail him now."

"You still have faith in him then?" The voice of the strong, dark-eyed woman quivered a little. But before he could answer light steps came down the stairway that led to the upper floor, and she freed herself gently and whispered, "*She* is here. We must tell her."

"Who is here?"

"His mother."

All bitterness departed on invisible wings as they braced themselves to meet a pain infinitely greater than their own.

Claudia Procula was dreaming. The Rabbi Yeshua was standing before her husband, who was blind, and he touched his eyes and said mildly, "Open your eyes now and see." But Pilatus put his hand over his eyes and said in that stubborn tone of his she knew so well, "I cannot see. Nobody can see", and she felt an intense pain racking her because she knew that she ought to have told him that it was easy to see—she had known for a long time.

And then she saw that Yeshua's eyes were sadder than ever, and he too was suffering because there were blind people everywhere, and they stormed against him and tried to cut their way through him with swords, thinking that he was in their way. He looked at them with compassion and let them wound him.

She cried out to him to resist them, to ward them off, but he said, "Blessed are those who hunger and thirst for holiness; they shall have their fill", and at that moment her blind husband stabbed him.

She screamed and screamed, but he would not hear but went on stabbing like the others, and Yeshua said, "Blessed are the merciful; they shall obtain mercy", and still they stabbed him. Then there was a terrible noise of trumpets, and Yeshua began to grow and grow to immense size, his head gained the clouds, and still he grew, and she awoke.

The trumpets were still blowing the morning call, the signal for the soldiers to rise.

Her head ached. The place beside her was empty.

On his way back from the Dung Gate to the Temple Judah saw the former High Priest's litter and the men with it. He did not want to stop for a closer look, as he felt it was very important that he should get to the Temple, to the treasury, because of the money. It was the money that gave at least some shade of justification to Zakkai's bad opinion of him, and it was just possible that other people might think like Zakkai. The money therefore was important. He must give it back to the treasury, and then—then—he could not think further at the moment.

He staggered a little as he walked, he did not know why. The little procession passed by rather close, and he could not help seeing that *he* was there, his hands still tied together with a rope. With a rope. With a rope.

Temple guards in front, at the flanks and at the end. Priests and priests and scribes and priests, and that one, the dark one, was the one who had given him the money, and he must take it back, he must take it back at once.

Judah staggered up to the priest with the dark face. He raised the little bag with the money.

"Take it back", he said. "Take it back. I have sinned. You must take it back."

One of the guards pushed him away, but he managed to seize the priest's robe. "I have sinned", he told him wildly. "I have betrayed an innocent man."

The priest shook his hand off. "That has nothing to do with us", he said angrily. "It's your money. Do what you like with it."

They went on. They went on. They would not take the money back. They were going to the Antonia. They were going to the Romans.

So Zakkai was right.

Judah stood quite still. They wanted him killed. *They* could not kill, but the Romans could. They wanted him killed.

He had to do something. Action was required, action, now, at once.

He ran back, across the square, to the Temple, to the treasury.

He threw the money on the floor, a tinkling, silvery little river, and ran away so that they could not force him to take it again.

He passed the large hall in the Temple, where they kept the animals brought in for sacrifice. At the door he saw the ropes, hundreds and hundreds of ropes. There was a man standing in the door, looking at him curiously.

"A rope", Judah said hoarsely. "I want a rope."

The man nodded. He said nothing.

Of course, he would want money. Judah searched in his bag. The silver pieces were all gone, but he found a half shekel. A half shekel—that was what every good Jew sent to the Temple once a year.

He gave the man the half shekel.

"Choose", said the man, pointing to the array of ropes.

Judah chose.

IX

Feeling ill, tense, and worried, Claudia kept to herself.

From time to time she could hear vague noises and shouting coming from the direction of the Lithostrotos, the judgment place in front of the praetorium, but it was fairly far away from her rooms, and she paid no attention to it till Judith came running in with the news that the Rabbi Yeshua was on trial at the Lithostrotos and that a great crowd of people was shouting for his death.

Claudia blanched. Her hand flew to her heart. Her dream . . . With an effort she asked, "But why? What has he done to them?"

"Good", Judith said fiercely. "Nothing but good."

Claudia's lovely face showed contempt. "And that is how they pay him for it."

"I wish my lady would not say that." The little maid stood upright and stiffly erect, although her eyes were brimming over with tears. "It is not we who are doing this", she said in a strangled voice. "Not the Jewish people. It is the priests, the sons of Eli, who have gone rotten, and others whose learning has made their minds go sour, and the dregs of the city. I have seen some of the priests outside the gates barring the way to some and letting in only those on whom they think they can rely. Oh, they are very clever—"

"And—the procurator?"

"He is getting tired of it. He has that impatient look, my lady, just like the time he smashed that vase only because a slave had—"

"My writing tablet and my stylus, Judith, quick."

Claudia Procula scribbled a hasty note, just two lines. There was no time for more. "Do not meddle with this innocent man. I dreamed today that I suffered much on his account."

"Take this to the procurator at once and let no one stop you." Judith took the note and ran.

When the procurator was told that the mail from Caesarea had not arrived, he had known that it was going to be a trying day. The mail ship from Rome was overdue, the one regular contact with the larger world. Everyone was waiting for it; everyone was disappointed and therefore in a foul temper.

He smiled grimly when his breakfast was disturbed by the officer on duty reporting the arrival of a large deputation of Jews.

"Some of the chief priests among them, sir, and a prisoner."

That meant that he had to see them in person; and it could not be done in the praetorium, the main office building, but outside, on the Lithostrotos. These Jews firmly believed that it would make them unclean if they entered under his roof, and then they could not eat their paschal lamb. The things one had to put up with as a procurator of Judaea!

Couldn't be helped. Imperial policy was never to discourage local beliefs, never to interfere with colonial prejudices and superstitions; on the contrary, a show of respect was the thing prescribed. Any other attitude caused trouble, trouble caused punitive expeditions, and punitive expeditions cost money. Provinces were there to bring in, not to cost money.

Pilatus pushed back his plate, put on his toga, and walked over to the praetorium, where he picked up Vindex and a couple of centurions. Together they went outside.

The deputation was almost a hundred strong, almost all of them Sadducees, as far as Pilatus could make them out, and indeed including some of the chief priests. The prisoner was a tall man in a white robe. That would be the fellow they had worried so much about that they had asked for legionaries to have him arrested; Vindex had told him the whole story, of course. A lestes, they said, but Vindex was not sure, whereas the centurion making the arrest, Varro, was quite sure he was nothing of the kind. According to Varro the man behaved perfectly well about his arrest, offered no resistance, told his followers to behave.

The priests were both vociferous and nervous. Pilatus cut them short and asked the two questions that seemed to be relevant. What was the charge? And why didn't said.

No power to kill. So the matter appeared to them to be a capital crime.

Very well, what was it?

Three of them began speaking at the same time, but he got their meaning. Sedition. Preaching sedition. The fellow said Jews must not pay taxes. The fellow said he was the King Messiah.

Messiah, Messiah—time and again that came up with these people, the King Messiah who would come and make them great and glorious, the liberator of all and sundry. The King of the Jews.

Pilatus looked at the prisoner, who had not said a word. The man was bruised, seemed to have been ill treated. Maybe he was intimidated by his accusers? Pilatus turned to the nearest centurion.

"Take that man into the praetorium. I want to interrogate him myself."

The Sadducees did not raise any objection to that. Apparently it didn't matter to them if the prisoner became unclean.

Back in the main office the procurator sat down behind his table. He had a secretary called in to take down questions and answers and began the interrogation of the prisoner. Was he the King of the Jews?

He was, the prisoner affirmed, but his kingdom was not of this world. He was born and had come into the world only to bear witness of the truth. Then came a strange sentence: "Whoever belongs to the truth listens to my voice."

A kingdom not of this world. Truth. Pilatus had heard philosophers debate Truth and go for each other tooth and nail, Epicureans, Stoics, Peripatetics, and the gods knew what else. The priests of Jupiter Optimus Maximus said they had the truth, and so, probably, did all the others.

The man was a harmless idealist, poor fellow, and the Temple crowd was nervous because of the feast, that was all.

Pilatus went outside and told them that he could not find anything wrong with the man.

They did not like it. One of them yelled that the accused had been preaching sedition over the entire country, from Galilee to Jerusalem itself.

Galilee? A very welcome remark, that. Was the man a native of Galilee? He was? Ah, well, not Roman jurisdiction. Herod's.

"The case can't be dealt with before this tribunal", Pilatus declared with ill-concealed satisfaction. "Herod must deal with it. But you are lucky, you know. King Herod happens to be in the city for the Passover." Herod wasn't a Jew, of course, but he tried hard to be regarded as one, so no one could dispute his royal rights.

They didn't like that either, but there was nothing they could do about it, so they took the man away with them to Herod's palace.

Excellent solution. Very useful solution. Pilatus looked at Vindex, and Vindex grinned admiringly.

Herod had a grudge. Some of his precious Galilean subjects had been tried in Judaea, his royal prerogative had been slighted, and there was a fairly unpleasant note from him somewhere among the papers in the praetorium. This was a nice gesture, a diplomatic gesture in response to his note, and it should please the old good-for-nothing.

Now one could inquire again about the mail and then resume breakfast.

But the mail had still not arrived and the First Centurion Abenadar came in and reported that the people outside on the Lithostrotos would not leave and that more were arriving all the time.

Vindex went out to have a look, then came back and said he had smuggled a couple of agents into the crowd and they would soon know what it was all about.

By now Pilatus had lost his appetite. He remained at the table, writing. After a while Vindex came in with the report. He looked worried.

"Many of them have come, sir, because today is the eve of their feast day, and they claim their right to have one prisoner freed."

Of course. Pilatus cursed roundly. He had forgotten all about that idiotic custom. Well, they would have to have somebody. Nothing worse than breaking an established custom.

Suddenly it occurred to him that they might ask for Bar Abbas. If they did it might very well mean a great deal of trouble later on. Might be a good idea to have that man sent out to the crucifixion hill immediately and have done with it. Then they would *have* to choose somebody else.

He began to reproach himself for having kept Bar Abbas so long instead of dispatching him earlier, but it had seemed such a good idea to have him crucified just on their feast as an example.

Vindex should have warned him that this might happen. But then, Vindex wasn't a first-rate man, never had been and never would be.

What mattered now, obviously, was what kind of people they were out there. If they were quiet citizens, they wouldn't be very anxious to have Bar Abbas freed. He had caused too much trouble for that; peaceful citizens didn't have much taste for riots and bloodshed. Bad for business.

Old Abenadar came in again. He too seemed worried about something. No, not worried. Angry.

"They're back from King Herod, procurator—with the prisoner. Just coming in."

With the prisoner. Herod hadn't kept him. Now the whole thing would start again.

Vindex came with a new report. "Zakkai is in the crowd, sir—he's supposed to be the present leader of the Freedom Party. They are starting to shout for Bar Abbas."

Pilatus banged his fist on the table. He gave Vindex an ominous look, rose, and went outside, where he was greeted by a howl from at least a thousand throats. Crowds. They always made him feel like vomiting. Same thing in Rome, same thing everywhere.

Still more people were crowding in. By Jupiter, they were trying to make a big issue out of this.

He decided he would not allow more than two thousand to enter and gave Vindex orders accordingly.

The centurion who had taken the prisoner to Herod stepped forward and saluted. A young man; who was he? Ah, yes, his name was Mela.

As Pilatus told him to report, his eye fell on the prisoner, and he frowned. The man, his hands still tied, was now dressed in a scarlet cloak, a king's cloak. What was the meaning of this nonsense?

Mela explained. King Herod had only just got up when they arrived, but he seemed to be quite delighted with this official visit, as he was pleased to call it. He wished to convey his warmest regards to the procurator and to thank him for his exquisite courtesy. These were the King's very words, Mela said uneasily.

"What about the prisoner?" Pilatus asked.

"Well, sir, as I said, King Herod seemed quite delighted—he said he had been eager to meet him, because he had heard so much about him."

"Go on", urged Pilatus, as the young officer hesitated.

"Well, sir, he said he wanted to see a miracle done by the prisoner. Any miracle would do. But the prisoner was not responsive, sir. The King asked him questions—a great number of questions—and the prisoner did not say a single word. The the learned men or priests who came with us also asked questions, with the same result."

"You told the King that the prisoner regarded himself as the King of the Jews?"

"No, sir, I didn't, but one of the priests did. I—I think he wanted to upset the King a bit, sir."

"Quite likely. Go on."

"Well, sir, the King was not very much pleased at that, although

313

he laughed. Then he ordered his attendants to bring that cloak and put it on the prisoner. I had no orders about that, sir—"

"No, you hadn't. Good report. Thank you."

Mela stepped back, decidedly relieved.

A jest. Two things about it good and useful. Herod had acknowledged the Roman procurator's courtesy in letting him judge his subject; and he had proved, by his action, that he did not regard the prisoner as dangerous. Therefore there couldn't have been seditious talk, at least not in Galilee. But unfortunately the prisoner had been returned.

Noisy groups kept shouting for Bar Abbas. The Jerusalem garrison certainly needed a new intelligence officer as soon as possible.

A number of Pharisee leaders joined their Sadducee colleagues. They were not responsible for the judgment given by the Sanhedrin in last night's session, but when it came to getting rid of the man who had insulted them so often and so thoroughly, they were going to render assistance.

Vindex mumbled something about the potential usefulness of this Jesus or whatever his name was as a weapon against the power of the orthodox ecclesiastics. Trust him for saying the obvious thing; it had been on Pilatus' mind all the time. *Divide et impera.* The Emperor's favorite phrase.

From four or five places in the court shouts rose: "Death to the seditionist!" and "Death to the accused!"

Vindex, in a whisper, asked for permission to alert the first cohort. "The men could assemble in the inner court, sir, where the crowd can't see them. Just in case, sir."

But at that moment the procurator was given a note. Looking up, he saw that it was Abenadar who handed it to him.

"One of Domina Claudia's maids brought it", the first centurion said. "Domina Claudia says it is very urgent."

With a couple of thousand people yelling at him and this absurd case on his hands he must read his wife's note! Snorting,

Pilatus glanced at it, crumpled it up, frowned, opened it again, and read it once more.

He remembered now that she had seen the man; he had had to rebuke her some months ago for going into the city to hear the man talk while the city was still unsafe after the riot. From what little she had told him then, the man had talked metaphysics, certainly nothing seditious. Claudia wouldn't stand for that sort of thing.

Oh, well, he might easily have made *some* remarks that could be interpreted politically, but he certainly was not a political man; they were out for his blood because they hated him for some other reason. Probably scolded them for their bad habits, like that other fellow whom Herod had dispatched for the same cause.

Vindex babbled something about the man allegedly having performed a variety of miraculous feats. Herod seemed to have heard that, too. Strange, the man didn't look like a trickster.

The crowd kept yelling at him all the while, trying to persuade him that the man was dangerous. He was hot and angry, and he hated the noise. Abruptly he raised his hand. "Silence", he said sharply. And across the heads of Sadducee priests and Pharisee leaders he called out to the people on the square: "You have a custom of demanding that I should release one prisoner at paschal time. Would you have me release the King of the Jews?"

Zakkai's bull voice rang out: "Give us Bar Abbas!" His men took up the cry. So did Sadducees and Pharisees, some of them glancing at each other knowingly. It certainly was the first time they had voted for Bar Abbas, and they were not likely to again, but at the moment only one thing mattered.

Zakkai barked an order at the men around him, "Shout louder for Bar Abbas! Death to this man. Freedom for Bar Abbas!"

And for the first time the terrible cry went up, "Crucify him! Free Bar Abbas! Crucify this man!"

The procurator hesitated. Vindex whispered to him that it

looked rather ugly and repeated his suggestion to alert the First Cohort.

"Do so then." Pilatus turned to the crowd. "I will scourge him, and then he shall go free", he said angrily.

But the whole mob seemed to be shouting for Bar Abbas now. Vindex was right; it did look ugly.

Pilatus shrugged his shoulders. "As you're so anxious for Bar Abbas, you shall have him. See to it, Vindex."

With a long face, Tribune Vindex passed on the order to the Centurion Varro, who clanked away to the dungeons. Then Mela had the prisoner led off for the scourging.

Varro came back with Bar Abbas. Six months in the dungeon had left their mark on the Freedom Party leader. His reddish beard had gray patches, and he had lost a great deal of weight. He did not understand what was happening to him and stood blinking in the unaccustomed light of the midday sun. When Zakkai and his men started shouting his name, he recoiled a step or two. Varro patted him on the back, very much as if he were patting a horse.

Then the Centurion Cassius Longinus came up from the praetorium and reported to Vindex that the First Cohort was ready in the inner court. "Some of our men are having fun with a prisoner there", he added.

"Scourging", Vindex said, frowning. "The usual thing."

Cassius said nothing. So the scourging was official; he had had the idea that young Mela might be acting on his own. He looked at the crowd, still restless and shouting up at the procurator. What was this all about? He had been working all morning with the legate on routine stuff, while here . . . Then he saw Bar Abbas, free and surrounded by welcoming friends.

"Surprised, eh?" It was Abenadar's voice, very low, only just audible. "They chose Bar Abbas. They condemned the man who is being brought in just behind you."

Cassius turned quickly. He saw the man whom they had

flogged and made sport of in the inner court. Two soldiers were supporting him. He wore a tattered scarlet cloak, and they had put a kind of crown on his head, made of thorny twigs; he could not see because his eyes were full of blood. They had put a reed in his right hand to look like a scepter.

"Who is he?" Cassius asked.

Pilatus glanced at the prisoner. "See, here is the man", he said almost jovially. All over now. Numerous strokes with the leather whip, with little pieces of lead inserted in the ends: "the half death" they called it in the army, and many a delinquent had died under it. Now surely that was enough.

It was not enough. Not for the pale, excited priests. They went on demanding death, insisting on death.

"We have our own Law, and by our Law he ought to die for pretending to be the Son of God."

All of a sudden Cassius knew who the prisoner was. He paled.

Of all the stupid things, Pilatus thought angrily. But—was it so stupid? Those "miracles" the man was supposed to have performed, the extraordinary influence he had on so many people. . . . Even Claudia had been carried away. Was it so stupid? For a moment something very much like fear welled up in the man who had long ago discarded any belief in either Roman or foreign gods.

Pale, staring faces, spitting hatred, hands gesticulating—he could not think straight here.

"Take the prisoner back to the praetorium", he ordered curtly.

The man seemed to have recovered a little, from the way he set his feet.

Pilatus followed him and sat down heavily at his table. "Where hast thou come from?" he asked. What if the man answered that he came from the seat of the gods? What if he suddenly showed himself, revealed himself as—not human?

But the man remained silent. And it was not due to the pains or the shock of the scourging. He was very weak, but he was fully conscious. He did not *want* to speak.

Pilatus began to drum on the table with his fingers. "What, hast thou no word for me?" he said. "Dost thou not know that I have power to crucify thee, and power to release thee?"

His Aramaic had never been good, and he was disagreeably aware that he was talking down to the prisoner when he should not. It was almost like using the language of signs to a philosopher. "You be good or I'll punish you—you understand me?" He was angry with himself for not being able to talk to the man as he would have liked to; he was irritated by his entirely irrational feeling of embarrassment, and at the back of his mind he was afraid. Just a little afraid. But afraid.

Then the prisoner spoke at last. "Thou wouldst not have any power over me at all if it had not been given thee from above." And, after a short pause, "That is why the man who gave me up to thee is more guilty yet."

Pilatus fairly gaped. He had had legal training, but he was first and foremost a soldier, and as a soldier he reserved his deepest respect for courage. This was the most scathing retort he had ever received from a man on whom he was about to pronounce judgment. Sullen silence he knew. Indignant protestations. Insolence and even impudence, the hurling of abuse, curses, and oaths. Or pleadings, entreatings, cajoling, begging, flattering, tears of self-pity and of hatred, of remorse and of moral indignation. The flamboyant honesty of the dishonest he knew and the outrageous smile that said, "I know I can't say anything to please you; whatever I say you are going to condemn me, because you are a cruel man or because you have been bribed." He knew the apathy of the dullard and the dumb anger of the downtrodden. And he knew that all these attitudes and many others could be the signs of innocence or the signs of guilt, mankind being what it was.

But this was different. This was judgment given on *him*.

This prisoner, this wreck of a man, with several thousand people yelling for his blood, scourged, jeered, mocked at, could make a calm, objective statement of guilt—but of the guilt of his betrayer and of his judge, whom, incidentally, he equally calmly acknowledged as his judge because of power "from above". And according to the prisoner's judgment the betrayer was even guiltier than the judge. Of course, this presupposed as a given fact that he regarded himself as absolutely and perfectly innocent. But that was only by the by. The thing that mattered to the prisoner was to differentiate between the guilt of his betrayer and of his judge—and in the same breath to pronounce them both guilty.

And the trouble was that he was right. His judgment, the judgment of the prisoner, was correct.

Many a lesser man would have regarded it simply as the most incredible insolence. "After all I am the judge here. I am the representative of the Roman Empire, and according to the best brains of his own people this fellow is a criminal." For lesser men like to cover up their less edifying actions as individuals with the cloak of national grandeur or national necessity, as the case may be.

Perhaps it was the finest moment in the life of Pilatus the judge that he replied nothing but went back to the Lithostrotos, fully resolved to set the man free.

And there was one other thought that had got a hold in his mind, once more primarily a soldier's thought. A soldier was always up against the problem of authority. He knew something about it. He knew the difference between true and false authority, and he knew a true leader when he saw him. This prisoner was a leader. He was not a military leader. He was not a political leader. He was not a philosopher either—cocksure of his concepts or vague and muddleheaded. There was something royal about his manner that almost made one forget that the scarlet cloak had been hung on him only as a mockery.

From then on Pilatus referred to the prisoner invariably as the King. After all, why not? The man was ten times more of a king than that rascal Herod.

In the meantime the Sadducee priests had asked for and had received reinforcements, which consisted of one man, a tall, well-favored man in his late fifties, with a beautifully kept black beard, sprinkled with silver.

Aza had slipped out to fetch him, and the sentinels now guarding the gates against further arrivals could not very well stop this one. The newcomer and the priests were talking together in whispers.

The moment Pilatus said, "I cannot find any fault in him", one of the Sadducees cried aloud, "If you say that, you are giving justification to his claims." And another, "Thou art no friend to Caesar if thou dost release him; the man who pretends to be a King is Caesar's rival!"

A rival of Caesar! Pilatus gave a sign to bring the man back to the Lithostrotos. When they saw that pitiful sight, they would have to acknowledge that this sort of statement could not be made in earnest.

But the moment the man in the scarlet cloak and crowned with thorns appeared again, the howl went up: "Crucify! Crucify!"

"What, shall I crucify your King?" Pilatus asked coldly.

The tall, well-favored man stepped forward. He looked Pilatus straight in the eyes and said in a sonorous voice, "We have no king except Caesar."

As the procurator recognized the reigning High Priest, he instinctively lifted his right hand in a greeting. But his mind was racing. This put an entirely new face on the whole affair. It no longer merely involved an individual, guilty or innocent. It had become a state affair. First of all, the High Priest had made official acknowledgment of Rome's absolute rule over Judaea. That it was pure hypocrisy did not matter. Here was submission absolute under the Roman rule, from the mouth of spiritual rulership and in front of two thousand witnesses.

But in the same breath, the High Priest had also made it

impossible for Pilatus to release the prisoner without laying himself open to an accusation before the Emperor. Tiberius, of course, might dismiss it with a laugh. He was an experienced statesman, and he knew—or he used to know—sufficiently well what was going on in every province of the empire. He would know, or else could easily be convinced, that the High Priest's statement was no more than a clever argument for getting rid of a hated enemy who in reality was a perfectly harmless man and might even be of use to Rome as an influence against the arrogance of the orthodox priesthood.

Tiberius was sequestered on an island. . . . An upstart like Sejanus would take the High Priest's words at face value. The supreme authority of the country had asked the Roman procurator to destroy a man who declared himself to be the King of Judaea. The supreme authority of Judaea was loyal and would accept no other King than the Emperor himself. If the procurator released the prisoner now—in a few months' time he would be standing before Sejanus, trying to justify himself, and somebody else would be procurator of Judaea.

The High Priest had maneuvered him into a situation from which there was no escape. He had forced his hand. The impudence of it made the Roman grit his teeth. What joy it would be to remain adamant.

The crowd was howling like savages. Savages. Pilatus thought of Varus in the German forest, savages howling all around him in the dark. Advance or withdrawal? Varus made the courageous decision. A couple of days later he was dead. It did not pay to be courageous.

Pilatus passed a weary hand across his forehead. Action was required—immediate action. And as Judah of Kerioth asked for a rope, Pilatus now asked for a bowl of water to be brought for him to wash his hands.

"I have no part in the death of this innocent man; it concerns you only."

A great shout of triumph went up from the crowd, the wild, uproarious, soulless, and merciless triumph of the mob which has got its wish. "His blood be upon us and upon our children."

Thus they accepted responsibility, chanting the ancient formula: the pack of Freedom Party men who knew that their leader Bar Abbas was now safe; the Pharisee savants, myopic from too much reading and unable to see the storm clouds on the horizon; the Sadducee priests, jealous of their privileges and their wealth; and a couple of thousand people, some of them irresistibly drawn by the scent of bloodshed and catastrophe, while certain others were present under orders and did not know or care about anything except shouting what they had been told to shout.

Outside the walls thousands upon thousands of pilgrims were preparing for the feast, the great feast of liberation from bondage. They did not know what had happened on the Lithostrotos.

As Caiphas walked away, calm and dignified, Zakkai glowered at him angrily. Bar Abbas was free—but that priest had no right to talk like that. The hour would come when the party would show him and his like whom Israel regarded as her leader and what regard she had for Caesar. He said so to Bar Abbas, standing beside him. But Bar Abbas did not answer. He stared dully into space.

Zakkai looked at him anxiously, and the thought struck him that the great man might no longer be what he had been before he was cast into the dungeon of the Antonia.

Many Pharisees and Sadducees pressed Caiphas' hands as he passed among them. He hid his contempt behind an enigmatic smile. There would be no revolution now. And in the future a man would think and think again before professing to be the Messiah. Perhaps this would lay that ghost once and for all.

There was one man who shared this thought with him. It was Pilatus.

He had had to let them have their way, but at least this would

322

be the end of that Messiah story that was haunting the country. They had had their Messiah, and they would not have another.

He asked for a piece of parchment, for pen and ink, and wrote, "Jesus of Nazareth, King of the Jews", in Latin, and then again, in Greek.

"First Centurion!"

Abenadar stepped forward.

"Have somebody write the same text underneath in Hebrew. It will be fixed on the cross, over the man's head. Make the letters big. You are in charge of the execution party. There are three men to be crucified, the two lestes who were with Bar Abbas and the King of the Jews. The King in the middle. Take as many men with you as you think necessary."

Abenadar had turned as white as chalk. He was struggling for words. But just then a Pharisee leader bent forward, read the inscription, and said furiously, "Thou shouldst not write, 'The King of the Jews'! Thou shouldst write, 'This man *said*, "I am the King of the Jews"!' "

Icily Pilatus said, "What I have written, I have written." And he turned away abruptly and walked back to the praetorium.

Abenadar wrote the text in Hebrew himself; he had learned to form these letters when he learned to read the Scriptures. It did not take him long. But when he had finished, the procurator had gone, and so had Vindex. Only the Centurions Varro, Mela, and Cassius Longinus were still there and the fifty men that Vindex always insisted on having present when the procurator had any kind of dealings with a crowd — and of course the two soldiers on either side of the prisoner. Everybody except the prisoner was looking at him.

He was in charge now. And he was the only senior officer.

"All the men here will form the escort", he said in a quiet voice. "Centurion Varro: take twenty men of the cohort in the inner court; fetch the other two prisoners and the—things we shall need. Centurions Longinus and Mela are dismissed."

X

A bath. Nothing in the world was as important now as a cool bath. Pilatus shouted for the bath slaves and went to the swimming pool. It was not much of a pool, of course, compared to that in the palace in Caesarea, to say nothing of the baths in Rome. Ah, to be in Rome; to strip leisurely in one of the Thermes, first a hot pool, then a tepid, then a cool one and a skillful massage, and friends to talk to . . .

To be in Rome and to forget all about these infernal people, their shouting, their gesticulating, their obstinate insistence on having things their own way. He had done the only thing he could do. He had tried so hard to—he refused to think of it. Cool, cool water, refreshing.

What a crowd it had been; it fouled the air. This would wash it off, wash it away from body and mind once and for all.

A judge had so many cases. Even the best judge, surely, gave the wrong judgment sometimes. It could not be helped; there were circumstances . . .

He was bound to forget it sooner or later, so why not now? What difference did it make if they were at work on the man at this particular moment, or the next? Time? What was time really?

The water was too cold. It made one feel restless. He got out, and the slaves rubbed him dry and helped him into a fresh tunic, fresh sandals, everything fresh, a new man. He was a new man now.

He decided to go to see Claudia. She would know by now that he had not been able to save the fellow, and she would want to talk about it, but he could always wave that aside—enough for today, my dear. I've had it all morning; I cannot talk about it anymore. A woman's voice, a woman's chatter, the perfume that always surrounded her.

But that little Jewish maid of hers was standing before her

door. Would the master please excuse the domina? She was not feeling well and had gone to bed again. She was sleeping now.

The maid's face looked ugly, all swollen up. She'd been crying, apparently. Perhaps Claudia had been crying too, tears, a swollen face, reproaches, explanations . . .

Pilatus turned abruptly and went back to the praetorium and his office. A curse on all women, Pharisees, Sadducees, lestes, crowds, and all the rest. By Jupiter, one might think the world was going to pieces because he had a Jewish rabbi executed. He'd execute a dozen—all of them, if he thought it was necessary.

With what desperate seriousness they all seemed to take it! In twenty years, in ten years he would have forgotten the whole thing completely. After all, he had been confronted by so many problems in the course of his life, both in the army and as an administrator—worse than this one—this was just another case, not a nice case, admittedly, but what else could he have done? There—thinking again. He swore under his breath.

In his office he found Vindex with a letter he had composed, a letter to Herod. "Don't you think it's an excellent opportunity to restore good relations, sir?"

The fellow was obviously trying to make up for his blunder about Bar Abbas. But it wasn't a bad idea.

"Even better," Pilatus said, after a moment's thought, "I'll pay a courtesy visit to the old fox. Now. Get me a couple of centurions and an escort. We'll ride over."

A few minutes later Pilatus was on his way, on horseback, with the two centurions Longinus and Mela and twenty men.

Herod. He at least had not taken that man so seriously; he'd had his fun with him. Clever fox, Herod.

The streets seemed strangely empty. Just as well. He'd seen enough of their faces.

Had they all gone to watch that man being nailed to the cross?

Nonsense. Most of them would never go near that place. What did they call it? the Skull. Golgatha.

The air was leaden.

Pilatus had never before visited the King in his Jerusalem palace. Herod did not often come here. He stayed most of the time in his own realm, and lately they had not been on good terms.

When the cavalcade arrived at the palace gate, Pilatus sent young Mela to announce his arrival. "We must give the man a minute or two to put on his paraphernalia, can't embarrass him."

It seemed to be getting dark. There was no wind at all. Almost as if a thunderstorm were brewing. Not likely, though, at this time of the year.

A stream of servants in the gaudy Herodian livery came pouring out. There was the usual bowing and scraping while Pilatus dismounted.

A moment later the King himself appeared, smiling, with outstretched arms. What an unexpected pleasure, if only he had known, he would have made suitable preparations . . .

The King's wine was excellent, always was; one had to say that for him. Altogether, he knew how to live, magnificent carpets and vases, slaves beautifully trained . . .

Pilatus inquired courteously for the Queen and the Princess.

Herod explained regretfully that the ladies had preferred to stay at home; they did not like Jerusalem, hated it, to be frank. Most courteous on the part of the procurator to send over that unfortunate man. Was it true that he was—to be executed?

Well, yes.

The King made a wry face. He scratched his chin, a habitual gesture—his beautifully perfumed beard was always a little in disarray because of it. Executed, eh? On the cross? Was it not a little hard?

Pilatus was playing with his cup, a beauty of a cup, worth a small fortune. A little hard? Well, a matter of viewpoint. The man claimed to be the King of the Jews. A political claim of some magnitude. And the Jews did not like it. They had shown an almost surprising loyalty to the Emperor.

Herod laughed heartily and then shouted for lamps to be brought in. The darkness was deepening steadily.

"Of course, the man was a little strange", Pilatus went on. "When I questioned him, he said his kingdom was not of this world."

Herod put his cup down. He shook his head, as if he wanted to shake off a thought. "I don't like it", he said suddenly. "I don't like it. Such men are very troublesome. I've had some experience with them myself. That dreadful man Jochanaan—you remember him, perhaps? Went around baptizing people, as he called it, all quite harmless—but saying terrible things about the Queen, about myself. . . . I tried to ignore it for a long time, but the Queen was upset and no wonder. In the end I had to arrest the man, and *then* the real trouble started. Much better if I had gone on ignoring him. One mustn't touch such people, my lord procurator. One must leave them alone. It will end one way or the other; everything ends . . . "

He looked waxen and ill, but perhaps that was only because of the artificial light.

Pilatus said nothing. After a while Herod continued. "They always talk as if they knew something that no one else knows, as if the deity had let them in on all kinds of secrets." He grimaced, as if he had bitten on something bitter. "They have a knack of making one feel like a worm, and one doesn't like to feel like a worm."

"Exactly . . . " Pilatus nodded. "That is   I mean—they are awkward people." He was perspiring a little.

"That's why I didn't want to have anything to do with that Rabbi Yeshua of yours", Herod went on. "That's why I sent him back to you so quickly. He wouldn't perform any miracle for me—well, I didn't expect him to, not really, you know. I—I heard a good deal about what he had done or was supposed to have done—"

"Do you think he can do anything miraculous?" Pilatus asked with somewhat uneasy sarcasm.

327

Herod spread out his hands. "It is not reasonable, is it? I mean, if he could he would not be—where he is now."

There was a sharp, metallic noise, and the King stared down, naked fear in his eyes, at the two cups, which had clashed as if by their own volition. Now they were gliding away from each other again. They seemed to have a life of their own. They were dancing up and down.

"An earthquake!" Pilatus ejaculated.

For a few seconds the two men felt that they had been lifted up bodily and were dangling in midair. One of the cups fell with a crash, and the wine poured onto the tablecloth in a dark stream.

"An earthquake", assented Herod. He stared with disgust at the wine. "A very slight earthquake", he said. "A perfectly natural thing to happen, is it not? Absolutely natural." His voice rose rapidly to shrillness. "You see what I mean? Such men—one should not even talk about them. They make everything appear—come in, somebody!"

Slaves, gray faced with fear, entered, and he had the cups and tablecloth removed and replaced.

"We are rational men." The King managed a smile. "We are not influenced by such—occurrences. Nevertheless I must say I'm glad I didn't—condemn that man. Oh, I suppose you had to", he added hastily. "You couldn't help it. Somebody had to. Have some more wine, will you?"

"No, thank you, my lord King." Pilatus rose. There was that feeling which always came after an earthquake, that nothing was firm or solid or safe. "I think I had better go back to the Antonia now—to see whether there is any damage."

"Oh, there won't be, noble procurator, there won't be; the tremor was much too slight for that. But if you feel you must—I admire your sense of responsibility."

Pilatus stared at him. You never knew with that old fox, but on the whole it was not likely that he was being sarcastic. He was still too frightened for that.

"Miracles or no miracles, my lord King, you and I must be for law and order, and that means we must be against anybody who threatens to upset law and order."

"Exactly, exactly—"

The usual compliments followed, and the King went so far as to accompany the procurator to the palace door; most courteous, really; perhaps the visit had been a success after all.

Outside it was almost as dark as night, and the air was still heavy.

"Let me help you, sir", the Centurion Longinus said. "The horses are a bit nervous."

"You don't appear to be nervous anyway", Pilatus said when he was finally in the saddle.

"No, sir." Cassius grinned.

"Good. We are going back now."

The clatter of hooves seemed to be the only noise in the world. The streets were deserted.

"What is the time?" Pilatus asked casually.

"Going on for the ninth hour, I should say, sir", Longinus replied.

There was a lightning flash with thunder following so quickly that the center of the storm could not be very far away. Longinus' horse reared and almost threw him, but he managed to quiet it down again and to resume his place in the escort.

The man did not seem to have any nerves, Pilatus noticed with envy. Young, of course. And nothing much to think about. He was wrong about the time, though. The trial had been over before the sixth hour—noon—and surely since then less than three hours had elapsed.

The trial. Now he was even calculating time in terms of that trial. Absurd.

They reached the Antonia. No damage was visible there. Pilatus dismounted, gave the two officers a short nod, and walked to the praetorium. As he passed the Lithostrotos, he hesitated, stopped, and walked over to the judgment seat. The whole place was empty now, and the seat looked very small. That was strange. A few hours ago he had felt as if it were the whole world, with all the world's people shouting at him.

So many more cases would appear before him here. He really must stop fussing about this one.

Out here the prisoner had not said a single word. Threats, insults, curses had seemed to be scurrying about like rats through thick layers of hatred and anger and vindictiveness.

Thundering again. But the thunder did not come from above—it was a rolling, groaning noise from under his feet.

Once more, more strangely than before, he felt that he was not standing on solid ground at all, that everything was shaking and trembling and hanging in midair, as if the whole world had hanged itself and were dangling at the end of a gigantic rope.

The judgment seat too was rocking.

He staggered toward the praetorium. The way seemed to go uphill, steeply uphill.

A whistling noise came from afar. It grew and grew, and now a gust of wind blew across the Lithostrotos with such force that he would have fallen if he had not been seized by strong arms from right and left. His two officers, Longinus and Mela. He was glad they had been looking for him; they all had to struggle to keep on their feet, but here was the entrance at last, and he was safe.

Kohen Gadol, Aza, and a small retinue were on their way back from the house of old Annas when the second, heavier quake began, and they took shelter under a heavily built doorway.

Caiphas' first thought was that he would have to return to his father-in-law as soon as this was over. The old man had been having convulsions, and twice at least Caiphas had thought he was dying. In between the fits he muttered incoherent words.

Aza maintained he had said something about the vengeance of the Galilean or the magic of the Galilean or words to that effect. After two solid hours of nursing, the old man had become quiet and finally fallen asleep. But this upheaval might well bring on a severe relapse.

Then the sudden gust of wind came, of such strength that a number of people were thrown to the ground. Clouds of dust and sand filled the streets and made it almost impossible to breathe.

As soon as the worst was over Caiphas stepped out into the street, drawing a corner of his cloak over nose and mouth, and the others followed his example. They had walked only a few yards when they heard somebody screaming something that stopped them, all of them, as one man.

"The Temple—the Temple!"

A man came running and Aza seized hold of him. "What is it about the Temple? Speak up, man!"

"Split—split!" The man was babbling like a lunatic. "The curtain ..."

They all turned and ran toward the Temple square.

When they saw the Temple, they stopped in their tracks and stared, incapable of speaking.

All the four outer curtains of the giant building had torn loose and were fluttering wildly in the strong wind. And the inner curtain, shielding the Holy of Holies, was split from top to bottom, laying bare what must never be seen by a human eye except that of Kohen Gadol.

Kohen Gadol looked at it in horror. Some strange impulse made him think of the moment the night before when he had torn his mantle.

At about the same time a small delegation of men in black, fringed robes hastened to the Antonia and asked to be received by the procurator.

"Outside the praetorium, I take it", the centurion on duty said dryly.

"If you please", said the leader of the delegation politely. He was Rabbi Josaphat.

Pilatus swore when he was told, and Vindex offered to go out and hear what they had to say. He came back after a few minutes. "It's about the bodies of the executed men, sir", he said. "Their sabbath starts at sunset, and it's an abomination to them if their people are killed on the sabbath. They call it a desecration."

"I shall never understand these people", Pilatus snorted.

"So they are pleading for the usual procedure, sir — to have the legs of the executed men broken and to have them carried away to be buried together, when they're dead, I suppose."

"Tell them they can go bury them themselves", Pilatus rasped.

But Vindex shook his head. "Sorry, sir, but there is an imperial edict — I've got it here somewhere, if you'll bear with me for one moment —" He began a frantic search among documents and papers on his desk. "Here it is, sir. 'Caesar Augustus, Pontifex Maximus, Tribune of the people, ordains thus: since the nation of the Jews has been found grateful to the Roman people — and so on — it seemed good to me and my counselors — and so on —'" Vindex flushed and began to mumble, as the next passage dealt with an imperial promise that the korban was not to be touched, but then he got hold of the relevant passage: " 'And that they are not obliged to go before any judge on the sabbath day, or on the day of preparation for it, *after the ninth hour*' — you see, sir, that's the thing, the ninth hour will start shortly, and their interpretation is that from then on they are exempt from all legal proceedings, including torture. That's their case, sir, but what they chiefly have in mind, I think, is that their sabbath must not be desecrated."

"All right", Pilatus snapped. "Centurion Longinus!"

Cassius stepped forward.

"Take a dozen men and some carts, ride out to the execution

place, have the legs of the three men smashed, and carry them off wherever they are supposed to go. Where is it, Vindex?"

"Burial place for executed criminals, in the Hinnom Valley, sir."

"You heard, centurion."

"Yes, sir."

"Vindex! Tell those people outside that their wish is granted."

The tribune obeyed. The little group in the fringed, black robes listened attentively, expressed a coldly polite gratitude, and withdrew.

As they left, the Centurion Cassius Longinus was already ordering the carts to be brought from the stables. A few minutes later he and his twelve men were under way, up the same road that the soldiers with their prisoners had taken a little over three hours ago.

The sky was clearing a little now, but it was still very dark.

As Cassius turned a corner of the twisting road he saw the execution party on their way back, with Varro riding alongside the column. They were marching in double file, leaving just enough space to pass them.

Cassius gave a curt salute and then stopped Varro simply by halting opposite him. "Is Abenadar still up there?" he asked. "And what's the . . . "

He broke off. He had seen Varro's face.

"What's the matter with you, man, are you ill?"

"Let me pass", Varro said thickly. He pressed his horse on so vehemently that Cassius had to give way.

What *was* the matter with the man? He had been in the army all his life—he was bound to have been on execution duty before. A crucifixion was not pretty, but it was not a rare occurrence.

Cassius stared at the returning soldiers and did not like what he saw. They looked like men retreating after a disaster.

The magician seemed to have bewitched them all. Five men were missing. So was Abenadar.

Cassius spurred his horse and rode up the hill. It was only just clear enough to see the silhouettes of the three crosses. Something dark on one of them was moving a little.

Suddenly he pulled at the reins with all his strength, so that the horse reared up and recoiled.

There was a split in the rock just ahead a yard in width.

The earthquake. Maybe that was what had frightened Varro and his men. The quake seemed to have been very strong up here. He had seen little damage in the city, except here and there a bit of fallen masonry.

Varro might have warned me of this, Cassius thought angrily, and he led the trembling horse up a different path. Turning in the saddle he shouted back to his men, "Careful here. Split in the rock. Follow me."

Then he reached the top of the hill. It was a fairly wide plateau.

From where he stood the three crosses looked huge and black in the half-dark. The one in the middle was that of the Galilean; he could see the parchment attached to it. Nothing moved there. The man had probably lost consciousness.

The two lestes on the outside crosses were squirming feebly, and he could hear them groan.

The shadows of a few soldiers hovered near the crosses. Perhaps Abenadar was one of them.

No wonder Abenadar had sent Varro and the others back. There were scarcely any people left here now. Only small groups of veiled women and far away, at the outer edge of the plateau, a few men. That was all. No one stirred.

A thought whispered that this was the loneliest place in the world.

The sound of the carts rumbling up the hill came as a relief. When they reached the plateau Cassius raised his hand. "Wait here", he ordered. His voice sounded hoarse and yet much too loud.

He forced his horse nearer to the crosses.

At the foot of the one in the middle women were kneeling. One of them was Naomi.

She was looking up to the shadowy figure on the cross.

Cassius clenched his teeth and rode on. But as he approached, the women rose, turned, and walked away to where the others were standing. She had not looked at him at all.

Then he saw Abenadar. He had both arms around the upright of the cross, and his head, like that of the crucified man, had sunk on his breast. As Cassius dismounted, he looked up.

"Order of the procurator", Cassius began. Then he stopped. Varro's appearance had been bad enough. Abenadar's expression was terrifying; his face seemed to have shrunk, and the eyes under shaggy white brows burned like coals.

"The Son of God", Abenadar whispered. "He was the Son of God. He was the Messiah."

"Was?" Cassius asked sharply.

The old man nodded. "He is dead", he whispered. "And by his wounds we were healed."

Lost his reason. But if the man was dead—

"He has prayed for the transgressors", said Abenadar tonelessly. "He has prayed for me—and for you. He was the Son of God."

"Come with me", Cassius said gently, and he tried to loosen the old man's fingers from the cross. But he would not let go, and finally Cassius shrugged and stepped back. Turning toward the carts, he raised his arm and beckoned, and they rumbled up to him.

"Three men for each of the two crosses right and left", Cassius ordered. "Break their legs and take them down." He looked at Abenadar. The old man did not seem to have heard him. He was still clinging to the base of the cross.

Cassius raised his chin toward one of Abenadar's soldiers, and the man came up. He took him aside and asked in a whisper, "What's the matter with the commander?"

The man looked past him. "You haven't been here, sir", he muttered. "You're lucky."

One of the two lestes gave a wild shriek as the clubs smashed his shinbones; then he was quiet. The other one howled, a long-drawn animal howl.

"What was so terrible about it?" Cassius asked, when at last the howl had ceased. "The earthquake, I suppose?"

The soldier shook his head. "It wasn't that, sir", he whispered. "I've been through many quakes. Nothing to them, unless you get swallowed up by a sudden split or unless you're hit by something falling on you, more likely." He became eloquent suddenly, in a kind of conspiratorial way. "It's just that one's not accustomed to a god of flesh and blood, sir, that's what it is. And that one on the cross is a god, sir. I know it sounds crazy, but it's true."

"Then why didn't he come down and kill you all?"

But the heavy sarcasm was lost on the soldier. "I think he could have, sir. I think he didn't want to."

Cassius said scathingly, "You are all stark, raving mad up here."

The soldier nodded. "May well be, sir. We killed a god, sir. That could most likely make a man mad."

Cassius thrust out his jaw. "Tell me just one thing", he said. "What in the name of madness makes you think that this executed criminal was a god?"

The man looked past him again. He said nothing.

Cassius turned away. The groups of women were all kneeling now. Naomi was kneeling to that man on the cross. He was dead, gone, finished, yet she was on her knees before him. A god.

They had driven nails through his palms and through his feet, and he had squirmed and twisted on his cross as they all did. He had sweated and bled and cried as they all did, and then he died. But he was a god.

And she preferred to look up to her dead god rather than look at her lover . . .

Then he saw the soldiers. They had finished their work with the two lestes and were looking at him for further orders.

No sense in breaking the legs of a dead man. Not too much sense in it even when a man was still alive. It was an old army regulation. Sometimes during a war or the quelling of a rebellion a condemned man had to be taken off the cross before he was dead, especially when there were many to be crucified and little wood was obtainable for the crosses. So they took the man off and smashed his legs. That way he could not possibly escape, and he was sure to die, helpless as he was, as soon as the wounds began to suppurate and to get full of maggots. It would be simpler to kill him outright, but a rebel's death had to be painful, to deter others. In any case the cross was then empty and could be used for the next man.

But this man on the middle cross was dead. Or—was he?

Abenadar had said so. This idiot of a soldier had said so. But those two were in a condition to say anything.

Everybody up here was mad, except himself and the men he had brought with him and who had not yet been affected by the spell of this Galilean miracle worker. Abenadar was his commander, but in his present state he was not capable of making any kind of decision. Cassius knew it was up to *him*.

It was up to him to dispose of that god of theirs. Abenadar's god. Naomi's god.

He approached the cross again. The shadowy figure hung motionless. If only one could see in this infernal darkness.

He was probably dead. Probably. But why did Abenadar hang on to the base of the cross? Why were the women kneeling?

Did they think that his shadow, his ghost, was still about? There were a lot of superstitions about that sort of thing. A ghost, a disembodied soul or whatever they called it, could return into its body and use it again. Maybe they believed that? But even a magician could no longer use a body after its vital organs were destroyed.

337

And now he knew that he must make sure, absolutely sure that the man was dead. He beckoned to the soldier to whom he had spoken. The fellow came, reluctantly.

"Give me your spear", Cassius said roughly.

The man obeyed. His hands were trembling. No use letting him try; he'd only botch it. It was a regulation six-foot spear, the blade almost two inches wide and near the shaft a little over half an inch thick.

Cassius weighed it in his hands to get the feel of it and then tightened his grip. Raising the spear with both hands, he thrust it with all his strength forward and up, through the crucified man's heart.

For one split moment he thought that he had been hit by a bolt of lightning. Everything around him lighted up with terrifying clarity, and he saw the long, lean body, pale and golden, with its arms outstretched as if to embrace him, and his spear entering it. He heard the thud, and he felt the resistance, either of the body or of the wood of the cross behind it.

Then it was night again, a dark-red night splashing all over him and blinding him completely, and he staggered and would have fallen if he had not held on to the spear in the crucified man's heart.

Blood. He was full of blood. The whole world was full of blood. He was suffocating in it.

From far, far away came the sound of crying. The world was crying.

He wiped the blood from his face.

It was still day. The sun had broken through the clouds just as he had thrust in the spear, and for one moment he had seen clearly, for that one moment. Then darkness again . . . It had not been lightning but the sun.

The long, lean body hung before him, pale and golden, with its arms outstretched, as if to embrace him. The head with the crown of thorns had sunk on the chest.

He must withdraw the spear now. Softly. Softly. Blood came flowing again, dark red—and water. Blood and water.

For some strange reason it made him think not of death but of birth. He shook off the absurd thought.

There was the soldier; he must give him back his spear. But the man raised his hands, shaking hands, and turned and walked away.

"Centurion . . . "

Cassius turned. A tall man, gray-haired, his face the color of old ivory. Very richly dressed. Beside him, smaller and even older, a scholarly-looking man in the black, fringed robe of the Pharisee rabbi. Behind them a few servants, carrying a stretcher, a few vases, and some sheets of white cloth.

Cassius saw it all quite distinctly. He was no longer blind.

"I am Joseph of Arimathea", the tall man said with distant courtesy. "This is Rabbi Nicodemus. The lord procurator has given me permission to bury the body of Rabbi Yeshua." His long, thin fingers produced a letter.

Cassius glanced at it. Joseph of Arimathea. Permission to bury the body. It was Pilatus' handwriting. "Take him", he said. He saluted and stepped back.

The Arimathean gave him a slight bow and went at once to work. He would not allow his servants to touch the body. Only Nicodemus helped him and after a short while a third old man who at last had let go of the cross. It was not easy. They had to use ropes. Twice Cassius made a motion to assist them, and twice he drew back. It was not right. He must not.

He watched, leaning against one of the carts. Once a thought came, hard and rational: How did Pilatus know that he—that the man was dead? But the answer came to him almost at the same moment: Varro, of course. Then he watched again, concentrating only on what was happening, his mind a blank to either past or future. They got the body down with infinite care and put it on the stretcher. Then they carried the stretcher toward the group of women, and there they laid it down.

One of Abenadar's soldiers came up to him and said in a whisper, "That's his mother, sir."

Cassius stared at the man. "His . . ."

"Yes, sir. She's been here the whole time. Once he spoke to her from the cross. He . . ."

"Be quiet", Cassius gasped. "I don't want to hear about it. Be quiet."

"Yes, sir."

Cassius whirled around. "My horse", he ordered. "We're leaving." He started off the instant he was in the saddle. He did not look back.

Only when the Place of Skulls was out of sight, he stopped and waited for the carts to catch up with him.

They had to ride a fairly long way. The Valley of Hinnom was at the southern end of the city. They took the way alongside the western wall, past the palace of Herod and Mount Zion with the house of the High Priest.

All the dirt and debris of the city was carried off to that valley, and it looked it. There were no trees, no groves. Not even grass would grow in that desert of stones and mud.

Yet people lived here—outcasts of all kinds, beggars and, segregated by a moat even from outcasts and beggars, most wretched of them all, the lepers.

Here, too, was the burial place for criminals: a foul-smelling fire, made of dried camel dung.

The carts came to a halt, and one of the soldiers reported that the two lestes had not survived the transport.

Cassius nodded. "Get the men to have them burned."

The half-naked, swarthy servants of the burial place pocketed their coins, carried the bodies away, and threw them into the fire. They would have done exactly the same thing if the two lestes had been still alive.

This would have been the Galilean's end also if the man from Arimathea had not turned up.

Staring into the flames, Cassius saw the head with the crown of thorns, the lean, outstretched arms. He was here. Even here, in the underworld, the nethermost Hades, the land of flames and shadows and of the dead. . . .

It was dark when they clattered back into the court of the Antonia.

Cassius dismissed the men and went to report to the procurator. Never in all his life had he felt so tired. "Perhaps I too have become old, like Abenadar", he thought. Perhaps everybody who had been up there on that accursed hill grew old in a few hours.

There was no sign of life in the praetorium. After a search he got hold of an orderly.

"The procurator is in the banquet hall, sir—everybody is."

Wherever Pilatus was, he had to make his report.

But when Cassius entered the large hall, he saw that it would not be possible. The procurator was lying half across the table, dead drunk. Almost everybody was drunk, and all those who could still register some kind of emotion seemed to be in a state of enormous hilarity.

He was just going to withdraw when one of the older officers spotted him, one of the Caesarean tribunes; he did not remember his name. The tribune had a cup in his hand and was leaning heavily on the shoulder of young Mela. "What's the matter with *him?*" asked the tribune. "Been in the wars?"

Cassius looked around. Abenadar was nowhere to be seen. Vindex was here, though. He was lying under the table next to the procurator, fast asleep. There was nothing very unusual about any of this, except the hour, for it was still early in the evening.

The tribune walked up to him, the wine splashing over his hands.

"C-centurion Longinus, aren't you? W-what's the matter? The enemy at the gates?"

"No, sir."

"Then w-why run about like this? Great Jupiter, the man has brought a spear with him into the banquet hall. Whom do you want to spear, centurion?"

It was still in his hand. He should have left it outside, of course.

"Sorry, sir."

The tribune shuddered. "Don't stand there as if you were going to attack me at any moment", he said reproachfully. "And don't be so serious, man. I can't bear it. This is a day for rejoicing, surely."

A day for rejoicing . . .

"Is it, sir?"

The tribune narrowed his eyes. "Don't tell me you loved that cursed criminal—or did you? Not one of his cursed crowd by any chance, are you? B-because if you are, I see black in the future for you." He passed a finger across his throat. "Come now, own up: Was he the lord and master of your black heart? Did you spy on us for his sake while the going was good? The man is hesitating, I believe—hi, friends, I think I've caught an enemy of the Emperor right in our midst!".

The Centurions Mela and Calvus came up, and Calvus asked angrily, "Are you insulting a centurion of the Italican cohort, tribune?"

"I can insult whom I like", declared the tribune belligerently. "This man has been one of Sejanus' spies."

"Sejanus?" Cassius asked dully.

"Don't tell me you never heard the name before", jeered the tribune. "Don't know who Sejanus is, do you?"

"The chief of the Praetorian guards." Cassius shrugged. "And you, tribune, are drunk."

"Wrong", declared the tribune triumphantly. "Quite wrong. Sejanus is a corpse. A putrefying corpse. A dead corpse. S-s-so is everybody who had anything to do with him. What did you bring that spear here for, tell me?"

"What is he talking about?" Cassius asked bewildered.

Calvus suddenly struck his forehead. "Of course, you weren't here when the news came. You were out on some duty, weren't you?"

"Yes", said Cassius. "What news?"

"The mail arrived at long last. It was held up for several days in Caesarea. They wanted to check and countercheck; that's why it was so late. Rome is in turmoil, friend, or at least it certainly was when the mail ship sailed from Ostia. The Emperor discovered that Sejanus had conspired to have him killed and to put himself on the throne. So he secretly named a new prefect of the Praetorian guards—it's good old Macro—and had dear Sejanus arrested. Then he brought the case before the Senate. The Senate, as you may imagine, was delighted, no more bowing and scraping before that upstart, no more humiliating receptions in the guardroom. There never was a trial that went so quickly. They could say like Caesar: the news came, we condemned the man, and we had him strangled. All in one day."

"Sejanus is dead?" Cassius asked in a low voice. "Dead . . . ?"

"Look here, man, are you drunk, too? I just told you he's dead. That's what this banquet is about, that Sejanus is dead. Greatest event of the century! Have some wine."

"And it's not only Sejanus", Mela interposed. "The Emperor took the opportunity to clean the stables."

"And he's very good at that", Calvus affirmed. "We have a list here of all those who were cleaned out in the first two weeks—there must be many more now."

"Ab-absolutely cleaned out", said the tribune. "M-musht get some more wine." He staggered away.

"I hope no friend of yours is among them." Calvus grinned. "Barbutius Cimber, Aulus Metellus, Quintus Jovianus—who else was on it, Mela? You've seen the list."

"Gaius Fuscus, the Praetor Verranus, Marcus Balbus, Terentius Piso—"

"Marcus Balbus?" Cassius asked listlessly.

"Yes. Opened his veins. Most of them did. Friend of yours?"

"No", Cassius said.

"Well, that's all right, then. Come and have some wine. Only just come back, haven't you? You must be dried out. Not eaten yet either, I suppose?"

"I think I'll turn in", Cassius said. "Good night."

He clanked away.

"What's the matter with him?" Calvus asked.

"I have no idea." Mela yawned. "Maybe it's the weather. Been queer all day, hasn't it? Thunderstorm, earthquake, sunshine—"

"True." Suddenly Calvus' eyes widened. "By Jupiter, boy—don't you understand?"

"No. What?"

"It was an omen!"

"What do you mean?"

"Where are your brains, man? Think of it! A thunderstorm and an earthquake—and a couple of hours later we get the news about Sejanus!" Calvus wagged his head. "I used to think religion was all nonsense", he said. "But this shows you, doesn't it? Doesn't it? I'll never make fun of that sort of thing again."

"Let's have some wine", said Mela uneasily.

XI

The news of the fall of Sejanus reached the High Priest's palace about two hours later than the Antonia received it and was the topic of several conferences and discussions. They were resumed the next day. The outlook so far was extremely vague. It was impossible to foresee with any accuracy what importance the news would have for Judaea or for any other province of the

344

East. Sejanus had never shown any particular interest in Jewish affairs—the banishment of four thousand Jews from Rome some years ago had been initiated by the Emperor himself. Tiberius was too old to resume full powers for more than the emergency period; some successor to Sejanus would be appointed, but no one could guess who it might be.

It was not even possible to guess whether the present procurator of Judaea would be affected by the new development, although he had come out here on direct orders of Sejanus.

When the report came in that the procurator and all his officers had celebrated the fall of Sejanus with a sumptuous banquet, it was at first disbelieved and later regarded as a perfectly obvious show of loyalty to the Emperor.

"If Sejanus' conspiracy had succeeded and he had had the Emperor killed and assumed the purple, the procurator and his officers would have celebrated that", suggested Rabbi Josaphat.

Caiphas nodded. "Sound judgment. What is your opinion, Rabbi Nicodemus?"

The old Pharisee leader sighed. "Men are sorry creatures, my lord High Priest. Yesterday they were shouting for Sejanus— today they are shouting against him." After a pause he added, "Who knows what they will shout tomorrow?"

Rabbi Josaphat shot a quick glance in the direction of the old man. "Whatever it may be—the dead are quickly forgotten."

One of the Sadducee leaders gave it as his opinion that the office of the governor general of Syria would be the touchstone: if a change came there, it would come in Judaea as well. In the midst of the debate Aza entered with a document. Frowning, Caiphas read it and gave his secretary a few whispered instructions. Aza withdrew.

"I must interrupt the discussion", said Kohen Gadol. "I have just received the news that the body of the executed Nazarene was not taken to the Valley of Hinnom."

A sudden hush went over the assembly. The governor general of Syria, Sejanus, and the Emperor were forgotten.

"Only the other two executed men were taken there", the High Priest went on. "The two lestes, Dysmas and Gestas. The Nazarene himself was buried—elsewhere."

Rabbi Josaphat jumped to his feet. "The procurator promised explicitly . . . Is it known where the Nazarene is buried?"

"Yes", said Caiphas slowly. "In the new tomb which belongs to a member of the Council of Ten, Joseph of Arimathea."

"How did he get hold of the body?" demanded Rabbi Josaphat. "He must have had permission. He must have gone to see Pilatus. This is news more dangerous than that of the death of Sejanus."

Rabbi Nicodemus shook his head. "Why is it dangerous news that a dead man was buried?"

"Did you by any chance have a hand in this?" Rabbi Josaphat stared at the old man. "Have you been to see the procurator?"

"No", said Rabbi Nicodemus. Boldly he added, "But I was present at the burial."

"And you a Pharisee leader", stormed Rabbi Josaphat. "Don't you know that the Nazarene was forbidden the synagogue? *And* that the same applies to those who follow him? Neither you nor Joseph can partake of the paschal lamb now—you have made yourselves unclean and . . . "

"Just one moment." Caiphas' voice was calm, but the excited Pharisee broke off at once. "I think there are more important issues at stake."

"You are right, my lord High Priest. Indeed there are. I know what you mean. That is why I said it was such dangerous news."

"The Nazarene", Caiphas went on, "said on several occasions that he would have to die but would rise again on the third day."

He had their full attention now. A few of the leaders laughed rather uneasily.

"It has been established also", said Caiphas, "that on one occasion at least the Nazarene said, 'Destroy this Temple—and in

346

three days I will raise it up again.' He often used symbolical language. There may well be a connection between this saying and the others. We know that the man had many followers. If they succeed in getting hold of the body and then show the empty tomb to all and sundry . . . "

"Do you see now what you have done?" Rabbi Josaphat shook both his fists at Nicodemus. The old man's answer was lost in the general uproar.

It subsided only when Caiphas raised his hand. "The third day starts tonight at sunset", he said crisply. "But I am not taking any chances on a fulfillment of this—this prophecy. I have just sent an officer and ten guards to watch the tomb until the third day is over. But I think it would be even better to have Roman soldiers there as well. The more official the matter is, the less the possibility that there will be any talk about another miracle."

One of the priests looked worried. "There is just one dangerous point about that, my lord High Priest. If the Nazarene by any chance succeeds—then we have made it impossible to deny it."

Caiphas smiled coldly. "I think we can regard that possibility as remote."

"Not again", said Pilatus incredulously.

"I'm afraid so, sir." Tribune Vindex grinned wryly. "The same deputation as yesterday, plus a few Sadducee priests. They are worried about the man's burial."

"But surely I fixed all that yesterday—with that man Joseph of Arimathea. High-ranking man, one of their Dekaprotoi. He came specially for that!"

"Yes, sir. But apparently he is no longer persona grata in the more orthodox circles." Vindex liked a little irony when he had reason to believe that his views coincided with those of his superior.

"Sort of black sheep, you mean?"

347

Vindex grinned. "Black among the white or white among the black. That's not for me to decide, sir."

Pilatus eyed him a little suspiciously. "I have a splitting headache", he complained. "Can't you deal with them?"

"I think they would appreciate it if the procurator talked to them in person."

"I daresay." Pilatus heaved himself out of his chair. "What do they want anyway?"

"A guard for the tomb, sir, as near as I could make out. They seem to be afraid that his followers will steal the body."

Pilatus shook his head. "What next? You know, Vindex, it is rather strange. Man said he was a king. Herod laughs at him but has him dressed in a scarlet mantle. Joke, of course. But he *does* have him dressed as a king. I have him executed. But I give him a written testimonial that he was a king. Didn't exactly do it to honor him—just wanted to annoy the blackrobes. It did annoy them, too. But I did call him a king. Now they want a guard for his tomb, because they are afraid that his body will be stolen. But only a king has a guard to watch his tomb. Strange, isn't it?"

"Are you going to give them the guard, sir?" asked Vindex.

"No", Pilatus exploded. "He was the King of the Jews. He should have a Jewish guard. I told them yesterday it's their business and not mine. Rome has nothing to do with it. I want the officers who were in charge of proceedings yesterday."

"First Centurion Abenadar is ill, sir. I gave you the sick list this morning."

"Haven't looked at it yet. What's the matter with him?"

"High fever, sir. Physician's report is not very satisfactory. I shall get the two other officers—Centurions Varro and Longinus."

"Very well."

A few minutes later the procurator and the two centurions stepped out to meet the delegation.

It was again led by Rabbi Josaphat. At least he was doing most of the talking. The procurator had promised them yesterday to

348

have the Nazarene Yeshua taken off the cross, to have his legs broken as was the custom in such cases, and to have him taken to the Valley of Hinnom to be burned there, again according to custom. It was now reported that this promise had not been fulfilled. The procurator replied that he had given orders accordingly. That the Centurion Longinus had gone out to the Place of Skulls with twelve men to carry them out. That immediately after he left, a member of the Sanhedrin, Joseph of Arimathea, appeared before the procurator and asked for permission to bury the dead Nazarene.

"I was surprised to hear that he was dead after only a few hours on the cross", Pilate said. "And despite my respect for the rank and dignity of my visitor, I called in the Centurion Varro, who was present at the execution, to verify the information. He confirmed it. In the circumstances I granted the member of the Sanhedrin the permission to bury the body. He went to the place called the skull where he received the body from Centurion Longinus. And it seems to me", he added caustically, "that our relations consist of you asking me for favors, me granting them, and you complaining about it."

But Rabbi Josaphat was no coward. "Joseph of Arimathea did not visit the procurator as a member of the Sanhedrin but in a purely private capacity. Ours is an official delegation. Will my lord procurator permit me to ask the Centurion Longinus a few questions?"

"If you must", growled Pilatus.

"Thank you, my lord procurator. Centurion, when you arrived at the place of the scull, did you have the Nazarene's legs broken?"

"No."

"Why not? Surely you were ordered to do so?"

"He was dead."

"How do you know? Because your superior told you so?"

"I know", Cassius said bleakly, "because I pierced his heart with this spear."

Instinctively Rabbi Josaphat made a step back. The Centurion Varro gave an involuntary exclamation of surprise, then clamped his lips together and stared straight ahead.

Pilatus frowned. A centurion had no business carrying around a spear, except in the field. He began to speak out of the corner of his mouth, always a danger signal. "Have you now quite finished cross-examining one of my officers?" he asked. "And will you admit that your wishes have been fulfilled beyond expectation? A man with his legs broken may live. A man with his heart pierced is dead."

"My lord procurator is not fully aware of the matter that is troubling us", Rabbi Josaphat had found his voice again. "After all, in this as in other matters we have exactly the same interests: that no further trouble comes from this deceiver. He said more than once that he would rise again on the third day after his death. Therefore two issues are important. First, to establish with absolute certainty that he is dead. Some people live a whole day or even two days on the cross, and he is supposed to have died after only three hours. Very well—his death has been established without doubt. But now we must see to it that his disciples do not steal the body and then proclaim that he has risen. I am very sorry to inconvenience the lord procurator about what must seem to him, as indeed it does to us, a story for the credulous and the superstitious, unworthy of reasonable and intelligent men. But unfortunately there are many credulous and superstitious people, and we must remember that the Nazarene was regarded as a miracle worker. And that is why we would be grateful for a detachment of Roman soldiers however small, to keep watch at the tomb until the end of the third day—which would be tomorrow evening."

"No", barked Pilatus.

Tenaciously Rabbi Josaphat tried again. "My lord procurator, if the followers of the Nazarene succeed in stealing the body and then tell the people that he has risen, this last deceit will be more dangerous than any that has gone before. And if . . ."

"You have guards of your own", interrupted Pilatus. "Go, and secure everything as well as you can." He turned abruptly and walked back into the practorium. Somehow he enjoyed the fact that for once he had not given in. And he would have no further dealings with the matter. He would tell Claudia that as soon as she was better. It would please her. She was still far from well. All because of that case. Well, it was finished now, definitely finished. No more delegations, official or otherwise. The man behind this last one was, of course, the same man who had brought about the decision at the trial. Caiphas. Not that obstinate little Pharisee. Caiphas was the man.

One of these days he would have to do something about Caiphas. Provided, of course, the upheaval in Rome left him an opportunity.

XII

The day was quiet. Cassius had to do some routine work for the Legate Sosius, who kept himself very much in the background while the procurator was in Jerusalem, at least since the Feast of the Tabernacles, which now seemed to have occurred in the far distant past rather than a few months ago. At the midday meal the general mood was one of sobriety. The first enthusiasm about the drastic changes in Rome had disappeared. On more careful perusal of the reports many officers found that the proscription list of the Emperor contained names of friends and even of relatives. Cassius observed that Varro seemed to avoid him. He went straight up to him after the meal: "Have you seen Abenadar?"

"He is ill", Varro replied curtly.

"I know. What is it?"

"I don't know. Saw him only a minute or two."

"I'll have a look", Cassius said.

"I wouldn't if I were you."

"No? Why not?"

Varro looked at him. "I don't think your visit would do him much good", he said bluntly. "I thought you'd understand, but apparently you don't. He—he cared about the man he had to crucify. It did something to him. I don't think he'll ever be the same again. I don't think he'll be able to stay in the army."

"As bad as that, is it?"

"Yes. I didn't want to talk about it, but since you started it: Did he see you—spear the—man?"

"Can't see how he can have missed it."

Varro drew breath, as if to say something. Instead he turned away.

Cassius grabbed his shoulder and swung him round. "Don't you understand? I arrived at that cursed place to find the old man a gibbering idiot, hugging the base of the cross. The soldiers with him weren't much better. You had left, but from what little I had seen of you I should say the man exercised some influence on you, too. Somebody had to keep his head."

Varro freed himself. "I see. Oh, yes. That little Pharisee fellow ought to give you a prize. Ask him. Maybe he will."

Cassius stared at him. "I didn't crucify him, Varro."

"No. You were well out of it—thanks to Abenadar. So you had to go and perform a great, heroic deed on your own—and pierce a dead man's heart." Varro shook his head. "Your family crest shows a spear, doesn't it? Bear it proudly then. But don't go and see Abenadar. Let his heart go on beating for a while."

He walked away.

Cassius stood quite still. After a while he turned and walked toward Abenadar's quarters.

He arrived just as the physician was leaving.

"How is he?" Cassius asked.

"Not too well, I fear." The physician of the cohort was an Alexandrine Greek. "Were you thinking of paying him a visit? It would not be advisable. Besides, he is delirious. Keeps repeating the same things again and again."

"What things?"

"Well, some of it is in Aramaic, and I know almost nothing of that language. I understood 'I am thirsty.' He said that many times. But when I tried to give him water, he would not drink. Ah, yes, there was one other thing—about some people who did not know what they did or something like that. I wish my Aramaic were better, but even then—his voice is very low. There was only one short sentence he said several times in Latin: 'Lord, forgive me my duty.' It doesn't make much sense, does it?"

It did not make much sense. A god was a god, and a man was a man. "The idea of the gods mingling with mere mortals is crude and unworthy of the reasonable thinker." Cassius did not remember who had said that. But the most important difference between gods and men was that men existed and gods didn't. Neither gods nor their sons.

He must get rid of that spear. Pilatus had looked at him queerly. It was really absurd to go on carrying it around with him all the time. Why was he doing it?

There was nothing wrong with the spear, of course. It was a perfectly good spear. Not the latest army issue. Provincial troops would not get that, but a decent enough weapon, well balanced and well kept. That soldier was going to find himself in trouble for not taking it back. The thing for him to do was take it to the armory, have the man issued a new spear, and forget the whole business.

There was nothing wrong with the spear.

There was nothing wrong about what he had done with it on the place of the skull. You can't kill a dead man. Abenadar was delirious. Varro, too, must be ill. If Cassius hadn't thought so he would have administered a sound thrashing for those insolent remarks about the Longinus family and its crest. There was no question of any heroic action. No one seemed to realize how necessary it had been to make absolutely sure that the man was dead. The spear did not kill him. He had been dead before. But now they could all sleep quietly—the procurator, the Roman Empire, the Jewish High Priest, and his men, everybody.

The man was dead. Dead. Now it could be forgotten that he had once saved Naomi. He had not saved her for Cassius Longinus. He had saved her for himself, at the cost of the freedom of her mind. She was saved from a death by stoning in order to live "in him", as she called it, whatever that meant.

He had taken her away. Piercing his dead body with a spear, before her eyes, was a pitiful revenge. But even so it was more than he could do about his enemies in Rome. Sejanus was dead. Marcus Balbus was dead. Only the lanista Spurio remained—perhaps.

Abenadar was right: life went its course, and revenge was impotent before it.

What remained, then? A cohort at the end of the year—a legion in a few years' time—and if he got himself the right connections and flattered the right people, an army, and after that a province. Then he would sit on the judgment seat and give in to a lot of noisy local dignitaries and condemn a man to death against his better judgment. He had been cheated out of his enemies, his hatred, his reason for being alive.

But it was not surprising. In a world of ghosts, why should any desire be fulfilled? The strange thing was that there should be any desire at all.

They were right, these bumptious little Pharisees. They were right in insisting that a dead man was dead and should not come back to haunt them. Death, putrefaction, dissolution, the end.

But Naomi went on praying, on her knees, to a dead man on the cross.

He had failed, he had so obviously and blatantly failed, that god of hers. He had allowed himself to be scourged and mocked and insulted and tortured to death—and yet she prayed to him, to his dead body, as if it still had life.

But then, of course, he had promised to come back, hadn't he? To rise again on the third day.

Was there some hint of fear in this insistence to have the tomb guarded?

Surely not. These Pharisee fellows were intelligent men, erudite in their own peculiar way, men with a keen sense of logic who knew about the laws of cause and effect. Up to a point they were logical even in their belief in a god, insisting as they did that he should be entirely different from man, invisible, bodiless, and holy. Perhaps Seneca would agree with them about that—if Seneca was still alive and still believed in the existence of a godhead of some kind.

Only once had Cassius felt he had something to live for other than revenge. The Nazarene had cheated him of that. And though the man was dead, dead and his heart pierced by a spear—Naomi was as lost to Cassius as in the days when he was searching the city for her. She prayed to his dead body, she thought he was a god and would rise again, because he had said so.

Well, by tomorrow he would be proved a liar.

No one could believe in a god who was a liar.

They were right, the bumptious little men. It mattered. And Pilatus would have done well to give them a Roman guard, picked men, too, who would not be affected by any kind of spell, like poor old Abenadar and the wretched Varro.

Well, the Temple guard would watch the tomb. They would take all the necessary or rather unnecessary precautions. It was absurd for grownup men to have to sit in front of a tomb all night and the whole of the following day—but it was important to prove that this "god" was a liar.

Perhaps then Naomi would say that his spirit was still alive—or some such rubbish. But it would not help. Not in this case. He had raised that man Elazarus or Lazarus from the dead, Naomi said. Well, either the man had never been dead but only unconscious or something, or Naomi had fallen for another of those famous spells of the magician. There was one good thing about it: she could not claim that her "god" had fulfilled his promise because his "spirit" was still alive. If he could raise a man from the dead and the man walked about and was alive again in every sense of the word — then he should be able to do no less in his own case, surely!

All or nothing, Naomi. All or nothing. By tomorrow everyone will know your god is a liar.

And no one will need to fear him any more.

Even so, Pilatus should have given them the guard they wanted. Why didn't he, if there was any danger that the man's followers might steal the body and then pretend that he had risen?

Could Pilatus be afraid this god might rise on the third day?

Fear was a powerful factor, strong enough, it seemed, to perturb not only credulous women but Roman officers and Roman soldiers.

What exactly were they all afraid of?

And why, in the name of Hecate and all the other gods that didn't exist, must he think about it all the time?

The day remained quiet. It seemed to be the sabbath not only for the population of the city but also for the garrison of the Antonia, who remained within the fortress, avoiding any display of military might. The story of a man found dead, hanging on a tree near the Valley of Hinnom, did not create much commotion. News did not travel fast on a sabbath, and even if it had, there were not many who knew the man. He was not a Jerusalemite. He was a stranger. From Kerioth.

356

Mela was the officer on duty when the Centurion Cassius Longinus left the Antonia. It was close to the time of sunset.

Strictly speaking, Mela should have asked for the password and inquired on what authority Cassius Longinus was leaving the fortress, but he knew better than to pester an officer senior to himself in service years, if not in rank. Besides, it was fairly obvious that Cassius was going out on some secret or at least confidential errand. He was wearing a white cloak. He did not seem to have a sword, as far as one could make out. Instead, incongruously, he was carrying a spear. And on foot, eh?

Some great and wonderful idea of Vindex and his intelligence people, of course.

XIII

The path to the place of the skull was not very long and not too steep either, if one did not have to carry a cross on one's shoulders.

Cassius was passing the place where he had met Varro coming down the road with his detachment. Soon he would reach the place where the rock had split. He could see the outline of the three crosses. Nothing moving this time.

Here was the split in the rock. Unchanged. Well, of course unchanged. Why should it have changed?

Just one more uphill stretch. Cassius was breathing heavily. This part of the way seemed to be steeper than he remembered it, but before he had been on horseback.

The plateau was empty. He walked across it.

The strip of parchment was still fixed to the middle cross. "Jesus of Nazareth, King of the Jews."

Perhaps he was the King of the Jews. You never knew for sure whether Pilatus was being ironical or whether he meant what he said, but he had seemed to make a great point that the man who had hung here yesterday was a king. Perhaps he was the last king the Jews would ever have.

How would it feel to be his successor? And would a successor wear a crown of thorns too?

"Lord, forgive me my duty." What a strange thing to say, even in delirium. "He is dead—and by his wounds we are healed." Poor old Abenadar. "He has prayed for his transgressors; he has prayed for you and for me. He was the Son of God." "It's just that one isn't accustomed to a god of flesh and blood, sir, that's what it is."

Quite right, soldier. One isn't accustomed to such a god and never will be.

"That one on the cross is a god, sir. I know it sounds crazy, but it's true."

How do you know it's true, soldier? How do you know anything is true—except the fear in your heart? Fear, fear, fear, that's what's wrong with all of you, superstitious fools. You're afraid of ghosts, of shadows, of a poor, wretched, crucified man. It makes you all shrink and tremble. It makes you behave like madmen.

"May well be, sir. We killed a god, sir. That may most likely make a man mad."

Fear. But Cassius Longinus was not afraid. He never had been. He himself was a ghost, living among ghosts. Nothing really mattered.

Cassius leaned on the spear. He looked around. Over there was the place where Naomi had knelt, and the other women.

"That's his mother, sir."

It couldn't be true. There had been that one moment only, when he had been afraid, blindly, terribly afraid.

"She's been here the whole time. Once he spoke to her from the cross."

His mother. Here the whole time.

She had seen what Abenadar saw—and Varro—and the soldiers. "You weren't here, sir. You were lucky."

But she had been here; she had seen her son nailed to the cross; she had seen him hanging, writhing on those nails that held him and tore at him.

How did she have the strength? What upheld her when old fighters, gray under the helmet and unrelated to the crucified man, went to pieces and talked gibberish and became ill?

The place where she had been sitting was not far, no more than thirty yards away, perhaps less. But it was not easy to go there.

It must be done, though; he did not know why. Proving something to himself, perhaps?

He shouldn't have come, of course. Why had he? To prove to himself that he could walk up here, alone, and stare at the crosses and tell himself that everybody else was afraid and he was not?

What double-cursed nonsense was this that made him stalk about in this place when he could be sitting in his quarters, drinking or dicing with Varro, no, not with Varro, but with Calvus or Aufidius?

Whistling in the dark like a little boy.

It was getting dark, too. But this time the honest night was coming up, not some magic earthquake or thunderstorm, and the living were alive and the dead were dead—and stayed dead.

And still it was difficult. Why should it be? Because the mother had been there when it happened? Was he afraid because a poor Jewish woman had watched her son hanging from a cross? Because of what she must have felt when he took the spear, this spear, in both hands and weighed it carefully and drove it into a dead man's heart, into her son's heart, before her eyes?

He had not even seen her. He had left as soon as he knew that she was there. Be honest—he had run away. In a panic. In a panic that she might look at him, look into his eyes. *And pity him. . . .*

That was it. Now he knew. That was what he was afraid of.

Her pity.

He prayed for the transgressors. He prayed for you and me.

His pity. Mother and son were united in their pity for those who made them suffer—in their terrible, their monstrous compassion. "You weren't here, sir. You were lucky." Well, I'm here now, soldier. And I know. I know now, Abenadar, I know what troubled you.

And then Cassius saw the men.

They were huddled together, below him, in what looked like a small clearing between rocks and shrubs. About a dozen of them. They looked like Temple guards.

It was too dark to see clearly. He would have to get nearer.

The way down seemed fairly smooth, but he moved carefully. A few loose stones rolling away from under his feet, and they would take alarm. No need for them to know that there was somebody watching the watchmen—if that was what they were. And if not, he had to be doubly careful. The spear helped him descend.

They were Temple guards. And all around them was a fairly large garden. He should have worn a darker cloak. If they saw him and thought that he was one of the dead man's followers, they might rush him on sight. Now if he were in charge of a troop of the man's disciples, he'd attack the post from three sides at once with, say, fifty men, and the whole thing would be over in five minutes. Carry the twelve bodies away and bury them; any place would do; then take the Nazarene's body out of the tomb—and rumor would soon have it that the guards had vanished by the power of the risen Nazarene, and his disciples could proclaim that his prophecy was fulfilled. But—were they the men to do that?

The Sadducee and Pharisee fellows seemed to think so. Perhaps they thought so because that was what they would do.

Would Naomi, for instance, lend a hand to such a thing? Or would—bah, pure nonsense.

Still, *he* said he was going to rise. And the third day had just begun.

You can't rise. Not with a pierced heart. But I am almost—almost sorry you can't. I *am* sorry you can't. For your mother's sake, although I have never seen her face.

Twelve of them. No, eleven. Officer and ten men. The stout man with the turban was the officer. Spears, shields, swords, everything. Not a very soldierly lot. I wouldn't need fifty men, twenty would do amply, and even ten would be safe enough. Not like the Freedom men, these Temple guards. No wonder either. Used for ceremonies, mostly, or for the arrest of civilians—unless there was danger that the civilian might resist, in which case borrow sixty Roman soldiers under Centurion Varro.

They were not here as soldiers, anyway. They were witnesses—witnesses that nothing happened.

Shrubs and rocks. Excellent vantage point. Here one could see without being seen.

Stars coming up. Many of them. A clear night. Cool, too.

Some of these fellows were sleeping. But only half of them. Probably arranged for a shift. Two watches. Sensible enough.

That was the tomb, over there, hewn straight into the rock, a lot of work. Big, too. Large stone set into the opening, the way they did it here. Something affixed to it, a round thing, like a seal. It probably *was* a seal. They sealed it off. Not a bad idea. No one could tamper with it that way.

The tomb of a rich man. That fellow Joseph of Arimathea, one of the Dekaprotoi, the Council of Ten. And that's why they sealed it. A rich man might be tempted to come out here and offer the soldiers a nice, fat bribe, and then make off with the precious body.

Probably the seal of that big man with the black-and-silver beard, the High Priest—or that of their High Council, the Sanhedrin. Don't touch. Religious property.

They weren't taking any chances. Even if those disciples were the kind of people the priests seemed to think they were and even if they overcame the guards and got rid of their bodies—they couldn't get hold of the dead Nazarene without breaking the seal.

Cassius felt more comfortable. There were people here, men, soldiers of a kind, guarding something for a purpose, a logical purpose. Just by being here, alive and awake, we can prove that the man lied; we can prevent the start of silly rumors. No one will play any tricks on us. We know better. We know that the living are living and the dead are dead.

Up there on the plateau it was different. Up there were the presences of yesterday with a kind of life of their own, and it was not only memory. . . . Or was it? It was *something,* something that seemed to lead thoughts and feelings into some kind of new country, a weird and terrifying country in which one was a very small and very dirty entity full of questions one didn't like to ask because one might get answers. Fear and pain and suffering and other things hovered over the place; a man had no protection there and felt naked and ashamed of being there. It was as if the man who died on the cross was the only man and the woman who watched was the only woman—and all the rest were ghosts, shabby little specters, moving feebly.

This was better, much better. You may not be the best possible company, you eleven fellows there, thirty yards away. I wouldn't choose you by preference; you're a poor lot of soldiers, more likely than not; but you are thinking of food and drink and women, and you are telling each other the kind of stories soldiers tell, and you smirk and grin and belch and spit, and you're no mystery to anybody.

I've spent years and years among your kind, and I know you. And part of myself is like you, and whatever there is in me that isn't like you I'd rather forget about.

We are alive, aren't we? Down here we are alive. Up there on the plateau it's different, but you won't go there, and I won't either, not again. I'll stay here and smirk and grin and belch and spit with you. It would be even better if I could step down a little farther and sit with you, one more watcher. I am a Roman centurion, and I shall be a first centurion before the year is out, but all I want is to sit with you and talk a bit or let you talk to me. It doesn't matter which; it's noise, human noise, and that's what I need.

I wonder what you think that Nazarene was? A blasphemer, a deceiver, a poor crazy fellow? A wise rabbi, a prophet—or the Son of God, whatever that may mean?

You don't think. You don't think at all, and you're quite right.

Tomorrow morning, or rather this morning, they'll come and relieve you, at least I hope they'll be decent enough to have a relief ready for the day watch. And by evening, the relief can go home, too, and that will be the end of the story. In three months, in six, the Nazarene will be forgotten, and someone else will take the stage and get himself elevated or struck down, crowned or crucified.

In the meantime he sleeps peacefully, at last, behind that big stone, nicely wrapped in the sheets they wound around him and anointed with spices and balms as is the custom with you people.

And what you are doing, my friends, is what most soldiers the world over do most of the time—waiting for something that doesn't happen. I know. I've done it myself, in this god-forsaken, dusty, stony country of yours, this little province of the great Roman Empire. There are many provinces, fellow watchers, most of them larger and more important than this, and each has its own little set of gods and sons of gods and goddesses and daughters of goddesses, among them even some who died—like Hercules, for instance. But that was before he became a god. And once he died, he was dead. He never returned. And the Egyptians had a god called Osiris, and he was murdered by another god and dismembered. And he also never returned. The dead don't come back, fellows—that's about the one sure thing we know. Everybody who was born must die, and none of those who die return. That is the truth; there are no exceptions.

363

But of course, you people always want to be exceptional, don't you? Abenadar told me a lot about that when we were still friends. You only have one God, and he invisible. You won't recognize anybody else's gods, not even the smallest. Only your own. Jealous of your God, aren't you? And you are the Chosen People of your God, and that is that. The only thing that never occurs to you is that he himself may not exist either. You've never seen him, but you believe he exists. By Jupiter—who doesn't exist either—I think if this Nazarene should rise and walk about and be seen by you, you would not believe it—but you would still believe that the invisible one exists.

Never mind, fellows; we are no better than you are, and maybe in some ways we're worse, with our packs of gods who are vain as we are, adulterous as we are, murderous as we are. Maybe there should be only one God; after all, there is only one Emperor.

The stars were paling. Could it be the dawn? Already?

They were changing the guard at the tomb. Cassius grinned. The ceremonial consisted of waking up some of the sleepers by poking them in the ribs. Two of the men seemed to be frightened. Perhaps they thought the dead Nazarene was waking them up. No, he went on sleeping; in that way the dead fared better than the living.

The stars were really paling.

There was a wind now too, a soft breeze, first wind of the morning.

No, not so soft. Blowing quite hard. Increasing in strength, blowing steadily, with a strange high note. Blowing from every direction at once.

The guards were on their feet, looking about; the sleepers woke up, jumped up, chattering and shouting, Cassius knew because their mouths were wide open; he could not hear anything but the sound of the wind.

And then the trembling began.

This was not like the earthquake of the day before: no rolling

364

underfoot, no heavy air, not as if something were stirring deep down in the earth.

This trembling came from above, as if the heavens were quaking, were twisting and turning. And the sound of the wind covered the earth like a mantle.

The curtain of high heaven split from top to bottom, and the earth moaned, and Cassius clung to the rocks for dear life's sake—this would pass; it was only an earthquake . . .

Lightning descended, lightning poured in streams over the rocks, in blinding streams, and the rock down there was alive with a life of its own, and the stone of the tomb came out obediently, slipped out and up and turned in midair and spun dizzily around, and the streams of lightning circled and became one and took form and moved, mountain high and all aglitter and agleam—spheres and circles and patterns moving over the tomb and in the tomb and all around it, in a glory of intense, intolerable, consuming light.

Suddenly Cassius realized it was all over. The next thing he realized was that it had taken very little time, only a few moments, only one moment, one short moment. He was exhaling now, and it was the breath he had inhaled when he first heard that strange high sound. It had happened in a breath, a pulsebeat, in no time at all.

The guards were not dead, as Cassius had thought. They rose from the ground faltering and stumbling, reeling like drunks, but alive.

They stood, gawking at the open tomb and at the stone that had come to rest a few yards away from it.

Then they turned and ran.

The place was very still. Only the stone cried out. The stone alone gave witness.

Cassius knew he must go down. There was nothing else to do but to go down. He felt dizzy and sick. He was a child again, a small child on shaky legs. He leaned on the spear. The spear was very heavy, but he did not dare drop it. He knew he would fall if he did.

He went down; it took him a long time, but at last he stood in front of the stone. He looked at it, incapable of thought. He looked at the gaping opening of the tomb.

He did not want to go nearer, but he must. He would die, of course. But he had to go.

Clothes. Winding sheets. A veil wrapped around nothing.

"Here I am, Lord", he said. "Kill me."

BOOK FOUR

I

Visitors never ceased coming to the little house in Bethany. But for the last two weeks they no longer came to see Eleazar. They wanted to speak to Miriam, and they wanted to hear the same story from her. Many came several times, only to hear the story again and again. Some would come at night, stammering something about their position and the dangerous gossip of their neighbors. Miriam only smiled. "They came to see my Lord at night, for the same reasons. Shall I feel offended, where he did not feel offended?" But many came quite openly in daylight.

There were still all kinds of rumors in the city, both credible and incredible. The former High Priest Annas was supposed to be very ill; Kohen Gadol himself was said to have spent a whole week without either food or drink after he had been told what had happened at a certain tomb; some people were led "by those who knew" to a closed tomb, and it was pointed out to them that this was the tomb of the Nazarene, and they could see with their own eyes that nothing had happened to it at all. But a great many took for granted that the body had been stolen by the Nazarene's disciples. Why, the guards had confessed that it was so!

This story, actually, was the reason why a young Pharisee of the name of Joel came to see Miriam. He had heard it from no less a person than Rabbi Josaphat. But his logical mind rebelled when he found out that neither the officer nor the men of the guard had been punished; a few subtle inquiries in the right quarters revealed that the officer had since bought himself a nice little piece of land. Now of course he might have got the money from the disciples, but these Galileans were notoriously poor. Joseph of Arimathea was rich but very unlikely to bribe anyone for any purpose, and in this case Joseph of Arimathea had nothing to gain—and a great deal to lose. So something was wrong somewhere.

Joel's logic made Miriam smile. She told her story for the hundredth time. She would tell it another thousand times and more and never tire of telling it. How she went to the tomb with special balms and ointments to preserve the body of her Lord. How she found the tomb open and the great stone rolled away and ran back to the city to tell the apostles, the nearest and closest of all the disciples, and how they would not believe her at first. Two of them, Simon, whom the Lord called Peter, and Jochanaan, came to look for themselves and then went home again, bewildered.

But she had remained there, weeping. And she saw a man whom she took for the gardener and asked him whether he had carried the body away and where he had taken it. And the gardener turned and called her by her name, and it was he and she fell at his feet . . .

Joel listened carefully. After a pause he said, "You will forgive me, I hope—but I very much fear that many people will think that there is a natural explanation."

"What explanation?"

"Well, you see—you had been through much suffering. You were overwrought. You were quite ready to see—*him* in any man you met at that moment. So naturally you saw the gardener and thought it was *he.*"

"But I didn't", said Miriam cheerfully. "I saw my Lord and thought he was the gardener!"

Joel was so perplexed that she broke into happy laughter.

"It's a point", he admitted finally. "It's a very neat point. What a pity you're not a rabbinical scholar. You would do well."

"I am happy to be what God wants me to be", she replied with dancing eyes.

"But—but if this really happened—"

"Exactly." She nodded. "But you must have the courage to think that sentence through to its end. It is not easy, I know, for those who have not seen. It was not easy even for the apostles. They thought, as you did just now, that I was overwrought. Then they saw him themselves— He appeared to them, spoke to them, ate with them—"

"Ate—"

"Yes. And now no one can say that it was a ghost. But only ten of the apostles saw him. The eleventh was absent, and when he came home and they told him, he would not believe them—not till he also had seen him and put his fingers into his wounds—"

Joel rose. "I can take no more today", he said. "It is too much." He looked past her into the peaceful garden. "I only met him once", he said in a low voice. "It was a few days before—before it all happened. He was teaching in the Temple, and I asked him a question: What did he think was the greatest commandment of all? And he said, 'Listen, Israel; there is no God but the Lord thy God; and thou shalt love the Lord thy God with the love of thy whole heart, and thy whole soul, and thy whole mind, and thy whole strength. This is the first commandment, and the second, its like, is this: Thou shalt love thy neighbor as thyself. There is no other commandment greater than these.' And I praised him for saying this and said that this was a greater thing than all burnt offerings and sacrifices. And he said to me, 'Thou art not far from the kingdom of God.'" Joel's eyes were moist. "I shall never forget it", he added softly.

He sighed. "Whatever he was—he was a good man."

"Oh, no!"

Miriam rose, her eyes flashing. "But that is impossible", she cried. "That cannot be. My Lord said he was the Son of God. He said that he and the Father are One. He said to his apostle Philip that he who had seen him had seen the Father. He said, 'Before Abraham came to be, I AM.' If it is not true, the man who said it was a blasphemer, and no one could call him good. But if it is true—then he is more than a man, and again it is not possible to call him a good man and leave it at that."

Joel had turned pale. "That makes it very difficult", he stammered. "I can see the logic of your thinking, but—"

"But it shocks you. I cannot help that. It is a question you must face. It is a question everyone will have to face sooner or later. *Who is he?* Think about it, Joel—and ask yourself also whether God would think fit to raise a blasphemer from the dead!"

In the afternoon of the same day young Joel was sitting very humbly at the feet of a great man who was old and frail and wrinkled. But his years had been spent incessantly in the service of God; his frailty was due to the intensity of work and to fasting; his wrinkles were furrows on the field of God that was his face. He was a Pharisee, but in his presence men like Josaphat and Mordecai became quiet and uneasy. He was a member of the Sanhedrin, but the High Priest and the Sadducee clique much preferred to leave him to his studies and his teaching instead of inviting him to participate in the sessions of the High Council, unless they felt sure that absolute probity and compassionate wisdom would help rather than hinder what they had in mind.

Rabban Gamaliel had been Joel's teacher for years.

The relation between teacher and pupil was patriarchal in every sense of the word. And many a student, when thinking of Abraham, saw at the back of his mind the wise face and the venerable white beard of Gamaliel. There were some who regarded him as wiser even than his famous grandfather and teacher, Hillel, but he would never tolerate any such statement in his presence. He had the same veneration for Hillel as his pupils had for him and never tired of quoting his old teacher, who had been head of the Sanhedrin to the day of his death, twenty years ago.

Kind as he was, it took courage to interrupt the flow of Gamaliel's thoughts and the course of a lecture to make him think and speak of what was so much on Joel's mind.

Gamaliel knew less about the events of the Passover week than most of the simple citizens of Jerusalem. The study of the Torah absorbed his interest—and the forming of his pupils in his image.

He listened attentively. He remained silent for a long while, and Joel could hear the pulse of his own heart.

At last he spoke. "They were wrong in what they did to my relative."

Joel's quick mind understood at once. Both Gamaliel and the Nazarene descended from the royal house of David.

"They were wrong", Gamaliel repeated slowly. "For if this thing is not from God, it will vanish of its own accord. And if it is from God, they will not be able to stop it."

Joel gave a long, deep sigh. "What is your advice to me, rabban?"

"To you? Remember what the wise Hillel said: 'Be a pupil of Aaron—the peacemaker, a friend of all men—and draw them toward the Law.' You are a student; you have chosen wisely. For an ignorant man cannot really be devout, and he who does much commerce will not become wise. Who will look for the salvation of your soul if you do not do so yourself? And now."

"But—the Messiah, rabban. What am I to think of what happened?"

"I told you that."

There was a pause. Gamaliel closed his eyes. Of what was he thinking? Of what had happened during that fateful session of the Sanhedrin to which they had not invited him? Of what happened on Golgotha? Of the Messiah?

After a while Gamaliel nodded. "It is over thirty years ago now", he said. "You were not yet born."

He was quiet so long that Joel dared to ask, "What happened then, rabban?"

371

Gamaliel opened his eyes. Never had Joel seen him look so sad.

"Hillel and I conferred throughout a whole night, my son. We thought and spoke of many things. And when the dawn came we agreed that it would have been better if God had not created man."

II

It was from Miriam that Naomi learned the meaning of what had happened on Golgotha.

She had seen it happen—though not all of it. For Miriam had drawn Naomi's veil over her eyes when she felt that it would be too much for her. "You were not strong enough, little one—"

"But his mother saw it all—"

"No woman can dare compare herself with her, Naomi. There is no woman like her in the world and never has been from the days of Eve. Do you know what you witnessed?"

"The saddest day—"

"Yes, and the most glorious. There has been a curse on mankind ever since we ate of the fruit of a tree—the Tree of Knowledge. On this day the curse was taken away from us. For the cross of our Lord is the Tree of Life. Remember the word of God? That if we ate of the Tree of Life, we would never die? Now it has been fulfilled. Do you understand now the words of our Lord when he told us that we must eat his flesh and drink his blood if we were to enter the kingdom of heaven? Those who are reborn in the Christ will live forever."

Naomi kept very still, so that Miriam would go on talking. There was an empty place, an aching place in Naomi's heart; listening to Miriam she felt bigger than herself. She could hope that her love of him would satisfy all her wants as she knew it should. But she was not like Miriam, Naomi thought sadly.

"All the Passovers before", Miriam continued, "were in memory of the liberation of Israel from the bondage in Egypt. But that liberation itself was no more than a symbol of the liberation of the world from the bondage of sin and disharmony with God. It is God's way to talk to the world in symbols, and it is the destiny of his Chosen People to be those through whom he speaks to the whole world."

"To the Gentiles, too?" Naomi asked, and thought, "Oh, Cassius, if only *you* ... "

"Has he not created them as he created us? From now on it will be the memory of *this* Passover that the world will celebrate—when a Lamb without blemish was led to the slaughter. Now we know what he meant when he said to Martha, 'I am the resurrection and life.' "

Naomi said nothing. It was more than ever difficult to keep pace with Miriam's thoughts since she had seen him again. But then, everything had grown to such tremendous size. That terrible place, Golgotha, seemed to be the center of the world; and Rabbi Yeshua, her Rabbi Yeshua, had grown most of all, so much that the whole earth was like a grain of wheat on the palm of his hand.

How could she believe that he still listened to her, as in earlier days when she talked to him in her mind: "Lord, make Cassius change and see you as you are." Once she had even asked him to give Abigail back to her, as a child might ask to be given back a loved toy; she had been so stupid. He had too many things on his mind now to bother about her and her little problems.

Besides, she must not even think of the Roman any more. She forced herself to call him "the Roman", to make him impersonal, to push his memory back to the time when all Romans looked and were alike to her.

She had seen him thrust the spear into his side. She dared not even pray for him after that. She had been too ashamed to tell Miriam that he, he was the man she once had loved.

There was only one prayer she could make about Cassius: "Let me forget him, Lord."

"Naomi . . . "

"Yes, Miriam?"

"I want to go to the city. Will you come with me?"

Naomi thought at first that Miriam wanted to go to the tomb again as she often did; she never went back now to the place where Eleazar had been buried. But Miriam took a different way this time, and they entered the city proper. The pilgrims had left, and the city had its usual ways. There was something unbelievable about that. Several times Naomi felt that she wanted to cry out, "Don't you know what has happened?" and Miriam must feel it even more.

Once she stopped and looked back.

"What is it?" Miriam asked.

"I—I just saw the head servant—Boz' head servant. I am sure it was he. He saw me too and looked away. There he goes into the street of the coppersmiths. The one who is carrying that big package."

Miriam nodded. They went on. There was nothing really surprising about encountering the man—or in the fact that he seemed to wish to avoid her. Probably Boz had sent him on some errand and—and there was the house. Boz' house. There was the step where she sat waiting, till the head servant opened the door and told her, "The master says you are not to enter his house again." It was yesterday. It was a hundred years ago.

And the door opened, and a woman stepped out and looked up and down the street.

Naomi's hand flew to her heart. It was not true. It was not possible. "Abigail . . . "

The woman saw her. Speechless, trembling, she opened her arms. Naomi rushed across the street, half blind with tears.

"Abigail, Abigail . . . "

They clung to each other, sobbing. It was a long time before Naomi had the strength to speak. "I see it now. It was all a lie."

"I don't understand . . . "

"He told me you were dead, Abigail. He told me they killed you . . . "

"Who?"

"Why, Cass—the Roman. He told me you were killed. He lied. There is nothing, nothing he will not do . . . "

"Well, they very nearly did kill me", Abigail said, and there was something of her old grimness in her tone. "Stabbed me, they did, and that Roman found me—he may well have thought I was as good as gone. Three months on my back I was, and only now am I back to normal."

Naomi laughed, her eyes still full of tears. "To hear you talk, Abigail, to hear you and see you! He didn't raise you, but it's he who did it all the same . . . "

"What are you talking about, little one?"

"I talked to him about you . . . "

"To whom?"

"The Messiah", Naomi told her simply.

Abigail looked over her shoulder and then gave a shrug. "I forgot there's no one here to listen", she said grimly. "They all ran away when . . . " She broke off. There was an expression of anguish in her face. "I shouldn't have allowed you to touch me", she murmured. "What if . . . "

"Now you are talking in riddles", Naomi said impatiently. But as she stepped forward, Abigail recoiled.

"Stay where you are!"

Naomi looked at her in blank surprise. For a moment she thought that she might be under the ban, as one of those who were followers of Rabbi Yeshua, so that no one was allowed to approach her nearer than four cubits. But Abigail! It was impossible.

"What is the matter, Abigail?"

"Well, if you must know, he is ill." Abigail jerked back her head. "No one knows quite what it is, but it's—very ugly. The servants couldn't stand it any longer. They ran away, all of them.

They stole everything they could lay their hands on. Now only the head servant and I are left and I can't find *him*."

Naomi asked, "Why did they leave Boz?"

Abigail looked embarrassed. "It's—ugly", she repeated. "They refused to enter his room and—do things for him. And it may be catching; it probably is. Never mind, little one. Don't you worry your sweet mind with such things. I'll . . . "

"What does the physician say?"

"He says there is nothing he can do. It—it must take its course, he says. But if the master were a poor man, they would have turned him out of the house and out of the city months ago . . . "

"Oh, no, Abigail! Abigail! He hasn't got—leprosy?"

"I don't know, little one. I told you, no one knows what it is. But the physician was always glad to get out of the room—as long as he still came at all."

Naomi took a deep breath. "I am going in", she declared.

"Child! You can't. It's out of the question."

"Let him turn me out again, if he wishes to. But my place is now at his side."

"Naomi, you mustn't. You might catch it. And he is in such a state, he won't even recognize you . . . "

"What does that matter?" Naomi walked up the stairs to the entrance. Then she thought of Miriam. She must tell Miriam, of course. She turned.

Miriam had gone.

And Naomi knew that the time was past when she had to be told what to do and when she could find protection under Miriam's wing. Resolutely, she stepped into the entrance hall.

The large house, where everything used to run so smoothly, was deserted. There was a dusty, stale atmosphere, the odor of neglect. But there was something else: a fetid smell of corruption and death that made her feel sick.

"Little one, little one, don't go any farther, I beg of you. You won't be able to stand it. Even I can't bring myself to go in . . . "

Naomi did not listen. She braced herself and went straight to the bedroom. The air grew worse with every step. It became almost impossible to breathe.

But she drew the curtain aside and walked in quietly.

The thing that was lying on the bed seemed scarcely human. It was a skeleton, covered with suppurating ulcers, exuding a nauseating stench.

Abigail, close behind her, held her hand over her nose and mouth. "He can't see you", she whispered. "He's almost blind."

"Fresh water", Naomi ordered crisply. "Oil. And bandages."

Abigail obeyed automatically.

Naomi went down on her knees beside the bed. With infinite tenderness she took up a clawlike, ulcerous hand and breathed a light kiss on it. "Forgive me", she murmured with swimming eyes.

When Abigail came back, she found Naomi sitting by the bed, still holding Boz's hand.

"I shall stay with him", Naomi said quietly. "You go and get that physician back. Better yet, get another physician."

"I don't want to leave you here alone, little one. When the head servant comes back . . . "

"Why did you send him away?"

"I didn't."

Naomi remembered the heavy package the man was carrying. "He may not come back at all", she said. "Go and fetch the physician."

Again Abigail obeyed. She came back an hour later with a robust, florid-looking man who entered the sickroom holding a piece of cloth drenched with vinegar to his nose and mouth. He looked at the patient perfunctorily and went out again as quickly as was decently possible.

"The young woman is doing all that can be done", he said. "Olive oil for the ulcers, fresh bandages, fresh waters. I doubt whether the man will be able to take much food."

377

Naomi was standing in the door. "But—what is it?"

The physician raised his stubby hands. "There are so many things we do not know", he replied. "I don't think it is leprosy, but I very much fear he is *tama*—unclean—all the same. He should not remain in the city. It really is my duty to tell the authorities to have him removed to the Valley of Hinnom."

"There is no need for that", Naomi said quickly. "I shall look after him."

"It may take a long time", the physician warned.

"It is what I have to do. You do not know of any cure?"

"There is no cure, lady."

She nodded. "Give the good physician a piece of gold, Abigail."

"There is no money in the house, little—Lady Naomi. The servants stole everything before they left."

Naomi saw the face of the physician darken. "Take anything you like", she said. "There are chairs inlaid with mother-of-pearl in the large room on your left. Take one of them. It will sell for more than a piece of gold." She went back into the sickroom.

For three weeks she looked after the stricken old man, attending to the lowliest tasks. From time to time he woke up from his usual torpor, but he never fully regained consciousness and he never recognized her. Once she said, "No one seems to know about his illness."

Abigail replied, "It is because they know that they do not come." After a while she added, "Except for the servant of the lord Serubabel."

"What about him?"

"He comes every day, always at the same time. I always go to the door then. He mustn't see you. He only wants to know whether the master is still alive."

The old man died on the twenty-second day after Naomi's arrival.

When Serubabel's messenger came, Abigail told him about it, and he hastened back to inform his master who was now the heir.

As soon as the man had gone, the two women left the house. They went to Bethany.

III

A man walked slowly across the desert. He was almost naked and lean to the point of emaciation. The sun of many weeks had burned and blistered his skin. He walked several miles till he reached the Jordan, to bathe and drink. Then he went back the same way to a small cave where he was living. This was his habit every morning.

There are few places on earth where a man can find solitude as he finds it in the desert.

There are few ways in which a man may find God as clearly and intensely as he will find him in solitude.

The desert had known such men for a long time. There was nothing unusual about this one, except that he carried a spear.

Birth, on the whole, is more painful than death.

The death of the old life was amazingly easy. It had not hurt at all.

When Cassius came back from the place where all the laws of the world had been shattered, he had gone to his quarters first and dressed meticulously. He put on armor, helmet, and sword. It was like performing a funeral rite.

He went to the praetorium and told the officer on duty he wished to see the procurator.

When he stood before Pilatus, he saluted stiffly and asked for permission to resign from the army.

Pilatus was surprised. The dossier of the Centurion Longinus mentioned great military ambition as well as skill and courage.

"Why?"

"I have come to the conclusion that an army career is not for me, sir."

The shortest way. Senseless to tell him what he could not understand. All the more senseless, as he did not understand it himself.

Pilatus nodded. It was the news about Sejanus, of course. He had picked up Longinus straight from the arena. He would never have been in the arena if he had not had powerful enemies. The political changes were playing havoc all round. One had to be cautious and prudent.

"What are you going to do when you're back in the Eternal City?" he asked jovially. "Take up politics?" The Longini were a well-known old family.

"No, sir."

He did not want to talk. Just as well. Better be a good-natured superior. It was a risky time.

"Well, well. You signed on for five years, didn't you? The time will be up in about six weeks' time anyway. No need to resign. You simply don't sign on again. In six weeks I can get you transportation to Ostia."

"I have no wish to go back, sir. And I beg to be allowed to leave now, immediately."

Pilatus frowned. "Most irregular. Why? You must have a special reason, surely."

"I'd rather not answer that, sir."

"If you have committed a criminal offense, you'll be better protected in the army."

"I have committed no such offense, sir." (I have, I have—but you would not understand. And you couldn't protect me. Not the whole Roman army . . .)

"You're not going back to Rome?"

"No, sir."

Pilatus looked at him sharply. The man had had a shock. Last person likely to have one: imperturbable, never lost his head before. But now—all the signs.

"I shall have to know more, you know, before I can grant such an extraordinary request."

It could not be helped, then. "The One whom you called the King of the Jews, sir—he has risen from the tomb."

There was a pause. "You mean—the body was stolen after all?"

"No, sir. He has risen. I have seen . . . "

"Be quiet." Pilatus leaned heavily on the table before him. "Six weeks' leave", he said hoarsely. "After that you'll come in and get your discharge at the tribune's office."

"Thank you, sir."

"And I forbid you—do you hear?—I forbid you to mention what you just said to anybody else. You may go."

"Thank you, sir."

He was halfway down the stairs when he heard the rustle of a woman's dress. Then Claudia stood beside him. "I heard it all", she said tonelessly. "You know now too, don't you?"

He said nothing.

"We are all guilty", she said. "All of us, without exception. Where are you going, Cassius?"

"I don't know."

He saluted courteously and went on. He heard her weeping softly as she returned to her rooms.

The death of the old life was amazingly easy.

But birth was slow and painful beyond belief.

The first days in the cave he could think only of hiding. He must not be found; that was all that mattered. There was a god loose somewhere who had been killed but had risen again, and now he was out and about, and a man must hide. Again and again he saw that thing moving, glittering and gleaming, streams of lightning forming spheres and circles and patterns, and yet the whole was a living thing and a thing of tremendous, overwhelming power, and it was there and it was gone in one breath.

The earth was no longer solid. It could no longer be trusted. Life and Death had exchanged parts like actors. How was a man to know which was which?

But there was always the spear, leaning at the entrance of the cave. It seemed to be looking at him, reminding him that it was all real and that he could not get rid of it by pretending to be mad.

He should not have taken the spear with him. But it had never occurred to him to leave it behind. Where could he have left it, anyhow? In the armory, to be picked up at the next opportunity by some soldier—to be used perhaps? That was not to be thought of. He would never be able to get rid of it. He would have to carry it for the rest of his life.

That was the least that could happen to a man who had pierced the heart of a god.

There once was a boy of twenty who said to a girl he wanted to impress, "I've always wanted to do something—something really big with my spear. I know I'm good at it. I have always felt I didn't have my skill for nothing and that one day I'd do a very big thing . . . "

He had done it. He had pierced the heart of a dead man. He had pierced the heart of a god. And now he must hide.

Was there a purpose? Was this god all-foreseeing? Was it he who had given the Longini the crest with a spear? Was everything linked up in some strange pattern? Nothing was impossible. Nothing.

It did not absolve the deed. Even if this god had foreknown it, had allowed it to happen—that did not mean that he had brought it about. No good putting it on the god's shoulders.

Curious thoughts came out of the darkness. That Life had started anew altogether when a double stream of blood and water flew from the Heart of the World; that it was a new sun that had broken through at that moment and that it shone on a new earth. But there was also the fear, growing and growing, that he who had thrust the spear was cursed and excluded from the new Life, the new sun, and the new earth. There was no place for him anywhere. Everything to which he had ever aspired was totally insignificant and worthless. He could not go back to the past. That life was dead. Once more he was a ghost—but no longer in a world of ghosts.

And thus came temptation, stealthily at first, then bolder and ever more demanding: to do away with himself. Death, corruption, putrefaction, the end.

He certainly would not rise again. Make an end.

He was weak with hunger, but the idea of food disgusted him. Ghosts needed no food. Make an end. He had a weapon, had he not?

But his hands would not seize the spear. It was not for him. The very thought made him shudder.

During the first weeks he dreamed a great deal, and most of it was incoherent and wild and very frightening. Later the dreams ceased altogether. He spent his nights in a tomb of black, bleak sleep.

The day came, leaden and merciless, and with it the wheel of thoughts. He was an outcast. A time had been when he was made a slave and was treated as a slave. But in his heart he had known that he was a man born free and of ancient lineage and that right was on his side. There had been a time when Naomi and Abenadar spoke to him of a Messiah, a Christ. But he could withdraw into being a Roman. Theirs was not really his world at all. Rome was his world—the Rome he despised for what it had done to him. Nothing could happen in Judaea that would matter fundamentally. Judaea was an episode, to be watched serenely and a little condescendingly—as one watched the strange rites of the Jews from the gallery of the Antonia, looking down on their Temple.

Now there was no corner into which he could withdraw. He was no longer observing a picture. He was part of the picture. There was no escape.

It was senseless to try to hide while the spear was there—never out of his sight, saying, "Here we are, you and I, we did it together."

But there was worse still. This god was after him in some subtle, incomprehensible way: "Suffering, are you, Cassius Longinus? I am your brother. I also suffered. Despised as a slave, were you, Cassius Longinus? Mocked? Jeered at? I am your brother. I also was despised and the most abject of men, and they mocked and reviled me. Delivered to the arena to die, were you, Cassius Longinus? Although you were innocent? So was I, my brother Cassius Longinus. But I did die—in my arena. No longer can a man say in his pride, 'Maybe God can do many things that I cannot do, but there is one thing that I can do and he cannot: I can suffer and die.'"

There was no defense. And hiding became stupid when the god was in your very heart.

He had never seen the Nazarene's eyes. They were covered with blood, back there at the Lithostrotos. They were closed in death on the place of the Skull. But those eyes gazed at him now all the time, at the fool who thought he could escape from him by hiding in a cave.

He had asked him to kill him that morning, as the dawn came.

But death was not enough. That was the secret: death was not enough. You must give yourself up first. Surrender.

He seized the spear and held it up. "Here is my offering", he said dully. "And I beg—do you hear?—I beg for your pity and your compassion."

Then he saw a man coming across the sand.

"You rose to your feet", said the stranger. "You raised your hand to greet me, and then you fainted. Have a little more wine now."

Cassius drank from the mouth of the wineskin.

"Now eat this fig", the stranger ordered. "But chew it slowly. I can see that you have been fasting for a long time. Don't speak yet. You must gain strength first."

Strength welled back with every gulp, with every bite. Never in his life had he eaten such good figs.

He could see the stranger now. The blurred shadow became the figure of a young Jew, simply dressed, with a quiet, thoughtful face and beautiful black eyes. "Better stop eating now", said the stranger, smiling. "You can have more in an hour or so. I can see that you are feeling better. Fasting can be overdone, you know. Not everyone can keep it up for forty days."

As soon as his voice obeyed him Cassius asked, "Did the Nazarene send you?"

The stranger raised his head in surprise. "I am Judah, the son of Alphaeus from Galilee", he said. "What do you know about my Master?"

With an effort Cassius managed to sit up. "That he suffered an unjust trial under *my* former master, Pontius Pilatus, and was crucified; that he died and was buried; and that he rose again."

Judah's eyes widened. "You know *that?*"

"I saw it happen."

"You were one of the guards, perhaps? But no, you are a Roman. . . . How did you come to be there?"

"I wish I knew. I—I had to. I think he had power over me, ever since—never mind. You didn't answer my question. Did your Master send you here?"

"Perhaps he did", Judah said slowly. "I'm on my way to the city—to Jerusalem. He told us all to go there. We are going singly, it is less dangerous."

"*He* told you to go to Jerusalem? When?"

"The day before yesterday. By the shore of Lake Tiberias."

"He was there?"

"He has been there with us for nearly six weeks."

There was a pause.

"You cannot be—mistaken?" It sounded very lame.

Judah smiled. "We were with him for almost three years before his death. But in these past weeks he has taught us what we never

385

would have grasped if it hadn't been for what happened in Jerusalem. We were like blind men—all of us. He has opened our eyes. He taught us—he ate with us—"

"Forgive me", Cassius said. "Please forgive me for asking once more—you cannot be mistaken? It was he, just as you had known him before?"

"It was he", Judah replied simply. "But not entirely as we knew him before. There are five wounds in his body."

Cassius looked past him across the desert. "He was betrayed, wasn't he?" he asked almost in a whisper.

"Yes", Judah said. "And the betrayer had the same name I have. It will be cursed by many."

Cassius looked straight at him. "So will my name be", he said hoarsely. "But for a deed of my own. Did he say anything about the fate of those who did him harm?"

"He said that such hurt must come into the world, 'but woe to the man through whom it comes'."

Cassius nodded. "It is as I thought, then. There is a curse on me. You cannot help me. No one can. There is no hope."

Judah shook his head. "Suffering is not the same as damnation", he said. "And no case is hopeless."

Cassius struggled to his feet. He took the spear and held it out to Judah. "This", he said tonelessly, "caused one of the five wounds. I pierced his heart with it."

There was a pause. Then Judah reverently bent over the spear and kissed its blade. "The unfortunate man who bears my name betrayed him with a kiss", he said in a low voice. "If atonement is possible for him, I will suffer gladly. As for you, my friend—yes, friend!—you only did what all of us have done. For every time we sin against almighty God we drive the nails deeper into the wounds and pierce his heart again. You are guilty—but no more than everyone else, and perhaps less than many. I know now who you are. Jochanaan saw it happen. He is one of us, and the Lord loved him greatly. He said to me, 'This is the proof that our Lord was really dead, when they took him down and buried him.' He is right. In doing what you did, unknowingly you made yourself a witness for him—"

Cassius stared at him, trembling. "You mean—you think—there is hope for me?"

Judah said gravely, "He prayed for you as well as for those who nailed him to the cross. I need not ask you whether you believe in him. Your life since that day is proof enough. He has drawn you to himself because he loves you."

"Loves me?"

"More than you love yourself."

Cassius pressed both hands to his temples.

"What does he want me to do? I'll do anything—anything. What does he want me to do?"

"He wants you to be his witness as long as you live. Come with me to Jerusalem. I shall tell you more about him."

IV

Seven weeks after the Passover, Jerusalem celebrated the Feast of Asartha, which the Greeks called Pentecost, the Feast of the Fiftieth Day. A sacrifice was made of a loaf of leavened wheat flour and of two lambs. A burnt offering was made of three bullocks and two rams, and of fourteen lambs and two kids, "for the sins of the people". And frankincense was burned in the sacred fire where the offerings were burnt. The High Priest himself sacrificed twice a day. There were some who worried for fear the city would see riots and bloodshed as on the last Feast of the Tabernacles or a trial and execution as on the last Passover.

But Zakkai had told the hotheads of the Freedom Party to keep quiet for the present. "The time is not ripe." They scowled and grumbled, but they obeyed. They did not care very much for Zakkai. He was no Bar Abbas. But Bar Abbas himself had vanished. For a while he was seen shuffling through the streets, looking like an old man, bleary-eyed and disheveled, with a twisted smile, muttering foolishly to himself. Whenever he was spoken to, he repeated the same words again and again: "I knew it. They must choose between him and me. I knew it." Then one day he was gone; no one knew where.

The Tribune Vindex had satisfactory reports from his agents. There was little danger of any serious rioting on the occasion of this feast.

A small band of men came out of a house — a dozen men, no more. They were obviously Galileans, simple men from the countryside. But there was something strange about them. They came out like soldiers, going into battle, each one intent on his own objective.

At a dozen different points — squares and street corners — they stopped and began to speak. They spoke with an intense determination and with a complete disregard for whether people listened or not. It was as if they were making an official proclamation in the name of an authority. They were like heralds.

Some people stopped and listened. After a while small crowds formed, which increased.

"Where did that man learn to speak Arabic so well?" asked Selim ben Dawud. He and three companions had come to Jerusalem to buy earthen dishes for their tents. "And who is that man Yeshua he is talking about?"

"Arabic? What do you mean? The man's speaking Greek", declared Stratocles of Ephesus, who had come to sell his silverware.

A tall, lanky Egyptian looked at him with pity. "You must not display such ignorance, friend. This is the pure dialect of Memphis, my home, though how he learned it I don't know."

"A Galilean without an accent", said a Jerusalemite astonished. "What are we coming to!"

"You are all crazy", said Selim ben Dawud in broken Aramaic. "He just said in perfect Arabic, 'He has risen from the dead', but as no one can rise from the dead, he must be crazy."

"He did say that", Stratocles agreed, also in Aramaic. "But he said it in Greek."

They stared at each other, dumfounded. And so did men around the other speakers. There were people who laughed, and others who grew angry with each other. It was so obvious that this man was speaking in the Pamphylian dialect, but this cross-eyed Persian good-for-nothing would insist that it was Persian, and the legionary Gallus, on his way home from a visit to a tavern, smiled contemptuously because these idiots could not understand Latin when they heard it.

It was really a huge joke, and the crowd decided with the strange logic of bewildered men that the speakers must be drunk.

Groups were forming within groups; twenty, fifty, a hundred arguments started. How was it possible, how could it be true, what these men claimed, that they had conversed for weeks and weeks with one who had been executed at the time of the last Passover? These men were drunk. No, they were mad. They spoke the truth; the executed man was a prophet. He was a seducer; he was the Son of God. Anyway, the whole thing was an obvious lie, for how could anybody come back from the dead?

Who were these men? Why did they tell this story? What did they hope to gain by it? Surely they were exposing themselves to grave danger. They were accusing the procurator of having conducted an unjust trial; they were accusing the priesthood of having committed the most terrible mistake: worse, of being as guilty, more guilty, than the court of the Gentiles.

What was the country coming to if peasants from Galilee could preach such things to the people, and on a feast day, too?

On the contrary, it was about time these things were said; at last somebody was speaking up. It was vicious to condemn a good man like the Rabbi Yeshua to death; it was a crime to deliver a good Israelite to the injustice of the Gentiles.

"Now listen, Rabbi Josaphat said—"

"Yes, but Rabbi Nicodemus said—"

"Rabban Gamaliel would have nothing to do with it. He stayed away from the trial—"

"Prince Ephraim didn't attend it either. He wouldn't stand for that sort of thing. He told the Sanhedrin what he thought, too. Told them off properly, he did."

"Bah, the time for kings and princes is past. And Rabbi Mordecai says it was the only thing to do."

"Now listen . . ."

"Men of Judaea!"

The thunder of the deep voice silenced half a hundred discussions and quarrels. Everybody stared at the speaker. He was a big, broad-shouldered man, in his late thirties perhaps, standing on the top step of a staircase.

"Who is he?"

"Don't you know? That's Simon, Simon bar Jonah. He was with Rabbi Yeshua all the time. A simple man, a fisherman. They're all simple men, you know."

"Then they should keep quiet. Are we to be preached at by men who know nothing of the Law and of Scripture? Now I tell you . . ."

"Be quiet yourself. I don't want to hear you. I want to hear him. He's got a good face; he's like a lion, with that broad forehead."

"Reasoned like a woman. Are we to judge a man by his looks, God forbid?"

"Well, your Rabbi Josaphat looks exactly like a fox."

"Can't you keep quiet over there?"

"What for? To listen to these drunks?"

The lion-faced man on top of the staircase was speaking again, and suddenly laughter rolled back from those around him and across the square.

"What did he say? What did he say?"

"Well, it was a neat one, I'll say that for him. Said these men couldn't be drunk, as it was only the third hour . . . "

"That's a good one. Did you hear that?"

"Will you be quiet!"

"This is what was foretold by the prophet Joel", boomed the voice of Simon bar Jonah. " 'In the last times,' God says, 'I will pour out my spirit upon all mankind, and your sons and daughters will be prophets . . . ' "

A hush fell over the assembly, vast now, for all the groups had contracted, and the other speakers had lined up beside the lion-faced man who now spoke for them all, as he had done so often in the past.

"He has grown", Miriam whispered. "He has grown beyond all comprehension." She and Eleazar, Martha, Abigail, and Naomi were standing close together. "They all have", Martha said. "What's come over them?"

Miriam said nothing. She knew that the apostles, twelve again now that they had chosen a new man to join their ranks to take the place of Judah of Kerioth, had assembled at daybreak in the same room where they had partaken of the Passover meal with Yeshua on the day before the crucifixion; she knew that Yeshua's mother had been with them.

Something had happened there, something tremendous, something that had changed these vacillating, timorous, simple men into what they were now . . .

"They all look like rulers", Naomi whispered.

They did. But Simon, whom the Lord had called Peter, was the greatest among them; not for nothing was he singled out, again and again, to feed the Lord's lambs, to feed the Lord's sheep, to "confirm" the other apostles. A headstrong man, an impulsive man, the only one who had raised his hand in his Lord's defense, in vain, true enough, but he had raised it, and there was splendor even in his failure, in that one, futile blow that caused the Lord's last miracle before the greatest of them all.

"What is it, Naomi?"

"N-nothing. I thought I saw—I must have been mistaken."

" . . . Such were the miracles and wonders and signs which God did through him in your midst, as you yourselves well know. This man you have put to death; by God's fixed design and foreknowledge, he was betrayed to you, and you, through the hands of sinful men, have cruelly murdered him."

The multitude was deathly quiet now.

"But God raised him up again, releasing him from the pangs of death; it was impossible that death should have the mastery over him."

The simple man who never studied the Law and the Scriptures had given them a lengthy quotation from the Book of Joel; now he quoted David as his witness that the body of the Messiah would not see corruption.

The learned men in the assembly looked at each other, bewildered. How did he know this? Who had taught a fisherman from Galilee to quote difficult passages of Scripture by the page, as if he were the head of a school?

Peter went on, "God, then, has raised this man, Jesus, from the dead; we are all witnesses of it. And now, exalted at God's right hand, he has claimed from his Father his promise to bestow the Holy Spirit; and he has poured out that Spirit, as you can see and hear for yourselves—"

Little, bowlegged Joram, the former agent, listened, beaming.

Joel, the young Pharisee, listened, and the Rabbi Nicodemus and Malchus of the Temple guards and Joseph of Arimathea; about one hundred and twenty disciples of Yeshua were in the crowd, and besides the main contingent of Jerusalemites there were Parthians and Medes, Elamites and Cypriots, Cappadocians, Pontians, Phrygians, Egyptians, Libyans, Cretans, Arabs and Romans, Greeks from the isles and from Attica and the Peloponnesus.

Gravely Peter ended, "Let it be known, then, beyond doubt, to all the house of Israel, that God has made him Master and Christ, this Jesus whom you crucified."

"Not all of us", murmured Rabbi Nicodemus, pressing both hands to his heart. "Not all Israel, O Lord God, not all Israel", he cried bitterly.

Naomi said in a quivering voice, "At least no woman of Israel took part either by word or deed."

But Miriam said, "This has grown beyond our understanding. Peter is speaking to all the world. And all the world is guilty, for all the world has sinned against God."

The crowds pressed forward now, closer and closer to their accuser.

"What must we do? Tell us—what must we do . . . "

They stretched out their hands; they tugged at Peter's rough tunic.

One man, his eyes swollen with tears, shouted, "I was one of those who cursed him! I said, 'May his blood be upon us and upon our children.' What can I do?"

"His very blood will save you; your very curse will be turned into a blessing, because you repent."

"Repent?" the man stammered. "Is that all? Can it be that easy? And my children—my children . . . "

"It is not easy and never will be easy." Peter's voice rose to full strength again and thundered across the square, "Repent and be baptized, every one of you, in the name of Jesus Christ, to have your sins forgiven; then you will receive the gift of the Holy Spirit. This promise is for you and for your children and for all those, however far away, whom the Lord our God calls to himself!"

They came by the hundreds. For hours the apostles and disciples baptized and went on baptizing. By noon there were three thousand, and still they came.

"This may be a new party forming", Zakkai said to one of his henchmen. "What I don't understand is how they can dare to do it all so openly. Surely the fate of their master should be a warning to them."

"Well, if it's true that he was raised from the dead . . . "

"Nonsense."

"Maybe, but they certainly act as if they believed it. That man over there, with the short beard, Philip they call him, he told me half an hour ago that he and the others had seen him every day for weeks in Galilee and that he was teaching them all the time . . . "

"Not after his death?"

"After his death. That's just the point."

"They were overwrought with grief—they just thought they were seeing him."

"What, eleven men? For weeks, day after day!"

"Or it was some kind of an apparition."

"He shared their meals, Philip said."

"By the vestments of the High Priest! You seem to believe in this, Tubal."

"Look here, how do you explain the sudden courage of these men? A few weeks ago they were frightened out of their wits. The biggest and boldest of them all, that man Peter, told me he denied then that he was a follower of this Yeshua; he denied even that he knew him at all out of sheer fright. And now they're shouting their belief from the housetops. What's come over them? Now, if they have actually seen him, then I can understand it. They *know.*"

"Go and tell it to the Pharisees", Zakkai said angrily. "Let them find an explanation. It is another party. But they won't liberate Israel. I can't see these people driving out the Romans, can you?"

"I'm not so sure."

"How?" Zakkai jeered. "Didn't you hear that this Yeshua said his kingdom was not of this world? He said it to the procurator, and one of Pilatus' officers heard it and told others about it . . . "

"And?" Tubal asked. "Go on. What happened? Who told *you?*"

"Another Roman officer. He didn't tell it to me; he told it to your friend Peter. I overheard it an hour ago. Peter baptized the man."

"Exactly." Tubal nodded. "Just as I thought."

"What do you mean?"

"It's spreading to other peoples. It may spread to Rome itself."

"Now that's absolutely ridiculous."

"You never know. And if it spreads in Rome as fast as it is here, this kingdom from within may conquer Rome—from within."

"You are mad." Zakkai snorted. "If you think so much of them, why don't you go and have yourself baptized, too?"

"Maybe I will", Tubal replied.

The Greek Stratocles turned to a compatriot. "One of these fellows here seems to think this creed may spread to Rome."

"Out of the question."

"Why, Lysander?"

"Because it is such a typically Jewish thing. It will never create beauty and joy. And Rome has become too Greek to accept anything devoid of beauty and joy. Can you imagine this Messiah creed doing anything for art, for an example? A new style of architecture, shall we say? Or music? Painting and sculpture are barred altogether, of course. The Jews allow nothing of the kind."

"Well, you know more about that sort of thing than I do. . . . "

"Depend upon it, this is a belief for Jewish consumption only. Even here it won't last long. It will fizzle out and be forgotten. But the idea that it might spread across the world and be accepted by Greeks and Romans, by Numidians and Germans and Britons— this story of an unfortunate little Jewish carpenter from Nazareth— well, he would certainly have to be a god, and more than just *a* god. He would have to be all the gods of Olympus rolled into one."

"Well, the way you put it, I can see that it was a foolish idea. I really thought for a moment . . . "

"You mustn't be taken in by a wave of local enthusiasm, my Stratocles."

The wave of local enthusiasm increased.

Soon it was known that Peter had healed a man who had been lame from birth, a beggar who had been sitting day after day at the Beautiful Gate of the Temple, and the crowds began streaming toward the Temple square.

Once more Peter spoke of their guilt: "You gave him up and disowned him in the presence of Pilate, when Pilate's voice was for setting him free. You disowned the holy, the just, and asked for the pardon of a murderer, while you killed the Author of life. But God has raised him up again from the dead, and we are here to bear witness of it." He pointed to the beggar now standing beside him. Most of them knew the man. Every morning he was carried to the Beautiful Gate to sit there and beg for alms. Now he moved about like a normal person. "It is the faith that comes through Jesus that has restored him to full health in the sight of you all. Come then, brethren. I know that you, like your rulers, acted in ignorance . . . "

Abenadar was in the crowd, leaning heavily on Varro's arm. Two weeks ago he had received his honorable discharge from the army, and two hours ago both he and Varro had been baptized by the man whose tremendous voice could be heard all over the square. "Hear that, Varro? He is saying what the Christ said, 'Father, forgive them; they do not know what it is they are doing.' They're all of one mind now."

Again the call to repent: "And all the prophets who spoke to you, from Samuel onward, have foretold those days. You are the heirs of the prophets, and of the covenant which God made with our fathers, when he said to Abraham, 'Every race on earth shall receive a blessing through thy posterity.' It is to you first of all that God has sent his Son, whom he raised up from the dead to bring you a blessing, to turn away every one of you from his sins."

"Your mother was a Jewess, wasn't she, Abenadar?" Varro asked.

"Yes, thank God. If it weren't for what she taught me, I might not be here today to hear this."

Suddenly they both stiffened, as their trained eyes saw the armed men emerge from one of the buildings near the Temple. Apparently no one else noticed them.

"Temple guards", Abenadar said. "And priests. They're going to arrest Peter."

"And the others. I was afraid this might happen. Peter was too bold. Shouldn't have spoken here right under their noses. Abenadar, is it all going to start again?"

The old soldier nodded. "Again and again—as long as the world lasts. Nothing is more difficult to bear than the truth. But I'm not afraid for Peter, Varro—I'm not afraid for Peter."

There was no need to be afraid for Peter. He and the other apostles spent the night in prison, and with them the cripple who was a cripple no longer. On the morning of the next day they were taken to the council chamber.

Kohen Gadol presided. Aza was standing behind his master. Old Annas was present, looking like a mummy and staring at his gnarled hands, and all the Sadducees of rank.

Peter spoke to them exactly as he had spoken to the people. Yeshua of Nazareth was the Messiah, the Christ. He was the stone, rejected by them, the builders, that had become the chief stone of the corner.

"Salvation is not to be found elsewhere; this alone of all the names under heaven has been appointed to men as the one by which we must needs be saved."

A Galilean fisherman. Who had taught him the Scriptures?

And next to him stood the beggar; they all knew him, had known him for years, the beggar of the Beautiful Gate. He stood there a little clumsily, grinning with cheerful embarrassment at being a figure of general interest instead of a figure of pity.

Caiphas had them taken out. There was a short conference. Reports arrived: these men had baptized over five thousand people the day before, and the city was buzzing with talk and excitement.

The council agreed on a stern warning to stop all further preaching and recalled the prisoners.

The prisoners refused pointblank to accept the court's judgment.

"Judge for yourselves whether it would be right for us, in the sight of God, to listen to your voice instead of God's."

Wearily, Caiphas reiterated his warning and dismissed them.

"We haven't seen the last of them, I fear", said the Sadducee Alexander grimly.

Caiphas gave no reply.

At the corner of the street of the coppersmiths Cassius found the man for whom he had been looking—Abenadar. He walked straight up to him and seized his hand. "Will you forgive me?" he asked. "I was baptized yesterday. I know you and Varro were, too. I saw you, but I couldn't get through the crowd. Will you forgive me?"

"What for, son? That you saw it a little later than I did? It is only natural."

"Where is Varro?"

"At headquarters. He's still in the army, you know."

"I have so much to explain, I don't know where to begin."

"You don't have to, son."

"But I want to, Abenadar. I told you once that some people in Rome killed my father. But I didn't tell you the circumstances . . ."

"Your father", Abenadar said, "was General Longinus. He was cheated out of everything he had by some scoundrels in Rome. You sold yourself into slavery to save him, but they killed him anyway and they planned to kill you. So they matched you in the arena against Baculus. But you won."

398

"How do you know all that?" Cassius was bewildered.

"People talk, son. You came from a good family, yet your ear was slit. Why? Some of all this I knew when I first met you, but the most important bit I found out only a short while ago, after you had gone on leave."

"What is that?"

"That you gave up your freedom for your father's sake." There was a warm light in the old soldier's eyes. "One of the officers from Caesarea had heard about that. And I think that was why you were allowed to come in touch with the Christ."

Cassius gave a start. "I only thought of vengeance", he stammered. "Remember when you told me it wasn't going to be worth while? You were right. My enemies are dead. The worst one was Sejanus—"

Abenadar shook his head. "Your worst enemy was—Cassius Longinus. But all you went through and everything that happened to you were necessary; it was part of the way, son. But tell me, why are you carrying a spear? Or—or is it . . . "

"Yes", Cassius said. "I—I don't seem to be able to—I don't know what to do . . . "

"Go and ask Peter", Abenadar said, and his voice was again that of a military commander. "He is over there, in the large house at the corner, teaching. He'll tell you."

Naomi's eyes widened, and she hastily drew her veil over her face.

"What is it?" Miriam asked. Then she, too, saw the man with the spear. So did Abigail, who drew a sharp breath, raised her arm as if to put it round Naomi's shoulder, and then dropped it again.

The big room was full of people, easily more than a hundred, and most of them were gathered around Peter.

The man with the spear made his way through the crowd. Naomi lost sight of him. She was too small; she could not see him. . . . But he was here, here in this room.

"He is talking to Peter", Miriam said. "He must be one of us now, or he would not be here."

Naomi said nothing.

"Peter is giving him his blessing", Miriam told her gently.

Suddenly Naomi leaned against her shoulder, sobbing.

Cassius had to find the cross.

It was the custom to bury the implements of execution near the place of the execution, and the place of the Skull was not very large. Even so it was not an easy task.

But Peter had said, "Let the spear be where the cross is."

Cassius had to find the cross.

"The staff of Moses", Peter said, "drew water from a rock, so that the children of Israel could quench their thirst. This staff of yours drew blood and water from the Sacred Heart of our Lord, and all those who partake of the Blood will live eternally, and all those who are washed in the Water will be free of their sins."

He had to find the cross. It was a long, lonely search. The sufferings of the past were watching him, but they were pale and powerless. Everything had changed, even the place of the Skull.

Then he found the place—a small cave with three crosses in it. They no longer looked like crosses. They looked like—wood. Just wood. Yet one of them was the Tree of Life.

Cassius raised the blade of the spear to his lips, as Judah had done. He laid the spear next to the crosses.

The Lord's own cross and those of the two lestes. Bad company, Lord. That's what they so often accused you of, didn't they? Keeping bad company? Thank God you did. Where would we all be if you had not?

"You need the spear no longer", Peter said. "*Be* a spear in the Lord's hand. Let your words and deeds open the hearts of men for him."

Can I do that, Lord? Not alone. Alone I can do nothing.

"He loves you", Judah said. "More than you love yourself."

Someone once told me about the sevenfold love. A brilliant man, Seneca. But he did not know you, Lord, or he would have known that there is a love beyond those seven, encompassing them all, ennobling them all and surpassing them all. *Your* love, which makes everything holy.

Cassius turned away and began to walk back to the city.

When he reached the road again, he saw a solitary figure standing there, waiting.

It was a woman.

It was Naomi.